W9-BVE-606

LAIRD'S CHOICE

Other Novels by Rosamond Marshall

Kitty
Duchess Hotspur
Celeste

LAIRD'S CHOICE

a novel by

Rosamond Marshall

—————

Prentice-Hall, Inc.
New York

Copyright, 1951, by

ROSAMOND MARSHALL

*All rights reserved, including the right to
reproduce this book, or portions thereof, in
any form, except for the inclusion of brief
quotations in a review.*

Second Printing, March, 1951
Third Printing, March, 1951

PRINTED IN THE UNITED STATES OF AMERICA

LAIRD'S CHOICE

One

The Spell of the Spitting-Stone

EARLY MAY DAY MORNING, THE MAIDENS OF BEN FADA
went up to the high meadow to gather May dew,
about twenty, all single, eager, pining for husbands—all
except one. Laurie could hear her companions laughing
and tittering and jesting as they trudged up the stony
path, a few climbed in sleepy-eyed silence with their
plaidie shawls nipped under their chins.

"What dream ye, lasses?" mocked a plain-faced girl
named Janet, who had long crossed the stile to spinsterdom. "There ben't husbands enough in all the Laird's
lands! Aye! E'en if we'd wed the paupers, the brawlers
and the ne'er-do-wells! Glickety, that's what we be, each
year this same foolishness!"

"An it be foolishness, why do *you* come, Janet," called
the slim and agile Nan who was leading the way, "an ye
think it foolishness, why do *you* go gatherin' the dew every
May Day?"

They laughed and climbed all the faster, cleated shoes
clicking on the pebbles, skirts catching on the brambles
that were sprung up hardy and green. Beyond the low
stone walls on either side stretched the meadows like a
bolt of the Brodie tartan unfurled, and over all a morning
sky of tender blue.

Laurie was a newcomer to Ben Fada and this was the
first time she'd gone May-dew gathering. There was no

such thing at Great Marlow-on-Thames where she was sent to school when she was twelve, this being the age when a girl begins to dream of love and marriage. She thought it a somewhat childish custom but without harm and not foreign, for Laurie was born in Scotland of Clan Macneil of Barra, in Inverness County, the badge of her clan was the wild thyme and the clan slogan was for careful folk who looked before they leaped—GANG WARY. The words glowed in gold lettering on the clan arms—she could never forget, for is it not true that memories of olden lore stay buried in the breast like a token laid in a coffer, but open the coffer and you find the token whole and sound, kept perfect through the years?

Up forward, the first of the turnout had jumped the stile and were scattering in the pastures like a flock of robins lighting. Laurie watched the brown and the gray and the green skirts mushroom and spin as the girls scooped up the dew in the palm of their right hand and dashed it over their left shoulder.

The Laird Duff-Drummond's tartan, which was scarlet and blue and gold, clashed brazenly with the meadow green. Laurie liked her own dear Macneil better—blue on blue with a single scarlet thread—how much richer, nobler, quieter than the brash Duff-Drummond! Her Granny Macneil had shorn and cleansed and carded and dyed and spun the wool and woven the sett with minute care for the thread count so that no Macneil alive could say the colors were not true. "Keep the plaidie safe," she bade her grandchild when Laurie started for the border, "e'en though the speech o' the Hielands be bred out of ye, there's no sayin' when ye may need the plaidie ag'in!"

Well sprinkled with allspice to ward off moths, the Macneil shawl had lain four long years at the bottom of Laurie's school locker; she never dreamed that someday she'd need it sorely, having no fashionable bonnet to cover her head and no city coat to keep her shoulders warm.

4

"Laurie!" called Nan shrilly, "toss the May dew! Hurry!"
—a pretty custom, but Janet of the sour tongue spoke the truth! How few would find good husbands! Ben Fada was a village of two hundred and forty souls. The Laird's entire domain did not number more than two thousand five hundred, and the women outnumbered the men three to one. Cock-o'-the-walk lads took their pick of the bonniest lassies, especially of those who had at least five pieces of "siller" for a dowry. The plain and the penniless were left to spin beside the hearth.

"Laurie! Dinna ye want a good lad?" scolded Nan. To please the anxious girl, Laurie knelt and scooped the twinkly dew into her palm.

"Och! Brush toward ye!" screamed Nan. "For certain ye'll fecht with your husband!"

Laurie laughed. Little did Nan know how true was her faith to the slogan of her clan—Gang wary! Wary indeed with the lads, and warier still with the grown men, sly ones with pincer fingers, bold ones with a hook for an arm, sweet ones with syrup on their tongues: "Laurie, your hair is like the gold on the wing of the rooster atop the steeple o' Killmalie."—"Lass, did naebody e'er note that ye've a form like the sweet, bare statue-lady up Spittal Way?"— yes, they tried all manner of approach but their meaning was the same, and when you've done four years' service in a public house and listened to the kerls, piping four thousand tunes, all with the same ending, you know when to turn a deaf ear! Nevertheless, to please Nan, Laurie scooped up some dew and tossed it over her left shoulder; to please, also to yield to the heart's natural hope for love and happiness in wedlock. Was there in all the world a man for Laurie Macneil? Laurie feared there was not, especially in these Braes of Angus where the men were almost on the level of the kine—so unlearned and rough-mannered! If a finer sort there were, she'd not met them yet!

5

"Dry your hand i' the sun and do it over again," cried Nan, "or ye'll hae only ha a love and ha misery!"

"Silly one! Come along!" laughed Laurie. "The others are starting home!"

"Ye don't gie faith to the May dew, do ye, Laurie," said Nan, earnestly. "Ye don't believe in the Green Lady who is put under a spell, and if she answers your call, there is nought she won't do? An' ye gie no faith to the Morag—the Monster who carries away the lass he likes best and keeps her in his underground cave!"

"*Ga unseadh do na clachan!*" answered Laurie in the Gaelic, "Go tell it to the stones," and even as she spoke she was surprised that she should remember this old saying! It was Granny Macneil's way of putting her off when she came with some chatter-box tale—always Granny would answer, "Tell it to the stones!"

In England, Laurie learned that in ancient times, long before the Romans came to the Isles, those stone circles or monuments found strewn here and there in remote places of England, Scotland and Wales, were places of parliament as sacred as Westminster itself. When the people had a grievance or wished to make new laws or dispense justice, they met together to "tell it to the stones."

Nan glared. Some said she was "fey" and Laurie could well believe it! She was unlike any other girl in the domain. If there were people on the moon, Nan might be of their breed; her hair was straight and silver-light, her eyes were pale gray, flecked with bright specks and her skin was like a beam of the moon. Even her hands, though roughened by hard work, were small, milk-white and veined with blue. If not a moon maid, Nan might well be a descendant of those seafarers from Icelandia who boarded the eastern coast of Scotland long, long ago and hacked their doughty way to a new life among the ancient hills.

"Ye dinna hae faith, Laurie! Your heart is flinty and
6

your brain is like the crystal rock. I'll show ye!" Nan dug deep into her petticoat pocket and brought out a small piece of gray stone three or four inches long and polished smooth as leather. "See this! It is a spitting-stone that has magic. I'll make a spell for you and it shall come to pass."

"All right, Nan, make a spell," answered Laurie to placate her.

"What shall I make?"

"Anything you wish."

"No! It's for you, Laurie Macneil! It must be for you! I'll wish that within the hour ye may set e'e upon the one whose sweet love ye will be!"

"Very well," answered Laurie straight-faced. Nan held up the stone to the sun and spat upon it. She rubbed it on the grass and spat a second and a third time. Had Laurie told her that she was invoking the gods of the sun, the soil and the four winds, like her ancestors a thousand years ago, she would have cried, "Blasphemy!"

Eyes tight-closed, lips moving, Nan made her spell. "Now ye'll see!" she nodded, hiding the stone in her pocket. "Ye'll ne'er mock me again!" With that she turned and ran down the path.

Laurie was in no haste to follow. This was the first time she'd looked down upon Ben Fada like a bird from the air. There at the widest part of the vale was a speckling of slate houses. The largest was Rocktree Grange, the house of Mister Ronald Clargy, who was the Laird's bailiff. Mister Clargy's house, his barn, his cowpens, his dairy were all neatly boxed inside a four-foot wall of stone. Outside the wall the meadows sloped upward to a crag on the left, on the right to the Laird's castle—Duff's Rock they called it, because the stones of the natural mountain and those of the keep were the same. Glowing angry red by sunset, brooding black and still by midnight, the Crag and the Rock were like two crouching lions. "Look! The twa

7

beasties!" the traveler would say when he beheld their outline from afar. "Now we're on Duff-Drummond's land."

Laurie drew in a deep breath. The sun warmed her face. What bliss if she could lie down in the young grass with a book—her favorite Robbie Burns who had a rhyme to fit every mood.

> One morning, by the break of day,
> The youthful, charming Chloe,
>
> . . . .
>
> Girt on her mantle and her hose,
> And o'er the flow'ry mead she goes . . .

Youthful, charming Chloe indeed. She was Mister Clargy's dairymaid and she must hop to her duties! The milk to be skimmed, the dairy floor to be cleansed.

Scrubbing brush in hand, Laurie was on her knees in the dairy when a shadow fell across her wet floor. No one in Ben Fada wore a hat the shape of Mister Ronald Clargy's except Mister Ronald Clargy himself!

"Good mornin', sir," she said, rising in respect for the one whose orders she obeyed.

"You're a diligent girl, Laurie," said Mister Clargy.

"Thank you, sir."

"I like the way you keep our dairy! It is spotless!"

Laurie thought of Nan's "spell": "I'll wish that within the hour ye may set e'e upon the one whose sweet love ye will be!"

"Thank you, Mister Clargy!" she said, holding back a laugh that longed to burst out. If Nan's spell were true here was her future husband!

Mister Clargy poked the thick cream rising on one of the pans with his forefinger. The surface dented but it did not break. A few drops of skim rose and rolled over the rim of the covering like pearly beads on a round of cream velvet.

"Fine cream! Very fine!" Mister Clargy didn't look at

8

the cream, he looked at Laurie. "I've had it in mind to speak to you for quite a while, lass."

"Yes, sir?"

"What I hae to say may be of an unexpected nature. The fact is, Laurie, I've come to view ye i' the light o' someone more dear than a hired servant."

Surprise made the blood rush to Laurie's face. Mister Clargy's meaning was clear—oh, very clear! And if words were not enough, the look in his eyes said the rest!

Lord Duff-Drummond's bailiff, Ronald Clargy, was a big-built man with reddish hair and beard. His skin was white and his eyes were sometimes gray and sometimes greeny blue. The girls often argued different ideas about him.

"Mister Clargy is a fine-looking man."

"I think he is plain as a bear o' the mountains!"

Laurie could not agree that Ronald Clargy was handsome, neither was he downright plain—a man rough-hewn, outspoken, kindly, who seemed to know what he wanted.

"You're very kind, sir," she said, stammering a little.

" 'Tis not kindness," said Mister Clargy, " 'tis somethin' more—tell me lass, do ye like our braes?"

"Oh, yes, Mister Clargy! I was born and bred in mountain country until my father took me across the border."

"When was that?"

"I was going on twelve when I went to school in England, sir."

"I know, I know," muttered Clargy, "and it didna turn tha pretty head to learn fine ways like it wud some! Tell me, Laurie, I was gi'en to understan' your father and mother passed away—your closest kin are the Colquohoun family o' Edinboro?"

"Yes, sir."

Mister Clargy's manner changed subtly, became in fact quite like that of tavern admirers. "Tell me, lass, hae ye ne'er gi'en thocht to the r-romance o' life?"

"No, Mister Clargy," answered Laurie, wishing she could take wing and sail right out of the milk-house and far away.

"How ca' it be?" said Mister Clargy, pushing out his lips and sucking them in again as though he were rolling some tidbit on his tongue. "Ne'er lover for this bonnie hand?"

He took away the scrubbing brush to which Laurie clung. Bonnie hand? She wondered if his eyesight were good? Her hands were red and rough from water. The nails were broken and there were calluses on her palms.

"A free heart and the face of an angel!" muttered Clargy. Was he joking? She'd almost a mind to ask him, but he stepped up close and seized her two elbows and squashed her hard against the wall, so hard that she could feel his heart bumping against her breast.

"Hear me out, lass!" he said in a pleading voice. "You're all I want beside that which I have—my house, my fields, the trust of my Laird. Laurie! Tell me, could ye learn to care?" And before Laurie could get breath enough to answer, he hurried on, "Hark lass! I've a ring o' siller. . . . See! Here it is! Solid silver metal. I wager it will fit that pretty finger like a glove!" He folded the ring into Laurie's palm, and with heaving chest, "I've more . . . a fine wool dress . . . cost a fortune! The wee room at the rear o' mine is empty and waitin'. . . . Say the worr'rd and I'll creep in nichtly . . . creep so stilly thot no one will kna' . . . and for all ye will be to me, I'll gie a better wage . . . no more scrubbin' floors . . . I'll make ye my house-keeper. Nanny Biel longs to returrn to Edinboro!"

Laurie let the bailiff rave himself out. The offer did not shock her, for this was a way of men—urging their lust upon a girl as though it were their gift from heaven!

When Clargy made a move to take her in his big arms, Laurie threw the ring in his face and let fly with all the force of her strong right hand. The slap cracked like a popgun in the quiet milk-house. Clargy's cheek blotched red, then he broke into wild, exultant laughter. "Gude for ye lass!" he roared. "I thocht as much . . . but I must make sure! Och, Laurie! Laurie! You and I will make a famous pair—bra' spouse and bonnie bride!"

Too startled for words, Laurie could only stare, gulp, back away as her ardent suitor tried once more to embrace her. She backed into a corner and could go no further. "Please . . . please Mister Clargy . . . your proposal honors me . . . but . . ."

"But me no buts, lass!" Clargy pleaded with arms abegging. "I've luved ye since the firr-rst moment I saw ye! 'Twas when ye fetched me the pint o' ale. . . . I luve ye! luve ye! luve ye!"

"You may love *me*, Mister Clargy . . ." gasped Laurie, "I cannot say that I love you. In fact I've never been in love, so I don't exactly know . . ."

"Fiddle-de-dee!" said Clargy. "I'll tell ye what it is to be in luve! 'Tis a fury here." He put his large hand over his heart. " 'Tis a weaking here!" He touched his forehead. " 'Tis both pleasure and pain! Lass! Come into my arms! Gie me your pretty lips and maybe ye'll discover . . ."

Laurie fought for breath as she was drawn into a bear-hug that nearly cracked her ribs.

> Humid seal of soft affections
>
> . . . .
>
> Dearest tie of young connections
> Love's first snow-drop, virgin kiss!

rhymed Robbie Burns.

Mister Clargy planted moist, resounding busses on her temple, cheek and eyelids. She laughed nervously, and this seemed to rouse him all the more. At last he found her lips and his questing hand found her breast. The smoky scent of him mingled with a clean man-odor. Like a wise swimmer caught in the boiling surf, she gave up the struggle and let the tide carry her down . . . down to greeny depths yet unexplored. A thought tolled, clear as a bell: "You don't love Clargy. You don't want Clargy but you want a man!" It was true! Too long she'd kept feelings pent and womanly instinct in leash. This sudden flowering of the senses was warning clear that she could not go on in chaste singleness forever and deny herself the right to be loved and bear some honest man's children.

Perhaps amazed by his own daring, Clargy let her go and stood there panting, blinking, licking his lips that were still moist from her sweet mouth. "Laurie, angel, say the word! 'Tis married we will be! I canna' promise tha' my wife may sit always i' the parlor and fold her pretty hands, for 'tis verra true tha' a godly marriage is not all made of sweetkins, but a'so pullin' the yoke together. Naturally, I mean it as a figur-re o' speech, for my wife need ne'er harness to the plow!" He backed slowly to the dairy-house door. "Think it o'er. An ye're a mind to say yes, put a posy in your hair. I'd ne'er find courage to make my wish known a second time." He stumbled out of the dairy and walked away with the step of a tipsy man. Laurie was trembling. She'd never dreamed she could be so aroused by a kiss. Other times she'd felt only disdain and rage that a man should dare—she who never gave a look that said, "Come hither!"

> Tho' women's minds like winter winds
> May shift, and turn . . .

Was this the climatic change from freeze to thaw, that Burns described so well?

Looking down, she saw her reflection in the water bucket—the face of an angel, said Clargy. She'd fair hair and a rosy complexion. One might even stretch the point and say that she'd goldy hair that curled—she'd never much admired fair-haired persons, especially a lass! Long ago her granny told her that it brought bad luck all the year to see a fair-haired woman wi' the first-foot on

12

New Year's morn! Granny said the best first-foot was a man with dark hair, and next to the best was a dark-haired maid! At this moment she saw herself in a different light, a strange new creature aglow with "passion wild and strong," round, voluptuous hips and swelling breasts—how Clargy nestled them in his great palm and she'd let him! Shame on you! Shame on you. Nerves all racked up, Laurie flung the scattered curls out of her eyes and finished scrubbing the floor until it was spotless. Then she wrung out her wiping cloth and emptied her pail outside the milk-house door.

"Laurie," called Nanny Biel from her kitchen window, "hurry to Mcilrey's and pick up the four dozen eggs he promised!"

"Very well, Nanny Biel! I'll come for a basket," Laurie answered.

"Nay! Take your milk pail! Hurry!" screamed the old woman. "I've batter begun . . . and nary an egg!"

Laurie started for the stone gate. So intent was she on her own worrisome thoughts that she did not see a horseman approaching. She stepped through the gate as he came galloping in. Too late she saw him! With a scream of fright she dropped the pail, stumbled and fell. The rider spurred his mount and jumped her like a hurdle. She smelled the odor of horse-flesh and sweaty leather as rider and mount vaulted her prone body. Too terrified to move, she lay in the dust with eyes closed. Was she dead or alive? A strong pair of arms lifted her up.

"Hey! Lassie! Are you hurt? Do you feel pain?"

Laurie looked into a pair of dark eyes. "I . . . I don't know. I think not . . ."

"Tell me for sure," said the stranger. His fingers crisped into her shoulder. "I thought I saw Ebony's right front hoof strike you . . . here!"

"No."

"Here . . . ?" The gentleman's gloveless palm slid satin-soft

13

across her bosom. Then Laurie grasped the message of those dark, magnetic eyes.

"Let me go, sir!"

"So soon?"

"Please!"

"Why? 'Tis pleasant to cradle so fine a doll, wi' hair like spun gold and eyes of blue! And your Maker gave you a shape like the goddess of love! What is your name, lass?"

"My name is my own!" cried Laurie, struggling to free herself.

"You speak with the accent of England. Who are you?"

"I say . . . let me go!" cried Laurie. Though dressed in the Duff-Drummond tartan, this man was no uncouth Highlander. He put on the speech of the braes and took it off, like a cloak.

"Is it so much, to ask a girl's name? I'm in the habit of receiving a civil reply to a civil question! Answer or I'll take a fine from those red lips!"

What sparks of merriment in his dark eyes, merriment at her expense!

Putting forth her full strength, Laurie sought to free herself—in vain! This man was not to be denied. And even as she struggled, Laurie knew she had no desire to be free. Forgetting that only a while ago another man had also held and kissed her, she gazed at the one whose arms now kept her captive—willful cleft chin, tumbled raven locks, a shape like a gladiator. Who was he? From whence did he come?

"Very well, then. Pay the tithe!" Warm lips took the very breath of her life . . . or so she imagined. Such soaring bliss was not of earth! She wished she'd ne'er felt this kiss, yet she wished that heaven had created the giver for her—a man embued with powers to bind and enflame!

Straining in the sweet prison of his embrace, she returned the kiss with interest tenfold. Time, the place, the reality of her being, the name of the one who wooed her?

14

All vanished. Pride, modesty, chastity? She saw the three fly away like witches on the wind.

"Plague it!" muttered the stranger as he put her from him.

Laurie turned and saw a gentleman riding through the gate. Behind him rode a gnomelike fellow, the bagpipes slung over his shoulder batting him with every step of his hip hobbyhorse-nag.

"Angus," called the man who had just kissed her, "catch Ebony." He turned to the gentleman. "Jean . . . an accident . . . fortunately nothing serious. My horse nearly trampled this Highland lassie!" He turned to Laurie and said in a quick aside, "Adieu for now, my bonnie! Fate may be kind and let us meet again!"

The three newcomers were halfway across the courtyard before the bemused Laurie heard a shout of welcome.

"The Laird! The Laird! Hail to the Chief!"

She watched numbly as Bailiff Clargy, Nanny Biel, young Davy the cattleman, the girl servants, old Deek Byrd, all pressed around the tall stranger and his companion. So—this was Sir Colin Duff-Drummond of Gillian and Barra, the almost legendary Laird whom she served with scrubbing brush in hand! Forgetting her errand, forgetting everything except the sudden despair that cut her like a cold blade, Laurie ran panting up the ladder to the loft that she shared with little Nan and threw herself sobbing on her cot of straw.

Two

My Love Is Like a Red, Red Rose

LAURIE!" IT WAS NAN, SPEAKING FROM HER TRUNDLE BED which leaned against the opposite wall of the loft.

"Yes, Nan?"

"Do ye believe, now?"

"Believe what?"

"The spell, Laurie! The spell o' the spitting-stone! Dinna dare deny that Mister Clargy went to the dairy to speak marriage! We saw it writ on his face when he stepped i' the kitchen."

"You're always imagining things, Nan!" said Laurie faintly. "Now go to sleep!"

"I canna sleep for thinkin' o' the power o' my spitting-stone! Verily 'tis magic!"

"Nan!" exclaimed Laurie. "Believe what you will but don't talk foolishness to me!"

"Blasphemy!" cried Nan in a squeaky voice. Moving into a square of moonlight, she sat up in bed and peered through the darkness which hid Laurie from her sight. "Blasphemy is mortal sin!" she cried. " 'Tis punished ye will be, Laurie Macneil!" The child looked like the Sea Lady herself, with her fair, straight hair streaming around her pale cheeks. "Do you dare say Mister Clargy didna beg you to be his bride? Coom nu! He told Nanny Biel as muckle! And Nanny Biel said, 'Laurie may feel sae honored tha' a fine mon like the Bailiff wants her.' Nanny

16

said too, 'Laurie had best say yes, or she'll find herself on her way back to Edinboro.'"

Laurie's heart quailed. Back to Edinburgh? Back to the Royal Scot Inn? Even if Uncle Colquohoun would have her, and she doubted he would, the Royal Scot never! No! She'd go to Glasgow—Dundee—anywhere except Edinburgh!

"You said you liked Mister Clargy," chided Nan. "You always stand up for him when the others run him doun."

"Mister Clargy is a kind man," murmured Laurie.

"Then marry him and we'll hae a fine weddin' and dancin' and a'!" Nan began to laugh in glad anticipation of pleasures to come. "The lads will flock fra a' corners o' the domain. Especial one certain lad I ken . . . from Fairlie. His name is Tommy. Ye ne'er saw Nan dance a fling, Laurie! I ca' foot it wi' the best! Wait nu! Games there'll be, and prizes. How fine tha' the Laird has coom! He'll likely gie Clargy a bull for his ain and a gift to the bridie, too." At last Nan's voice was hushed in slumber.

To be sure, marriage would make a poor girl snug and safe. Ronald Clargy was an earnest man, and sincere and what a difference between a greasy-handed dairy-maid and being Mistress of Rocktree Grange, between a tavern servant and the wife of the Laird's bailiff who had five villages under his sole rule! Except for the infrequent visits of the Laird—so infrequent that his lordship's coming this morning had thrown everybody into a fever—the Bailiff was in full authority, wearing the keys on his chain as if he were master of the doman. Oh, Clargy would make a solid husband!

A hired maid would scrub her dairy floor—*her* dairy floor! Laurie smiled as the pronoun slipped past her tongue! The dairy was the Laird's, but Clargy was his bailiff and if she became Mistress Clargy, then . . . Oh, silly Laurie, counting chickens before they were hatched! Well, today she'd discovered that Clargy was a warm suitor with

17

plenty of push and press and she liked him the better for it. Sparing but not too sparing—he hadn't even bothered to pick up the silver ring, leaving it where she had thrown it —did he intend her to keep the bauble? She fished it from under her pillow and slipped it on the ring-finger of her left hand; ere the silver warmed she took it off.

The whole trouble was the Laird *had* come! How could she say yes to one man when spears of memory probed her flesh? Laurie recalled that moment supreme when the Laird pressed his lips to hers, memory so disquieting that she dug her nails into her pillow and thrilled with a thrill more real than she had ever known.

What was this sudden boiling of the blood, this pounding of the heart, this lifting of the breast with windy sighs? It seemed that she could still embrace that phantom shape and kiss those shadow lips! So real the illusion that she fell back on her pillow in sweet exhaustion. But a dousing of the fires within brought a change of mind. Was she daft that she could dream of one who was as far above her as the Rock above Ben Fada? He, the Chieftain—she, a penniless dairy-maid, bound to earn her daily bread by the sweat of her brow.

A Bible, a book of Burns' poems, a copy of Shakespeare, Mr. Wordsworth's lyrical ballads, the tragedies of Racine in French, the clothing on her back, were all Laurie Macneil had owned when she came to Ben Fada; and who was she, pray, to play the choosy? So she argued, trying to still the voice of the imp who whispered in her ear, "You'll never love Roddie Clargy now that the Laird has held you in his arms!"

"A pauper lass has no right to say a good man nay," she argued right back. "That luve of which Robbie Burns speaks is but the raving of a poet who puts his dreams in verse: '. . . my luve is like a red, red rose . . .'"

The idea of Ronald Clargy being like a red, red rose was laughable! Honest and forthright, yes! A love with

warmth and the will to please. But another man there was
who fitted the poet's description to a T.

> . . . my luve is like a red, red rose
> That's newly sprung in June.
> Oh, my love is like the melodie
> That's sweetly play'd in tune.

The Laird was the mirror of all male beauty! What
dark and curling hair! What dark and fiery eyes! All the
grace to make a gentleman! All the daring of a lover!
And there was a spark of mirth in that dark eye when
he said "Highland Venus" as if he didn't believe his
own words! Then shortly he was surprised to find that the
lass he'd kissed could speak the King's English!

A woman would run through fire and water for such a
man! Twirly-brain Laurie—all aquiver and aquake because a cavalier had stolen a kiss! "Forget him!" she whispered to the dark. "Think only of Clargy who did you the
honor of asking you to be his wife! A good steward is a
good man, and a good man makes a good husband!"

So Laurie reasoned that night, like a market wife who
puts her best apples on top o' the basket: Mister Clargy
was not cruel. He did not starve his lambs so that his
household could drink the milk of the ewes, and he did
not order that their little jaws be bitted with wood to keep
them from suckling. This was a practice she could not
abide, so much so that she never liked to watch the lamb-
kins gamboling in the spring, for she knew that soon a
heavy hand would fall upon their tender heads.

Mister Clargy dealt fairly with the tenants who paid on
time. Of course, there were always the wormy apples.
Clargy had a bearish temper when his blood was up, but
hadn't all men tempers? After all, the Bailiff's duty was to
stand for the Laird's rights.

Perhaps what pleased her most was Clargy's abstinence.
To her mind, a man spare of mirth and a bit on the dour

side was better than one whose blood heats in the flame of whiskey, whose wit curdles and sours, and whose strength finds outlet in brawling, beating, or worse. She knew because her father had drunk himself to death. She knew because she had served four years in her uncle's public house in Edinburgh.

'Twas the boast of whiskey lovers that Edinburgh, a great and majestic city of seventy-five thousand, had two thousand public houses. Ben Fada, a village of two hundred and forty souls, had two; Macpherson's at the Crossroads and Macroy's in Glen Road, but Mister Clargy never set foot over their thresholds and he poured no whiskey at his own table.

How oft Laurie had sorrowed that her own father did not die before she had reached the age of understanding, that she might have kept his memory without blemish.

MALCOLM MACNEIL
DISTILLER OF FINEST HIGHLAND MALTS

That sign should be carved on her parent's gravestone. "There's no finer or more elegant whiskey made than that which comes from my still!" was his boast. Father loved his product so much that he would rather drink it than sell it.

Outstanding among her childhood memories were the times she had played on the floor of the distillery, building castles out of wet mash, sampling droplets from the plugs. Before she was eight years old she could tell whether a sample came from a plain cask or a refill—that is to say, a cask made of plain oak wood or one that is first steeped in madeira or sherry until it is tasty and mellow, then emptied to be refilled with spirits. She also knew the exact peaty flavor her father preferred and she could tell the approximate age of the spirits almost as well as he could.

The finest whiskey, so Father said, was made from

north of an imaginary line drawn through Dundee to the east and Greenock on the west. The spring waters of the Spey River were the best for distilling. Great controversy arose among buyers who held that the Islays were the king of whiskeys in all the world.

"Much too peaty!" insisted Father.

"Aye, but they are big!"

"I prefer the elegant!"

Miss Big-Ears drank in all this talk like other children the stories of Jack the Giant Killer and Sleeping Beauty.

Her father's distillery was built of gray stone, "on "Speyside." The crystal waters that went into the making of Macneil's Finest Malts came down from their mountain cradle under Cairndearrg to Glenlaggan, and here they met Truim River waters near Glentruim House which belonged to Macphersons. At Invernahavon, where the two rivers wed, was fought the great battle between Clan Cameron and Clan Mackintosh.

From the wide stone arch of the distillery, one could see the peaks of Ben Muich Dhui and Braeriach to the north and the Cairngorm mountains to the south. Wreathed in summer mists or capped with winter snow, they were always Laurie's friends. She was certain that she could make out giant faces in their shapes—kings of auld lived in their fastnesses, the white clouds that lay so soft upon their summits were the bridal veils of the kings' daughters, the black clouds that galloped over their heads were the raven steeds of suitor princes come to claim them.

In autumn, the forests that clothed their slopes took on the colors of the clans—Ferguson and Graham and Forbes and Brodie, Macdonald of Sleat and Macdonald of Clanranald, Macgregor and Mackenzie, Macleod and Macnab, Macarthur and Macalpine, Campbell and Duff-Drummond —her father had taught her to recognize a hundred or more clan tartans. She could call them like a kennelman calls his pack, each one by name!

"Father, why are Scots named Mac?"

"Mac is another way of saying son! Son of Fergus—Son of Nab—Son of Neil."

"Like the Bible?" said Laurie eager to show her knowledge, "Son of Jacob—Son of Abraham?"

Father promised that when she was older he'd take her over Laric Pass and she would see the woodsmen cutting in the forest of Rotheimurchus and the ruins of the castle on a lonely little island, where in ancient days a great Scottish lady shut herself away from the world to mourn her lost warrior husband. Laurie never did go to the forest or to the castle. Instead, she went to the Lowlands, orphaned and alone, her father having died of a stroke when she was eleven. So reduced was his estate that when all was sold, nothing remained but sixty-nine pounds, ninepence ha'penny. The only will they found was a note on the back of a bill for six dozen gallon-size kegs in seasoned oak:

> Should I die, I want any monies that remain to
> be put to my daughter's education in an English
> boarding school. This is my wish, made in sound
> mind.

Mr. Dury, the lawyer who settled the legal business, picked Miss Weston's, at Great Marlow-on-Thames.

Laurie arrived at school in time for the fall session, so numb with grief and strangeness that at first she hardly noticed the difference between this England and her own darling Highlands; but soon she opened her tear-blinded eyes!

How different this Southland, where the cows grazed up to their teats in lush meadows, the flower gardens, the quiet Thames River flowing beneath leaning willow trees —here nature was combed and tidy. Houses were larger and finer. The people seemed fatter and more open-faced than the Scots who battled the cold, the rain, their fields uptilted against high mountains, their fields growing an ever-ripening crop of stones!

How different the ways of the English, their speech and manners! At first she was ashamed of her uncouthness. But Miss Weston, a prize among educators, asked her to stand up in class. Then she told her pupils that they could learn from Laurie Macneil for she'd traveled farther than any other girl in the school and could tell them about the great events of Scottish history. It never had occurred to Laurie that salmon fishing was an art. She'd always been able to hook her twenty-pounder like a man. How the girls marveled!

Soon her tongue lost the native burr, she learned to say have and can, instead of hae and ca'. She never breathed to anyone that her father was a distiller of whiskey.

After two years at school, Miss Weston called her Scottish pupil into her study.

"The money you had when you came is gone, Laurie. We'll have to decide upon your future course."

"I've two more years, Miss Weston!" cried Laurie in a sudden panic of fear.

"I know."

"Must I leave before I receive my diploma?"

"Not if you place an education higher than your pride."

"What must I do, Miss Weston?"

"Earn your way."

"How, Miss Weston?"

"Make fires, scrub floors, clean windows, polish knives, help with the laundry."

Laurie swallowed hard. This was a comedown! The brightest student turn kitchen drudge. "Skudgy," as they said in Scotland.

"Of course, I'll do it, Miss Weston," she answered. The beloved teacher put her arms around her and kissed her on the cheek.

23

"You'll find it easy if you keep the main goal in sight," she promised.

There were two other "paupers"—one, a dullard named Eliza; why she wanted to go to school was more than anyone could see; but Annie was dark and pretty and very clever and her ways were wild. She ran away one night and never was heard from again.

Laurie was sixteen when she stood facing an uncertain future with her sheepskin in her toil-roughened hands.

Miss Weston could not make room for her—there were new "pauper" girls eager for her place in schoolroom and scullery. The teacher list was filled with experienced women.

Laurie pondered a surprise letter that came from Edinburgh.

> MY DEAR NIECE LAURA,
>
> News of your scholastic success reached us by way of Mr. Dury who settled my poor brother's affairs. Would you care to come and be part of your only relative's household? I'll send travel money and welcome you in the name of your father, my dear deceased brother Malcolm.

Laurie had heard her father mention his only sister Emma in none-too-cordial terms. According to him, she'd married beneath her.

"By all means, accept your aunt's kind invitation," said Miss Weston to whom Laurie appealed for advice. "It is good for a young girl alone in the world to find haven among her own kith and kin."

Laurie wrote her Aunt Emma, expressing her gratitude, and received another letter from Edinburgh.

> Mr. Colquohoun (your Uncle Thomas) will be in London on business, June 30, at the Post Inn, Charing Cross. You may travel North to Edinburgh in his company.

24

In the letter paper were four sixpences, with the notice, "fare from Great Marlow to London."

Dick Whittington did not set out for adventure with a more fervent heart than Laurie! Sixteen—the world before her, enough knowledge in her head to keep her from foolish or idle thoughts, God's love in her soul. She was neatly dressed in blue challis and a cinnamon-brown wool shawl with long fringe; her bonnet of brown straw was trimmed with a blue ribbon bow, her brown kid shoes had bright metal buckles that looked like silver. This was the first new clothing she'd had since she put on the dark blue school uniform four years before. Miss Weston helped her to buy and paid for everything out of her own purse, saying that she'd earned the money in faithful service and excellence in her studies.

Laurie felt like a queen as she boarded the London stagecoach, all the more so because, with the exception of a gentleman who sat opposite reading a newspaper, she was the only passenger out of Great Marlow that morning.

Her box and bundle atop the stagecoach contained her precious books, her tartan shawl and a few odds and ends accumulated during her school years. She clutched her reticule tightly. Miss Weston had put in an extra shilling "for good luck"! Her luncheon consisted of two hard-boiled eggs, two buns and a stick of sugar sweet. From time to time, she stole an admiring glance at her white crocheted mittens, her white stockings, the frill of her white petticoat that peeped out from beneath her skirt. So pleased was she with her appearance that she did not notice her fellow passenger until suddenly the coach lurched and she was thrown forward, her knees bumping his knees.

"I beg your pardon, miss!"

"I beg yours, sir!" Red-cheeked, Laurie settled back into her corner.

The gentleman folded his newspaper and sat looking

out of the window at the passing landscape that was very lovely in the spring sunshine. He was a tall man of middle age, of vigorous frame and high in color. He had large, round eyes and a chin so heavy that it overbalanced his Roman nose. His hair was spare and carelessly trimmed. His coat of fine blue broadcloth was spotted and soiled. There was a small tear in one sleeve, not poverty but neglect, for his boots were handsomely made and his steel-gray breeches were immaculate. After a while, he drew from his pocket a sketchbook like the schoolgirls used to take on outings with the art teacher. Soon Laurie realized that she was the subject of his drawing; yes, her poke bonnet and her mittens were there in black and white and from time to time he stole a glance her way. Well! Really! Then as though the artist had read her thoughts, he handed her the sketchbook.

"How do you like it?" He'd caught the likeness, of that there was no mistake! But what a mischievous pencil! This was a caricature of a young girl, preening herself in fatuous awareness of her fine looks and new apparel!

"Capital, sir!" said Laurie, laughing gaily.

"I like your sense of humor, young woman."

The artist hoisted himself halfway out of his seat with a low bow. "My name is Gillray, James Gillray."

"James Gillray!" What schoolgirl or boy didn't wait in laughing anticipation of Mister Gillray's comic pictures that poked fun at "Boney" Bonaparte, John Bull and the weaknesses and foibles of men and women.

"Here!" The artist tore the page from the sketchbook. "Keep it in memory of your first trip to London. . . . I take it this *is* your first?"

"My first *to* London, Mr. Gillray," answered Laurie, "thank you! I'll cherish this drawing until I die, as a reminder not to be a foolish peacock!"

"Peahen!" corrected James Gillray. They burst out laughing, laughed and chatted all the way to Wargrave which was ten miles from Marlow. There Mr. Gillray took his leave with a grand sweep of his beaver hat.

"Good fortune to you, Miss Macneil! I trust we shall meet again!" Laurie tried to remember what her traveling friend had said to make her laugh, it was not easy. His jests were subtle like his caricatures. She was delighted to have met so distinguished a person first-off—good augur for the future, or so she thought.

From Wargrave on the journey was humdrum and the passengers also—a stout gentleman with a solicitor's brief-case, a farmer, an elderly lady in puce silk, a preacher. The highway hugged the banks of the River Thames except where it clipped off a bend or ran through a hamlet.

Laurie ate one of her boiled eggs with a bun and broke off half of her sweet stick and sucked it enjoyably. While they were changing the horses at a pretty village named Pangbourne, she followed the lady in puce silk to the drinking fountain and quenched her thirst. From Pang-bourne on, the Thames flowed between low, wooded banks. Her head nodded, soon she fell asleep. A voice awoke her calling loudly, "London! All out please! All out please!"

The stagecoach had come to a halt. The darkness was pierced with rays of light from the inn windows. Bonnet askew and one foot stinging from pins and needles, she hopped out, the last passenger to alight.

"Is this the Post Inn, Charing Cross?" she asked a boy.

"Yes, miss," he answered. "W'ch box is you'n?"

"The black one with the rope."

Laurie inquired of the innkeeper who was standing at the door, "Where may I find Mr. Thomas Colquohoun, if you please?"

"Mr. Colquohoun is seated at yonder table, miss," he answered.

"So . . . this is Malcolm Macneil's daughter!" said her Uncle Thomas. He did not rise or even put down his knife. "Weel, weel, beggars canna be choosers! 'Tis a pity your father dinna hae the thrift to put aside a bit for his only child's future."

Right then and there something prompted Laurie to say, "Yes, Uncle Thomas." It was not servile catering; she sensed that to argue with her uncle was to waste her breath.

"Sit down, lass!" Mr. Colquohoun motioned with his knife to the bench opposite. "Put your bundles under your feet." He bent beetling brows upon his new-found niece, sniffed and jabbed his nose with the fleshy part of his thumb, a habit he indulged in frequently. Then he proceeded to serve her some of the remains of his potpie dinner, muttering as he did so, "No use makin' up extras on the bill . . . travel light, say I . . . a mon is a' the better for it!"

Laurie was hungry! Fortunately she had one egg and an extra bun left. When she had eaten, she took stock of this stranger, her uncle. He was a man of middle size, stout, and with gray in his curly hair. His cheeks were florid and full like the cheeks of a squirrel carrying nuts; this odd effect was heightened by fuzzy, gray sideburns that he wore long. His coat and trousers were fashioned English style, but they were made of indestructible Inverness weave that a Scot hands down, complete with wrinkles and bulges patches and snags, from father to son. He made no concessions to English ways in his headgear! His tam-o'-shanter stuck with a grouse feather brought back sharp memories of olden days on Speyside. How long since she'd set eyes on a tammy!

But it was Uncle Thomas' purse that fascinated. Large, round, made of stout leather, the flap decorated with a brass plaque on which were engraved the initials T.C., it hung from his belt by a brass chain. Every time he had need to pay out even a ha'penny, he unbuckled two buckles, fumbled in one of three compartments to find the coin, then quickly fastened the two buckles again. A highwayman would have had to saw through belt and chain to separate Uncle Thomas from his money.

Oddly enough, there was another side to Mr. Colquohoun's nature. He had a high, and to Laurie's mind a somewhat too-mighty, ambition for his three daughters. "I take it ye're conversant wi' the habits o' educated people, Laurie?"

"What do you mean, Uncle Thomas?"

"They told me Miss Weston's was a finishin' school, so ye should know how to greet a person above yoursel' in station, how to write a letter, how to come into a parlor, make polite chitchat and pour tea."

"Yes, Uncle." Laurie bent over her plate to hide a smile. She wondered what Uncle Thomas would say if he knew that she'd also taken a degree in fire-kindling, floor-scrubbing, window-washing?

"Verra gude, verra gude! Tha's the chief reason I'm payin' to take ye hame—so ye can gi' your cousins some pointers. They've not had the advantage of an English school like yoursel'."

"I'll be happy to teach them anything I know," murmured Laurie politely.

"Verra gude! Verra gude! Pick the Scot's burr out of their tongues. Show 'em how to curtsy!"

Laurie had dreamed of seeing some of the sights of London, but this was not to be. Uncle Thomas put her in a boxlike room on the top floor of the inn and told her to stay there until he came.

There were bugs in the bed. She sat up most of the night, gazing out of a dormer window over miles and miles of housetops, steeples and belfries. This was the London of the Abbey, Temple Bar, the Tower, Fleet Street and Westminster Parliament; the greatest port on earth; the most fabulous market; the meeting place of genius and wit; the playground, gallows and tomb of kings and queens.

Smoke from thousands of chimneys mingled with the early mist to catch the pinking rays of the sun. Oh, why couldn't she have roamed those famous streets that bore names more ancient than the memory of the oldest living man! She'd have willingly given her new bonnet to see Hyde Park where grand folk take their outing, London Bridge and St. Paul's!

Far from fulfilling her wish, she was forced to wait and wait—hungry and disappointed until ten o'clock, when her uncle sent for her. She joined him to share in an economical breakfast of porridge and tea.

"I had i' mind to take a remembrance to the wife and daughters," he said. "I purchased twelve gross o' pins."

Gravely, he shook the contents of a box onto the table and began to count the pins while Laurie looked on in amazement! "One thousand seven hundred and twenty-seven, one thousand seven hundred and twenty-eight!" He looked up and said almost with regret, "I cude 'a sworn the tally was short . . . but I was mistook! The count is cor-rr-ect!"

Three

The Royal Scot in Princes Street

UP THERE, LAURIE," SAID UNCLE THOMAS COLQUOHOUN.
He pointed to a door at the top of a narrow stair.
"Speak soft to your Aunt Emma, she suffers from chr-r-ronic
vapors."

Laurie's first thought when she saw her Aunt Emma
Colquohoun was, "How did she ever squeeze up this
stair?" The poor lady was very stout. She must have
weighed "twice twelve stone i' the saddle," as they say of
a person overweight. Her outmoded wig crowned her like
the turban of an oriental potentate; decorated with loops
of false pearls, feathers, bows and a flower or two for good
measure, it sat awry on her head; powdered curls hung
like rolls of pastry dough down her left shoulder.

Almost as strange as the aunt's appearance was her bedchamber, the most peculiar museum of faddism Laurie
had ever set eyes on! It was the shape of a halved circle,
and lighted from a flight of five round windows in the
outer curve that faced down upon Princes Street. The
walls were hung with buttercup cottonade, unwashed since
it was nailed there. Piled in disorder on the bureau, on
tables, the whatnot, the floor, were all sorts of things—old
shoes, bundles of rags, chipped cups and plates, broken
statuettes, a torn engraving, a box of seashells, a pail filled
with bits of rusty metal. Was Mistress Colquohoun a
scrimpet?

"Come here, child!" she called, as Laurie stood gaping

31

on the threshold. "Let me look at you, stand over there in the strong light."

Obediently Laurie faced the sunset rays that poured through the windows.

"Yes . . . yes! You're my brother's child! Did you have a good journey North?"

"Yes, Aunt Emma," Laurie replied, with a charitable lie.

The ride North had been wearisome indeed, and she was hungry all the way! Uncle Thomas Colquohoun's idea of a low-cost meal for a "young thing" was a cup of tea, two slices of bread and a dice-size piece of cheese. Then she was hustled off to sit in the coach while he sated his appetite with more filling fare.

"Let me see you curtsy, Laurie," demanded Aunt Emma. "Go on, curtsy like a real lady who stands before their Majesties!"

Wondering, Laurie did her best to content this strange woman and when she rose from an imitation of a court curtsy, she was rewarded with a childish smile. "Good! Good! I see that you know. Oh, Laurie, take my girls in hand. They've sore need to learn genteel ways. I am an invalid! See my miserable condition? I've been bedridden these twelve years! And my girls have come up helter-skelter, their father caring nothing what they learned. Promise me you'll take 'em in hand!"

"I'll do what I can, Aunt Emma," answered Laurie. "Where are my cousins?"

"You'll see 'em quick enough! I sent 'em away until you and I had a little talk. I wanted to be sure . . . perfectly sure you could act like a lady."

"Could she be a wee bit off her top?" speculated Laurie, in schoolgirl idiom. Her suspicion that her Aunt Emma was not quite sane increased when that lady threw off the covers, rose and strode over to a highboy.

"See, child! I keep a few goodies in this bottom drawer. Come! We'll enjoy a slice of sausage and a fresh roll! I'll soon have water boiling for tea!" She put the kettle on, and coaxed the hearth fire to brighter flame with the bellows.

Laurie's mouth dropped open as she watched the "invalid" set out a substantial high tea of sausage, pickles, rolls, butter, seed cakes and jam. Aunt Emma was no more bedridden than her husband. In fact, under her kirtle she was dressed to petticoats and stockings.

"Mr. Colquohoun is a sparing man," she said in a sibilant whisper. "He thinks a light diet is good for the stomach. I always keep something tasty on hand—yesterday I had the best lamb pie! Sit down, Laurie, child! Eat!"

Poor woman! Poor, foolish Aunt Emma! Some great trouble must have unbalanced her mind, making her not only a recluse, but also the strangest kind of snob.

"What interesting things you have, Aunt Emma," said Laurie in a feeble attempt to make conversation.

"Ssh," whispered Mistress Colquohoun, a puffy forefinger pressed to her pursed lips, her pale blue eyes round and full of sudden fear, "don't let Thomas know! He would take everything away from me . . . all my treasures!"

They had barely finished tea when Mrs. Colquohoun exclaimed, "There! There are my girls! I hear their footsteps. Help me to hide the tea things! They mustn't know! Especially Kate! She'd tell Mister Colquohoun!" The deluded woman had crammed the food back in the highboy and climbed into bed where she lay fanning herself with a lace handkerchief when her three daughters entered.

"Kate! Margit! Jinny! Your cousin Laura Macneil, from England."

"Good day, Cousin Laura!"

"Welcome to Edinburgh, Cousin Laurie."

Kate and Margit gave limp handshakes, but Jinny, who was the youngest, kissed the newcomer's cheek warmly. Were there ever three sisters who differed more than these?

Kate was the eldest, nigh onto thirty, the spitting image of her father. Uncle Thomas Colquohoun's Roman nose and squirrel cheeks were passable in a man—poor Kate! Tall, angular, vinegary—Laurie sought to find some redeeming feature, her hands perhaps! They were beautifully shaped.

"You've such dainty hands, Kate!" Her eldest cousin spread her tapering fingers and looked at them as though she were seeing them for the first time.

"Don't spoil the girl with flattery, Laura!" said the mother.

Laurie intercepted the venomous beam that sped from her aunt's eyes to those of her eldest daughter. Could it be that they detested each other that much?

Margit was the fairest of the three. She had that much-prized "Black Scottish" beauty, blue-black wavy hair, dark wistful eyes, olive skin—a Bible Rachel come to life. Her nature was closed and melancholy. Laurie often wondered what dreams she dreamed as she bent over her embroidery frame, making petit-point chair covers by the dozen!

Right from the start, Jinny was the favorite—a rollicking miss with an amazing talent for mimicry! Where did she pick up the songs she sang, in perfect imitation of the strolling funnymen and balladeers who performed in her father's taproom? Neither she nor her sisters were ever allowed to set foot on the premises.

"How are you this afternoon, Mother?" asked Jinny.

"Much the same as usual, thank you, Jinny," her mother answered in a plaintive voice that conveyed the exact opposite meaning. "Now girls, and you, Laura, leave me alone! I can't stand so much chatter and excitement. My nerves, you know!"

"I'll show Laurie where she is to sleep," said Jinny. "Are you coming, Margit?"

"Yes," murmured the girl with the ebony hair.

34

"I'll stay with Mother until she is comfortable," said Kate.

"There's no need to, Kate," protested her mother.

"But, I must."

"I'm all right. Quite all right."

"Mother . . . there's no use arguing."

"Oh, come on Laurie!" cried Jinny. She had closed the door to her mother's bedroom with a sharp click. "That's the way it is between those two. I wish Kate would let Mother alone! She just bothers her, fussing and fussing, it always ends the same way. 'Now Mother, there's no use arguing!'" Jinny mimicked her elder sister perfectly.

"Mother's a bit queer—up here," she added in a whispered aside.

Laurie turned on the landing to look for Margit, but she had disappeared.

"Don't mind her," said Jinny, "she never wants to be with the rest of us. Come along! I'm afraid you're not going to like your room. I tried to make Father give you a better one but . . ."

Laurie choked back an exclamation of dismay. Her bedroom was a dark closet under the stairs. The bed, if one could call the hard cot with a wafer-thin straw mattress a bed, almost filled it—should she want to sweep, she'd have to drag the bed out onto the landing. The only other furnishings were a tin basin on a three-legged stool and three wooden pegs on the wall, presumably to hang clothing.

"You may wash in my room," said Jinny, "and if you are cold or lonesome, you may sleep in my bed. I have a feather mattress. Come and see!"

Jinny's snug little room overlooking the rear court was the only haven Laurie knew during the four years of her life at the Royal Scot. Here she read nights until her eyelids closed. Here, in safe hiding, she kept her own precious

35

books and a new treasure of ancient volumes that she found all dusty and neglected in a corner of the cellar of the Royal Scot. Here, when fatigue or discouragement weighed her down, she found the solace of friendship and the balm of quiet. How did Jinny insure her privacy? Simply by keeping a cageful of white mice of which prying Kate was mortally afraid. As for Margit, she never set foot over her waggish sister's threshold.

Any hope Laurie might have held that she was to find a lasting refuge in this house vanished like smoke in the wind when she discovered why her Uncle Thomas had brought her to Edinburgh—to become not only governess to the Misses Colquohoun, but also charmaid, barmaid and maid-of-all-work to the Royal Scot. A strange life, all hard labor except for an hour now and then when she was supposed to coach her three cousins in the arts of the drawing room—she who knew so little about those arts herself. "No . . . no . . . do not simper, Kate. Speak up plainly! Be natural in manner . . . yes, the widowed queen is named the Dowager Queen . . ." Lessons were often curtailed by a voice bellowing from downstairs, "Laurie! Coom doun and knock the mud off my boots!"

Laurie sometimes looked at the sketch laughing James Gillray had made of her on the way to London. Could this prim miss be the same girl who carried out slops, fetched coals, tended bar and dodged public house customers today? Long after the family had retired, skudgy Laurie was on her knees, washing the filthy taproom floor; and this was not the worst of it! More than once she had fought to preserve herself from lecherous stableboys and alehouse patrons. A black eye, bruised ribs, blue marks on her fair arms were proof that her would-be gallant had come close to having his way. Was it any wonder that after four years of such a life she had been willing to take the first chance that came along, to improve her situation?

36

"How would ye like to wor-rk in a dairy, lass!" said the traveler who occupied a modest room in the Royal Scot's top story.

"I've never milked a cow, sir," answered Laurie.

"There'd be no milkin' o' cows, lass. The labor is less than what you perform for Mister Colquohoun."

"Just what would my duties be, if you please, sir?"

"Skimmin', scaldin', cleansin' and helpin' the cheese-maker."

"Would there be washing of linens, sir?"

"No."

"Carrying coals?"

"No."

"What would be the wage?"

"Four pounds annum and found."

"Let me think it over, sir."

A blind person could see that Mister Ronald Clargy was eager to hire and that he'd treat his hireling well. Laurie talked to Jinny about his offer.

"Take this chance to be sure!" she exclaimed. "Take anything to get out of my father's clutches. But wait—I'll ask father in a roundabout way who the gentleman is. I'll say he gave you a sixpence gratuity. The idea of anybody giving sixpence away will shock father into speech."

Soon Jinny found out that Mister Ronald Clargy was the bailiff of Lord Duff-Drummond whose holdings were in Angus County. Moreover, Mister Clargy was noted among Highland growers for having introduced the Ayreshire methods of cheese-making on his laird's estates. "'A worthy mon,' father said, 'one who'll go far to keep his laird in comfort, aye and also himsel'.'"

It was another matter when Laurie told her uncle that she was leaving his "hospitable" roof. "You'll come to no gude at a'," he muttered, "a young thing traipsin' into the wild Highlands wi' a purr-rfect str-ranger!"

Nevertheless, Laurie packed her heavy bundle. Mister

Clargy said she could take her books. So had ended her servitude to her Uncle Thomas Colquohoun, in Edinburgh.

She and her new master had boarded a coastwise hooker bound for Dundee and by happy chance they had excellent sailing weather. From Dundee they traveled north by stage through Coupar Angus and Alyth to Kirrimuir. Hark! Music of the glens broke upon Laurie's enchanted ears—running brooks, the sighing of wind through the fir trees! Here were the ancient hills again! How fresh the night breeze blowing down from snow-capped peaks! Still further north was Ben Glas, the heart of Angus Braes, where the travelers took to pony-back, "for a short-cut," as Mister Clargy said. The pony path climbed the east bank of the River Esk among green pastures bounded on either side by craggy hills.

"Look up!" said Mister Clargy. "There is the Laird's castle—Duff's Rock as it is called—it is only four miles more to my laird's domain which contains five villages—Ben Leva, Ben Fada, Grailie, Fairlie and Cortach by name."

Laurie was astonished to find that the mountains at the head of the River Glas swept upwards to a broad moor which Mister Clargy said was three thousand feet above sea level. Here on these moors or braes pastured a new kind of cattle—new for her. They were small and shiny black and without horns.

"They are the Polled Angus, also called Aberdeen," said Mister Clargy, "fair milkers but great beef makers, and much in demand at the moment, what wi' a war goin' on overseas and the need for salt meats. The truth is, I get a higher price for this beef than is usually paid; the Navy seems to prize it."

Mister Clargy gave his companion an oblique glance as he clucked at his pony, "One thing to lear-rn, lass . . . a basket o' the best is worth more than a bale o' the middlin'!"

Four

Nanny Biel Makes the Bridal Haggis

MISTER CLARGY'S PROPOSAL OF MARRIAGE CHANGED THE very air of the kitchen when Laurie walked in the morning after. Nanny Biel who cooked for the household; Nan who was maid-of-all-work; Ayreshireman Deek Byrd, who had come to Ben Fada to make cheese for Mister Clargy; young Davy the cattleman; they all looked up from their porridge bowls. The mere thought that the new dairymaid might become their mistress made them quick to bid her an extra-kind good morning, and Laurie marveled to see how willingly they shifted their position from companions-at-toil to that of underlings!

"Good morning to all," she answered as usual and started to serve herself from the porridge pot.

"I'll ladle for ye," said Nanny Biel. She gave her an extra spoonful and pushed the jug of skim milk to her hand. When the others had gone to their toil, Nanny said, "Bide a wee, Laurie!"

"Yes, Nanny Biel?"

"I'd hae a few worr'rds wi' ye, lass."

"Yes, Nanny Biel?"

The old servant seemed to find it hard to begin. "Child . . . I kna', as does ivery soul in the grange, tha' Mister Clargy hopes to plight ye his troth. An I'd like to speak oop, plain. A lass wi' not much more'n her fine looks canna be too proud. What I mean to say is . . ."

"I understand, Nanny Biel," said Laurie quietly.

" 'Tis na to speak doun your learnin', Laurie! Readin' and writin' are fine! Even I learned to take pen i' hand so's I cude write to my bairns and lassies, far awa. Five bairns and three lasses! Aye! They're scattered far and wide." Nanny Biel chuckled. "I vow they've peopled the New World wi' their offspring! Scots blood was always mighty and blessed! 'Thy seed shall inherit the earth' as the Scriptures say. Aye, lass, after the Great Rebellion, thousands upon thousands o' Scots put forth i' ships . . . onywhere . . . everywhere. . . . Here i' their ain land they'd starve, for the wars had wasted the countryside."

What was Nanny Biel coming to? Why the sermon on Scots history?

"I bring oop a' this to make you see why 'twud be wise to accept Mister Clargy's proposal," Nanny Biel continued. "Of a' the unmarried lassies i' the domain, his e'e fell i' the right direction. 'Nanny Biel,' said Clargy to me, 'yon lass wud make a fine baillie's wife. She'd help raise the people. We mought e'en build us a school.' "

"Clargy said that?" exclaimed Laurie in surprise.

"Aye! And he said more. Our laird is not like The Hamilton and The Douglas and The Penmouth. For a' I luved Sir Colin when he was a babe and suckled him at this breast— For a' I gloried in him when he grew to manhood— For a' I luve him still, I cannot boast that he's ony great Scot wi' strong feelin's for his clansmen."

"So . . . that's why they call you Nanny Biel!" cried Laurie. "You were the Laird's nurse!"

"Aye," answered the old woman. "I luved his poor dead mother like my ain child and to this day there's nary a lady i' the land more gracious than his grandmother, e'en though she do be full o' years and a bit forgetfu' o' auld Nanny Biel."

"Why do you say you cannot boast about the Laird, Nanny?"

"'Cause he's gone English."

"The English are not bad people."

"I dinna say the're bad or gude. I say they are softies."

Goose-bumps rose on Laurie's flesh as she remembered the strength of the Laird and the power in his lithe frame when he held her close in his arms.

"I . . . I saw him," she murmured. "He struck me as being a handsome and hardy man . . . not a softie."

"Handsome—aye! Heartbreaker, aye!" smiled Nanny Biel meaningfully. "But I recall The Duff's great-great-grandfather Nu! there was a man who cude call out twa thousand yeomen in defense of his lands and lead them in battle. And I recall The Duff's great-grandfather who fell only when he had slain two score English on the field! But our Duff has let his sword rust and his battle-horn n'er does blow."

"The wars are over, Nanny Biel!" cried Laurie in defense of her liege. "What foe could he kill?"

Looking about to be sure no one overheard, Nanny said in a whisper, "Warring ain't the whole o' life! A' my big bairn cares for is frivolities and sin."

Nanny Biel's conception of sin was so wide as to embrace almost every activity of mankind except church attendance on the Sabbath. "Tell me, Nanny, what kind of sin?" Laurie questioned.

The nurse shook her head like a wise old crow. "The de'il breeds a number o' sins and the Laird adopts 'em a'! Gamin' and bettin' . . . consortin' wi' jocks!"

"What is a jock, Nanny?"

"A jock is a tiny mon who rides the races. The Duff has his favorite jock thot he prizes more than a child o' his ain blood."

"There's nought so sinful in racing, Nanny Biel!" argued Laurie. "Many good, fine gentlemen race horses, in England."

"I kna', lass!" said Nanny Biel. "There's more . . . The

41

Duff will na settle doun, a quiet married mon! Och! I've heard his poor granny weep in sorrow that he wudna take some fine Highland lady for his bride and gie Duff-Drummond an heir! But the female who ca' take the Duff has ne'er been born! He breaks a' the nets that are spread!"

Nanny Biel's words brought to mind the thrashing fight of a King Salmon who rips the mesh and away like a silver streak into dark, free waters. Laurie's cheeks were burning red and her heart was beating to suffocation. What if Nanny Biel were to find out that the Laird had kissed her? "I must go to my dairy, Nanny," she pleaded.

"Nu . . . tarry awhile," said Nanny Biel. "I've na' doon speakin'! An the Bailiff wants ye, take him, lass!"

"I'm not certain I'd make the Bailiff a good wife."

"Fiddlesticks! You're the age when lassies go skittery thinkin' o' the pleasures o' luve! You're ripe as a peach on the bough! An' Mister Clargy is no weakling! Why wait, lass? An we hold the weddin' soon, the Laird will be bridesman as is the Scots custom. Think what an honor for Mister Clargy! And for you."

All the forenoon long, Laurie struggled with her conscience. "Can I be honest in marrying Mister Clargy?"

"Go to, little hypocrite!" whispered that small voice from within. "All you want is to justify your secret yearning!" How foolish to compromise a fine future for a myth! "Fate may be kind and let us meet again," said the dashing Laird. To what end? With what purpose? Another kiss? Another caress—Laurie clapped her hands to her flushed cheeks.

"Nu . . . thee looks like a boiled crayfish," said little Nan who came at noon with bread and bowls to eat the luncheon curds. "Has't thee bin i' the sun?"

The two girls sat down on the dairy step and began to eat. "The Laird's comin' has set the grange on its ears," said Nan. "Mister Clargy had to go to the castle again. The Laird wants village women to clean and set the Rock to rights. He was in a rage wi' Angus; he called him a clumsy oaf . . . no good except to blow the bagpipes! You should 'a seen Angus coom runnin' to Nanny Biel's kitchen to fetch soap and brooms! He's still there, dippin' his dirty fingers into the shortbread pan!"

"Women . . . to clean?" said Laurie. A wild thought struck her—that she might go to the Rock and catch another glimpse of the man whose memory haunted her night and day.

"Aye! Mistress Mcpherson and Mistress Saunders are gone. They took Mistress Saunders' walleyed spinster sister with 'em. Aggie's death on dust and cobwebs!"

Laurie's hopes sank. "Why doesn't the Laird have a caretaker?"

" 'Cause the Laird has no luve for the Rock," Nan declared. "I heard say he wish't 'twould slide down the mountain and disappear forever!" Nan giggled. "What a thumpin'! A' that armor! Those swords and spears!"

"Have you been in the castle, Nan?" asked Laurie breathlessly.

"I? No. But I've heard describe how it looks! A grand auld place wi' rooms bigger 'n the kirk, and everywhere the arms o' dead chieftains! Why it takes a whole tree to warm up the hall! This mornin' six lads were sent to the forest to cut wood! He was fair wroth, was the Laird that a' the wood was gone. I heard Angus say the last time the Laird was here was on his twenty-first birthday. Now he is thirty-four! And Angus didn't count right. He said . . . eleven years! It's twelve! I added on my fingers, and two thumbs over."

"Thirteen years, Nan!" smiled Laurie. "You haven't thumbs enough!"

Nan looked abashed as she spooned up the last drop of curds. She nudged Laurie's arm. "Hark! There's Angus, nu! Tha' stocky-built mon wi' a red beard and hair to match. The Laird's piobaire. The lasses fear him worse than a wild bull! Whisht! Here he comes . . . gie him not a glance!"

Laurie and Nan turned their backs on the piper but he did not pass them by. With his mouth stuffed full of shortbread, Angus strutted to the dairy door and looked the girls over.

"Nu, my proudfoot lassies! Gie auld Angus a wee smilie!"

"Awa' wi' ye, Angus!" scolded Nan.

"I dinna speak to thee!" grinned the red-bearded gillie. "'Twas yon goldilocks caught my e'e!" Grinning and combing the crumbs from his beard with blunt fingers, Angus strolled away.

"Like master, like servant!" giggled Nan. "When ye ken the Laird, ye'll see wha' I mean!"

All week there were comings and goings from the Rock to the grange and from the grange to the Rock. Granny Biel baked breads and cakes for the castle, the Bailiff brought ancient wine kegs and bottles to light, village men hunted game and fished the upland streams so that the table of the Laird could be well filled. The Laird wanted horses. The Laird wanted messengers to run with invitations to neighbor chieftains. The Laird ordered beef killed for a banquet—the best Angus steer Clargy could find among the herds!

News of carousings at the Rock filtered down to the grange. The Laird called for stone-putters, javelin-throwers and wrestlers from the villages to amuse his guests.

Occasionally Laurie caught a glimpse of a cavalcade of gentlemen riders going up the glens—their varicolored tartans looked like the plumage of the pheasant in the sun. Once she was able to single out the tartan Duff-Drummond but only once and the wearer was too far away for her to see anything but the colors.

Clargy's services being in constant demand at the Rock, Laurie had time to consider, pro and con. When Clargy spent an evening at the grange he talked of little else but the Laird.

"Last nicht, the Laird took on Wrestler Sandy from Grailie . . . floored him! Nu . . . Sandy might ha' drunk a bit more than was gude for his muscles . . . but the Laird is a bra' mon. And what a sight to see when he doffs his shirt and steps out in the loincloth alone! One wud n'er believe his chest were so wide and so deep! And smooth like yon hearthstane."

Laurie could not master the sensuous stir of her awakened body when she heard Clargy describe the one for whom she yearned. In vain she scrubbed and scalded until her wrists ached and her back seemed to break! Weary and beat, she could not sleep nights or find peace by day. Neither did Nanny Biel give her any rest, prodding her daily to hasten and make up her mind about Mister Clargy.

"It takes time to prepare a weddin' feast! Time to make the haggis!" And again, "How long will The Duff tarry i' the Rock? One day he'll get astride his horse and ride awa' —no noble bridesman for Laurie! No giftie o' siller!"

Came young Davy the cattleman with new fuel for the fires that consumed Laurie's heart. A strange youth, Davy. His speech was unlike any she'd heard before; and he spoke of God and His Angels like other young men speak of their earthly loves. He had come from the northermost part of County Caith where he was born, and he told Laurie about the surging waters of Pentland Firth and the swirling mist that blotted out the Isles of Orkney, "like a veil, to hide the face of the bride." It was wonder to behold the light in his eyes when he spoke of the Laird Duff-Drummond.

"I saw him yestereve. He'd been a-hunting. What a Chief! His brow is open like the marble cliff! The very manner of his gait bespeaks him Leader! He rises on the toe—'tis the heart tha' lifts him!"

"You should write poetry, Davy," smiled Laurie but her pulses were hammering. This young cowherd spoke the truth with a bard's tongue. "His brow is open like the marble cliff! The very manner of his gait speaks him Leader. He rises on the toe—'tis the heart tha' lifts him!" If untutored young Davy of Caithness could so clearly discern the magnificence of the Laird, was it any wonder that Laurie Macneil could be bewitched, enthralled, daft as a lamb in a daisy field?

True to his word, Mister Clargy did not make any further attempt to press his suit. But Laurie knew he was growing more and more impatient. Clargy not only wanted a bride, he wanted a fine wedding with his laird standing as bridesman. She knew the Bailiff would not wait much longer . . . that soon he'd come right out and say in his blunt manner, "Nu?"

What would her answer be? Laurie's practical sense told her, "The Laird was only playing with me." His remark, "Fate may will that we meet again," was gallant banter!

"Nu Nan, lass," said Nanny Biel one night as the servants of the grange sat at supper. "Soon ther'll be no more fine shirts to launder!"

"What shirts do you launder?" Laurie asked Nan when they had finished the meal.

"The Laird's and those of his French gentleman friend," Nan answered complacently. "You n'er saw the likes . . . so fine, so silky! Dost wish to take a look? I've a basketfu', ready for Angus to take up, tomorrow mornin'.'"

Laurie turned pale when she touched the fine garments. There was a little mark embroidered in blue silk on the bosom—The Twig o' Juniper, emblem of Duff-Drummond.

"Nu! Are ye ill?" exclaimed Nan. "Your cheeks are the color o' skim!"

Thursday was Deek Byrd's day for drawing the whey, a day of work from dawn until dusk. Laurie could almost believe what the cheese-maker vowed, that he had a "wee mon" who sat on his shoulder prompting his every move—how else could he make the identical cheese, week after week, without measure, without a clock or thermometer, by "feel" alone? It was her task to feed the fire under the giant milk kettle. "Na the thick stick!" warned Deek, "they gie too big a flame."

Heating, dosing, dipping, pouring, reheating, "Coom, lass! Nu, lass, we draw the whey!"

The old man hotted a long iron bar to blackness, and taking a handful of curd from the tub, he squeezed it almost dry and pressed the hot iron to it. When the curd was "right," the iron drew fine silky threads about a quarter of an inch long. Stirring to cool the mixture, Laurie could smell dripping udders, cream souring in the cat's dish, a babe who has sucked his fill—the very spirit of the milk itself. Now came the pressing process. She had learned to turn the press-bar slowly, and form the molds with gentleness, "not to bruise the curd."

The cheeses were then taken to the curing house and placed on racks. The rest was Deek's business; only a man of antlike patience would feed the fire, twig by twig, so that the air was not too hot, not too cold for curing.

"Whisht, lass," exclaimed Deek Byrd, "where's thy brains, today! Up i' the clouds are ye?"

"I . . . ?"

"Ye left three forms i' the milk-house."

"I'll get them, Deek," said Laurie, reddening.

"Is't thocht o' marriage, lass?" asked the old man kindly. "I kna' a lassie's wits do scatter . . . tell me, Laurie, what are ye minded to say to Mister Clargy?"

To her own amazement, Laurie sputtered an angry, "Oh, mind your own affairs!" and ran to her loft. Her wits were indeed scattered! She could think of nothing but a pair of dark sparkling eyes, the kiss of warm lips, the vital embrace of a man's strong arms and those arms were certainly not Clargy's!

Laurie doused her face in cold water and tidied her hair. She'd walk out a bit and let the wind blow the cobwebs from her brain!

The volume of Burns' poems under her arm, she climbed swiftly to the stone fence at the edge of the meadow. There she sat and pondered—marry Clargy or not? Marry him—she'd say farewell to worry and want. Marry him not —she'd have to pack her bundle and go! Clargy was not large-hearted enough to take "no" with good grace and jog along as before, master and servant.

It was true what Nanny Biel said when she was pressing Mister Clargy's suit. There was much that a woman of education could do to improve the lot of the people of the braes. Laurie had eyes to see the need of Duff-Drummond men and women. The Education Act of the Scottish Parliament of 1696 notwithstanding, the Laird's villages had no schools. The only person in the domain who knew how to read and write with scholarship was the Reverend Macbride, though Clargy knew enough to keep his tallies and read his Bible and Nanny Biel boasted she could write a letter. Often when Laurie was a child, she had heard her father rant that "Scots genius was left fallow for lack of the plow of education." A bailiff's wife might well be the one to stir up the yokels! There was no lack of natural talent in the braes—young Davy of Caithness a poet born, and in the village of Fairlie a youth named Abraham Warrack who was always building water conduits and wheels. He'd invented a crude wing-shaped plow with which to remove the snow in winter. Neither Davy nor Warrack could read one word of English or Gael. What would they accomplish if they had access to books, the inventions of the Modern Age?

Year after year, as Nanny Biel said, the finest youth of Scotland tramped to the seaports and sailed away to lands where they hoped to find opportunity. Why need they go? Give to the land like the English, and the land would give to you! Scotsmen knew nothing about tree planting and soil enrichment!

The sin of Scotland, of any people for that matter, was to raze primeval forests, leaving only bleak, barren wastes. Oh! heather was a pretty sight when it was blooming, but how much better than the purple heath a fine stand of elder, larch, maple, oak, fir, laburnum! Few Highland people had ever tasted a pear, a cherry, a walnut—even the apple was a rarity. Those who believed that the roots of trees spoiled the ground, the shade killed the grain and the branches fostered the birds that devoured their crops could be instructed in the modern science of forest husbandry. Why, a few broad thinkers could change the very face of Scotia! Spurred by noble thoughts, Laurie climbed higher and higher through the meadows. Yes, why not? Marry Clargy! Set forth upon a career of service to her native land! What higher ideal? And deep in Laurie's mind was the thought: "I'll show that kissing, carefree Laird that I'm not just a peasant maid!"

She plumped down on the grass and fluttered the pages of the poems until her eye fell upon the lines:

> O scenes in strong remembrance set!
> Scenes, never, never to return!
> Scenes if in stupor I forget,
> Again I feel, again I burn!

Alas, Robbie always had the right word! "Scenes if in stupor I forget, again I feel, again I burn!" Laurie buried her hot cheek in the crook of her arm. It behooved her here and now to lay the ghost of memory and quit crying for the moon! Marry Clargy! Forget the dream for fleshy reality! Cease to burn with will-o'-the-wisp fuel! Cease to shape the lips for phantom kisses! Kiss Clargy's good red face! Clasp him fondly! Bear his children! Clargy would make a fair, strict father.

First a lad and then a lass—she'd have them schooled and teach them manners. Yes! Yes! Marry the Bailiff.

A sharp, joyful barking warned her that sheep dog Charlie had spied her from afar. He came bounding up the hillside, took a stone fence in one flying leap and nuzzled his cold, wet nose against her cheek.

Then she saw Mister Clargy climbing toward her with purposeful clatter of hobnailed boots.

Deliberately she picked a buttercup and stuck it in her hair! Seeing the flower, Clargy turned red, then pale. He dropped on the grass and pulled her to him.

"Lass! Do you mean it . . . the posy? Do ye?"

At that moment Laurie wished she could cast the flower away, but it was too late!

Throwing restraint to the evening breezes, Clargy squeezed her in his powerful arms and whispered in her ear, "I luve ye lass! O I luve ye! We'll hae a fine weddin', wi' our chieftain to stand as bridesman! But we must make haste! The Laird will not tarry much longer. Say we set the time! Twa weeks fra today? Nu! Kiss your Roddie to seal the pact!"

Laurie closed her eyes and yielded her lips, but this was not the kiss she longed for—not the kiss that sent her whirling like a leaf in the wind!

Little knowing, Clargy kissed all the harder! "Let him!" thought Laurie. "I'll make believe. 'Tis not honest! 'Tis not decent! O Roddie! Kiss me! That I may feel the thrill of the Laird!"

The wedding was not to be like that of a Highland-born girl; Laurie would not go out of her father's house to meet her bridegroom, she being a servant under her bridegroom's roof, and no blood kin to swell the throng of guests; as for Ronald Clargy, his kin lived far away in Sterling County.

"The Five Villages will be our guests!" he said, "and no

payin' for vittles either,"—he would stand the expense, alone.

Plans went ahead for festivities on a larger scale than Laurie might have wished, but there was no holding the Bailiff, now! He was like a man drunk with his own conquest. Nothing was too good for his "bridie."

"For you, bonnie!" said Clargy, setting a large hamper at her feet.

"For me?"

"Aye! Open up! See what's inside!"

On top, wrapped in rustling white paper was a wedding gown! Oh! It was pretty! A high-bosomed dress of white muslin with a ruche at the neck and a sash of white satin!

"But . . ." Laurie cried in amazement, "when did you buy it?"

Clargy's eye twinkled. "In Edinburgh . . . after I met ye. Look underneath; there's two good dresses for a married woman, also other needful things such as shifts, hose, shoes and a bonnet."

"How did you know I'd say yes, Roddie?" cried Laurie.

"I . . . just . . . hoped!"

"Spend so much money . . . on a mere hope?" Laurie was deeply touched. "Thank you Roddie!" She kissed his cheek. "You're a dear, thoughtful man!"

Clargy smiled contentedly and scratched his head. "No, the ony worrit is . . . a bridesmaid to walk wi' the Laird! There's nary a girl comely enough to do him honor!"

"I've a bridesmaid in mind," said Laurie.

"Who might she be?"

"Nan."

"Our maid-of-all-work?"

"Yes. She has always been my friend. Please, Ronald, let Nan be my bridesmaid."

"Aa . . . verra weel!" Clargy consented.

"I, to be maid, and the Laird bridesman!" squealed Nan

when she heard the news. "I ne'er hoped for a better bridesman than Mr. Tweedie!"

"Who is Mr. Tweedie?"

"How owns the still. He makes the Cortach Dew from Glen Dollwaters. Coom, Laurie! Try on the weddin' dress!" Nan clapped her hands in delight when Laurie showed herself in bridal white. "Now try on the green poplin!"

"How do I look?" asked Laurie.

"Fack!" giggled Nan. "Now you look like a jimpy Salome, sharpin' to tempt poor Apostle John."

"Jimpy?"

"Jimp-middled! Slim i' the waist! Aye! The green color comes off in your eyes. Put on the bonnet, Laurie."

Clargy had chosen a new-style bonnet of black straw with a wide poke brim and green streamers that tied under the chin. Where in the name of common sense could one wear such headgear in this part of the world? If she wore it to church, would people listen to the Reverend's sermon?

"I like the bonnet best of a'!" sighed Nan. "I think if I had such a bonnet I'd die content!"

Laurie had never seen a Highland wedding though she'd heard them described. Highland brides wore no veil, only white flowers in their hair.

There was the ceremony of the scarf. "What does one do with the scarf?" Laurie asked Nan.

"You'll see when the day cooms!" giggled Nan. "'Tis a' so beautiful and so sad! Och! I wisht 'twere me was to be a bride!"

One of Laurie's doubts was soon answered—whether Clargy would break his rule and serve the indispensable *uisgha* for his wedding—when several barrels of the "dew" came pony-back from Cortach. Not even an abstainer like Clargy would dare go against custom and hold a "dry" wedding feast, in the braes.

Swift-running lads went out in all directions, to bid the guests to the feast. A steer was slaughtered, the pit was fired for roasting. Trestle tables were set up in the inner court, a platoon of lassies came to give kitchen aid. The busiest person of all was Nanny Biel. She made bread and a dozen kind of cakes. She brewed barley broth, "for coolin' the head," boiled fowl, roasted duck, pickled sheepsheads, and set frothed buttermilk to chill in the running brook. Her masterpiece was the festive haggis, for which she was renowned. "There's nae thing the Laird luves like a haggis!" she declared as she hashed and pounded, minced and steamed. "Cauld or hot . . . he'll revel in it just the same. Coom, Laurie! Watch close! Someday 'twill be your tur-rn to make the haggis for the Laird."

Laurie watched, she even jotted down quantities, ingredients and order of cookery on a fly-leaf of her book of Burns—a haggis recipe was a valuable item in the wedding chest of a Scotswoman. Would the day e'er come when she'd hear the name of the Laird without a quickening of pulse?

"Nanny Biel, what is the part the bridesman plays? I know so little of Scots weddings."

Before answering, Nanny Biel hooked a monster meat pudding out of the boiling kettle and poked it like a farmer pokes a piglet.

"They're done!" she exclaimed. "Nu, gie me aid!" The last of five monster meat puddings and one midget left-over raised from the kettle and put out to steam and set, Nanny nodded with contentment. "Weel, as I said before, first there's the giftie-trade. Bridesman's haggis for bride's siller."

"You didn't say, Nanny Biel!" cried Laurie.

"Nu! 'Tis na' to do wi' the weddin' morn. The giftie-trade takes place the eve o' the weddin'."

"What does it consist of?"

53

"Patience! I'm trying to get it off me tongue. The lass to be wed dresses in a decent dress . . . not white o' course! Your new green poplin will do! Then wi' the wee haggis, i' the basket, you go to the castle and knock three times, and when the door opens—no matter who it may be, you say, 'I am the bride, wi' meats for the Chieftain.' And you receive a gift o' siller."

"The Laird does not appear?" asked Laurie with dry lips.

"Nay! I doot!"

"And . . . that's all?"

"Aye. In aulden times, 'twas custom for the Laird to slice and taste the haggis on the threshold. But those were the auld days."

Laurie's springing hope was dashed, that she'd see the Laird again—just they two, face to face!

True, they'd come together at the wedding, but how different, to meet him in a crowd!

The coming of a pair of piper sergeants, home from the wars, and their two learners of the bagpipes was a sharp reminder to Laurie that she would soon trade her cot for the marriage bed. The four tootled and wheezed and blew all day and some of the night, practicing the old Scots air, "Fye, let's a' to the bridal."

Laurie's position in the Bailiff's household had changed, a buxom lass named Alice having come to take over her duties in the dairy, she was no longer servant, not yet mistress, something in-between—and Mister Clargy blocking her way, pleading for kisses! She laughed, escaped with a lock dangling and apron strings pulled, not daring to admit, even to herself, that his touch filled her with sensations quite divorced from love!

The morning of the last day before the ceremony her nerves were strained to the utmost, and so were the nerves of Nanny Biel. Nanny snapped at the maids like an old turtle. "Do this. . . . Fetch that. . . . Make haste! Clumsy!"

She heaved a great sigh of exasperation when Nan put a dish in the wrong place. "Mightn't I find bricht helpers e'en for our weddin'!"

"Our weddin'," giggled Nan, "anybody'd think 'twas you, Nanny Biel, not Laurie who is to be wed."

The old woman turned on the giggler. "N'er forget I was the Laird's nurse!" she said proudly.

"But . . . 'tisn't the Laird's weddin' either!" teased mischievous Nan. "Ye ken, Nanny, 'tis Mister Clargy and Laurie who are the bride and groom!"

Nanny Biel glared at the teaser. "Nu, wiseacre! Dost thee na' know tha' ony weddin' takin' place on the Laird's lands is like the weddin' o' the Laird?"

Laurie heard the echo of a voice long silent when Nanny Biel spoke so reverently of the Laird.

Her own father had been proud to teach her the duties of a clansman to his chief. How grand, he used to say, to be a *duinne uassal* or chieftain like the Duke of Hamilton or The Macleod of Macleod who maintained the ancient customs and honor of the clan. She had even been taught to recite the "parts" of a chieftain's *luchdtachk* or "tail"—a body of selected young men whose duty and pride it was to attend and guard him. Laurie could hear herself now, reciting in a childish treble: "The *gillie-coise* or henchman attends the person of the chief and stands behind him at table. The *bladair* is his spokesman. The bard tells his exploits in song and rhyme. The piobaire or piper accompanies the laird whe'er he goes, walks in front of the castle whilst the chief is dressing and plays at meals. The *gillie-more* bears his armor. The *gillie-piobaire* is the piper's servant and carries his instrument. The *gillie-casfluich* bears the laird on his shoulders at river fords and on rough and dangerous paths. The *gillie-truarneis* is his baggageman."

Today, only a few lairds preserved the ancient splendor and trappings of their forefathers—among them, the Duke of Hamilton and The Douglas.

But even London Duff-Drummond kept some traditions alive. Nanny Biel grudgingly admitted there was no more able huntsman and sportsman than The Duff.

"A pity he'll not contest!" said Nanny Biel. "He'd knock 'em all doun like ninepins!"

Watching from the kitchen window, Laurie saw Clargy's guests streaming to the feast. A merry lot they were! Clansmen and their wives rode pony-back with a wee bairn in Duff-Drummond kiltie up front. Athletes who would contest for prizes came with their "stanes" and spears and clubs. The dancers wore their swords. By middle-afternoon, some hundred guests had arrived and were searching for a place to bed in the barn, the hay-mows and outhouses. All this time, food and drink were served! Small wonder Nanny Biel and her army of helpers had toiled for a fortnight to make ready!

With every passing hour, Laurie became more nervous.

"When must I go to the Rock with the haggis?" she asked Nanny Biel.

"After sundown."

"But the sun sets so late!"

" 'Tis the custom, lass!" Nanny gave Laurie a sharp look. "Art afraid? The ony mon thee has to fear is Angus. . . . Look! Over by the hogshead!" Laurie followed Nanny's pointing finger and saw the Laird's gillie capering like a monkey around the trestle on which the whiskey barrel was set up.

"Dr-runk as a Liverpooler!" smiled Nanny Biel. "I'd niver ha' let ye go to the Rock if Angus were at large! But there's nought to fear, nu! Go, lass! Take thy bucket o' hot water for thy bridal bath. Dress nice and slow. 'Twill be sundown soon."

Laurie's knees were wobbly as she climbed to the loft. The din and laughter in the court was deafening and the pipers were letting go with all their lungs! Even sheep dog Charlie joined in with loud barking. She put down

56

the two heavy milk buckets full of hot water that she had brought from the kitchen. What was the matter? She felt so queer . . . hot, cold . . . first a chill and then a fever! Was it the warm evening? Had she stayed too long in Nanny's hot kitchen? The smell of cooking *was* a bit overpowering!

Laurie undressed to her shift, and searched in the kerchief bundle where she kept her most precious possessions for a piece of scented soap that her cousin Jinny had given her for her birthday . . . this was the time to use it! The scent of lavender was more agreeable than that of brown soap!

Dousing her hair, she lathered it clean and rinsed it carefully over a wide milk crock that Nanny Biel had let the girls use because it was cracked. She threw the water out of the loft window and poured a fresh crockful. Undressing, she bathed. Then she dried her fresh, sweet-smelling body and fluffed her hair into red-gold curls.

She had just finished tying it with a ribbon when Nan burst in.

"Oh, Laurie! Ye *are* the prettiest! I n'er saw ye true naked before!"

"Never mind!" Laurie slipped on a clean shift.

"But ye hae sich pretty tits!" cried Nan. "They are round and white like a snowball with a moss rose stuck i' the snow! Whee! Clargy is a lucky mon!"

Embarrassed almost to tears, Laurie bent to hide her flaming face and began to pull on a pair of white stockings.

"Nu, is there no hot water left?" said Nan who hadn't noticed her friend's embarrassment. "My laddie from Fairlie has came! Tommy Maclevy! And here I be, all dirty and mussed!"

"You'll have to fetch a pail from the kitchen," said Laurie. "I used the two."

"Niver mind! I'll wash my face and hands wi' cauld water! And a bit o' the neck and behind the ears! 'Tisn't my intention to marry Tom Maclevy, not this nicht, ony-ways! though he might try to win me wi'out a ring!"

Nan tossed away her work dress and began her sketchy toilet, talking all the while.

"Mister Clargy is lettin' go wi' the uisgha mug, too! And him so sober! But he's fair wild wi' joy! I guess a mon o' forty year is tha' proud to take a young wife . . . he'll be tipsy by midnight! But Nanny will sober him wi' her barley brew! Ye needna fear! He'll hae his senses complete for the bridal nicht!"

Dressed and combed, the light-hearted Nan dashed away to her pleasures, leaving a Laurie unstrung.

"Roddie Clargy . . . my husband?" she murmured to her reflection in her little pewter mirror. It was the old story—a girl in love, readying for marriage to one whom she did not love. How different if the bridegroom were . . . but no! The idea was absurd. In real life, a noble lord and a dairy-maid were not destined for each other.

Five

An Auld Scottish Custom

COUNT JEAN D'ANTIMES HAD TAKEN IT FOR GRANTED THAT he knew his friend Duff-Drummond to the core, but Colin of Mayfair and Colin of the Highlands were two different men. Was it the air of Scotland that wrought the change, as heat alters iron, cold the running brook? South of the mystic border, Colin had worn Bond Street clothing; crossing to the other side, he had put on kilt, sporran and tam-o'-shanter—but that was not all; there was a subtle change of way and mood. Always a lighthearted fellow, liking his liquor blended and his food well seasoned, liking his women in silks and jewels, now he would drink nothing except raw Highland whiskey—and too much of that! His favorite dish, venison *saignant* and a dreadful gruel of coarse grain. In the matter of women— zero!

Four weeks *sans tremper le bec!* Colin seemed not to miss the Duchess Diana d'Alboli, Lady Arabella Dorkington, Mrs. Maude Lowes, with whom he played love games in England. Even his latest favorite, the beauteous Lady Jane de Cruselle—forgotten. Was it the climate of Scotland, strenuous days of clambering among the crags in pursuit of mountain goat, nights of drinking? Rough games with Highland wrestlers, stone putters, javelin throwers? D'Antimes had marveled to see the aristocratic Duff-Drummond floor a hulking village champion in a Greco-Roman wrestling match! He'd always known that

Colin frequented London's wrestling clubs, to meet gentlemen wrestlers like himself. The match he had waged with one of his tenant lads was no lace-handkerchief game! And what would the lovelies of London say if they could see their darling now?

Duff-Drummond had assembled a pile of ancient spears and javelins from the panoplies on the wall. A giant stuffed bear, rampant, was his target. The spear hurtled the length of the hall and pierced Bruin in the underbelly. With every throw, the stuffing flew! Poor Bruin was rapidly becoming unstuffed!

"Zing!" went another spear. "Bumpfh!" grunted the bear.

"I say, Colin! How long do you intend to carry on?" laughed d'Antimes. "Let's play a game of chess."

"I've no patience for chess tonight," answered Duff-Drummond. He turned to the firelight and his friend saw the sweat glisten on his face and chest. In order to do his spearing more freely, Colin had bared himself to the waist. His nether parts were encased in Scottish trews, a tight-fitting garment made of Duff-Drummond plaid so cleverly pieced and fitted that the sett formed a lozenge-like pattern from hip to instep. With this odd garment, not unlike the diamond-patterned garb of Harlequin on a more muted color-key, Colin wore a heavy silver belt of antique design, and soft black slippers with lacings—a kind of evening shoe made after the model of the sturdy Highland brogues that he affected by daytime.

It was the first time French-born émigré Count d'Antimes had visited Scotland, though he'd long been intimate with Duff-Drummond—also a protégé in exile of Duff-Drummond's grandmother.

"Go with Colin to the braes, Jean!" said Lady Inverkleith when pleading with her grandson to visit his domain. "Watch over him! See that he behaves as a Scotsman should!"

Colin had needed no watching! He eased into the plain

and barbarous ways of his ancestors like a man eases into an old shoe.

"Why not tonight in particular!" laughed d'Antimes. "Haven't you exerted yourself sufficiently to want to sit awhile?"

"There's not time enough to finish a game," Duff-Drummond answered. "I'm expecting a female visitor."

"Ah-ha!" smiled Jean d'Antimes. "The Highland Venus?"

"I wish it were she!" said Duff-Drummond. "It's only my bailiff's fiancée, some overage dodlip!"

"What's a dodlip?" laughed d'Antimes.

"A cross-patch in petticoats. Clargy's bride-to-be could hardly be anything else. He's well past the skittish age. He values a good housekeeper and cook more than a pretty face! Have you noticed, Jean? When our Highland girls reach spinsterdom, they thin down . . . become stringy!"

"Can't say I've noticed. How can you tell a spinster, first-glance?"

"By the shawl, Jean. By the plaidie shawl. A married woman wears a black and white shawl. The unmarried girls wear the plaidie—on my lands, the tartan Duff-Drummond."

"I see," said d'Antimes. "And why should your bailiff's bride-to-be come calling at this late hour, and on the eve of her nuptials?"

"It's an old Scottish custom," Duff-Drummond answered. "The bride is supposed to bring a haggis to the Laird . . . token that she will furnish her share of marching rations in time of war."

"You seem especially well versed in old Scottish customs, Colin," laughed d'Antimes. "I'd never have believed it, to hear the way you faced your grandmother down, when she asked you to visit your domain."

"I detest my domain!" exclaimed Duff-Drummond, letting fly with another spear and piercing the bear squarely through the heart. "I'm baffled and distressed by the ignorance of my people. My skin creeps at their filth. My stomach revolts at their eating habits!"

"Habits you seem to share!" jibed the fastidious d'Antimes. "You dig into your bowl of porridge like a real Highlander."

"True," conceded Duff-Drummond, aiming another spear. "Habits and tastes of childhood are hard to change, never forgotten. Watch this! I'll get him in the neck!" He threw the spear and ripped the place where Bruin's carotid used to be. Hafting a rusty javelin he added, "It would be impossible for you, a Frenchman, logic to the core, to understand a Scot. We're a queer lot!"

"Really?" D'Antimes laughed sarcastically. "I hadn't noticed . . . just that you're the maddest Scot of 'em all!"

"Laugh if you like," said Duff-Drummond indulgently, "One half a Scot is a crusader, a defender of the faith, an expounder of truth, a reformer of sinners. The other half is a bolluxman of the worst—a spender, a drinker, an all-around no-good. I stood up to Granny also because I hate being told, 'Do this! Do that!' And I detest the hold she has over me, her million pounds sterling! When she dangles a gift before my nose as she did, to force me to pay a month's visit to the domain, 'Five thousand, dear boy, if you'll be good and do your duty!' I feel like throwing the money in her sweet old face!"

"But you won't!" grinned d'Antimes. "You'll be glad to get it."

"Of course. My creditors are breathing down my neck! Five thousand pounds will be like red meat to a pack of hungry wolves. They'll stop to devour it. And with luck, I'll take a purse or two during the racing calendar."

"If I were Scots-born I believe I could fit my ways to those of this country," said d'Antimes. "A far cry from my native Touraine to Angus County; but here, you stand on soil that is yours, live in walls that are your own. I talked with Sir Ian Hamilton the other evening during dinner and afterwards. He and his father the duke are all for Scotland. Sir Ian says that in time, and with much-needed agricultural reforms, the Highland Counties will flourish again. He says that his own herds have increased fourfold with the importation of English stock. He went further . . . said that when Scotland is returned to Scottish rule, there would be a change for the better in every way."

"The Duke of Hamilton is a rabid Covenanter," said Duff-Drummond. "He trained his whipper-snapper son in the same way."

"A handsome young man!" said d'Antimes warmly.

"Handsome, if you like rosy cheeks and red hair."

"I liked his looks and his spirit."

"Bah! Men with a cause are all the same, one-minded, fanatic! The Hamilton still preaches the Covenant of Jacob at prayer meeting. Would you like to see a document, the very existence of which most people outside Scotland ignore?"

Duff-Drummond opened a great carved dresser and handed d'Antimes a sheepskin roll covered with archaic writing. The signatures at the bottom were threaded with some twenty varicolored ribbons. At the ribbons' ends, the signers' seals in red and green wax.

"What is it?" asked d'Antimes.

"The Scottish Declaration of Independence, written in 1320," Duff-Drummond answered. "The exact replica of the original which is preserved among the national treasures in Register House, Edinburgh."

"Indeed!" exclaimed d'Antimes. "I confess my ignorance, also my inability to decipher so much as one word!"

"My old tutor, Dominie Macgregor caned me into a fair understanding of the text," said Duff-Drummond. "The language is medieval Latin. See, the j and the i, the u and the n are interchangeable. I was a lad of fourteen when the Duke of Hamilton sent the document to me. He'd had copies made at his own expense for each of the remaining clan chieftains, I suppose in an attempt to rally their pride and support to the cause of Scots rule. The thing fascinated me! For as long as a fortnight, I saw myself, a new Duff of Duff, risen to save the nation from the English! Here's my ancestor's seal, right next to that of King Robert The Bruce. The Duff died in 454 A.D. after a reign of forty years. He was descended from King Kenneth I and Margery of Drummond. 'Twas then that our clan name changed to Duff-Drummond . . . seems Margery brought quite an estate in her wedding chest."

"454 A.D!" exclaimed d'Antimes. "You don't mean 1454 A.D.?"

"Oh, no!" Duff-Drummond smiled. "There are still older records of our ancestors! We descend in line direct from the Old Testament kings. As for The Duff, he's a modern man compared to my earliest recorded ancestor who lived and died in 500 B.C. That was King Herremon, a Prince of the Scarlet Thread. See this red thread running through my tartan? It proves descent without a shadow of a doubt."

"And what might be the meaning of the Scarlet Thread?" asked the incredulous d'Antimes.

"Shades of Dominie Macgregor!" laughed Duff-Drummond. "Don't you remember? When Judah's twins were born to Tamar, the midwife bound the first babe's hand to come forth from the womb, with a scarlet thread so that the father would know his first-born and heir?"

"Come come, my friend!" laughed d'Antimes, who was of literal mind, "you can't expect me to believe you're descended from Judah!"

Duff-Drummond put a finger to his lips. "Ssh! Don't tell our Roman scholars, but it's the truth! We Scots are all sons of David, Judah, Dan, Levi . . . sons of the Covenant of Jacob—Israel. Hence . . . the name Covenanters. Ask Duke Hamilton! He can trace our tartans to the Twelve Tribes."

"I thought the tartan colors were the inspiration of your skilled Scottish weavers," said Jean d'Antimes.

"By the Albanoch, no!" exclaimed Duff-Drummond. "The colors take their origin from the Bible! Remember the verse: 'Now Israel loved Joseph more than all his children, because he was the son of his old age and he made him a coat of many colors'? The tartans are the remembrance of Joseph's birthright, his coat of many colors. Why, even the Juniper Twig and many other clan badges have Biblical significance. Remember Elijah who sat himself down under a juniper tree to die and the Lord raised him up? Here it is—the event commemorated by my clan badge in this brooch of silver which I'll give to Clargy's bride when she joins Clan Duff-Drummond."

"Pretty!" said d'Antimes, admiring the jewel. "I wish I could believe . . . but tell me what's written in this Scottish Declaration of Independence? It stirs my Voltairian sense to think that fourteenth-century Scottish kings were revolutionaries."

"Your Voltairian sense!" scoffed Duff-Drummond. "I suppose you thank Voltaire for having deprived you of your lands, wealth . . . your very heritage!"

"I thank nobody. But I can put the finger on many reasons for my loss. Voltaire had something, my friend, and we nobles of France were ripe for the guillotine. Believe me, I do not condone the abuse of power just because I myself am a victim of violent reform."

"I'm sorry, Jean!" said Duff-Drummond. "One sometimes forgets just how much you lost. Come here to the light. I'll try and recall what I read years ago. We'll skip the compliments to the Pope and translate roughly as follows:

". . . WE KNOW . . . THAT THE NATION OF THE SCOTS PASSING FROM GREATER SCYTHIA THROUGH THE MEDITERRANEAN SEA AND PILLARS OF HERCULES, AND SOJOURNING IN SPAIN AMONG SAVAGE TRIBES . . . COULD NOWHERE BE ENSLAVED . . .

65

"... AND COMING HENCE, ONE THOUSAND TWO HUN-
DRED YEARS AFTER THE OUTGOING OF THE PEOPLE
OF ISRAEL, THEY, BY MANY VICTORIES AND INFINITE
TOIL, ACQUIRED FOR THEMSELVES THE POSSESSIONS
IN THE WEST WHICH THEY NOW HOLD ...

"These 'Possessions in the West'—this ancestral land is
Scotland. And the name Scots is a derivation of the Greek,
Skuthia, or Scythia—a region north of the Black Sea where
our ancestors sojourned before setting sail through the
Pillars of Hercules, the Straits of Gibraltar as we call them
today. But the name Scots has another, older derivation—
sons of Isaac ... Isaacsons ... Saxons. I don't expect you
to follow me down the line, but I'll explain the historical
meaning of the text.

"King Edward II of England having failed in his attempt to subjugate the Scots and meeting with crushing
defeat at the Battle of Bannockburn in 1314, enlisted the
support of Pope John XXII, who sent emissaries to The
Bruce, demanding his submission to the English king. But
The Bruce wouldn't parley with Cardinals Gancelin and
Luke. Instead, he assembled the Scots Parliament and this
document was drawn up and dispatched to London and
Rome. The importance of the document—so Duke Hamilton affirms—is that it refutes false historians who hold that
the Scots kings are a myth, and that the tie between Scotland and the ancients of Israel is a folk legend."

"Sons and daughters of Biblical kings!" mused d'Antimes. "No wonder your Scots are all so headstrong, proud,
unbending. Reformers and Protesters indeed! And your
young girls ... beautiful as princesses of Jerusalem!"

"Do you mean that thumpin' lass I almost rode down?"
said Duff-Drummond with a quizzical smile.

"The same. Now there was a beauty. I thought certainly
you'd make an effort to see her again."

"I would have, except that it's unwise to go chasing

66

after the daughters of my tenants and clansmen," said Duff-Drummond. "If I were to attempt to play Paris to that village Venus, I'd be very unpopular indeed."

Duff-Drummond tossed the Declaration of Independence back in the oaken chest and picked up a spear. "We'll not be here much longer. I plan to leave immediately after the wedding. We'll ride to Melfonts' for dinner and on to Montrose. Then to Edinburgh by ship. I want you to see our grand coastline."

"I vow I am curious to witness a Highland wedding," said d'Antimes. "I've heard they're very gay."

"Aye," Duff-Drummond smiled. "A better word is raucous. But we'll not tarry for the feast that lasts all day and all night . . . sometimes the day after, depending whether the whiskey holds out!"

"I'd hoped to see your national games and dancing."

"Believe me, Jean. We'd better slip away before the solid drinking begins. I might go after that golden-haired charmer and get my head bashed in for my pains."

"Oh, very well," said d'Antimes. "I bow to your better judgment."

"I promise I'll show you a Highland wedding with all the trimmings, the day I marry!" said Duff-Drummond.

"You . . . marrying?" d'Antimes roared with laughter.

"I might."

"I'll wager no money on it!"

"You're wise, Jean!"

"But you *do* remember that golden-haired charmer," teased d'Antimes. He rose. "I think I'll leave you to your old Scottish customs and go to bed. I'm halfway through a fantastic tale in verse of wars and loves that I found on your library shelves. It breathes the spirit of heroic times, a kind of Scottish Iliad."

Borne by a light southeast wind, a needle-fine mist sprayed Laurie's cheeks and eyelids as she climbed the steep path to the castle. This was the first time she'd seen the Rock near-by. It was more massive than she had thought, a stronghold that must have cost back-breaking labor of those who piled stone upon stone. The ancient drawbridge was in disuse: the bridge was down, iron-studded outer portals stood open; what need for defense now? The bones of Duff-Drummond's ancient foes lay moldering in the chasm below.

The shades of evening, closing in, seemed to restore the old walls to their former majesty—impenetrable keep defending the inviolate standard of the clan chief. There were lights in the windows of the east wing. No sentinels on watch. No fierce dogs roaming, as of old. Laurie paused and brushed the misty dew from her eyes—if she could only see the Laird once more! Just once. Not in a crowd as they'd be tomorrow, but alone. It might well happen that her heart would cease yearning. "I've had my wish," she'd say. "I've gazed on his dear face and I possess the keepsake of his memory for all time!" She climbed with laggard step, well knowing this could not be. Old customs . . . dead as the dead of ancient wars! There were many good customs of old—for instance, a clanswoman could be pressed into service of her liege to supply food for his warriors. Thus the womenfolk were able to share in the adventures of their men. How grand to stand by Duff-Drummond when the horn blew!

Slowly, Laurie lifted the massive iron knocker. It fell with a thud. The door shook on rusty hinges. She listened to her own heartbeat in the stillness. Knock again! Three knocks, said Nanny Biel.

The door swung open at last.

"I bring the wedding haggis . . ." Laurie began. She stopped short! This man in half-naked splendor—this chieftain with spear in hand—"The Laird!" she gasped, and her surprise and confusion heightening, she held out the basket: "The haggis, milord!" and turned to flee.

"Wait!" A hand plucked at her shawl and bared her head. "You . . . Clargy's bride?"

"Yes, milord! They sent me . . . I didn't mean . . ." Laurie's tongue tripped and her wits failed her.

"Come in out of the damp, lass!" said the Laird in a kindly tone.

"Oh, sir, it is late! I must be on my way!"

But he coaxed her over the threshold. "Why all the haste, young woman? You know the custom. We must slice the haggis!"

"Oh, sir," stammered Laurie, "Nanny Biel said we'd not do it! She said milord wouldn't . . ."

"My old Nanny thinks I have no love for the customs of yore," said the Laird. "She's wrong! Come, lass, we'll slice the haggis according to clan ritual."

A hundred thoughts flashed through Laurie's mind. Nanny Biel said . . . slice the haggis on the doorstep, but the Laird was leading her through a great hall and up a stone stair!

The light from a single smoky torch brightened shredded banners and brought a glint from iron ghosts who stood with lance in hollow arm and helm on headless shoulder.

She gasped in wonder at the hall, a place to hold an army encamped! Soft rugs of Persia under foot. Rich old Flemish weave on the walls. A fireplace of stone carved with the arms of Duff-Drummond. Massive oak tables and high-backed chairs, and a great couch covered with tawny foxskins.

"I must apologize for my attire!" said the Laird as he pulled on a jacket of black velvet. "I was idling the time, throwing spears. See poor Bruin? He looks more like a porcupine than a bear."

The Laird's pleasant manner, his smile, his serene welcome set Laurie somewhat at ease. What a fine gentleman! What a cavalier! She dared peep as the Laird went to a dresser to fetch a great hunting knife. How handsome he was! Much more so than when she'd seen him first, all covered with the dust of travel and a three-day beard on his chin.

"Now let's see this haggis!" The Laird took the pudding from its wrapping and sniffed it. "Fine! Fine! Perfect aroma! Do please hand me that pewter platter, over there, young woman!"

As Laurie hastened to do the Laird's bidding, "Can this be I?" she marveled—"I, Laurie Macneil, here with the Laird of the domain?"

"Now!" The Laird placed the haggis on the platter and held the knife poised. His dark eyes flashed at Laurie. "You know the custom? If I approve you will be for all time duty bound to provide your share of marching rations for my army."

"I didn't make the haggis, Laird!" said Laurie shyly. "'Twas Nanny Biel."

The Laird frowned. "Indeed? Do thee wish to trick me, lass?"

Laurie cried, "No, no, milord!"

He burst into laughter. "Come! I was only jesting! Haggis-making is a job for old crones. Young beauties like you have better work for their pretty hands, such as combing their golden hair . . . love-making!"

Laurie blushed like a rose at this bold talk. The mere word, "love," from this prince's lips made her tremble.

The Laird sliced the haggis with a sure stroke of the knife and examined the texture with a critic's eye.

"Fine . . . smooth!" He broke the slice in two and gave half to Laurie. "Delicious! It's worth all the hardships of a journey to the braes, just to eat Nanny's haggis."

"I marked down the recipe, milord," ventured Laurie. "I think I could make a haggis, too."

"A lass from England, interested in haggis-making?"

"I was Scots born, milord."

"You must have gone to England when you were very

70

young. It's not easy to unlearn the Scots after childhood."

"I was put in an English school when I was twelve, milord."

"So, you are a learned miss too."

"A little, milord," said Laurie in trembling delight that the great Duff-Drummond should treat her almost like an equal. "I read Burns . . . Wordsworth . . . Shakespeare, and love them . . . especially Burns."

"You like the Bard of Ayr?"

"I do indeed, milord."

"Admirable taste. My own liking for good Robbie cost me some thrashings when I was at school. Our Eton masters said he was neither grammarian, poet, nor scholar—in short, a barbarian!"

Laurie listened in rapture. All this was so far beyond her wildest dreams that she could hardly believe she was sitting here—not like a poor village girl, but like a guest of the castle.

"Excellent haggis!" said the Laird. "I'll reward Nanny Biel with a flask of her favorite blackberry cordial. As for you, Miss . . . Miss . . ."

"Laura Macneil is my name, milord."

"Pretty name, Laura."

"Most people call me Laurie."

"I like Laurie too, but Laura suits you better. You have a kind of beauty as grave and meaningful as your namesake, the laurel tree. I am also reminded that your Macneil tartan bears the scarlet thread."

"What, milord?" said Laurie, who didn't understand.

"That scarlet thread in the sett," said the Laird, pointing to the plaidie shawl she had let fall from her shoulders. "Tartan Duff-Drummond has it too. Tell me, Laura, how came you to meet my good bailiff Clargy?"

"I was serving in my uncle's public house, the Royal Scot, in Edinburgh, when Mister Clargy engaged me to come to the braes as dairymaid."

71

"Poor child! So much beauty wasted!" said the Laird. His tone plucked at the heartstrings.

"Milord flatters me," cried Laurie. "Mine is not real beauty. Those with dark hair and dark eyes are the beauties."

Duff-Drummond lifted one of her curls. "Not beauty . . . this? And your eyes! Blue as the skies. Your skin! I've never seen the likes in London. Your figger—divine! I mean no offense, just that a shape like yours is hard to find. Especially the ankle!"

"Sir, you overwhelm me!" murmured Laurie. It was folly to listen. She must leave.

"Tell me, Laura, why does a girl so fair have to settle for poor Clargy?"

"Mr. Clargy is very kind, milord, and I am very grateful that—"

"Mr. Clargy should be the grateful one!"

"A girl who has to earn her own living soon learns to count only on her fitness for work."

"A girl with your looks could have London at her feet, like Helen had Troy!"

Now he was really jesting! "I think Helen had more ambition than I, milord," laughed Laurie. "Also she had two fine gentlemen named Hector and Achilles, both eager to win her heart."

"All this, and Homer too!" exclaimed Duff-Drummond. "Beauty, wit, learning. Jove, Laura Macneil! You could turn the capital topsy-turvy!"

"Now milord is making fun of me," said Laurie, with a pretty pout.

"I? I never felt less like making . . . fun!" Duff-Drummond's tone changed. He seized her wrists and pulled her to him. "Lass, from the very start you had me perplexed . . . bothered. Remember that day when we kissed? I said, 'Fate may be kind and let us meet again.' I've been hoping. You understand I couldn't go out and beat the glens. But

72

something told me— Oh, Laura, this is Fate's own hand pointing the way!"

Laurie trembled. Could this be the working of Nan's spitting-stone? "I wish that within the hour ye may set e'e on the one whose sweet love ye will be." Within the hour, Mister Clargy had asked her to be his bride. But she'd also set e'e on another, the very man whose arms were stealing around her waist at this moment!

"Laura . . . lovely!"

"Laird . . . I beg you, free me!"

"One kiss!"

"Have pity!"

"I kissed you once! You consented!"

"This is not the same—"

"Why? Are these not the same sweet lips?"

"I . . . I belong to another!"

"Not yet, my sweet!"

It was true. She hadn't plighted her vow to Clargy. But Laurie held back in fear of her own weakness . . . the Laird's commanding will.

"I promised to be Clargy's bride, milord! That is enough to obligate me."

"My! My! What big words!" said the Laird caressingly. "Is it a crime to kiss? Does the imprint remain? Secrets are sweet keepsakes. One . . . one kiss . . . just one. Who will ever know?"

"I would, milord," cried Laurie. "How could I ever forget—"

"That we kissed at first sight!" prompted the Laird. "That you stole my heart? Darling, ask my friend Count d'Antimes! I raved about you, raved like a schoolboy! Why only a while ago, Jean was teasing me, 'Why do you stay? Just to catch another glimpse of that girl?'"

Laurie ceased to struggle. How much easier to melt in the Laird's arms, let his kiss rekindle the flame she'd fought in many a tortured hour of remembrance!

73

When the Laird freed her, she was as breathless as though she had run a race.

"I said one kiss," said the Laird with earnest mien. "See. I keep my promise!"

Laurie's heart sank. Her conduct demanded a tongue-lashing. "Unashamed! Bold! Brazen!" But her pulse said— Only one?

It was not easy to assume an air of dignity, but she tried. Picking up her shawl, she started to put it on.

"One moment!" said Duff-Drummond. "I must not forget to give you the gift o' silver, according to custom."

He was trying to gauge the inroads he'd made upon the girl, virgin she was, by her trembling, by the drowned look in her eyes. Her mouth when he left it was chilled, as with flux and rush of new sensations a virgin's blood drains to her vitals. Evidently she'd never recovered from the shock of their first embrace! It was a maiden's way to treasure baubles of souvenir that had moved them from the land of innocence to the adult kingdom. A moment ago he'd thought only of a little sport—a kiss or two, a caress—now his ideas were changing, and to hell with tomorrow's bridegroom! Half tipsy with wedding toasts, Clargy would never know what his bride had lost—or care!

He opened the jewel casket and took out the brooch that he'd shown Jean d'Antimes.

"The Twig of Juniper. Wear it for the clan and for me." He pinned the brooch on her bosom.

Trembling at the touch of his fingers, Laurie stammered, "I thank the Laird. I shall wear the Twig forever."

"Gracefully said, Miss Macneil. Now will you not seal the giving of the Twig according to ancient rite?"

"I am of Clan Macneil, milord, instruct me."

"Very simple . . . I place my right hand on your left shoulder . . . my left, around your waist . . . draw you to me . . . thus . . . then I say, 'Grace upon my clanswoman . . .' and you answer, 'Grace upon the Laird.'"

74

With faltering breath and pounding heart Laurie repeated the salute. So near, the Laird's dark eyes seemed to burn. She couldn't draw away. She did not even want to!

"Now, we give the ceremonial kiss, one on each cheek," said the Laird. This done, his lips slipped and fastened upon hers. Sweet lass! Her response had the quality of dedication! Soft arms wreathing his neck, she strained him in close embrace, so close that her breasts rolled like golden apples on his bare chest! Cautious though! Fright not! Deal your assortment of sweets, one by one. First the sugarplum kiss of tender feelings, then the confessional kiss, "I adore you!" Next, the kiss of desire uncontrolled, passion unleashed! Now, cruelty takes a hand in kisses that finish on tooth's edge. Calmer, give the kiss that wanders like a minstrel. Cheek to throat, temple to heaving bosom! Lacings give way. Snowy cream with strawberry topping melts on the tongue! She's helpless now, caught in the web where a virgin dies! This is the moment to destroy the last barrier—a girl's *pudor*. Gown-hem turned up is like the trumpet blasting of Jericho. "Dearest! Beautiful! My Queen!" The foxskin couch is soft . . . soft . . . lovely limbs nestle among the furs. Quiet those cries with kisses while walls go crashing down.

Cheek to cheek with her lover-Laird, her red-gold head resting on his muscular shoulder, Laurie shut the door on returning consciousness. ". . . wish I might die, here . . . now!" What better time? She had riddled love's riddle! Limbs all lazy with release from longing, she was at peace. What greater joy could the world hold?

The Laird's eyes were closed. The flames painted dancing lights on his shapely body. Oh, to die, here in his arms, and so never have to face the truth—that she'd betrayed another's trust, given her maidenhood to this Prince of Love.

She was not sorry! No! Not at all—except for the one

betrayed. Poor Clargy! Go she must and face him—not to ask forgiveness but to announce, "I love another. I cannot marry you." Woe to the wedding feast and the guests assembled! Woe to Clargy who must sustain double shame —double loss—that of the girl he loved and his manly pride! But there was no other way. She was too proud to steal away like a thief! First, she'd have it out with Clargy.

"Mine! All mine!" her lover had whispered. "My own! My love!" he'd sobbed in ecstasy. 'Twas bliss to hear him! Delirium to imagine the future in his arms!

> While day and night can bring delight,
> Or Nature aught of pleasure give,
> While joys above my mind can move,
> For thee, and thee alone, I live.

"My darling!" murmured Laurie, pressing burning lips to her lover's cheek. The Laird stirred and opened his dark eyes.

"Ah, Laura! I must have had a catnap! Come here! Let's see you, in all your Venus beauty! He pulled her playfully to him and propped her against his knees. Her long, red-gold locks had come undone. They hung below her hips. "Wonderful hair," he marveled. "I didn't realize it was so long. You knot it like a seaman's line. There's a way to display what you have to better advantage!"

"I've never learned those arts, milord," said Laurie shyly. Her whole skin pinked under the subtle fire of his gaze.

"They're easy to acquire!" said Duff-Drummond. What a subject for a St. James' Street couturière and hairdresser! But wary now, lest the girl gather a snowball of ideas. He'd pother enough, keeping apart the mistresses he had. Too bad! This one would have added new luster to his collection.

He wrapped a lock of golden hair around his fist and pulled the captive down within reach of his lips.

"You're the prettiest lass I ever kissed!"

76

"Am I truly?" cried Laurie in rapture.

"I might even go so far as to say . . . adorable!"

She was not slow to reward him for his compliment. Gad! How the lass learned! Lips that could barely babble the ABC's of kissing now spelled out the Advanced Reader without stumbling! Even Duff-Drummond who had many strings to his bow could not help but wonder at the natural talents of this Highland girl for love! There was a quaint mixture of country freshness and schooled knowledge that enchanted while it amazed. Laura gave full rein to her feelings, at the same time she played the coquette better than Jane, Arabella, even Diana who was the surprise package of 'em all!

A pity such a gem of feeling, tenderness, passion was destined to be buried in Angus Braes! How this gel would shine in the setting of London—but no! Decidedly no! Lulled by a soft caress of a small hand—not so smooth that it would not snag a silken pillow—Duff-Drummond closed his eyes and let fancy wander. How the bucks would paw and gee! If only it were feasible to keep her in some out-of-the-way nook—but no! Diana, Arabella, Maude, Jane were not women to be deceived! They'd tolerate a split, four ways, of their lover-in-common's attentions—they'd never down a pill like this peasant beauty!

"Here!" laughed Duff-Drummond. "Waste no kisses, lass! We've miles o' lovin' ahead!"

Laurie thrilled. His meaning was clear. Oh, he wanted her as much as she wanted him!

The Laird rose and took her hand. "Come, lass." He led the way to a bedroom hung with scarlet brocade. "Stay by the fire and warm your pretty backside, I'll fetch a robe."

Laurie looked around in wonder. She'd never seen a room like this! The furniture was carved in massive oak. The bed was high and wide and hung with scarlet draperies. There were smoke-darkened paintings on the walls,

77

battle scenes led by chieftains on horseback. Truly, here one stepped from modern times into the past.

But the man who came out of the closet with a robe of blue wool over his arm was not a figure of the past.

"I find the strangest oddities in my ancestress' chests and boxes," laughed Duff-Drummond. "Here's something. I once locked my pet dog in it and got a caning for my fun. I've always had a mind to try it on the species for which it was invented."

"What is it?" asked Laurie, gaping at the metal cage.

"Turn your pretty buttocks! You'll see!" CLICK! CLANK! Laurie found herself encased from hip to thigh in a corselet of steel, her female parts quite beyond reach, unless one used a smithy's tools.

"Look at you!" laughed the Laird. He turned her to the mirror.

Golden hair in a waterfall, lips so red that they seemed painted, eyes full of stars—and under the silver cage, red-gold burning!

But Laurie saw only her lover. His fine head towered above her shoulder. His dark, naked skin formed a perfect background for her ivory body.

"What is this . . . this thing?" she stammered, pointing to the belt.

"A chastity belt. Don't you know? In olden times when the knights set forth on a Crusade or to wars in distant lands, they didn't trust their wives too much! My ancestor, Fiachadh the Duff, when he went to war in 1020, seemed not to have trusted the Lady Isobel. He called in a silversmith and had her fitted with this belt. Then he went to Jerusalem to fight the Heathen and stayed in confidence, eight years. Of course, the Lady Isobel was faithful! How could she be otherwise unless she had the double key! Anyway, there's only this one left. It seems the knights wore the key around their necks on a chain, like this." Duff-Drummond slipped the chain over his head and smiled as

78

he patted the little silver key. "Now, Lady Laura! Be faithful, while I fetch something to eat!"

He whistled gaily as he left the room.

"I'll be faithful forever!" murmured Laurie to her reflection in the mirror—strange picture she made! The silver cage was hardly a comfortable garment. With every step it cut her tender flesh. But love could endure even such torment. Shivering with a sensuous thrill, she pulled on the robe of blue wool and waited by the fireside. Those ladies of old must have been another kind of being, that they needed a cage to make them true to their liege!

"Lady Laura" he called her. Of course he spoke figuratively, meaning to evoke the olden days. But the thrill of it! Lady Laura! Lady Laura!

"Here I come with the head of Emperor Saladin himself!" said Duff-Drummond. He placed a huge platter on the table in front of the fire. "Roast wild boar . . . cheese. Bread. A bottle of white wine. Sit down, Laura."

"I find it hard to sit, milord!" said Laurie demurely. "This belt . . ."

"Ah, the belt! Of course!" The Laird took off chain and key and knelt on the rug. "Let down your robe. Turn around to the light. The padlock is so small. The keyhole is doll's size. I don't want to break the key in the lock and leave you like the Lady Isobel, belted and chaste for eight years!"

With every click of key on metal, Laurie thrilled. Strange vibrations struck her through and through. When at last the belt clanked to the floor, she let her gaoler take her in his arms. "Laura! Love!" Step by step, kiss by kiss they neared the huge bed. Kiss by kiss, caress by caress, love conquered again. This second bout with Cupid was more bitter-fought and sweeter won than the first. Laurie's last scruple was cast away, her last maidenly fear was vanquished. Dear love, for nothing less than this would she have broken troth with unspotted modesty—this blaze,

79

consuming all yet leaving all whole and restored like the sands when the tide has passed.

The Laird stretched his muscled arms and yawned. "Now . . . about that supper. I'll carve the meat. You'll find the necessary to refresh yourself in yonder cabinet."

What fastidious gentleman's array of soaps, toilet waters, razors, silver brushes and combs! Laurie had never even seen, much less used this article of furniture—a kind of basin, built like a hobbyhorse and filled with scented water. But instinct told her how to put it to use. She then tidied her curls and donned the comfy blue robe. Next it was the Laird's turn. He soon joined her, dressed in a style that she'd never seen—a kind of long coat of wine-red brocade with dashing revers and stand-up collar.

"What a beautiful coat!"

"Like it? I got the idea from a Russian friend, Count Malakoff. The Prince of Wales had it copied in six different colors! Georgie-Porgie always loses his head over some tailor's novelty. Sit here beside me, Laura. Your glass! We'll drink to . . . what?"

"To our love," said Laurie with a shy smile.

"Oh! Very well! To our love!" While restoring his powers with a hearty meal, Duff-Drummond was somewhat apprehensive lest his conquest should dream of attaching herself to her conqueror, time without end. Perish the thought! But it was not easy to dampen a maiden's fire once she was a-burning. Now it was she who wooed with amorous cooings—"Darling! Sweetheart! I adore you!"— she who scattered kisses like rose petals. What an enticing piece! Her long red-gold locks were scented with the spice of glorious youth and health. Her skin was satin-smooth— soft as a babe's. No paint or powder had e'er altered that cheek, no corset ever squeezed that slender waist. And her lovely breasts were Venus-shaped, in the heat of love they budded. And every part of her twinkled, vibrated, swayed to his tune. Great Juno! What a woman!

The clock was striking quarter to four when Duff-Drummond suddenly awoke and looked at the sleeping girl beside him—a grand night! But it was high time . . .

"Laura," he called softly.

"Yes, my love?" She awakened with a kiss, ready to enfold him again.

"It's getting late," he said, regretfully warding off her clinging arms. "This is your wedding day . . . Remember?"

A nerve rippled at Laurie's throat. No—she'd misunderstood!

"Laura." He rocked her gently as if to bring her wide-awake. "You'd better make haste, girl! Clargy's guests will soon be swarming. I wouldn't like you to be seen returning!"

Returning—what did he mean? Laurie sat up, stared at her lover.

"Come, lass." Duff-Drummond threw back the covers. "As much as I hate for us to part, your bridegroom will be waiting!"

"I . . . marry Clargy . . . now?" gasped Laurie, turning pale.

It was now becoming clear to Duff-Drummond that he'd ill-gauged the nature of this peasant lass. Just his luck, to pick one not only pure, but full of moral virtues. Searching for some logical reasoning that would salve her conscience and at the same time free him from impossible obligations, he remembered a legend of his clan.

"My dear child. Nobody, least of all Clargy, would question your right to go through with your nuptials as planned. You and I have done nothing wrong. Surely you know about the time-hallowed law of our clan: 'a maiden that the Chief covets shall present herself, willing, for the Laird's pleasure. This counts not as stain or blot on her purity, and nuptials may be consummated thereafter as before.' "

"I . . . I know nothing, milord!" cried Laurie.

"But Laura," argued Duff-Drummond with quiet insistence, "the law of Laird's Choice was written in our books in the year 1140. Ask Clargy . . . no, better not! Clargy will have no complaint! Anyway . . ." Duff-Drummond finished his argument lamely, "he'll never know the difference, if you're spry and get back to the grange before people are up and about!"

Raging waves, foaming out her own shame, broke over Laurie as she searched for her discarded clothing. She knew there was no use arguing, questioning; the Laird had had his amusement with a dairymaid. For all his talk that she'd turn London upside down, that her wit and beauty would take the capital by storm, he meant only to spend a pleasurable night with a pretty girl. Fool that she was! But coming to the fox-covered couch where first she fell, Laurie thrilled again. I love him in spite of everything! I'll never stop loving him!

Tears scalded her eyes as she slipped on her shift and petticoat, her green poplin dress, shoes and stockings. Could it by any chance be true? Was there some centuries-old law of Laird's Choice? She'd not admit it's validity in these modern times. But many were the laws that had gone into disuse—the torture rack, for instance. Trial by fire. The ducking-stool. It was common knowledge among Scots that tyrannical chieftain-kings of auld made and unmade laws to suit their own convenience. Each clan head was, indeed, a law unto himself, until Union and the spread of English justice—not that she could or would go through with the nuptials with Clargy as planned! Laurie was searching desperately to justify the immoral act of a seducer whom she'd enshrined on the highest altar of her heart.

"Laura! Are you ready?" The Laird had buckled on his kilt. He seemed not to feel the chill of morning on his bare chest.

"Dear child," he murmured, taking her in his arms, "this has been the most delightful night of my life."

O heart! Where was Traitor Death for whom she longed? Laurie followed the Laird through the dim hall and down the stairs.

"À Dieu va!" said Duff-Drummond to himself as he watched the shawled figure slip away. He hoped sincerely all would go well, that she'd be a good gel, marry Clargy as scheduled. But of course she would! Girls had a habit of falling and getting up again. He yawned cavernously. What he needed most was sleep! The wedding was not until noon. There was plenty of time. He closed the door and returned to his bed, still fragrant with a girl's youth.

On the drawbridge, Laurie paused to quiet the pain in her heart—pain like a knife. The eastern sky was like a scarlet canopy flung across the sleeping vale. She drew a deep breath and ran on. She was nearing the end of the bridge when a dark shape sprang. The impact hurled her to the ground. Sobbing and gasping, she fought the terror she could not see. Who was this monster? He reeked of whiskey and sweat. He was strong as an ox!

"Whisht! Lass!"

"Angus!" screamed Laurie. Her cry was stifled by a hairy hand that clapped over her mouth. "Noo! Lass! Be still! You and I ca' hae a bit o' sport . . . coom gentle, behind yon rock!"

Her captor picked her up as though she were a feather and pressed her face to his sweaty chest. Pinioned to the ground by a knobby knee, she knew she was lost! Punishment for her night's sin was swift and sure—to die a thousand deaths by rape of a drunken gillie!

"Noo, lass!" Angus' red beard scraped her face. "Noo . . . a kissie to Angus?"

Six

A Funeral and a Feast

LAURIE, IN HER TORMENTING DREAM, WAS STANDING IN A pool. Water touched her chin. She strained for thirst but could not drink. The water ebbed too soon. Her feet bathed in slime. She screamed but no sound came. Who was the silent watcher at her bedside?

"Whisht, lass, 'tis Nanny Biel."

Laurie opened her eyes, and saw the old nurse's face in the shuttered light. She could not link the present with what had gone before, she remembered only pain . . . fear . . . then as memory quickened, she sat up, lips framing to scream.

"Hush, hush!" soothed Nanny Biel. "Here. Sip this hot milk wi' a drr-rap to restore the spirits!"

But Laurie pushed the bowl away. "Nanny! How did I come here? Oh, tell me, or I'll go mad!"

Nanny Biel sat down heavily. "Och! Woe to thee, Laurie," she said with a labored sigh. "'Tis a sad day for a bride . . . twa men dead!"

"Nanny! I' heaven's name, what do you mean, twa men dead?"

The old nurse swayed back and forth in her chair. "'Twas partly my fault. I went to bed late. Cudna sleep for the bear-screechin' i' the court . . . so restless, I rose at four to stoke my bake oven. Lord knows why I took it i' me head to go see if you and Nan was safe. Nan was, but you . . . your cot was empty! Och! Laurie! I ran to look if Angus was still there wi' the drinkers! He was gone! I woke Mister Clargy . . . He didna remember rightly when Angus left. 'Clargy,' I said! 'Go quick! Search for Laurie! I fear Angus has got her!' He took off so swift I cudna follow. And young Davy on his heels! He'd heerd wha' I said about gillie Angus! Sure enough, there you were . . . Angus o'er ye, growlin' like thunder."

Laurie shuddered and hid her face.

"The end was foreseen," said Nanny Biel with the sad, inspired look of a prophetess foretelling doom. "Ronald Clargy, God rest his soul, was a strong mon. Angus was na' named the Bull for nought. I heard 'em scrabblin' and scuffin' and gruntin' . . . I was trying to bring you to your senses, poor lass! But Davy was in at the finish. Locked in mortal fray, Clargy and Angus dashed into the chasm!" Nanny Biel's voice dropped to a whisper. "I bade Davy carry ye to the grange. I made him swear he'd ne'er tell! He'd kiss the stones where you walk, Davy wud! Now he's gone wi' the men to bring the bodies doun."

Laurie began to understand. She'd been saved, she remembered, just as everything went black, Angus huffing in her ear, "Lass! Lass! Wake up!" No doubt the fainting spell had been her best defense! Not even a drunken gillie would take an unconscious girl!

"Nanny! Nanny!" sobbed Laurie, "I wish I were dead!"

"Twa corpses is enough!" said Nanny Biel. "All ye need do is . . . dress, tidy thy hair. Put on thy shawl and wait."

"Why? What will happen?" cried Laurie in terror.

"The Laird will hauld questioning," answered the old nurse, her head going up in instinctive loyalty to the chieftain. "The Laird is law of the domain . . . except when the Royal Guard is summoned. I see no reason, nu the murderer and his victim are both dead."

"Nanny . . . Nanny . . . what shall I say if they question me?" whispered Laurie with chattering teeth.

"Wait!" answered the wise old woman. "Wait 'til they question before ye plan to answer."

"Nanny Biel!" cried Laurie when the nurse turned to go. "Tell me . . . truly! Is there a law which says the bride can be the Laird's choice, before she weds?"

Nanny Biel came back to the bedside. "What nonsense is this?" she asked sternly.

"But . . . he said . . ." Too late Laurie caught herself.

"Who said . . . ?"

"The Laird."

"Soo!" Nanny Biel shook her head. "Tha's where ye were, wi' him! I might ha' known! Och! Poor dove i' the eagle's claw!"

"You haven't answered!" cried Laurie. "Was there ever such a law? Oh, tell me, Nanny Biel, for I love him more than all the world, more than life itself!"

The old nurse's anger was slow, but now she was aroused. "For shame, Laurie! Luve him, she says!"

"I do! I do!" wept Laurie. "I worship the ground he walks on!"

"Fie on ye!" cried Nanny Biel. "Laird's Choice, eh? If there e'er was sich a law, it was struck oot these five hundred years! Och, lass! How cude ye? What wickedness! Twa men dead for a wastling's pleasure! Och! Poor Clargy! God pardon the Laird, for I canna!" Nanny Biel stopped short. "Hark! The pipers! Hear 'em skirlin' the Cumhadh for the Dead! Dress quick, lass! I'll call when it's time."

Laurie ran to the window. There they came—four pipers ahead. The two dead men had been wrapped in their tartans and laid on crossed staves. Laurie could see Elder Donald Carmeichel of Ben Leva and Deek Byrd striding in the fore. Except for Davy, helping carry one of the improvised biers, the other marchers were strangers. Surging up to meet the procession, the kilted mob, the village women, the bairns, dancing as tho' bound for a fair. Laurie was too numb to weep. What said the psalm singer? I will be sorry for my sin!

She dressed and knotted her hair the best she could. Shawl drawn close, she went back to the window. The tragic procession was now entering the court. The bearers placed their burdens in the center of the court. The four pipers took their places at the four corners. They were playing the Cumhadh—saddest music ever piped!

It seemed to Laurie that the entire population of the domain was trying to crowd in around the biers—strange contrast to the grave demeanor of the crowd were the antics of a few drunks who hadn't the faintest notion what was happening! Strange contrast, too, the tantalizing odor of roasting steer—all the preparations for a wedding feast in full view!

Laurie heard a low murmur. Her knees nearly buckled as she saw the Laird riding in with his friend. The two gentlemen dismounted and the crowd parted to let them pass. The Laird was pale but composed. He was dressed in the tartan. First he uncovered the face of his dead bailiff, then that of his gillie. With measured step he led the way into the house.

Of violent impulse, these Scottish folk could also be masters of their emotions—so it seemed to Jean d'Antimes as he waited with Duff-Drummond in the office of the dead Bailiff—a small, unpretentious room with one window. The desk on which Bailiff Clargy was wont to count the Laird's lease money and tithes was nicked and marred by long use. A quill pen was stuck awry in an inkpot. Several worn ledgers stood on a shelf above the desk. A plain-faced clock ticked the minutes away. Duff-Drummond had seated himself in his bailiff's chair. Hands quiet, features composed, he was calm personified, the only clue to any inner disquiet—his extreme pallor.

It was not long before the room filled with dour-faced men and the air began to reek of uisgha breath, and fire-smoke. D'Antimes wondered at the ease with which Beau Colin could switch from the accent of Mayfair to his rugged, rattling Gael. The faces of the men grew longer as they listened. One man spoke briefly. The others chimed in with an "aye" or a nod.

There was a mystery here that might never be solved—so pondered the young Count from France. He'd wakened early this morning in keen anticipation of attending an authentic Highland wedding. But his host was grave as a stone image!

"Trouble, Jean," he'd said.

"What's happened?"

"My bailiff and my gillie had a fight. Their bodies were found at the bottom of the cliff."

"The bridegroom?"

"Yes. Poor fellow. I'll never find another bailiff so honest and hard-working."

"Then . . . the wedding?"

"Eat, Jean!" said Colin. "I'll have to go down and hold a kind of inquest. The nearest coroner is in Kirrimuir. Here on my lands, I act as officer of the law. After the inquiry, the feasting can begin—"

"Feasting?"

"A *draigie* instead of a wedding feast. Draigie means a funeral feast in the Gael. Highlanders have no preference, so long as good food and drink do not go to waste."

A singular man, Colin! His coolness amazed the sensitive d'Antimes whose every nerve was alert to some latent drama, some unsolved enigma.

"What was the cause of the fight, *cherchez-la-femme?*"

"You Frenchies! Always *cherchez-la-femme*," shrugged Duff-Drummond. "A Highlander will fight for a word misused, for a dour look! Angus would fight for the sake of fighting."

The longer d'Antimes watched and listened, the more certain he became that there was a woman in the case—Colin's icy demeanor, his close-lipped reserve, his lack of haste, as if he needed time to arrange his own thoughts, and now, the appearance of a young woman—bereaved fiancée of the Bailiff!

Jean instantly recognized the girl he'd seen in Duff-Drummond's arms the day they arrived. Not a spinster dodlip—Colin's Highland Venus was to have been Clargy's bride! And she was the girl who had come to the castle last night, "to fulfill an old Scottish custom!"

Flanked by a proud-faced old woman whom Colin called Nanny Biel, the girl withstood the bombardment of searching eyes without flinching. But as Duff-Drummond began his questioning, this time in English, d'Antimes saw her chin tremble and her fingers pluck at the edge of her tartan shawl.

"What is your name, young woman?"

"Laura Macneil, milord."

"Were you promised to wed my bailiff, the deceased Ronald Clargy?"

"Yes, milord."

"When did you last see Mister Clargy?"

"Last evening, milord."

"Have you any explanation why Mister Clargy and my gillie Angus should have quarreled?"

"No, milord."

"Nanny Biel tells me my gillie had accosted you before."

"He did speak, milord. But . . ." The girl tried to blink back her tears.

Jean d'Antimes saw Duff-Drummond's lashes flicker.

"That is all I need to hear, Miss Macneil. Believe me, I feel for you deeply in your bereavement." As the Laird added a few words in Gaelic to Nanny Biel, it seemed to d'Antimes that she answered him with a kind of brusquerie, while shooting a look to kill from snapping old eyes.

Duff-Drummond rose and spoke again in Gaelic to the dour gathering. The only word d'Antimes could understand was *uisgha*.

The clansmen then filed out of the room, and as the nurse and the girl turned to go, "Wait!" said Duff-Drummond. He pulled a silk purse from his pocket and offered it to the girl.

"No . . . no thank you, milord," she stammered.

"Take it!" urged Duff-Drummond.

"No, milord! I couldn't!" The girl turned and fled, sobbing. But the older woman took the purse with no "thank yous."

D'Antimes and his taciturn companion rode away immediately after the "inquest."

They had left Ben Leva far behind and were riding through a rocky gorge when Duff-Drummond reined in his horse and turned to look back over the valley.

"What will happen to that girl, Colin?"

"What happens to any girl? She'll stop crying . . . wonder . . . is love always like that? She'll try again, to find out. If her next partner fits, she'll soon forget last night. I'll return ten years from now and find a plump mistress Mac with her brood o' nine. Come, Jean. Let's ride on. I want to get to Melfont's before dark."

First a double burial—Laurie was forced to stand at the grave and hear the dirt fall on two coffins, forced to join the women in their keening for the dead. As soon as the draigie feast started she ran to her loft. All afternoon and night, the clansmen and women ate, drank, danced, sang, and the bagpipers skirled and tootled sad tunes and gay.

When night was dark and the revel was at its height, she carried her bundles down from the loft. Then she crept to the stable and saddled a pony.

She longed to say farewell and "thank you" to Nanny Biel but to stay an hour longer in Ben Fada was more punishment than she could stand. She had taken bread and cheese from the pantry—nobody saw her. Poor, tired Nanny Biel had gone to bed, the maids were out there dancing holes in their shoes! She had one royal fifteen, part wage and part 'a bit o' siller' that Clargy had given her—generous gift from a man ill-used to spreading his money. No—she'd not tarry a moment longer.

Laurie led the pony to the place where she'd left her bundles and slung them behind the saddle. It was not so long ago that little Nan had said, " 'Tis dreadfu' to hae nae hame, nae safety."

Loving the clear Highland waters that gushed from the snows, loving the scent of Highland fern and the cool caress of Highland rain, Laurie Macneil was doomed to leave it all and flee. Would she ever see again these green meadows where the small, black kine grazed, these homey cots where the orphan wanderer had thought to find warm shelter? Was there "nae hame, nae safety" anywhere?

Seven

Return to Auld Reekie

A THIN LITTLE MAN IN A BROWN COAT BOARDED THE STAGE-coach at Ben Glas, seated himself opposite Laurie and proceeded to watch her from under heavy, arching brows like a small brown owl watching a mouse.

She hoped that soon he'd turn his attention to some other passenger but he did not, and as the hours passed and the stagecoach rumbled its way south, she first grew restless, then frightened. Could Mr. Brown-Coat be sent by the constabulary to spy on her, waiting to arrest her at the end of the road? She changed her seat when a passenger alighted in a village near Dundee but this did not stop Mr. Brown-Coat. He stared and stared until she wanted to cry, "Why do you look at me?"

It was in passing a field where a herd of cattle were grazing that Mr. Brown-Coat remarked to nobody in particular, "This hae bin a poor year for calvin'!" He nodded, "Aye!" and lapsed into silence. Not a spy, a farmer! In Dundee Laurie hired a lad to lug her bundles to the waterside. A ship's mate told her that the *Highland Queen* would haul anchor for the Firth o' Forth on the mornin' tide, passengers could stow now. She paid her two shillings' fare and went aboard.

A stiff, nor'norwest wind drove the *Highland Queen* to Edinburgh with good speed. Laurie, who had always loved a ship and never felt discomfort on a bounding deck, was ill all the way. Her sufferings were made more acute by the chatter of a kindly-intentioned but inquisitive woman who ministered to her. Where was she going? Where had she come from? What was her name?

Her protectress would not be left behind when the *Highland Queen* came to dock.

"Share my hackney, child! I'm riding to Grassmarket where we have a greengrocery."

"I go to Princes Street," murmured Laurie, "it is out of your way."

The lady, Mistress Gough by name, hailed a hackney, piled in Laurie's bundles. "Where, in Princes Street?"

"The Royal Scot, if you please."

"The Royal Scot? We furnish greengroceries to Mr. Colquohoun . . . a fine man!"

Laurie's heart sank. She had planned, with the few shillings she had left, to go to cheap lodgings; as soon as she'd earned enough money for coach fare to London, she would journey on southward. Now, every turn of the wheels brought her closer to the public house.

No sooner had the hackney stopped than Laurie piled out and dragged her two bundles to the pavement. "I thank you, Mistress Gough . . . I thank you for every-thing!" She waved the driver on. Thank heaven it was early in the morning, the Royal Scot was still shuttered. If only she didn't have her bundles. Books, of all things. How futile to cling to these symbols of culture! What use had she for Rousseau and Racine? No matter how she tried to rise, she always fell back to the level of slop bucket and broom.

Laurie saw a caddie idling on the opposite street corner. She was about to call him, bid him pick up her bundles and direct her to cheap lodgings, when a window above opened. Her cousin Jinny looked out. "Psst! Laurie! Wait! I'll come down!"

Sickened by the odor of stale tobacco smoke in the public room, Laurie clung to her cousin's arm. "Jinny, I'm in trouble."

"I know," Jinny nodded.

"You . . . know?"

"Poor silly! 'Twas all i' the newspapers . . . Mister Clargy's dreadful end . . . the fair young fiancée, havin' to fold her weddin'-gown i' the lavender!"

Laurie broke down and wept, let her cousin help her upstairs. This was even worse than she'd anticipated. How could she have forgotten the newspapers that thrived on mishap, sorrow, murder, death! Who had given the known fragments of her story to the press? Not the Laird— but yes, it might be he! Even Lord Duff-Drummond would be obliged to report a double death on his lands to a higher law . . . some scribner might have seized upon the report . . .

"Now," said Jinny, eyes bright with excitement, "lie down! I'll take off your shoes. Tell me . . . tell me everything, Laurie. Tell me before Father finds out you are here. He says there's skullduggery somewhere, that you must have led Clargy on, then the other—what was his name, Angus?"

"It's not true, Jinny!" sobbed Laurie. "It's not true! I swear it!"

"That's what I said. 'Laurie isn't that kind!' I said. Poor Laurie, a widow e'er she becomes a bride! What will you do now?"

Mister Colquohoun's wrath rolled like ocean breakers when he discovered the prodigal beneath his roof. "How dare ye show your face i' my respectable house? Did ye think murr-rder cude be hid, and those tha' had a hand i' murr-rder cude go scot free?"

Laurie let the first wave ebb. She declared with firmness, "Uncle Thomas, Mister Clargy and the gillie were roused by liquor. I was in no way to blame. I do not ask to stay under your roof. I'll look for work this very day. But you have no right to accuse me of things I did not do."

94

Muttering darkly, Mister Colquohoun stomped down the stairs.

"You told him right, Laurie!" said Jinny with a toss of her head. "Father always sees the worst side of everything!"

Laurie asked herself which was worst: her uncle's anger, her Aunt Emma's maudlin sympathy or her cousin Kate's underlip smile, the contempt in her cold gray eyes?

Jinny alone stood by her. "Do not go to the Cross today. Who would hire you so wan and pale? Come! I'll put you to bed. Then bathe and wash your pretty hair. I'll clean your dress. Tomorrow will be time enough."

That night Jinny clasped her cousin to her bosom. "Goodie! I missed you Laurie! I had nobody to tell my secrets to. I've a big secret, beggin' to be told. Look Laurie!" Jinny pulled a ring that was tied to a ribbon, from her bosom. "Now you may call me Mrs. Baird."

"Mrs. Baird!"

"Yes. It's true. I'm a married woman. But it's a secret. Nobody knows!"

"Jinny . . . who?"

"His name is Walter Baird but I call him Wattie. He's a student at Surgeon's College, a wonderful young man. Poor as a mouse!"

"Where did you meet him?" asked Laurie in amazement, knowing how close Thomas Colquohoun kept his three daughters.

"Whisht! I was combin' my hair at the window one day when I saw him come walkin' down the street, his chest stuck out, tammy ribbon a-flyin'. . . . I happened to drop my comb . . . he picked it up. . . . I went downstairs . . . we spoke a few words. The next day he passed again, and the next. Then we made a tryst, and I stole out to meet him. When I asked Father if we could marry, he flew into a rage and said I must never see my Wattie again, that a penniless student was not for the likes of me! Then came the bad time. But we wouldn't give up. Night after night

I stole away. We used to climb up to the castle and sit among the stones and he'd smack me wi' kisses and we'd hug and look at the lights o' Auld Reekie . . ."

Laurie let her cousin ramble on, her own thoughts heading back over the long way she traveled—what was Jinny saying, her voice lowered to a cooing whisper? "Laurie, have you ever kissed a real kiss?"

"Whom should I kiss?"

"Someone . . . anyone . . . just to know what a kiss is."

How well Laurie knew. The word stirred her like a caress.

"Even a kiss is nae so much!" Jinny whispered. " 'Tis only play compared to loving, and that's the truth. My Wattie loves me so strong. . . . Oh, if you could know!"

Who knew better than Laurie Macneil who had lain in a lover's arms and tasted every delight, every thrill, every torment of love?

"I'm weary, Jinny!" she sighed, but her cousin was not to be silenced.

"I can tell you how 'tis done . . . first he kisses . . . then you kiss back. Then he touches . . ." Full of a wedded woman's daring, Jinny's fingers twinkled like the wee feet of a mouse.

"Oh, let me alone, Jinny!" cried Laurie in a ferment of remembrance. "Let me sleep, can't you? I must rise early and look for work."

"Don't you care to hear how Wattie and I got married?" Jinny pouted.

"Well, how *did* you get married?"

"You don't care at all—"

"Yes, I do."

Jinny's whispers tripped on and on over the stones of her bedfellow's silence.

Early the next morning, Laurie went to the Cross where city and farm servants waited—in truth the old City Cross had been torn down and hopeful hirelings loitered around

96

the door of the Tron Church, like beggars asking alms. She was not the first one there. Women young and old, men of all ages stood singly or in groups; a big girl with red cheeks and strong bare arms looked the newcomer over. "I've been for an hour by the Tron, Hinny! De'il an ane has speered my price and I've twice your heft to heave a hayfork."

Laurie stood until she could stand no longer. Would-be employers came, looked, went their way. By noon, hiring was over; as the crowd began to disperse, a hag in a gray shawl accosted her. "I ken a house, lass! There be on'y six girls, none so pert as ye be! The mistress treats gude . . . meat twice a week, no work and spirits on Sunday. Sixpence the pass." The hag's foul breath, her meaning, made Laurie's stomach turn! She picked up her skirts and ran as though fiends were in pursuit.

Day after day, she forced herself to go back to the Cross. The apple-cheeked girl was hired, so were other fortunates. Once a pleasant-faced woman asked Laurie many questions, said she'd speak to her husband, come back that afternoon. She didn't keep her promise.

"Trouble wi' *you*, lassie," said a vendor of hot scones, "ye look too muckle the fine lady!" She'd been dairymaid, skudgy, water-carrier, kitchen-helper, barmaid—why should they take her for a lady? Was it the green gown with a longer skirt than servants wore? Perhaps she had better trade it for a woolsey frock. Her place at the Royal Scot was becoming untenable. Mister Colquohoun never let her pass without some jibe— "So . . . the widow Clargy haen't found a new husband?"

"He begrudges every bite you eat," said Jinny. "I have to smuggle your food out of the kitchen." But Mister Colquohoun was willing to let his niece scrub taproom and kitchen floors, mop the stairs, dredge the pavement while family and servants slept.

"Laurie! I prayed you'd not find work today," said Jinny

when her cousin came home at the close of the fifth hopeless day of waiting at the Cross. "A gentleman came."

Laurie's heart seemed to stop beating. "A . . . gentleman?"

"Well . . . not quite a gentleman. The steward of a lady . . . a great lady, said Father. She's Lady Inverkleith who lives in George Street. Her ladyship is looking for a gentlewoman companion."

First one wild hope, then a modest one was dashed. "I . . . a gentlewoman?"

"Well, are you or are you not? I say you are. George Street is a fine street. The people who live there will never know you were a pub servant if you're clever."

"How did this steward know I was for hire?"

"He said he'd seen you at the Tron. Just as he was about to speak, you up and ran!"

"It must have been . . . Yes! I know what day."

"I warn you, Coz!" sermonized Jinny, "unless you lie, you'll never get out of your fix. Look at me! What would Father do if he knew about Wattie? Out! That's where I'd go! 'Let your husband feed and house ye,' he'd say. You know how Father is. I don't know how much longer he'll let you stay. I heard him ranting to Kate. Kate hates you too. Anyway it won't hurt to try. The number is 28, George Street."

Wearing her bonnet and kid gloves, Laurie crossed Nor'Loch Bridge that afternoon. She paused a moment to gaze at the turreted castle high up above the hunchback spine of High Street—St. Giles, like an open crown under a cloth of gold—not only to look, but to gather courage. Would Lady Inverkleith accept her as a gentlewoman companion? She wished her hands were not so rough and red! She wished . . . Oh! if wishes were horses, beggars could ride!

The front door of every house in George Street opened on a wide well-paved street. Malodorous gutters were sunk out of sight. What a change from the Old Town with its dark, crooked closes! Number 28 was built of stone as white as curds. It stood in a straight line with the neighbors, not a single front awry!

Laurie pulled the bell-wire at the service entrance and listened to the jangling of the bell.

"Follow me, young lady," said the manservant who opened the basement door. He led the way to an office where a soft-spoken man with gray hair received her.

"How kind of you to come, Miss . . . Macneil."

"Thank you, sir," said the amazed Laurie.

"Sit down, Miss Macneil. My name is Malcolm. I am Lady Inverkleith's steward. I saw you at the Tron. I must confess I was looking for a scullery helper at the time. But milady is also in need of a young companion. Tell me, do you care for dogs?"

"Why yes, sir," answered the astonished Laurie.

"The reason I ask is because her ladyship keeps a number of pets and one of the duties of her companion is to air the dogs . . . amuse them."

"I'd be happy to do anything required, sir! But . . . my fear is . . . I'm not experienced enough."

"Let me be the judge of your experience, Miss Macneil," said the kindly steward. "Lady Inverkleith will say the final word. The pay is generous, thirty pounds per annum. Will you come with me?"

The gray-haired man led Laurie up a service stair to the Master's Hall—a beautiful staircase soared to the second story. A velvet carpet muted her steps. A graceful fan-window threw a mellow light over all. Here were dozens and dozens of paintings in wall panelings made to fit life-size portraits of dogs—poodle and boarhound, pomeranian and spitz, terrier and sporting dog, bloodhounds, bulldog, greyhound, mastiff, coach dog and lap dog, even a humble turnspit treading his wheel. There were kinds of dogs that she'd never seen before—dream-animals created by an

99

artist's fancy, the most eye-catching, a picture of a beloved pug with wings, and a halo over his little snout-face! Underneath the picture was the inscription: "Pet of the Angels—My Bowzer."

Laurie's guide knocked at a door ornamented with cream and gilt carvings. "The young woman is here, milady," he said to someone inside.

"Bring her in, Malcolm," answered a flutelike voice. Milady was a dainty little old lady who looked as though she might have stepped right out of the pages of Monsieur de Perrault's "Puss in Boots." Unlike the fabulous Marquis de Carabas, she had no cat but she had a dog—many dogs. At first glance Laurie counted three . . . then five . . . she gave up counting! The room was alive with toy poodle dogs, fluffy and white as the new-fallen snow.

A curtsy was not simple to manage with a swarm of prancing doggies around her feet. One little rascal leaped into her arms and tried to lick her face.

"Ah! Prince already adores you!" cried the mistress of the house. "Splendid! Splendid! He isn't easy to please. Thank you, Malcolm. You have excellent taste. Come here, child! Careful, don't step on Dauphin. I taught him to thread between my feet . . . he'll trip you if he can! Look at Madame! What a beggar she is, she wants more cake!"

Chattering, waving a lace handkerchief, she nodded her powdered head that was covered by a high, starched bonnet of white lawn with blue ribbon streamers, her ladyship beckoned Laurie to a chair at her side. Immediately the dogs gathered around in a circle and gazed at her as though she were some choice tidbit for dinner.

"Aren't they the naughties!" crowed her tiny ladyship. "They hope you'll give them an extra treat—but no! They've already had their tea. Let me tell you their names. The one with the yellow bow is Prince. The blue bow is Dauphin. The white bow is Madame. The pink is Reine. The violet bow is Marquis, the green, Baron, the plaid is

100

Bruce. . . . Where is Duke? Ah! There you are, you bad boy. He wears a black bow. His Duchess passed away last year. I may say that I have owned every variety of dog known—did you notice my portrait gallery on the stairs? Each favorite was painted by a famous artist, even Treadle Tom who used to turn the spit in the Duke de Jussin's kitchen. The Duke was my first husband. Now I have only these eight poodles left."

Bewildered, charmed and amused, Laurie listened to the chatter in treble key that poured from the lips of this doll-like creature and tried not to stare at the diamond rings, brooches, bracelets with which she was bedecked.

"I am Lady Inverkleith, but I like to be called La Monette. You are too young to know that soubriquet. Everyone is too young nowadays. You are very pretty, child. Do you carry a lighted lantern inside your head that makes your skin translucent? I am joking. Youth makes you shine. Guess *my* age!"

Milady bounced out of her chair and made a pirouette that ended in a deep curtsy to the floor. Her dogs scampered and leaped around her like a miniature *corps-de-ballet*. She righted herself with ease. "There!" she exclaimed as she sat down. "Now guess—no, I'll tell you! I am ninety-eight! They used to say that La Monette had quicksilver instead of blood in her veins."

This amazing person was born in the year 1707, year of Union between Scotland and England. Anne Stuart was Queen. Prince Charlie plotted for the scepter of the Scots. *Le Roi Soleil* was King of France. Her lifespan was a century play in which Royal George and Royal Louis marched on and off stage to the fife-and-drum of war and revolution.

"I need not ask you if you like my pets. They like you," said Lady Inverkleith. "I've known those rascals to nip the ankles of persons they dislike. Tell me, child, will you help bathe and comb them and see that they are properly fed? Will you put them to bed every night with a caress for

101

each one?" Her ladyship did not wait to hear the answer. "Very well then, it is settled. I presume you will want to pack your boxes. Go, child, and be here not later than noon, tomorrow."

"I have no boxes, milady," said Laurie apologetically, "only a bundle and my . . . my books. I can leave the books in care of my cousin at the Royal Scot."

"Not at all!" said Lady Inverkleith. "Bring your belongings with you." She rang a little silver bell and when her steward answered, she said, "Malcolm, give Miss Macneil plenty to purchase new clothes . . . a box . . . you know." She turned to Laurie again. "My favorite color is blue. Do you like blue?"

"It is also my favorite, milady."

"Good! Pick a blue dress . . . and things to match."

Recrossing the Nor'Loch Bridge, Laurie paused again.

> Ev'n ev'ry ray of Hope destroy'd
> And not a wish to gild the gloom!

There *was* some helping Power! "Toil-beat nerves and tear-worn eye" would rest, tonight!

No sooner had Laurie announced her good fortune than her Uncle Colquohoun changed his manner. "Weel, noo . . . the Lady Inverkleith! I swear! There's nae gr-reater for-rtune i' the realm than that o' Lady Inverkleith! Castles to burn!"

"Companion to Lady Inverkleith!" cried Mistress Colquohoun.

"And to her ladyship's poodles," Laurie corrected.

Her aunt made her tell again what milady said, what she answered. She asked if her ladyship had handsome chinaware, silver, bric-a-brac? Were the walls covered richly with painting? Her collector's passion touched Laurie almost as much as her melancholy daughter Margit's remark, "How delightful to live in some new place."

"Margit would go anywhere to get away from Kate,"

102

said Jinny in her peppery way. "Did you hear Father when I asked him if I could go shopping with you? 'Yes daughter!' My! My! Lady Inverkleith *must* be rich! Do you know what? I'll send word by the college beadle for Wattie to be at Mrs. Creery's tea-shop, then you can meet him and tell me what you think of my husband."

This lean snippet, Jinny's rapturous lover? Laurie could hardly believe her eyes. Medic Baird was not only unprepossessing in appearance, he was less talkative than a clam. All he seemed to think of was eating. Four pork pies, eight tea cakes, five cups of tea—Laurie had said beforehand that the treat was on her—Wattie scraped the plates of the last crumb and to all her questions he answered only a timid "nay" or "aye." At last she gave up trying to draw him out.

"Poor Wattie," said Jinny after they'd parted, "he never has enough to eat. Why must he choose to be a surgeon? A baker, a butcher, always knows where his next meal is coming from."

Jinny's husband was of small interest to Laurie on this day; she had her new box to pack, her new dress to put on. She'd bought a frock of blue challis with a blue sash, a blue cape with three tiers of capelets at the shoulders, a summer bonnet with blue ribbons, also pretty black shoes with bows and a modest amount of underclothing, also a sleeping gown and dressing robe, the first she'd ever owned. Best of all, Lady Inverkleith's purse was only a quarter spent. She had also chosen a gift to send to Nanny Biel—a new shawl made of finest wool. Before leaving she penned a letter.

DEAR, KIND NANNY BIEL,

Even tho' you may never forgive me for running away, I know you understand. After some poor luck, I've had wonderful blessings. Lady

Inverkleith of George Street has hired me to be her companion and helper with her darling poodle dogs. I shall try my very best to please her. This gift is poor thanks for all your loving help. Trusting this will find you in good health and restored frame of mind,

I am your loving,

LAURIE.

Eight

Lull after the Storm

THE ROOM WAS SMALL—A DARLING HAVEN OF FLOWERED wallpaper and white ruffled curtains. The bed was softer than downy moss. There was a carpet to walk on. An alcove concealed a toilet stand with pretty china basin and jug. The comfort-chair was screened. Laurie never ceased to be thankful that some forgiving Power above had given her a refuge in time of trouble. Her duties were pleasant. Her little canine friends were no bother at all. Their bedroom opened on a covered gallery where they could cavort on rainy days without getting their tootsies wet. Each poodle had his bed, real beds in miniature, beautifully gilded and carved, with the appropriate crown at the head. A prince's crown for Prince, a ducal crown for Duke, a baron's crown for Baron and so on down to Bruce who was honored with the crown of an earl and thistle of Scotland! Each doggie knew his own bed and there was never any poaching or squabbling. The little pets also had their boxes that contained drinking bowls, eating bowls, brushes, combs, spare ribbons, little jackets for wet weather, jeweled collars and toys. A large garden plot was fenced off for their use; here they romped on fine days. If Reine or Madame were in what her ladyship called "a delicate condition," they were locked away from their suitors. Lady Inverkleith would not allow the dogs to breed; she said, "Eight adorable poodles are quite enough for one household!"

Laurie soon grew fond of her prancing, dancing charges. Each doggie was different, each had his quirk, caprice, trick. As for the poodles, they developed what Lady Inverkleith called "a veritable passion" for Laurie. "Never . . . never have they shown such affection for any of my other companions before," exclaimed her tiny ladyship.

It was Lady Inverkleith's custom to take the poodles— all eight—for a daily drive. They would sit politely on the seat facing their mistress and behave like the ladies and gentlemen they were! One day, Laurie tried in vain to shoo the pets out to the carriage. Milady called, "Here Prince! Here Bruce! Come, Queenie!" But the little rascals ran back to Laurie. Again Laurie herded them to the carriage —out they bounced and trailed her up the step and into the house, showing her such marked preference that she became worried lest her mistress might be piqued.

"Prince! Duchess! Brucie! Now mind! Jump in!" Laurie paused to catch her breath. "Milady, shall I put them on the leash?"

Lady Inverkleith smiled. "Try once more!"

This time, Laurie got the rebels into place. No sooner had the coachman given his team the rein, than eight white cannon balls shot out of the carriage, flew back to Laurie.

"Wonderful!" Lady Inverkleith clapped her hands in glee. "From now on, you shall come with us."

Driving in state through Edinburgh's parkways and streets, Laurie was ofttimes tempted to pinch herself to make sure this was not a dream.

Strange union of self and selflessness, artifice and candor, the marvel to Laurie was that her indulgent mistress seemed to have taken her youthful companion so to heart that she treated her like one of her own flesh and blood. Hardly a day passed that she did not shower her with gifts.

"Laura, this little bonnet—how fetching! Try it on. It becomes you." Lady Inverkleith waved to the milliner,

"Box it." So it was with "this sweet fall cape—how warm and . . . see! It is a perfect fit. We'll take it."

How hard to mislead so much kindness! How difficult to circumvent Lady Inverkleith's probing into her past history.

"You are Macneil of Clan Macneil?"

"Yes, milady."

"Good blood! And I like your manners, lady-like, my girl. Where did you go to school?"

"In Great Marlow-on-Thames, milady."

"The name of your headmistress?"

"Miss Weston, milady."

"Was your father in the trade?"

Laurie hesitated a moment, then she spoke frankly. "Father was a brewer on Speyside, milady."

"Honorable profession," nodded Lady Inverkleith.

"I would he'd chosen another, milady," said Laurie quickly. "Whiskey was the curse, not the blessing of our family."

"Poor child! Well, now all that is past and gone. You have only the future to plan for. What would you like to make of yourself?"

Laurie said wistfully, "Once I hoped . . . but now . . ."

"Now?" prompted Lady Inverkleith.

"I . . . I think my best chance would be to become a teacher like Miss Weston," Laurie answered.

"You . . . a teacher?" Lady Inverkleith smiled. "What would become of those fascinators, men?"

"I . . . I have no desire to marry, milady," said Laurie, blushing, "I like the single state."

"But you'd marry if you found the right husband?" teased Lady Inverkleith.

"No . . . no, milady!" cried Laurie. She amazed herself by bursting into tears.

"Poor child!" said Lady Inverkleith, when Laurie begged forgiveness for her outburst. "If you have a secret sorrow, confide in me. My old eyes have seen many things, forgiven many mistakes."

Casting about for a believable tale, Laurie hit upon a near-truth. "I was engaged to a good, honest man, milady. I lost him."

"One you did not love. And who was the other man?" said Lady Inverkleith, folding her tiny mittened hands.

"The other man?"

"Yes, of course. You are not the kind to fall in love with a mere . . . honest man."

"But . . . milady!"

"Milady nothing! Come, come! Was he person of higher station than you?"

"Ye . . . yes, milady."

"Of course he never talked marriage."

"No . . . no, milady."

"Poor girl! It is ever thus. The ones we love all have some wastrel streak, some flaw."

"He was a wonderful man!" cried Laurie in quick defense of her love.

"Handsome, eh?"

"Handsome as a god!"

"Of course! Now tell me . . . did the young rascal—"

"Pity, milady!" cried Laurie. "He was no more to blame than I. Perhaps he was less to blame. Those on whom fortune has smiled have different ways. I'd not call him a wastrel. He . . . he had the highest qualities, some seed of greatness."

"A paragon of virtue," laughed Lady Inverkleith.

"I think so, milady," said Laurie softly. "I'd give my life for him."

Lady Inverkleith sniffed audibly. "Such devotion is touching, my girl. Doubtless he is not so faithful to your sweet memory."

"It matters not, milady," said Laurie with a wistful smile. "I still wish him well."

"You speak of some seed of greatness?" probed Lady Inverkleith. "What do you mean?"

"I . . . I can't quite explain, milady. It is something one feels, as when, near a fire, one feels the heat. He comes of a great line. Many people would look to him for leadership." Laurie knew she'd been on the verge of letting the cat out of the bag when, happily, the conversation was interrupted.

In days to come, she began with maid Dubois' help, to piece together a picture of her mistress' fabulous past.

"See this screen, embroidered by Mademoiselle?" said milady's maid. "It tells the story of her loves."

The screen was made of apple-green silk drawn taut in a carved gilt frame. The silk was exquisitely embroidered with a tree of heraldic design, the branches hung with orange-colored fruit, each orange marked with initials.

"We begin here," said Dubois, kneeling in front of the screen. "The name Monette is written at the root of the tree. That is Mademoiselle, herself. She had no other name. She was a waif from the streets of Edinburgh who kept life in her frail body by dancing. But one day a dancing-master saw her being set upon by a minister who beat her with his cane, crying sin and wickedness—it seems it was the Sabbath but she, poor creature, did not know one day from the other. This kind dancing-master—he was from France—took the waif home, healed her bruises, fed her, taught her what he knew. But soon the pupil excelled the master. So great was her talent that he took her to Paris and offered her to the great master of ballet, Monsieur Dupré. Two years later she made her debut at the Opéra de Paris and when she was seventeen, she became the bride of the Duke Richard de Jussin—see, here he is, the initials R.J.? After the duke's death, Mademoiselle went back to the stage and it was during a dancing engagement in London that she met her second husbnad— here he is, the orange marked G.H., Lord George Hathmore, who presented his lady with Hathmore House in London! Wait and see! What luxury . . . what splendor!"

"Doesn't milady always reside in Edinburgh?" asked Laurie, trembling.

"Dear me no!"

"Malcolm spoke of travel. I thought perhaps she would go to some country retreat?"

"Mademoiselle goes where she pleases. Of course, now with the war, she cannot leave Britain, but she will go to London for the winter."

"When will that be?"

"Whenever milady takes the notion."

Laurie did not dare ask, "Will she take me?" She'd no way of knowing whether her services were satisfactory, except that her mistress was kindly, appreciative, generous to a fault. But Dubois had rubbed in the lesson—"La Monette is like the clouds . . . always changing!"

Laurie dared not think of London in connection with Lord Duff-Drummond. Two people might live eternally in the great maze of the capital and never cross each other's path. But there were moments when she let herself spin dreams. What if, someday, she were out driving with Lady Inverkleith and the Laird should ride by—what would her feelings be? Would she die on the spot, or live in hopes of glimpsing him again?

"Laura," said Lady Inverkleith one day, "I plan to journey to London next week. I've decided that you shall accompany me!"

A Noah's Ark for white toy poodles, Lady Inverkleith's coach-and-four pulled away from 28 George Street one fine September morning to the sound of a cracking whip, to the ear-splitting yelps of eight excited dogs.

A second vehicle soon overtook milady's coach and kept the lead.

"Malcolm and Dubois always precede me," said her ladyship to Laurie, "they make ready for my arrival at the inns. I like things just so."

Laurie marveled at the cleverness of the coach-builder who had made milady's coach. The interior was divided into two parts. Lady Inverkleith and her traveling companion sat in a comfortable back seat. The front seat had been removed to make room for two tiers of small wire cages. Each dog had his own cage, seeming quite contented with his cushioned prison quarters.

How different this leisurely journey from that bone-racking run in a public stagecoach, with her Uncle Colquohoun! Milady stopped at the best inns. The swiftest relay horses were reserved for her use. At each hostelry her apartments were transformed by her courier and maid —silk hangings, bed spread with silken sheets, milady's bath-tub, personal blankets, pillows, towels were used, even her dishes, silver and glassware.

Needless to say, this entailed endless packing, usually ten servants ran in and out with her boxes, bags and bundles. All this fuss over a tiny old lady might have seemed strange were it not that everybody liked to serve Lady Inverkleith. Her comings and goings were a royal circus in which everyone shared.

The white poodles, with their varicolored bows, milady's gowns fashioned in the rococo style of Louis Quinze' outmoded court, the magnificent jewels that she wore—all this was part of the spectacle. Laurie wondered—were her jewels safe, until Dubois confided to her that they were paste reproductions of the real gems, kept in a London vault.

No one took greater pleasure in the daily spectacle she created than her ladyship—she was always "on stage," and when she departed each servant was given a princely gratuity by her own hand, always with a kind word, a quip, or a gracious "thank you."

Small wonder that she was beloved, she loved everybody! "Are there finer people in the world than our Scots?" she beamed, as the coach pulled out of Berwick. At Newcastle, she praised, "What dependable people, our dear

111

English!" And speaking of her "dear Continentals"—"Ah! The French . . . what generous hearts!" "Those spirited Russians!" "The clever Germans!" "The charming Austrians!" "The fiery Spaniards!" "The good Portuguese!" "The gifted Tuscans!" "The witty Piedmontese!" She loved the "proud Greeks!" "The dear Hollanders!"

The comforts of the George Street mansion in Edinburgh were as nothing compared to the luxury of Hathmore House in London's fashionable Berkeley Street. A heavy screen of foliage gave seclusion to the residence, a building of classic design. The gardens were planted with every kind of tree, shrub and flower, opening enchanting vistas.

The mansion contained more rooms than one could count, a library with shelf upon shelf of books, a theater in miniature.

In London, Lady Inverkleith was royally served. Her chef was a Parisian named François. Tiny, mincing Monsieur Alcide, who had been her costumer during her years before the public, was now custodian of her wardrobe. He made her clothing, repaired old costumes, dreamed up new. Alcide painted and powdered. His white wig was made in the style of the Macaronis. His helpers were two pretty youths who sewed with nimble fingers, who pressed, fluted and pleated expertly.

Milady's greatest pleasure was to take her young companion to the room where her theatrical wardrobe was stored and display her costumes. Venus and Clorinda, Princess of the Night and Spirit of Spring, Elfin Queen and Diane Huntress—rags of silk and spangled gauze hung limp on the racks, awaiting the touch of La Monette to bring them to life. Pleasures, novelties, frivolities—a fairytale come true! The overdrawn was the order of the day. Fable changed to fact when this queen of make-believe waved her golden scepter. What amazed Laurie was that the almost centenarian Lady Inverkleith seemed to have leaped through the vicissitudes of life like a tumbler through a hoop of fire, without a scorch.

Four husbands—"and many, many heart's admirers," said Dubois with a smirk of double meaning—how could a woman retain a brow unmarked, the eyes of a child, the caprices of adolescence unless she were completely devoid of human feelings? But La Monette was not feelingless; else how would one explain the unflagging homage of those who gathered in her salon?

"Dear boy! Remind me to write my name at my bookseller for a copy of his forthcoming work. The title is *Waverley*. You may read to me when we have time." Lady Inverkleith was speaking of Walter Scott, whose very name Laurie breathed with awe. "Poor lad . . . how I admire his talent. What a pity he has a bad foot. It is the same trouble that afflicts poor George Byron!"

Laurie soon became used to hearing her mistress speak of the great of the times as "dear boy," or "poor lad." It took her much longer to overcome her amazement when those same "poor lads" and "dear boys" came in—treading laurels, kissed milady's hand, her cheek, chucked her under the chin, saying, "Good afternoon, Monette."

The Prince of Wales, General Wellesley, playwright Mr. Sheridan, the romantic Lord Byron were habitués of her Berkeley Street salon, also the dashing Sir William Smith, whom Lady Inverkleith nicknamed "L'Impatient." Sir William was on the verge of being promoted rear admiral of the blue. He chafed at the delay in securing a new naval command and a chance to "take the hide off that little monster, Bonaparte." No, the secret of Lady Inverkleith's charm was not fame or fortune, the magic balm that kept her brow unfurrowed was not concocted by a chemist. She possessed no elixir of life except her unawareness that she had passed the last milestone, survived the survivable, lived the unlivable.

The first month in London, Laurie's duties were to keep

Lady Inverkleith company when she was alone and air the doggies in the beautiful private grounds of Hathmore House. Somewhat to her disappointment, Lady Inverkleith never required her company on her daily carriage outings. But one morning she was called to her mistress' boudoir earlier than usual.

"Thursday fortnight, I am giving a dinner party, Laura. I wish you to be at table. I know what you are thinking, that you have no gown fit for elegant company. Well, I have attended to that. Mrs. Jack of Jermyn Street has brought a choice of evening wear . . ."

Mrs. Jack had already opened her boxes and shaken out a bewildering assortment of silks and gauzes; a hawk-nosed woman of middle-age, her black eyes gleamed when Laurie entered the room. "How fortunate that I brought the blue muslin! The very thing for Miss Macneil!"

After trying on the gown, Mrs. Jack decreed it "perfect" except that it was a "wee bit tight in the bust."

Lightly girdled with silver at the armpits, the soft, blue muslin fell in graceful clinging folds. The neckline was less to Laurie's liking. She longed to add a bit of gauze in front, a bow or something.

"They're very pretty," smiled Lady Inverkleith, "why hide 'em?"

Gazing into the mirror, Laurie's cheeks reddened with embarrassment. She looked like a bathing nymph! There was not even a petticoat to conceal the contour of her limbs. She did not know, of course, that this was the latest style from Paris and that daring blockade runners risked their lives to bring the newest fashion plates across the English Channel to fashion-hungry London.

"My good Jack," said Lady Inverkleith, "make up a wardrobe for Miss Macneil—the proper things for the fall season!"

"Some good furs, milady?" asked the dressmaker with a greedy gleam in her eyes.

"A little ermine pelisse and muff will do," said Lady Inverkleith. She turned to Laurie. "You may go to Mrs. Jack's rooms to be fitted. She will also direct your purchases." To the dressmaker Lady Inverkleith added with a taunting smile, "Jack dear, you've never been happy since I let Alcide make my clothes. But Alcide knows my age and he dresses me accordingly. Now you may allow your fancy full rein! I want Miss Macneil to be pretty and fresh as the springtime."

Laurie now entered a new and exciting phase of life—while Lady Inverkleith napped in early afternoon, she was driven to her appointments with Mrs. Jack of Jermyn Street, in one of her mistress' town carriages.

The dressmaker was a woman of keen wit and perception. She was also filled with inextinguishable curiosity about her new client.

"I've known and made for milady these past fifteen years. I've met all her companions—middle-aged creatures smelling of dog and moth-balls! Pfah! You are the first young thing she's ever engaged! Tell me, Miss Macneil, are you in some . . . er . . . distant way related to milady?"

"I?" laughed Laurie.

"Related . . . *de par la main gauche*," suggested Mrs. Jack.

"You mean . . . a long-lost grandchild of the bar sinister?"

"Exactly!"

"I wish I were!" laughed Laurie.

These visits to Mrs. Jack's busy sewing-rooms, the shopping forays in Mayfair were a marvel and a delight to Laurie. She watched the grand ladies sweep in and out of their carriages, watched their manners, their fashionable dress. Mrs. Jack was a walking *Burke's Peerage*. She named them as they passed. "Lady Craven. . . . The Countess of Warwickshire, Lady Dorkington. . . . There . . . see the one with the dark hair? She's the Duchess d'Alboli . . . a lady of the Italian nobility . . . rich as rich . . . and what a hussy with the men. Look, Miss Macneil. These slippers? Which do you prefer, the blue or the silver?"

Laurie soon found her wardrobe bulging with an assortment of day and evening wear—shoes, slippers, hats, gloves and underclothing, even a charming soft capelet of ermine and a muff to match.

"It's too much, milady!" she protested to her generous mistress.

"A beautiful girl can never have *enough* pretty things!" laughed Lady Inverkleith. "All for one aim and goal, remember!"

"What aim? What goal, milady?"

"Surely you know," said Lady Inverkleith gaily. "Dress to catch a man, undress to keep him!"

Laurie was amazed at her ladyship's unvarnished philosophy of conquest, but she did not judge. La Monette, spoiled of the gods, could not possibly reason like Laurie Macneil for whom a dozen gowns, a warm coat, a collection of exquisite chapeaux were undreamed-of luxuries.

When Lady Inverkleith ordered her faithful Malcolm to bring her jewel cases, the steward, aided by a footman, carried three large metal-bound boxes into the boudoir.

"Malcolm keeps my jewels locked in the vault," said Lady Inverkleith. "He is always afraid of burglars. Open the diamond case, Malcolm!"

Laurie's eyes were blinded by the flash and fire of diamonds worth a king's ransom. Necklaces, chokers, bracelets, stomachers, earrings, rings, pendants.

"I've one of the finest collections in the world," said Lady Inverkleith complacently. "My second husband, Lord Hathmore, adored to see me in diamonds. But I also have pearls and colored stones. Show Miss Macneil the emeralds and rubies, Malcolm, while I choose a trinket for her to wear to dinner."

As Laurie gaped admiringly at an empress' treasure, she

116

could not help but think, "One . . . just one of these jewels would build a fine school! And here they lie, in the darkness of a vault, except when their capricious owner trots them out." This ruby and diamond bracelet would provide snug new cottages for an entire village. This single ruby ring—the best wheat seed, the best livestock available. This gorgeous pearl choker, seven strands of perfectly matched pearls from which hung twenty-four graded, pear-shaped pearls, would build a hospital and pay doctors to care for the sick. New manufactories could spring into being with the proceeds of the sale of this flawless emerald brooch! And for every diamond in this tiara, ten thousand seedling trees could be purchased in England, and planted in Scottish soil.

Why were her thoughts always returning to the Braes of Angus? Why did she waken at night and hear the wind murmur, "Ben Leva! Ben Fada! Grailie! Cortach! Fairlie!" What did those poor villages signify in memory? Except for a few forbidden hours of enchantment, what had they held for Laura Macneil except back-breaking labor, and at the end—humiliation and loss.

"Here, Laura," said Lady Inverkleith, handing her a diamond necklet. "Wear this with your blue gown. It will light you up like Titania!"

The day of the dinner party, Lady Inverkleith had ordered the hairdresser at five o'clock—her French coiffeur who dressed her hair and elaborate powdered wigs. This was to be Laurie's first experience. Monsieur Edmond ran his comb through her curls. "Mon Dieu! What a head of gold! I shall do you *à la nymphe*—rising from a sylvan pool, shaking off diamond droplets."

Monsieur Edmond's poetic flight was mere rhetoric. He dressed Laurie's hair simply, in a way that suited. A blue gauze band held her curls in place at the temples, the ends laced into the curls that cascaded over her shoulders.

117

"Am I not too . . . undressed?" she said to Lady Inverkleith on presenting herself for approval.

"Dear me, no!"

"My shoulders . . . they are quite bare. I'll feel the cold!"

"The men's stares will warm you. But you do need something . . . here, this fan."

"I . . . a fan?" Laurie almost laughed.

"Then . . . this handkerchief."

Protected by nothing more substantial than a filmy handkerchief, Laurie followed Lady Inverkleith down to the drawing room where a dozen gentlemen were waiting. How right her ladyship was, their eyes did warm! Laurie found herself curtsying to His Royal Highness, the Prince of Wales, who said, "Demmed if you ain't the first leddy I've seen wearin' the Goddess of Liberty modes who does not look like she's in her nightdress!"

The Prince and several younger gentlemen whose high-sounding names Laurie did not retain were evidently patrons of the same tailor—they wore identical blue coats with high velvet collars and vast cravats, the folds held in place by jeweled scarfpins; breeches of close-fitting elastic cloth and low, slipperlike shoes that Laurie later learned were called "Hessians."

The Prince was nearing his middle forties, a man with heavy cheeks and jowl and a thickset body. But he carried himself regally and gave her a blast of daredevil eyes which, if one believed the gossipmongers, few females had ever resisted.

"Bein' a Scotswoman you ain't a Jacobite, are you, Miss Macneil?"

"No, your highness."

"Ah! Ah! I'm demmed gratified to hear it. Never did like Jacobites! They tell me they still thrive up there in the Highlands."

A slender young man with fair hair entered Lady Inverkleith's salon and surveyed the elegant scene. "Monette, cherie!" exclaimed Count Jean d'Antimes as he bent to kiss his hostess' hand. "Do my eyes deceive me or do I see a creature of the fair sex in your drawing room?"

"Your eyes do not deceive you, Jean!" retorted Lady Inverkleith.

"Then you've at last run up the white flag?"

"No, saucy! I'm still on the breach!"

"Who is she?"

"Go and be introduced." D'Antimes maneuvered for an opening in the compact mob around the lady in blue, without success. Each new arrival made his approach more hazardous. At table, d'Antimes found himself placed so far away that he could see only a head and a splash of blue through the table decorations.

"Who is the lady, my dear Charles?" he inquired of his neighbor, a beau of the Prince's entourage.

"Haven't the faintest, my dear Jean. Most unusual to see a lady at La Monette's board."

Laurie could have counted a dozen of the Isles' most distinguished sons, had she known who they were. A king's minister, two generals, two wits—a royal prince for a table-mate! She wondered who could be missing from the empty place on her right? Unable to identify Lady Inverkleith's guests, she saw only faces, uniforms, jeweled decorations, ogling eyes and smiles.

The Prince of Wales was indeed the cavalier servant, turning first to his hostess.

"Ah! Ah, Monette! How charmin' of you to match my blue coat!" The Prince nodded to the fanciful arrangement of blue iris, built up in the center of the board. Golden cranes held candles in their beaks. The plates and goblets were blue Bohemian glass, each piece carved with a scene from one of La Monette's ballets. The napery was of lace and finest linen dyed to match the blue tint of the glass-ware.

Laurie had heard that the Prince of Wales was the least modest and the most fashionable man in the realm, this must be true! His highness took over the conversation, telling of his new tailor recently arrived from Naples, the skill of his bootmaker from Padua, of his jeweler, "the cleverest since Leonardo!"

The Prince held up his watch-fob for Laurie to admire. "See these *breloques*—never wear more than seven; I say, look at this one!" The Prince singled out a large seal. "Did you ever see such workmanship? First time I write you a *billet-doux*, young woman, I'll seal it with this signet!"

Above the laughter that followed, one of the gentlemen called, "Will your highness go to the match race tomorrow?"

"Yes, Artie. Three-to-one on Plimpton Joe! What'll you take?" challenged the Prince.

"Two hundred, your highness. Can't afford more."

"Bet a thousand! Bet a thousand," reiterated the Prince. He turned to Laurie. "Mr. Brodbourne told me Cherami beat Corinna three times in 1800, giving something like seven or eight lbs. Now Corinna won the October Second with seven stone eleven; and Plimpton Joe gave Corinna sixteen lbs. over Ditch In, with seven stone on her back, mark you. The handicap went down to four stone, so one might say . . ."

Noticing Laurie's lost expression, the Prince guffawed, "Ha-ha! I take it you don't follow the races, Miss Macneil?"

"No, your highness."

"But they do race horses in Caledonia?"

"Oh yes, your highness! There is racing at Leith Sands in Edinburgh, but I know nothing of the sport."

"What *do* you know?" The Prince leered amicably—"How to kiss, I wager!"

"Your highness had better say cook," laughed Laurie.

"You . . . a cook? A Scottish cook? I say, Miss Macneil, do you know the recipe for haggis? Your countrymen

120

made one in my honor, sent it to London. Gad! What a dish! Never could get my chef to make it so good! How is it concocted?"

Laurie was amazed at so strange a request from a royal prince. "Your highness, it is a long recipe."

"Miss Macneil, I am all ears!" the Prince declared.

Laurie conjured up a memory of Nanny Biel's preparations for the wedding feast in Ben Fada—her kitchen fragrant with the nutty aroma of "bristling" oatmeal and suet frying in onions—a memory of a wee haggis, wrapped in a white cloth—the part that meat delight had played in her own life. "The ingredients are a sheep'd pluck and paunch, a pound of beef suet, your highness; a dozen small onions, peeled and scalded; a cupful of oatmeal . . . pepper, cayenne, salt, and vinegar if you have no lemon."

"Sheep's pluck?" queried the Prince. "What is that?"

"Pluck is a variety of innards, your highness."

"Ah, tripe!" exclaimed Royal George.

"Yes, your highness, and also the lights, liver and heart." Laurie wondered if her listener were not jesting. It seemed incredible that so fastidious a prince should wish to draw her out on the subject of haggis-making! But valiantly, she continued. "You must have a large stomach bag, and a smaller, or knight's-hood bag, as it is called. First you bristle—toast—a cupful of oatmeal in front of the fire. Clean the great bag thoroughly and soak it overnight in cold salt-water. In the morning put it aside with the rough side turned out. Wash the small bag and the pluck and put them on to boil covered with cold water, leaving the windpipe hanging out over the rim of the pot to let out the impurities. Boil for an hour and a half and then take it out and cut away the pipes and any gristle. Mince the heart and lights and grate half the liver."

"Why half a liver?"

"I suppose a whole liver would make the mixture too pasty, your highness."

"I see! What now?"

"You put all this in a basin with a pound of minced suet and two finely chopped onions, to which you add vinegar and cayenne crystals."

"Not cayenne in powder?"

"No indeed, your highness. The crystals spread the taste better. And do not forget to season highly with salt and pepper. Then you sprinkle in your bristled oatmeal."

"I like that word—bristle," guffawed the Prince.

"It means browned or toasted in the Scots, your highness," said Laurie. "Over all, you pour as much of the liquid in which the pluck was boiled as to make the composition sappy. Then stuff the great bag rather more than half full, say five-eighths, as it requires plenty of room to swell. Sew it tightly and plunge into a large pot of hot water to which you add a pint of milk, leave room to swell, be sure to prick it all over with a large needle to keep it from bursting. You boil the haggis in an open pot for three hours and serve very hot without any garnish."

Royal George nodded. "Haggis is not a *boudin* as the French know it"

"No, I think not, your highness!"

So absorbed were Laurie and her royal dinner partner that neither of them noticed the entrance of a latecomer until they heard Lady Inverkleith's birdlike cry, "Ah, Colin! Here you are at last! You deserve to be made to dine in the nursery!"

Colin? Laurie turned pale.

That night on the Rock of Duff-Drummond, the Laird had reeked of whiskey, sweat and fire-smoke! Today milord was the Mayfair elegant complete—'lastick trousers under a light-weight coat of dove-gray cloth, the flaring collar so high that it touched the lobes of his ears. His neckcloth of snowy lawn was artfully wound and tied. Watch-fobs tinkled with his every move, a single eyeglass swung on a wide ribbon band. His black hair was combed in a high curl over his brow, feathered at the temples.

122

"Forgive me, Granny!" Duff-Drummond turned to the Prince with a bow. "My humble apologies to your highness—and to all you gentlemen . . ." Then seeing the Prince's fair neighbor on the left, he froze to statuelike rigidity.

"Sit down, Colin!" commanded Lady Inverkleith with a sharp tug of her fan on her grandson's arm. "I declare, I've a mind to deprive you of sweets as I used to when you were a lad!"

Lifting himself in his chair, Jean d'Antimes was at last able to see the young lady who had received such unusual honors from La Monette!—a place between her fastidious grandson and George, whom Destiny was shaping to be England's next king. "By all the water in the ocean! Colin's Highland Venus!"

"How do you like London, Miss Macneil?"

"I like it very much, milord."

"The season is dull, at present, but it will soon liven." Here, Royal George broke in. "Miss Macneil brings her baggage of gaiety with her, my dear Colin! She's been entertaining me mightily."

"She has, your highness?" said Duff-Drummond.

"Yes indeed. Taught me haggis-makin'! Miss Macneil, be so good as to write the recipe and give it to me. I'll hand it to my chef. And if he succeeds, will you do me the pleasure of tastin' his product and passin' on it?"

"Your highness is most kind," murmured Laurie. "I'll be glad to write down the recipe."

Stunned as she was by her lover's out-of-the-clouds coming, she could not calm the wild exultance of her heart. At the same time she was hard-put to explain his icy demeanor, the edge on his tone when he addressed her. But, of course, having done so much to aid her to her present safety, he'd still be careful and discreet. She hadn't the slightest doubt that he and he alone had maneu-

vered her under his grandmother's wing. Not a frank pro-
cedure—Lady Inverkleith had no inkling—but how mer-
ciful! How wondrous his care! Seeking to hide her feelings,
she responded to the Prince's banter as best she could, but
every pulse was leaping in anticipation of the moment
when she'd be free to speak to the one she adored.

It was Lady Inverkleith's imperious way to ask the gentlemen to join her as soon as dinner was finished. No smoking or drinking in masculine company only—La Monette
would not relinquish her "dear boys" even for an instant.

She did not object to smoking in her presence. Neither
did she withhold fine liqueurs and brandies, which were
served with steaming Mocha.

"Monette darling," said Jean d'Antimes as he poured a
thimbleful of cordial for his hostess, "where did you discover that young beauty? You've never been a collector
of pretty girls, only of canine aristocrats!"

"Laura?" asked Lady Inverkleith with a smile of innocence. "I was in need of a companion. Malcolm spoke to
fourteen young women. I picked the one I liked best."

"Handsome choice, Monette chérie!" teased d'Antimes.
"May I try for an introduction to your little beauty?"

"Do so, dear boy," said Lady Inverkleith with a smile.
"Laura is over there . . . see . . . with the Prince?"

D'Antimes headed for the girl in blue to whom Royal
George was paying marked attention. Soon he found a
way to maneuver his highness from the field with the remark, "Your highness . . . our hostess hopes you'll pass on
a new brand of cognac." D'Antimes then circumvented
the attempts of three beaux to take his highness' place
and plumped down on the love seat beside Laurie.

"Miss Macneil, there comes a time when the last shall
be first. I doubt if you know my name . . . perhaps you
remember the circumstances under which we first met?"

"I remember both your name and . . . where we met,
Count d'Antimes," said Laurie.

124

"How gracious of you! I vow I never thought I'd see you here!"

"Neither did I, Count."

"Well, they say the hand of circumstance is more powerful than the horns of the ram!" laughed d'Antimes. He was watching the girl closely. She had not taken her eyes off the tall figure of Duff-Drummond who was standing before the fireplace, chatting with General Wellesley. Had Colin maneuvered the placing of his Highland mistress in his grandmother's household? Incredible! Colin was little given to tying strings on minor romance! "Love and leave *immediately!*" was his motto. Jean d'Antimes wondered if the girl had maneuvered her present enviable situation—but no! Not with that face! Doubt, apprehension, and the most outspoken adoration played on her exquisite countenance! Those blue eyes were now forlorn, now gay, now glad, now moisture-filled! No! Laura Macneil was innocent of intrigue. Prime mover and arranger must be Colin!

"Quite a difference between Berkeley Street and your charming rugged heath, Miss Macneil."

"Oh! Yes, Count."

"You seem to acclimatize with ease."

"Yes . . . yes . . ." Beauty was not listening. Her whole attention was fixed on Duff-Drummond—lucky devil!

In elegance and beauty, this girl could easily match the fairest young lady in London. Of course she had not yet acquired the arts of a coquette and her conversation was not out of the book, but how she could dazzle and attract!

Gazing in admiration at Laurie, Jean d'Antimes did not see Duff-Drummond approach. He uttered a startled "Uh?" when his friend said imperatively, "Jean, will you go help Granny entertain Georgie, there's a good fellow."

Laurie trembled as her lover sat down beside her. He was careful to settle the crease in his elastickers and arrange his fobs. He jabbed at the lawn handkerchief in his sleeve, and screwing his monocle in his right eye, he looked down at Laurie and said, "Perhaps this is as good a time as any for an explanation?"

"Explanation, milord?"

"You know what I mean, Laura. How came you here?"

"But . . . surely . . . you know, milord," stammered Laurie. "Lady Inverkleith hired me."

"Indeed? Mere chance, I suppose?"

This harsh tone, his fishy eye shook Laurie's belief that her lover was responsible for her good fortune.

"Milord, I couldn't stay in Ben Fada," she said pleadingly. "I left immediately and went to Edinburgh."

"Threw yourself on Granny's mercy, I suppose. Made yourself a sad, sad case. Confessed all!"

Laurie began to understand his true meaning. "I told nothing! I didn't even know you were Lady Inverkleith's grandson!"

"You fib neatly, Laura," said Duff-Drummond in cutting tones. "It would be impossible for anyone to live under my grandmother's roof ten minutes and not discover that I am her prodigal grandson, that Granny's third husband was my grandfather, Lord Duff-Drummond."

"It is your privilege to give me the lie, milord," said Laurie with dignity. "I still declare, I never knew you were related to Lady Inverkleith until you walked into the dining room tonight."

"You expect me to believe you?"

"I . . . I am in no position to expect . . . anything, milord. But I do not make a habit of lying. If milord will keep the truth from Lady Inverkleith, I'll make plans to leave this house as soon as possible."

Able judge of women, Duff-Drummond scrutinized the girl's charming face, searching for some outward sign of her inner thoughts. That he had gone too far—much too far—was quite apparent. The girl was fighting her tears. Dash it, why lose this pretty bird in the hand? Merely to be at her side spurred him with warming memories! Why

126

not seize this interesting situation? Granny, with her sweet old eyes closed!—a toothsome beauty under the same roof! Easy to skip through the corridors. With winter's coming, why face the snows to find a bed-warmer the likes of this Highland maid?

"Laura," he said in a gentler tone, "forgive me if I put you to the test. I believe you, truly I do. Your presence here is mere happy coincidence. Stay and comfort Granny's old days. I'll be a 'good boy' as Monette says. Now if you'll give me leave, the Prince is waiting for his game of cards."

Nine

Cupid Strikes Again

Happy thoughts crowded Laurie's mind as she readied for bed. O kind Fate that permitted her to breathe the same air Colin breathed, to see him, now and then! Her dream come true! London was not a maze where two hearts were lost—London was love's rendezvous. And even if love were only on her side—the high and noble Lord Duff-Drummond a creature quite beyond her reach —no matter! Just to watch through the open door of the cardroom the Laird's handsome head wreathed in tobacco smoke was joy. His manner courteous, softened, repentant, heaped joy upon joy.

Oh! Was it not true that the world was wide, peopled by a hundred million beings? Each with his own way, his caprice, his manner of thinking, his past, his hopes for the future, each one so very different? So it must be that the very act of living was a matter of every human's reaction upon the other. One should walk with the slenderest expectations, but with broadest tolerance; with love for little and great; and above all with that charity described by the Apostle Paul: *to find good in everyone!*

Her first fall had gone almost unpunished. She'd never fall again. Dedicating herself to serve La Monette, she'd find contentment in an occasional smile, a nod from the man she loved. But nobody—not even Conscience' thundering voice—could ever make her stop loving. She'd adore the Laird until death!

Laurie gave a last stroke of the brush to her bright hair and opened the door to the poodle room. All was quiet here. The dears were so well trained! She closed the door softly and climbed into bed. What contentment, to lie with open eyes and remember! "Stay and comfort Granny's old days," Colin had said. Oh! She'd do her very best! It was no task to serve and comfort so kind a mistress. "Mere happy coincidence," he'd said. No! No! Coincidence was an accidental power. Laurie was certain that Destiny alone had steered her course.

She was about to drift into the land of sweet dreams when she heard a scratching—that naughty Prince! Always begging to be let into her room! She raised herself on one elbow and called in a stage whisper, "Prince! To bed! To bed!"

The scratching ceased. Good doggie! But sleep had flown! Laurie lighted the candle and picked up her bedside favorite. What had Robbie Burns to say "On Having Found the Beloved Again"?

Her eye fell upon the lines:

> Jamie, come try me,
> Jamie, come try me!
> If thou would win my love,
> Jamie, come try me!

For shame, Robbie! She clapped the book shut and snuffed out the candle, but a voice spoke out of the darkness.

"Laura!"

"Colin!"—Oh, no! cried Laurie's better self. Her hunger cried, Yes! Yes!

"Where the deuce are you?" She felt groping hands atop the quilt. "Colin! Laird! I beg of you! Go! Leave me in peace!"

"Go? Are you mad? I couldn't wait to get here! Damn it, the servants were on a merry-go-round tonight! But nobody saw me. Where's the opening to this confounded bed?"

Laurie felt the cold as he lifted the cover. "Milord, it's wrong. Wrong! Please go! We mustn't! We shouldn't . . . !"

"Shouldn't . . . what?"

"Your grandmother trusts me. I've won her respect. Would you blast it all for . . . for . . ."

"I'd blast Westminster!" chuckled Duff-Drummond. "It'd be worth it to do a Guy Fawkes for your sake. Ah! Here you are!"

He'd found her at last! The bedclothing was no obstacle now! Quickly he slipped in beside her, entwined her warm limbs, wreathed her in his arms. "Gad! It's cold tonight! Warm me, like a good gel!"

Laurie protested one last protest before her lips were stilled with a kiss. "It's wrong!"—then the old spell was upon her.

Flesh turned to yielding clay. She was his, his again! Caressed and cajoled out of her scruples, too weak to resist, she closed her ears to the voice of reproof. This was what she'd cried for! Her man! Her lover-dear! Why try to say no? What folly to refuse the highest bliss the world could bestow? Away carping remorse! Think neither of yesterday or tomorrow! Think only of now, in Colin's arms.

"I missed you, lass. I cursed myself. You're deuced hard to forget!"

Loverly murmurs filled the night like stars, the sky.

"Have you been chaste? I should've locked you in that chastity belt! I deserved no better than that you should have picked a new swain!"

Heap ecstasy on ecstasy! Heap kiss on kiss!

"I'll never love again unless it be you, Colin dearest!"

"Sweet words, but I doubt—"

"I mean them! Oh, darling if you only knew . . ."

"Hush! Kiss me . . . kiss me like you did . . ."

130

Now as then, the Laird showed himself past master of ravishment. Sealed with his soft seal, her eyes were weapons of defense discarded. Her lips were searched by a treasure hunter after gold. Wild-wanton, he rolled his dark head on her tender breast. She heard him cry, "Laura! Laura!"

When at last the purple morn filtered through the curtains, he gazed at her, caressed her with strong, soft palms as if to commit her every curve to memory.

"Laura . . . mine!"

Laurie whispered adoringly, "I was reading 'Jamie, come try me,' when you stole in. But there's another piece:

> "Near me, near me,
> Laddie lie near me!
>
> . . . .
>
> Lang hae we parted been,
> Laddie my dearie;
>
> . . . .
>
> A' that I hae endured
>
> . . . .
>
> Here in thy arms is cur'd—
> Laddie lie near me!"

At dawn, the Laird stole away so quietly that Laurie was not aware he had gone.

Their reunion was the beginning of a mad new way of life—cool gentleman and obedient young companion by day, hot-blooded lovers by night.

At first, Laurie lived in constant apprehension that her kind patroness would suspect what was going on under her roof, but soon her fears dwindled and faded away. Lady Inverkleith was oblivious to the love affair, indeed she seemed delighted that her grandson chose to join her so often at dinner.

131

"I believe it is you who attracts him, Laura," she said to her blushing companion. "How foolish of me to have employed only older women. I must have forgotten that the best way to catch flies is with honey!"

Laurie was not so hardened that she did not feel pangs —Lady Inverkleith was so trusting, so very, very kind.

"I was certain you'd like my grandson, Laura . . . you *do* like him, don't you? Colin is the image of his grandfather, my own adored Colin, the only one of my husbands I really loved—the same unruly ways, the same keen mind, if he would only use it! Pour me another drop of chocolate, child! You see, Laura, I lost my husband, Lord Duff-Drummond, my only son and his wife all at the same time; their coach was swept away with a bridge that collapsed from the rains. Only the babe was saved, saved like little Moses from the Nile! If only Colin would see the serious side of life—I tried, Laura! Believe me, I tried! I even married the good, dull Lord Inverkleith hoping he would direct Colin's ways. We settled in our modest George Street mansion in Edinburgh and entered Colin in the University. For a while we thought he had changed, then we discovered that he was spending most of his time at Leith Sands wagering on the races. When Lord Inverkleith succumbed to illness of the heart, I could no longer endure life in Scotland. I promised Colin his own stables if he would finish his education at Oxford. He got through four years of readings in two years, finishing with high honors. 'Now I'll have those stables, if you please!' So it has always been: Colin has found every challenge too small. What he needs is a wife to inspire him, children to engage his loyalty—above all a son, to perpetuate our proud line! A son—oh, Laura! How I've prayed for an heir to the name of Duff-Drummond."

"Why hasn't your ladyship's grandson ever cared to marry?" asked Laurie in a thread of voice that she squeezed from the churning within.

"He's never found the right person," answered Lady Inverkleith. "Our London girls are either too bold or too simpering-shy! Never natural. Colin likes spirited women. Spirit comes from a natural mind—unaffected, uncalculating!"

Laurie ventured a question that haunted her. "It's unbelievable that Lord Duff-Drummond should never have fallen in love!" She spoke with a smile but her heart trembled as she awaited the answer.

"I think my Colin knows not the meaning of the word love," said Lady Inverkleith. "Caprices . . . yes, I daresay more than one! But deep affection? Loyalty? Never! Colin is as fickle as they come."

Lady Inverkleith was wrong . . . wrong! Her grandson was the embodiment of affection! Else why would he spend his nights with a girl named Laurie? He cares for me and me alone! thought the proud girl. If he did not, he'd stay away, skip a night now and then! But he always came back—sometimes late, sometimes early. She found it hard to breathe until she heard her door open—"Laura!"

"Colin!"

The thrill was never dulled. That first kiss was more rousing than a cheer, more warming than fire, more heady than wine.

In the course of daytime meetings, Lord Duff-Drummond was a model of deportment. In the intimacy of the bedchamber he forsook his formal ways, seeming more like a carefree lad. It was thus that Laurie loved him best —or was it? She loved him in every guise, at every hour, distant feigner, or plunderer of kisses.

Lady Inverkleith was the less aware of what was going on under her nose, because the more taken up with preparations for the *Venus and Apollo* ballet to be presented this year as in the past, on Boxing Day. Laurie had no part in these preparations except to watch the rehearsals in the miniature theater. A self-important personage named

Maître Ducase led the orchestra, a buzzing stage director whom everyone called "Candles"—his real name was Candelle—buzzed around milady's chair. Monsieur Alcide and his pretty-boy helpers came with costumes and stage properties, creating a joyous hubbub to the accompaniment of violins, flutes, oboes and violas. There were no female performers except Lady Inverkleith, who played the role of Venus. The rest of the cast were young men—graceful and agile terpsichoreans who leaped and bounded around the stage like gazelles. Watching the doll-like figurine of La Monette whirl and posture, Laurie could well discount the ordinary concept of age.

One evening as the ballet reached its climax, a footman brought a note, "for Miss Macneill!" Laurie at once recognized the labored handwriting of her cousin Jinny.

> Dear Laurie,
>
> I have come to London and I am staying at the Black Swan, Holburn. My purse was stolen so they are holding my things. Can you help your
> Loving Coz.
> p.s. 10 shillings will be enough.

Jinny in London? Laura was dumbfounded—also very much alarmed. The last person in the world she wanted to admit to her privacy was the inquisitive Jinny!

"A letter . . . ?" said Lady Inverkleith with the look of one who says, "Read it to me!" Her kind mistress twinkled. "Your cousin, in London? Why of course! Have her come! It will do you a world of good to have a companion your own age for a change."

Regretfully, Laurie dispatched the messenger with her answer. She never dreamed her cousin would make an immediate appearance—she was on the point of joining her lover when the door flew open and Jinny walked in, a startling vision in a bright scarlet frock and a gay feather-trimmed bonnet.

134

"Laurie! Heart! I couldn't wait," she called cheerily, then slammed the door on the footman who had carried her bundles upstairs. She walked across the floor in imitation of him—"Naow tyke it easy, my young loidy! Them marble steps is fair slippy!"

"Jinny! What brings you to London?"

"I'd enough of Edinburgh and the Royal Scot!"

"Your father . . . did he let you come?"

"Tut-tut! and 'sdeath, no!"

"Where did you get the money?"

"Nipped it o' the till."

"Then . . . your purse wasn't stolen?"

Jinny giggled. "Of course not, ducky. I spent every penny. But I had to make out a sad story."

"Your husband . . . your precious Wattie?"

"Wattie?" Jinny shrugged and tossed her gay red bonnet onto the bed. "I never want to see him again. Probably won't! He enlisted to fight Napoleon. Off to the wars . . . Ta-ra-ra!"

How long had Jinny been in London, that she'd already caught the twang of London's tongue? How many fibs had she told? Who bought her that mad bonnet and that scarlet dress?

"I got your letter," said the runaway. "It all sounded so grand. I was sick and tired of hearing Kate and Mother squabble."

"Margit will be lonely without you."

"I know. When I get rich, I'll bring Margit to London and find her a handsome love." Jinny had already begun to nose around the room, admiring everything she saw.

"This *is* a fine house! I shall have silk curtains too! And I'll have a down feather-bed and pictures on the wall!"

"How is Aunt Emma?" asked Laurie.

"Mother's just the same. She and Kate have it hot and heavy all the time, but . . . enough about me, Laurie! Tell me about you! How many fine gentlemen are groveling at

135

your feet? My, you've changed . . . quite beautifully pale! You're more slender! My deah! So becoming!" Jinny began casting off her clothing as she talked, her gown here, her petticoat there. Naked as the day she was born, she crawled into her cousin's bed. "Och! soft sheets! Laurie, heart! I was made to be rich and rich I'll be. Keep it in mind!" She lowered her voice to a whisper. "Laurie . . . want to hear about *my* latest? I met him in the coach . . . he's a dealer in grains . . . a nice, little man with a round tummy . . . name's Alfie! Dear old Alfie! Would you believe it, he bought me that red dress and hat? Come closer, Laurie! Let's nestle like we used to! Tell me *your* secrets!"

Laurie cast about for a way of escape from her tormentress. "Rest a bit. I must go to my poodles."

"Your poodles?" yawned Jinny. "Oh yes, I'd almost forgotten you were a poodle-lady."

Laurie slipped away to her lover who had just returned from his club. "Colin . . . not tonight!"

"Why not?"

"My cousin Jinny Colquohoun has arrived from Edinburgh."

"Well . . . what of it?"

"She's to sleep in my bed."

"Well, let her!"

Laurie backed away from her lover's arms. "Please, darling! It would be dangerous. Jinny is a dreadful gossip. She must never know about our love."

Lady Inverkleith seemed delighted with her companion's young cousin from Edinburgh—all the more so when the artful Jinny expressed her great admiration for La Monette.

"Surely you are too young to know of my fame, young woman!"

"Is fame a thing that can be measured by age?" flattered Jinny. "My dream was to be a dancer like La Monette, but my parents—milady knows how Edinboro thinks—that is why I came to London, to follow a career in the drama."

"I think you more suited to comedy, young woman," said Lady Inverkleith with a smile. "Let me see what you can do?"

For a moment Jinny was nonplused, then her natural daring came to her aid. "Would your ladyship let me act the part of a poor starving child who finds a gold piece in the snow?" She began a pathetic pantomime which she enlivened with a jingle composed on the spur of the moment.

> "I'm so cold, O have pity!
> My poor toes are blue,
> In this big, cruel city
> My heart's frozen too!"

Coming upon an imaginary gold piece, the "starving child" went into a frenzy of joy as she recited in gay, "stage" chatter:

> "This gold will buy me dilly love—and
>   that is no coat!
> 'Tis the arm of a charmer around me
>   and the heat of his kisses.
> Oh! Goodie gold piece! Come, let's away
>   to the market and buy me a love!"

"Comedy of course!" laughed Lady Inverkleith when the show was ended. "There may be something I can do . . ."

"What will she do?" questioned Jinny when they were dismissed. "She is a hundred years old, frumpy in her ways. I want to be with actors and actresses of today!"

But Jinny was a model of obedience the next time Lady Inverkleith sent for her. Milady was abed, "Candles" at her bedside.

"Here is the girl, my good Candelle," said Lady Inverkleith, "try her and see what she's good for."

It took Jinny only a moment to grasp Opportunity by the locks! She fell on her knees at milady's bedside and kissed her hand. "Thank you, milady! Thank you!" She hopped to her feet and turned a backward somersault, landing on one knee with arms outstretched and a "Ta-ra-ra."

Lady Inverkleith rocked with laughter. Even "Candles" gave a loud "Ho-ho," and pinched Jinny by the ear. "Come, I'll set you on your feet! There's no future in tumbling."

Laurie drew a sigh of relief when, a week later, Jinny left hospitable Hathmore House to embark upon her "career." It had been a hectic week. Generous Lady Inverkleith had showered Jinny with gifts of a wardrobe, a purse, promises of further aid.

She produced her newest protégée at an intimate supper. Even Lord-Drummond seemed to be heartily amused by what he called "Jinny's monkeyshines."

And Laurie was not overly pleased to hear Jinny rave about Lord Duff-Drummond. "A sweetheart! A marvel! A god in Bond Street clothing!"

Yes, Laurie was glad Jinny had gone and that she could return to arms from which she'd been a week estranged!

The Laird received her signal, "Tonight!" with a nod. No sooner was the coast clear, he slipped into her room, into her bosom! And bliss was found again, the sharper, the more eager for having suffered denial. But after the first flame was quelled, Duff-Drummond said, "I'm going out of town until the New Year, Laura."

Instinct told Laurie not to ask, "Where? Why? With whom?"

"I'll miss you," she murmured with breaking heart.

"I'll only be gone a fortnight . . . guest of the Prince. His highness' invitations are a command."

"Of course, dear."

"I'll have to be up early," yawned Duff-Drummond. "Put your sweet head on my shoulder. Let's sleep awhile, or I'll not be fit for dawn-rising."

Laurie could not sleep. Her lover gone, the sun of her life would set. Not to see him at all, not even a glimpse, was worse than the past weeks of separation!

She heard the clocks strike every hour, from one until four. Big clocks and little clocks, clocks with brazen chimes and clocks with silvery tinkle. A fortnight was more than fourteen days—it was eternity! The sleeper wakened on the stroke of half-past four.

A little time for kisses—one last ardent salute, and the Laird hauled himself out of bed. "I wish to heaven I could've said no to Georgie, but this end-of-the-year hunt is a ritual. . . . Now where did I drop that slipper? Ah! Here it is!" Duff-Drummond stooped to plant a good-by kiss on his mistress' trembling lips.

"A fortnight only. Promise!" whispered Laurie.

"I promise."

"I love you so! I can't bear to think of existing without you."

"You'll have plenty to occupy your mind . . . Granny's ballet and all!"

"Nothing occupies my mind except you!"

Her lover gone, Laurie felt a premonition of evil to come. She shivered. How cold the winter morn! The fire was spent . . . not even an ember! She huddled under the covers in her lonely bed. Why must they always part— their last kiss always farewell?

"You've been so pale these past days," said Lady Inverkleith to her despondent companion. "Come! Perk up! Take my carriage . . . go and visit your cousin. A change of scene will do you good!"

Laurie drove to Maître Candelle's residence at Number 14 Buckingham Street. Once the home of a noble, the house had been divided into small lodgings; a signboard under a lantern informed visitors that Maestro Giacomo Telletti taught the violin on the 3rd floor; that Mr. Beeks, mender of chinaware, clocks and watches was on the 4th floor rear. Madame Bland, Milliner, had her window display on the street. Jas. H. Gromes, Bookkeeper, lived in the basement.

Laurie found the sign she was looking for: "Maître Candelle and Madame Vesée-Candelle—School of Acting. *Étage Noble.*"

She groped her way up a flight of stairs lighted by the rays of the street lantern that pierced the dusty pane of a fan-window. Two masks in gesso, *"Comoedia"* and *"Tragoedia,"* designated the abode of the teachers. She pulled the bell-handle.

"Laura!" Jinny was bursting with excitement at seeing her "coz." She led the way into a vast, drafty room with a ceiling so high that the rosettes and apples of the stucco were almost invisible.

"This used to be a duchess' ballroom," she explained. "'Candles' holds his classes here now."

"Candles" and his lady were enjoying the evening air in a turretlike room that overlooked the moon-silvered reaches of the Thames. They welcomed their caller effusively and received Lady Inverkleith's gift of *petits fours* with the proper unction. Laurie looked around in amazement. The walls of the room were hung with puppets, their wires hooked to nails driven into the plaster. Punchinellos and kings, pirates and princesses, a crocodile, a black cat, a general in gold braid, a witch with pointed hat, all the characters of the child-theater were here.

"We used to travel with our own puppet show," said her hostess. "Candelle and Vesée. Perhaps you've heard of us? The wars on the Continent, the Revolution and all forced us to quit our travels and become teachers. Would you like to see our puppets perform? We made them ourselves. My husband is an expert wood-carver and I sewed their costumes."

Laurie was more anxious to talk to her cousin than to watch puppets but she had no choice. Jinny was all taken up with a tall young man who deigned to hoist himself out of his chair and salute her, then the two resumed their whispered conversation.

"Lord Radford is such a charming young man," said Madame Candelle with the leer of a *procureuse*. "Let me show you how our 'ballerina' can dance. We made her in the image of La Monette in her young days."

Madame Candelle was an expert puppeteer and her "La Monette" was delightful, but Laurie wasn't interested. Who was Lord Radford? How had Jinny managed to collect a titled admirer in so short a time? At last the young gentleman took his languid person, high stock, and foxnose away.

"Come to my room!" whispered Jinny when she had seen her swain to the door.

Jinny's room was a cubbyhole! Not much larger than the understairs quarters Laurie had endured at the Royal Scot.

"Now, tell me? Ain't Tommy horridly aristocratic?"

"Tommy?"

"Lord Thomas Elgin Radford of Radford Hall," said Jinny in a superb imitation of her languid admirer. "He's mad about me and he's fairly well off. I play him like a cat plays a mouse."

"Are you planning to make an end to mouse Tommy like you did Wattie Baird?"

"Wait and see!"

"Remember, you are a married woman."

"That's why it is so simple."

"If you are playing for the title of Lady Radford, hadn't you better first shed your husband in the courts?"

"Marry Tommy?" laughed Jinny. "Dear me, no! Tommy is not rich."

"You said he was well off."

"He has enough to live in chambers and belong to one club . . ." Jinny's lively face took on an expression Laurie had never seen before. "I want *real* wealth," she murmured, "wealth like your Lady Inverkleith. Did you know that

141

Lord Hathmore left Lady Inverkleith half a million pounds? She wasn't Lady Inverkleith then. She was the Duchess de Jussin. Tell me, Laurie, does Lord Duff-Drummond have many mistresses . . . love affairs?"

"I know nothing about his lordship's love affairs," said Laurie, turning her head to conceal a painful blush.

"A gentleman so fine . . . so . . . exciting," murmured Jinny, "he must have a hundred ladies at his beck and call!"

Laurie examined the contents of a book-shelf at the head of Jinny's cot. "What are these, plays?"

"Oh, those!" said Jinny with a shrug. "I know 'em all by heart. 'Candles' said he never had a pupil with a memory like mine. I look at a page—bang! I know every word. Let's talk about Lord Duff-Drummond! How strange the way things turn out—you might have married Lord Duff-Drummond's bailiff if he hadn't got himself murdered, and you'd be serving the Laird in Scotland! Instead you serve the Laird's granny in London! A much better place! I'd make the most of it!"

"Just how would you make the most of it, pray tell?" asked Laurie, not without a lively curiosity.

"Easy!" cooed Jinny throwing herself backward and tossing her slim legs in the air. "I'd make him fall in love!"

"Jinny! You're the mad one!" laughed Laurie.

"No. I'm practical! Give me that playbook!" pouted Jinny. "I'll show you! Soon I'll be the most talked-of woman on the stage. Tommy Radford is taking me to call on Mr. Grenville next week and I may get a part in *The Hitter Hit* or *Tansy in Trouble,*—an uproarious farce! I'll make 'em die laughing." Jinny went into her role, eye-balling it as though some wealthy patron were watching.

"You wait and see!" she said when she came to the end of the scene. "When I'm the toast of the Green Room, Lord Duff-Drummond will applaud. And I'll have a chance to nab him!"

Ten

The Venus Ballet

BEGINNING AT DAWN, THE FIRST SNOW OF THE YEAR FELL
on Boxing Day. A softening of the air, a quiet among
the trees heralded its coming. Soon the terrace was car-
peted with white and the trees and shrubs were dusted
with flakes that glistened like gems.

Laurie threw on a warm cloak and took the poodles for
a run. They went wild in the snow; they rolled and bur-
rowed and played like youngsters. Always the unruly
member of the band, Prince broke away from the others
and ran to the fence, barking wildly.

"Prince! Prince!" called Laurie. Usually her favorite
came at once. But this time he would not obey, so she
went down to find him. Then she saw what made him
bark, a crowd pressed against the side gate of the
gardens—a gray, silent crowd. As she came nearer, she
saw children of young age, and very poor. Their rags
scarcely covered their thin bodies. They had no shoes,
only sacking and straw tied in big clumsy wrapping
over their bare feet. Noses and eyes running, hands
blue with cold, they seemed to be waiting patiently—for
what? Did Lady Inverkleith distribute bread and goodies
to the poor on Boxing Day? Laurie asked a manservant
who was shoveling a path in the snow—perhaps he was
there to keep an eye on this army of waifs? "What are
these children waiting for?"

"The pantomime, miss," answered the servant.

143

"Lady Inverkleith's ballet?"

"Yes, miss. There's summat 'round fifty, now. This evening there'll be seven hundred and forty of 'em. They allus seem to know exactly how many will be let in. Seven hundred and forty and not one more, and that's countin' the babes."

"Do they have to wait here?"

"There's no other place, miss. They don't mind. They know what's in store."

Laurie herded her eight pampered doggies back to their warm playroom and went down to the theater, where she found a small army of people making ready for the evening's entertainment. Tables had been set up all around the walls. Fruits and nuts and *candis* were piled in baskets every few feet along the board. She could see no drinking cups or knives or even plates, but there were hundreds of pewter mugs and small, square trays made of wood. Soon the food was brought in, roast joints carved in thick slices, disjointed fowl, sliced ham and tongue, great trenchers piled with slices of buttered bread, sugar cakes and gingerbread men, great pitchers of sweetened milk, and dumped like pirate's gold enough Spanish oranges to fill the hold of a ship!

"Well, Laura, what do you think of our banquet for the children?"

It was Lady Inverkleith, surrounded by her court of mimes, dancers and musicians.

"Wonderful, milady!"

"Did you see them out there? Many spent the night at the gate, that they might be first to enter. It seems a pity that they must wait . . . heigh-ho! We must all sacrifice something to earn our Paradise. Come, Candelle! I wish to see the first half of the third scene—last night something went wrong. Music please!"

On the stage, the dancers pranced through a few measures of the ballet while in the dim theater, cooks' helpers,

144

footmen and lackeys came and went from kitchens, bringing more and more delicious foods, more and more surprises for the children waiting at the Paradise gates.

It was not until two in the afternoon that Lady Inverkleith stopped the rehearsal. She looked pale and fatigued as she climbed the stairs to her boudoir.

"I am still not content with the scene where—oh, never mind. It will have to do!" she sighed. "Sometimes I think Candelle is growing old. Next year I must find a new dancer for the role of Juno. That young Antonini is too foolish!"

What visions of a long and brilliant past swam before Lady Inverkleith's half-closed eyes as she rested in her great satin-draped bed? Did she see kings and princes standing in their loges to acclaim La Divine Monette, the glitter of jewels, the flowers tendered to her grace and genius—or did she see as Laurie did, that long gray line of children.

"Laura!" called Lady Inverkleith.

"Yes, milady?"

"Do not leave me."

"I shan't, milady."

"Sit here, near my bed."

"Yes, milady . . ."

"I am not tired!" said Lady Inverkleith petulantly, "I am troubled . . . here." She touched her breast. "Every year it is the same. I prepare these pleasures for the children. I say to myself, this time I will be strong and think only of the immediate need to provide beauty and happiness for those who have nothing. Then when the time comes, I find myself remembering the days when I was like those children, barefoot in the snow, my belly a cave of hunger. Wear your prettiest gown tonight, Laura! Nothing is too good for my children. Put on a white gown . . . here, hand me my jewel casket."

Lady Inverkleith's jewel box was of exquisite Italian

make. The lid opened at the snap of a secret spring, and a music box tinkled a tune, off key. The casket was filled with trinkets and souvenirs—a miniature St. George on a white enamel charger, a collection of jewel-studded Orders, a Chinese god carved in ivory, several small seashells and a string of glass beads.

"Colin strung these beads for my birthday when he was four years old," said Lady Inverkleith with a tender smile. "He gathered these shells on the sands of Normandy when he was seven." She handed the wide-eyed Laurie a diadem of diamonds set in lacy filigree. "Here! Wear this! The children will take you for Queen of the Elves."

Laurie had just finished dressing when she heard childrens' voices, and looking out of the window she saw a long procession trotting up the driveway, kept in line by several liveried lackeys. An endless horde of Graylings poured through the park. Their bare or rag-shod feet made no noise on the inlaid floor. Their voices were hushed. Their faces were half hidden by their unkempt locks, small dirty fingers pointed and mouths fell open in "ohs" of wonder. Then in the strange hush Laurie heard another sound—constant and over-all—a sound of sniveling and sniffing, the sharp rasp of coughing.

Soon the stench of the unwashed began to rise like a vapor in the air, bringing back stabbing memories—the stink of Edinburgh's medieval slums, drunken men staggering under pious legends: "Blissit be God in al his Giftis," carved in the stones, the fragrance of burned treacle that came from a near-by bakery where she went to return a gold-tipped cane that a lawyer named Kilrose had left under his table at the Royal Scot.

"Step in!" The lawyer's cook had poured a cup of tea; while Laurie was drinking, four youngsters came out of a dark room behind the kitchen. They were pale and unwashed and they coughed incessantly. "Are those your children?" Laurie had asked.

146

"Mine?" Cook tossed her head. "Those are the Master's childer."

"Why do they stay in that dark room?"

"Where else can they stay? The rooms upstairs are for the Master and his pleaders. The childer stay down here and rot, like sheep in a sunless fold."

"Dollop!" whispered a small urchin as he elbowed aside another boy. "Drop the bread! Save your belly fer meat! 'Ere! Tyke this, and see 'ow it feels to eat like a bloody Juke!"

By the order of Lady Inverkleith, lackeys stood with long candle snuffers, watching in case of fire, nor did they try to stop the onrush of hungry waifs.

Free to assault the food-laden tables as often as they pleased, the children did not hang back! Meat, sweets and beverages vanished like snow on a hot skittle. No sooner was the platter or the pitcher empty than a footman brought another filled full. How much could seven hundred and forty bellies hold? A few darted through the French doors into the garden where they vomited up the excess food, then came back for more.

Here sat a little girl with a whole cake in her lap, into which she dug with both fists. There, a boy stuffed his ragged shirt with oranges. A brother showed his sister how to strip the last tendon from a drumstick before grabbing another. Two lads fought for a platter of ham until a third said, "Garn! There's plenty more where 'at come from!"

Grayling hands plucked at her skirts as Laurie passed, mewing, "Loidy! Loidy!" She dared not heed a single cry for pity. Only God's wings were wide enough to cover them all!

The deep "bong" of a gong staunched her tears—stopped every cry and murmur, even the sound of champing jaws, the sniveling and coughing. Lackeys lowered the chandeliers and snuffed the candles.

On stage a Pierrot stepped to the footlights and Maître Candelle's voice boomed in the stillness.

"Your Majesties! Here is the Show! *Venus and Apollo,* or the story of a Contest of Beauty."

Laurie found a place of vantage near the stage, and leaned against a slender Corinthian column upholding the proscenium arch. With every action up on the stage, that sea of small bodies around her feet was stirred as by deep undercurrents. What did the Graylings hear? How much did they understand? Perhaps all they saw were the fairy figures of the dancers flitting in a wonderland; nor did they care what legend unfolded or that the Queen of Beauty was an old, old woman.

Faster and faster, the fairy throng leaped and spun and whirled upon the stage. The musicians played louder—louder—until suddenly the curtain fell upon the last tableau.

Laurie clapped her hands to her ears to shut out the piercing screams of the children. Again and again, Venus came to the footlights. They would not stop. There was a shrill note in their childish voices—dread of facing the freezing night outside those magic doors? They were striving to make Paradise last. But Lady Inverkleith spoke in her high, thin voice, the voice of the very old.

"Children . . . come back next year. I will dance for you again . . . but now I am tired and I must say good night! Good night. . . . Good night!"

Only then, Laurie realized that the ballet was ended. The children were herding slowly toward the exits. When she knocked at Lady Inverkleith's dressing room, Dubois answered, "Milady says you may retire. She will sup with the troupe as usual. No need for you to wait." Laurie went to her room with lagging step. So lonely she could scarcely refrain from bursting into tears, she went to say good night to her poodle family. The doggies were fast asleep —only Prince leaped from his little gilt bed. "Yes . . . you may!" Laurie consented when the pert animal sat up and begged. Prince hopped to his favorite place at the foot of her bed. "You're never lonesome, are you, Prince? You have so many little friends." The bright-eyed poodle cocked his ear and wagged his fluff-ball tail. "No . . . no games tonight!" There was nothing Prince liked better than a mad scamper over the furniture, under the bed, in and out behind the window draperies. "You're never jealous, either!" said Laurie, musing. Oh! it was foolish to be jealous! But her love was so far away. And it was not easy to forget Jinny's gossip—did Lord Duff-Drummond have many mistresses? A hundred, at his beck and call? Laurie knew the name of only one of the Laird's mistresses— Laura Macneil! She was no fine lady, just an adoring girl who would die for the sake of her beloved!

Laurie was restless, the room too warm and then too cold. The doggie was restless too. Up and down from the bed—sniffing under the door. She tried to keep him quiet but Prince had other ideas. At last, toward morning she rose and took him back to his own quarters. A chill seized her as she stood in nightgown and bare feet, wondering whether it was a drink of water she wanted. No—the mere thought of water turned her sick. She went back to bed. But the sick feeling worsened. She pressed a pillow against her middle and tried to stay calm. This nausea, this lump of lead in her belly? What was the reason? She'd eaten lightly, drunk nothing heavier than hot chocolate before going to bed.

The usual morning ceremonial got under way with the appearance of a young chambermaid named Pearlie, who brought kindling and coals for the fire.

"Good mornin', miss," said Pearlie. She pulled the curtains and knelt at the hearth. "It's fair nippy this mornin'! There's lace on the windowpanes. Frost, miss," Pearlie giggled. "I wish't I'd a dress made o' frost lace! I'd be the one, I would!"

Pearlie dumped the ashes into her bucket and cleaned the hearth. She laid kindling and started a fire from a live coal that she'd brought from the kitchen. Blowing the bellows until the flame started, she chattered cheerily. "Us'ns bin up since four o'clock, cleanin' the trash and mess! Whee! Them beggar children do be dirty. Of course it ain't for me to clean—that's for the chars and the footman, miss. But I 'elps put fings to rights. Just you rest warm 'til Clives comes up wif your tray, Miss."

"I want only a cup of tea, thank you, Pearlie," said Laurie.

"My, my!" exclaimed the maid as she lighted bedside candles to put to flight the gloom. "You look awfu' pale . . . Miss! Are you ill?"

The tea only made things worse! Fighting nausea, Laurie pushed the tray aside and got out of bed. She reached the comfort-stool just in time to vomit.

I'll feel better, now! she thought hopefully as she sponged her face with cold water. It was high time she dressed and got ready to feed the poodles.

Every morning sharp at nine, a footman brought a large silver tureen filled with mush and milk for the doggies' breakfast. It was Laurie's task to ladle the mush into separate bowls and see that each poodle got his share. Then she went to work, combing and tidying the little pets. Alas! A glance at her calendar told her that this was also trimming day. Once a fortnight, a bouncing chatterbox of an ex-Parisienne named Madame Deréchault came to trim the poodles according to style. She called herself a *coiffeuse canine,* and was much in demand among London pet owners. She cut fluffy coats, shaved slender legs, created gay pompons, pared claws, washed, brushed and made the poodles look like delightful toys. From a lumpy black bag she could produce all manner of strange objects at a moment's notice.

"Gloves . . . ? *Ma fille!* I've a friend in Soho . . . an Emigrée lady who makes the most exquisite gloves. I may even have a sample with me!" Veritable Mago's bag-o'-tricks, Madame Deréchault's carry-all contained such unrelated articles as fine laces and fancy dog collars, silk stockings and 'Wrinkle Destroyer Balm,' paste jewelry and potency potions, horoscope fortunes and the latest scurrilous pamphlet against the Royal Family. The poodle-trimmer was in the midst of operations when Laurie was again seized with nausea. This time she felt so ill that she reeled and almost fell. Madame Deréchault dropped scissors and comb and ran to her aid. "*Pauvre fille!* Lean on me! There. This pillow under your feet . . . your head down. Here, I'll set a basin on the floor. If you must vomit . . . vomit. Brandy would be good. I think I have some."

Laurie heard the click of bottles and jars as Madame Deréchault rummaged in her carry-all. Meanwhile the distracted poodles ran rings around the chaise-longue where their adored companion was resting, nuzzling her cheek with cold noses, touching her with delicate paws as if to say, "What's wrong, Laurie?"

Madame Deréchault shooed the doggies back to their own quarters, shut the door, and sat down beside the sufferer. "Pauvrette!" she said with a sigh that distended her ample bosom to the full. "Youth must have its fling . . . but . . . what are you going to do now?"

"What am I going to do?" echoed Laurie who did not understand.

"But . . . your condition!" exclaimed Madame Deréchault, shaking her jingling bracelets. "Surely you know you're going to have a baby! You're no fifteen-year-old! That pallor . . . green around the lips. Vomiting. Dizziness. And milady so particular about such things! Even if you were married—*are* you, Miss Macneil? But no . . . a poor

151

girl! What handsome rake seduced you? Alas! It is only human to listen to the call of love. But you should have been more careful, my girl. If you'd only asked old Deréchault! My 'Anti-Cupidon' would have saved you!"

Laurie fought desperately to conceal her terror. She knew with dreadful certainty that this woman had spoken the truth—last month's period skipped entirely, morning vapors, dizziness, lack of appetite, racking of the stomach. She was going to have a baby! Yes! Nature had at last caught up with two blithe lovers! The thought of a child —Duff-Drummond's child—should bring rapture, thankfulness and pride. What more could a loving woman desire? But in her poor estate—hireling and clandestine mistress of a great gentleman—what worse fate?

"Of course, it will be some time before your condition becomes apparent," said Madame Deréchault. "I know excellent pills that will stop the vomiting and restore your colors." From the all-containing bag, she produced a little round box. "How fortunate . . . I just happened to have some with me! Take one at midnight and one at six in the morning. The effect is stupendous. Only five shillings. But you must arrange to leave Lady Inverkleith's service well in time. In all the years I've served this house, I've never known milady to keep a companion who showed signs of being pregnant! 'Untidy' she calls it. 'An unmarried girl who is going to have a baby is . . . untidy!' Poor dear! Do you feel better? Can you go on with the work or shall I ask for a maid?"

Laurie shook her head, "No!" and got up. Knowing that she must placate this woman who already knew too much, she willingly paid the five shillings for the pills.

"Of course," said Madame Deréchault as she snipped away at Prince's thick white coat, "you might not want the baby—in that case I can recommend someone . . ."

"Why shouldn't I want the baby?" said Laurie faintly.

"I . . . I only thought . . . Well, since you're willing to

go through with it, I can also recommend a good midwife. Very reliable. She has a heart of gold. I think I may have her address . . ." For the nth time, Madame Deréchault delved into her carry-all, and brought out a printed card.

MISTRESS HUGGINS
gives motherly care.
Reasonable Prices
3 Fauconberg Mews, Soho.

"Better see her at once and make arrangements," said Madame Deréchault. "Her services are reserved well in advance. It is always nice to know one can be . . . er . . . discreetly cared for. Tell Mistress Huggins old Deréchault sent you."

The first free hour, Laurie hurried to near-by Soho. Fauconberg Mews was a dingy alley off Sutton Street. A drab—nearing her term from the size of her apron—answered Laurie's timid ring.

Mistress Huggins was a forbidding person with a shade of mustache and a pair of black eyebrows that seemed possessed of a life of their own.

"Well, speak up, little lady!" The right eyebrow quirked upward, the left managed to lower in a frown. As the midwife scrutinized her visitor's clothing, her figure, the size of her purse, her black eyebrows waved messages to one another. "Well, well. Who sent you?"

"A young woman from Waltonstowe," lied Laurie. "She said you were a good midwife. I . . . I'd like to know what you charge."

"Waltonstowe? I know nobody from—well, never mind! I charge a married woman ten shillin' the week. Those less fortunate may earn their keep providin' . . ." Mistress Huggins paused. Her left eyebrow nestled over her left eye—"Providin' . . . the mother will leave her child in my care."

"You mean . . . board my baby with you?"

153

"I mean . . . *leave*," said Mistress Huggins.

"Leave it . . . forever?" cried Laurie.

"I am not in business for charity, my girl. I find good homes for healthy babes."

Laurie did not wait to hear any more. So this was part of a midwife's traffic! Her knees shook as she hurried out of the Mews—how false the winter sunset that shed an ephemeral glow over old mansions and leaf-strewn grass-plots, the gray tombstones in St. Patrick's churchyard.

This icy hand that gripped her, this surge of despair were only the first fee of wrongdoing. The moralists call it, "The Wages of Sin."

> Wool of bat, and tongue of dog,
> Adder's form, and blind-worm's sting,
> Lizard's leg and houlet's wing,
> For a charm of powerful trouble.

Laurie's thoughts hung from her numb brain like icicles from the roof. Fear of signs and omens, fear of what pulpit-ranters called "damnation"—was it not all tied up with the fear of cold, hunger and shame to which she was now a prey?

Loving so deeply, longing with such passion, caring with such deep devotion, she dared not face her lover with the truth. A quirk of the eyebrow, some cooling of tone—even a look would be enough to let her know that neither she nor her child was wanted. There was nought in the world a man like the Laird detested more than a ball-and-chain! He'd told her so in a thousand ways—most of all by his refusal to take her for anything more than a playmate of the night!

Without this complication—dreadful name for a child of love—she'd have been content to live in his shadow, eat the crumbs from his table. She'd not endure his indifference or suffer the humiliation of knowing that the Laird would not acknowledge his own flesh and blood!

Laurie started to plan at once, an idea was beginning to form. What more could she hope than to plan for the nine months ahead?

Lady Inverkleith seemed quite rested from the fatigue of the last night's performance when at teatime she sent for her young companion.

She discussed the ballet at length—asked Laurie's opinion of the grand finale. "Were my *battées d'entrechat* perfect?"

"Entrancing, milady."

"My final *pirouette?*"

"Milady was like a silver top! Dazzling!"

"Good! I'm pleased. Now tell me about the doggies. Deréchault came this morning, did she not?"

There was nothing her ladyship liked better than to hear little stories about the pranks of her pets—what Prince did to Brucie, did Queenie turn up her aristocratic nose at her dinner! She never failed to have the poodles in for inspection of their "coiffures" after Madame Deréchault's visit.

While Laurie was exhibiting the pets' latest haircut, Lady Inverkleith said abruptly, "What is wrong with you, Laurie? You seem so downcast, not like yourself!"

Laurie trembled lest the sharp-eyed Monette should read her through and through. "I caught a chill while watching the ballet. I'm quite recovered, thank you, milady."

"It's the cold," said Lady Inverkleith. "I detest winter. I'd take us all off to my villa in Torquay, but they fear Napoleon may invade from the Channel. I say it's sheer nonsense! Well . . . patience! We'll both cheer up when my grandson returns."

Locking her door that night, Laurie dragged a box out of the closet. She packed only her plainest clothing—no evening gowns, no frivolous bonnets. She even abandoned

155

her beloved friends, her books! The less weight she had to carry, the better. Having done, she dressed in a warm frock and coat and tearfully penned a letter of farewell.

> DEAR LADY INVERKLEITH,
>
> In taking precipitate leave, I know I'm doing unpardonable wrong to One who trusted me and showed me angel-kindness. But circumstances stronger than my will have called me away.
>
> I pray your ladyship may find it in your heart to excuse and forget.
>
> Her disobedient servant,
> LAURA MACNEIL.

Knowing well the habits of Hathmore House's large staff, Laurie was waiting in the shadows on the grand staircase landing at midnight. Eerie scene in the feeble light of a few oil wicks. The marble banister of the grand staircase was ornamented every twelve steps with Janus-faced plaster busts of gods and goddesses dressed incongruously in the fashions of the time of Good Queen Bess. Their crowns, jewels, ruffs were painted in garish blue, red, purple, gilt and silver, Neptune-on-Newel Post, Venus and Apollo stared unblinking at those who entered the palace with the eyes at the back of their heads, at those who went up or down the grand staircase with the eyes in the front—or was it the contrary?

Precisely at ten minutes to twelve, the day footmen went off duty and the night footmen took over their watch in the hall. Evenings when Lady Inverkleith did not have guests there was always an interlude of ten minutes—the men went below-stairs for a mug of ale, a slice of cold beef and a laugh with the maids. The night footmen came on duty at the stroke of twelve.

She heard them laughing and talking on the way to the kitchens. Now was her chance! She ran down to the great front door, pulled the bolt, turned the massive key in the lock and slipped into the wintry night.

Eleven

Last Will of a Great Lady

"WENCH! A TANKARD O' PALE!"
"Girl, over here!"
"Hurry with my ale, maid!"

Familiar sounds to Laurie's ear. The clock was turned back, the scene, a London public house.

"Wot tyme do ye get orf, gel?"

"'Ow about you and me tippin' a few atter work?"

The time between, wiped out! Yes sir! No sir! Thank you sir. Run Laurie run, from kitchen to table. Hurry! Hurry! Work 'til you're numb. Fall asleep on a wafer-thin mattress in a stinking garret, rise at dawn, sweep, mop, dust, polish, scour!

Wandsworth's Ale House, Tottenham Court Road, was a thousand miles distant from Hathmore House, Mayfair, and Skudgy Laurie was back at the work she knew best.

Down on her knees one early morn, she was cleaning the steps when a man started nailing a poster to the board.

"You see this 'ere beauty?" he said with a wink at Char, "she's 'orth a hundred quid!"

Re-entering the inn, Laurie glanced at the board and nearly dropped her bucket.

The poster was illustrated with a reproduction of Mr. Gillray's thumbnail sketch of a young girl—passenger on a London-bound stagecoach—the details of hair and dress brought up to date so as to create a striking likeness of herself as she was today. Underneath, a printed notice.

157

ONE HUNDRED GUINEAS REWARD FOR NEWS OF THE
WHEREABOUTS OF THE ABOVE PERSON NAMED
LAURA MACNEIL, ADVISE SIR HENRY BANKS, TEMPLE
BAR.

It seemed to Laurie that the world was turning like a pinwheel. Trying to calm the fears that made her heart pound, she hurried to the scullery. The poster must be one of hundreds. How long before somebody would point a finger and say, "Laura Macneil!" Soon she found herself able to take a more calm view—if Sir Henry Bates advertised, surely it was not to do her harm.

"Well, naow, Duchess!" said the dish-washer, "'Ave ye ditched workin' for a livin'?"

"Today, yes!" said Laurie. She reached her decision suddenly. What could they do to her? She'd stolen nothing. Why not go to Sir Henry Banks . . . collect the reward and use it to help herself at birth of her baby?

"My dear Miss Macneil," said Sir Henry Banks, "what a pity those posters were not up sooner. It would have made Lady Inverkleith supremely happy to see you before she died." And apparently without noticing that his listener had dissolved in tears, the solicitor added, "I'd a had 'em out sooner but we discovered a youthful portrait-drawing of you among the objects you left behind. It seemed a good idea to use it and I was able to give the poster artist some pointers on your . . . shall I say . . . matured looks—fairly exact if I do say so." Sir Henry leaned across his desk and patted the fair weeper's arm. "Come! Miss Macneil, dry your tears! I can't endure the sight of a crying woman, much less a beautiful crying woman, one of the many reasons why I never married."

"Poor kind Lady Inverkleith!" Laurie said brokenly.

"Kind but not poor! La Monette lived a full life and she died the death of a princess! Not even the great Garrick himself could have staged the scene with greater art. Lady

158

nverkleith had retired. . . . Feeling the end was near she
ummoned her grandson to her bedside. 'Bless you, Colin
. . find Laurie!' were her last words."

"Why did she ask Lord Duff-Drummond to find me?"
ried Laurie from a new wellspring of hope.

"I'm not at liberty to disclose the exact reason until the
eading of the will," said Sir Henry Banks. "Lady Inver-
leith requested among other things that you return to
Iathmore House and care for the poodles. She set great
tore by the pretty little beasts, you know."

Laurie dared not ask: "Where is Lord Duff-Drum-
nond?" but the solicitor answered her unspoken query.
'Lord Colin has gone to Newmarket. He'll return to town
or the reading of the will, a week from today."

Long before the appointed hour, the staff of Hathmore
Iouse had gathered in the music room, and taken their
places on gilt chairs that were placed in rows as for a
ession of chamber music.

Awed, perhaps a little frightened, they sat stiffly, wait-
ng for what was to come. Every person who had served
Lady Inverkleith had received the same summons:

> Your presence is requested at Hatrmore
> House, Tuesday morning, January 18, 1806,
> at ten o'clock.

The card was signed, "Sir Henry Banks, Solicitor."

The first black fog of winter washed the windows with
crepy yellow-brown vapors that turned faces livid and
filled the corners with gloom.

A week had elapsed since this motley company of cooks,
footmen, musicians, dancers, costumers had rubbed elbows with a royal prince, three earls, four dukes and
other personages of rank and luster, at the graveside of
La Monette. So precise were Lady Inverkleith's instruc-

tions, that not one woman was there—not even the faithful Dubois. She had been obliged to station outside the iron railing of Grosvenor Chapel churchyard, and watch while the men paid final homage to the deceased.

She was the only woman at this gathering today, although the paint-bedizened Monsieur Alcide did look a bit like a mincing woman.

Dubois folded and unfolded her cold hands under a black shawl that she'd purchased for the occasion—if only Mademoiselle had remembered about the bed! More than anything in the world, except money, Dubois wanted her comfortable bed.

She turned to her neighbor, the major-domo who had exchanged his gold-frogged coat, powdered wig and knee breeches for more appropriate blacks. "Mister Chalmers?"

"Yes, Dubois."

"Why ain't Miss Macneil here?"

"I haven't the faintest!"

"I suppose she's not like us; she ain't served Mademoiselle a quarter of a century."

"I suppose," the major-domo agreed. He too was busy with speculations—how much her Ladyship had seen fit to leave him? All these years he'd been a good major-domo, never a slip, never a penny off in his books.

Chef François, the head gardener, the stablemaster, Costumer Alcide, Maître Candelle were all pondering the same question—how much will I get?

As time passed, the suspense became unbearable. It was bad enough to have been kept in the dark while milady's solicitor turned the country upside down looking for a runaway girl. Given to liking Miss Laura, the staff had almost come to hate her—because of her, the reading of the will had been postponed.

Would there be another postponement? No! A tremor ran through the nerves of the assembled company. Necks craned as the door opened. In walked Miss Laura, on Sir Henry Banks' arm.

160

Behind them, Lord Duff-Drummond, a notary and two clerks, laden with deed boxes and other instruments of the legal profession. Trailing the procession, milady's courier and steward, Malcolm.

The company rose, and at a signal from Malcolm, they all sat down again, chair-legs scraped the floor, a cough or two, quickly suppressed. Sir Henry Banks handed the pale-faced Miss Laura to a seat at one end of the long, velvet-draped table, while milord sat down opposite. The solicitor took the center, like a judge on the bench. Malcolm seated himself near Miss Laura. The clerks opened deed boxes and portfolios.

Many hands were cupped around listening ears as the solicitor began to read the last will of La Monette, widow of the deceased Duke de Jussin, of the deceased Lord Hathmore, of the deceased Lord Duff-Drummond of Gillian and Barra, of the deceased Lord Inverkleith.

The document was couched in plain language.

". . . To His Royal Highness, George Augustus Frederick, Prince of Wales, my French poodles, Dauphin and Reine, who are inseparable. Because His Royal Highness always teased me to part with a pair of my pets. To my faithful courier and friend, Malcolm Biel, and his mother, Janet Biel, beloved nurse and foster-mother of my grandson, the summer lodge at Lasswade and its furnishings and three hundred pounds annum, so long as either shall live. To my faithful maid, Marie Dubois, three thousand pounds and her bed and bedding, also my poodle named Madame and ten pounds of her favorite tea. To my old friend Alcide, I leave poodles Baron and Marquis, my costumes and stage jewelry and five thousand pounds so that he may set up his own costumer's establishment in the house in Soho that he coveted . . ."

To Maître Candelle and his wife, Lady Inverkleith bequeathed her poodle Duke, five thousand pounds, "and my stage properties, including scenery, for the purpose of establishing a School of the Ballet." To her chef, milady left her poodle Bruce, the contents of her cellars and money to open an eating-house "so that any man who has the price of a dinner may know the delights of his perfect cooking."

Laurie had long ceased to listen. The solicitor's mention of Janet Biel, as nurse and foster-mother of Lord Duff-Drummond was a new shock. Janet Biel—Nanny Biel! Of course! Malcolm even looked like Nanny Biel! Why had she never noticed the resemblance? Could it have been Nanny Biel who had directed her son to hire a girl named Laura Macneil for Lady Inverkleith's service?

If so, one could string the events of the past months, like beads on a waxed thread. Compassionate Nanny Biel, seeking to protect and aid the girl who had been made the victim of a lordling's hoax—Laird's Choice! Little did the kind old nurse guess that her protégée had not learned her lesson, that she had not lived chastely under Lady Inverkleith's sheltering wing—that the Laird was able to choose and choose again, until the inevitable came to pass!

Laurie trembled as she asked herself, What would the Laird say if he knew I was to become the mother of his child?

Her lover's face gave no clue to his state of mind. It was the first time they'd seen each other since that night, a thousand years ago, when she kissed him farewell. This morning when he walked into the room where she and Sir Henry were waiting, he had given her a bow, a polite, "Good day, Miss Macneil," that cut her deeper than a sword thrust! Words of sympathy choked in her throat.

"He doesn't love me now . . ." she'd thought with expiring hope. "Perhaps he never did!" Whatever his sentiments, milord sat like a man of bronze while the reading continued.

Coachmen, gardeners, stablemen down to the last kitchen boy were remembered, each one in kind. It was fascinating to see their reactions as the bequests were read. Surprise changed to joy, to tears of gratitude. Lady Inverkleith had not left money only—her gifts were freedom and opportunity, a school for a teacher, a restaurant for a cook. Milady set aside a large fund in trust, to provide for "her children"—enough to feast a thousand little ones, every year, on Boxing Day.

As the half-hours wore on and servant after servant received their gifts and withdrew, Laurie noticed that the Laird was becoming impatient. He shifted in his chair, drummed on the chair-arm. Occasionally his gaze flickered to herself, and away. There was no warmth in his eyes—no sign!

Feckless girl, to dream the Laird had ever thought of her except as a toy!

Suddenly the reading of the will was ended. Sir Henry Banks rose. "Well, now, Miss Macneil . . . Colin . . . since we've got all those good people behind us, why not repair to more comfortable surroundings? I vow my feet are ice-cold, there's nothing I'd like more than a glass of port."

Laurie glanced around, to discover that with the exception of the two gentlemen, the notary and the clerks, she was the only person left in the room!

"Your arm, Miss Macneil!" The courtly Sir Henry dismissed his notary and clerks with a nod, crooked his elbow, and led the way. "Lady Inverkleith's dispositions in your regard and that of her grandson are contained in separate documents," he said in tones quite conversational. "In fact they are set forth in two letters. I have the letters, here in my pocket."

"What's the joker, Henry?" said Lord Duff-Drummond abruptly. "Why were Granny's wishes not read publicly?"

"I'll explain, Colin. Kindly lead me to a warm fire, my teeth chatter . . . those I have left of course!" laughed the solicitor.

Was it Laurie's illusion, or did she feel her lover's burning eyes? Whatever they were, his emotions could not match hers. How well he concealed them as he led the way to the rose drawing room, saying, "I anticipated your wish, Henry! Here's port wine, a warm fire, a game patty. You, Miss Macneil? May I tempt you with a cup of hot broth?"

One could not help but marvel at the cavalier ways of these two gentlemen. Sir Henry Banks conversed about the weather and spoke of the crisis in Parliament. He drank his port wine, ate his fill of game patty and wiped his fingers with dainty gestures. At last he drew two letters from his pocket and placed them on the table.

"I shall be going, Colin," he said as he headed for the door. "Your servant, Miss Macneil."

Lord Duff-Drummond's quick "What the devil, Henry?" bespoke his anxiety. "Wait! I may want to ask you a question or two."

"Drop in at my chambers, Colin," said the solicitor, "you too, Miss Macneil. I shall be charmed to clarify any point that is obscure."

Sir Henry Banks slipped away so quickly that, for once, Lord Duff-Drummond was left without an answer.

Laurie watched him break the seal and open his letter, saw him flush . . . turn white. "What's this!" he exploded. "What's this farce? How'd ye manage . . . worm your way into Granny's graces?"

"Worm my way . . . ?" Laurie's tongue clove to the roof of her mouth. What was he saying? What did he mean?

"See! See for yourself!" shouted Duff-Drummond. He thrust the letter before her eyes and read in strangled

164

tones: "My dying wish is that you shall marry Laura Macneil."

"Milord!" cried Laurie. "I swear I had no part in this!"

"No? Don't talk piffle! Open *your* letter! Let's see . . ."

Laura tried to break the seal, but her hands would not obey. "Here!" Lord Duff-Drummond snatched away the letter, opened it and read, jumping from one paragraph to the next:

" 'It is my wish that you shall become my grandson's bride within the shortest possible time after this reading. . . . I appoint you executrix, guardian and steward of my fortune under conditions Sir Henry Banks will explain . . .' " Duff-Drummond almost choked as he shouted, "Now d'you deny you worked on the feelings of an old woman gone senile?" His hands trembled as he scanned the letter to the end. "So . . . you had no hand in it, eh? Granny wills you her jewels outright! Three hundred thousand worth. She leaves you Prince, your favorite poodle. Good riddance! And listen to this last paragraph! 'Give Colin not one penny to spend on any cause that you deem unworthy. . . . Bless him with many fine sons and daughters . . . restore the Clan to honor . . .' "

In his rage, Duff-Drummond crushed the letter into a ball. "Why you little conniver! You Machiavelli in petticoats! I've a mind to wring your neck! But this is absurd! This is farcical!"

Laurie rose. Outwardly she was cold and composed; inwardly the fires of justifiable wrath were kindling.

"A farce indeed, milord. As God is my witness, I knew nothing about Lady Inverkleith's will. And if I had . . . I say to you now . . . there's no power in heaven or on earth that could make me fulfill your grandmother's wish, and marry you!"

Lonely, fearful, dismayed, Laurie watched while the characters who had played their parts in Lady Inverkleith's lifetime drama made their exit one by one. Dubois was the first to say good-by. "Come, Miss Laurie, you can tell old Dubois what our kind mistress left you?" the inquisitive woman probed. "What will you do now, poor darling . . . all alone in the world? But you have kinfolk, haven't you?"

"I haven't decided what I shall do," said Laurie, not to let the truth leak out. "I may go to my people in Edinburgh."

Dubois gave crisp orders for the removal of her bed and bedding, her boxes and her bundles to a handcart. The two parts of the massive oaken bedstead were propped fore and aft, the six wooden crosspieces that supported the canvas-webbed stretcher were stuck upright along the sides, the feather-beds were plumped in the middle. Dubois tossed her poodle Dauphin onto the pile and his gilt bed after him—she took a hand-up from the carter and settled herself in among the feathers like a fat birdling in a nest. The departing vehicle looked very much like the tumbril that carried French *aristos* to the guillotine. But the good Dubois was going to a more gratifying reward, a tiny shop on Edgeware Road where she would dispense thread and needles.

Chef François' exit was more dramatic. From dawn to dusk he ran up and down the cellar stairs fretting, cursing *sacrebleux* and *morbleux*, while his priceless wines were carried out and packed in a straw-filled dray. Then, lest the burgundies, the ports, the sherries be muddled, he took the bridle of the dray horse and, on foot, led the animal while his poodle and the drayman enjoyed the ride in the driver's seat.

"May I have the little gilt beds?" Monsieur Alcide begged when he came for his poodles. The costumer and his pretty-boy aides had packed feverishly, filling six wooden boxes with costumes, armor, wigs, trimmings, tinsel, bolts of gauze, satin and velvet. When they were finished there was nothing left in the wardrobe room except a few scraps, and here and there a spangle on the floor.

"Candles" supervised the loading of the lavish stage settings and properties into two vans, and departed with Duke. Reine and Dauphin were taken, freshly washed, combed and full of fun, to their new master, His Royal Highness, the Prince of Wales. Only one doggie, Prince, remained—"your favorite" Lady Inverkleith called him.

Courier Malcolm's last greeting was respectful and warm.

"Will you see Nanny Biel in Edinburgh?" asked Laurie wistfully.

"No. Not in Edinburgh . . . in Ben Fada," Malcolm answered. "I'm proud to say, Miss Macneil, Sir Henry Banks recommended me to Lord Duff-Drummond for the position of bailiff of the domain, and I was accepted."

A clerk named Cibber from the solicitor's office had watched like a hawk over the execution of the defunct's will, and when the last bequest was made good and the great house all but empty of living creatures, he came to Laurie and said with a bow of ceremony, "Here are the keys to the jewel vault, Miss Macneil."

With difficulty Laurie restrained a despairing cry, "What shall I do with them?" Never had she felt so alone, so abandoned! Her sole companion and comfort the adoring Prince of Poodles. A chill spread through the great rooms like the cold of a tomb when the last stone is set and the floral offerings fade—the fires were not kept, dusting was left undone. She'd eaten only half-baked meats and unsavory puddings; a rough-spoken fellow in spotty livery brought food on a tray.

"What will happen to me, now?" Laurie asked the empty air. At last she could stand it no longer. "Come to my office," Sir Henry had said. She would do just that— and forthwith be freed from her intolerable position.

Dressed all in black, she hurried to the gate on foot, hailed a passing hackney and gave the solicitor's Temple address. But a clerk said Sir Henry was in Assizes, he would not return to the office that day.

"What name shall I give, miss?"

"Thank you, never mind. I'll call again." Laurie walked back to Berkeley Street—stony miles, stony solitude. Oh, her punishment was not over! The adored one was now the runaway—clear sign that he neither wanted the girl he once loved, nor did he care what became of her. He hated her more than he coveted his granny's gold.

Twelve

The Prince and the Pauper

LINGERING OVER A LATE BREAKFAST, SIR HENRY BANKS READ
the morning papers with a weather eye for news of
the courts and the bench. This was his favorite of all
hours. The day was burdened with professional cares, the
nights with social duties that increased with his professional success. This morning island, betwixt eight and ten,
was his to savor in lovely solitude. Sir Henry liked the
quiet of his handsome dining room, the elegant appur-
tenances of his breakfast table. He liked the morning meal.
Hot water for his third cup of fragrant tea simmered in a
crane-legged teakettle that straddled a tiny silver cup of
burning spirits. The shells of three eggs, a jackstraw pile
of bread crusts—Sir Henry found the crusts too tough
for his gums in which several essential molars were missing—a cold ham, shorn of three rosy slices gave proof of
his excellent morning appetite.

It was a dismal day. Fog breathed upon the windowpanes, but Sir Henry had a remedy he had borrowed from
Flanders, the art of turning fog into sunshine. A false
window of stained glass shed a motley red, amber, purple
and green over the breakfast table. His butler lighted a
few candles behind the window—simple, economic de-
vice, but how cheering when skies were low!

Sir Henry finished reading an account of the case,
Hoggins versus Neterby, a succession that had been fought
to the Lord Chief Justice's bench. Hoggins had lost just

169

as Sir Henry knew he would. Sir Henry reserved the *Gazette* for the last. Irrelevant and amusing scandal was to be enjoyed like a nip of good brandy at the end of the meal. His spine stiffened as he read.

> What noble gent plans to ditch racing for His Majesty's war ship? A certain Lord D-D of Berkeley Street and Newmarket is so hounded by his creditors, who received no satisfaction from a Lady's will and testament, he cannot longer abide the climate of England.

"What's this? What's this?" Sir Henry called for his boots. His servant bundled him into his greatcoat. Reluctantly the legal giant ventured into the fog and made his way to St. James' Street. Entering Brooks' Club on a day like this, t'was like calling on a duke with a duke lying dead upstairs—these stately rooms were gloomier than an open crypt!

"Lord Duff-Drummond?"

"His lordship is in, Sir Henry."

"What room?"

"Number 14. Shall I announce you, Sir Henry?"

"Never mind, Jergins!" The solicitor nodded to the factotum who had stood behind the members' key-desk for as long as he could recall.

A froggy voice answered his knock at Number 14. The solicitor's aquiline nose wrinkled disapprovingly—for a man of his fine looks, Colin could lose 'em quicker than a woman of sixty her ballroom beauty!

"I thought you might like to see . . . this!" He snapped open the *Gazette* and placed a tapered forefinger on the gazetteer's squib.

Duff-Drummond elbowed himself to a sitting position, rubbed his eyes and read. "Well?" he said with another yawn. "What's left for me? I plan to join Wellesley. I might as well get myself killed in glory as let my creditors squeeze the life out of me!"

170

"Are you quite mad, Colin?" exclaimed the solicitor. "I thought you were marryin' the young lady . . . that gold would soon gush into your pockets like cool water into a desert place."

Duff-Drummond bounced upright in the bed. "Let myself be snared . . . circumvented . . . hung up on the yes or no of a peasant lass? D'you think I'm clear mad, Henry?"

The solicitor was careful not to smile. Colin was in no mood for a jest, at his expense. "Dress, Colin. I'll wait downstairs. You'll feel better after a cup of the Brazilian Bean!"

By the time the gentlemen had finished breakfasting, Duff-Drummond's angry humor had changed to bleak ill-temper. Trudging through the fog to the Temple, he listened to the solicitor's arguments with a closed mind. Henry was oft wont to let go with too much frankness, stepping out of his role of legal adviser into that of god-father—La Monette's close friend.

"I've known you since you were born, Colin! Seen you waste your talents and your years, almost break your granny's heart. I was happy to write your grandmother's extraordinary testament. At last I could help to protect you from your own follies."

"I wish you'd kept hands off and let me go to the devil in my own way!" said Duff-Drummond bitterly.

"I wish you'd open your eyes and realize . . . at thirty-five a man can't sow wild oats forever!"

"I'm thirty-four!" growled Duff-Drummond.

"No matter . . . you've somehow got the idea . . . your sheaves are everlasting! Damme if I don't believe your granny was possessed of a sixth prophetic sense! She must have foreseen this very moment—you, sulking in your Club, your fiancée abandoned . . . weeping . . . forlorn!"

"My fiancée! You break my heart, Henry!" said Duff-Drummond, biting hard on the stem of his pipe.

Sir Henry entered his chambers and tossed hat and coat to his clerk.

"Sir Henry, a young person was here," said the clerk. "I told her—"

"Never mind!" snapped the solicitor. "If she comes back tell her I've gone to China! I want no interruptions for the next hour." He gave Duff-Drummond a penetrating glance. "The time has come to let you read a codicil to your grandmother's will."

Duff-Drummond waited in silence while his old friend and adviser unlocked a safe and took out a sealed envelope.

"It says here: 'To be opened in case of disagreement between Colin and Laura.'" Sir Henry watched Duff-Drummond's face covertly. The contents of that letter-codicil were well calculated to give the reader a slight case of apoplexy!

DEAR COLIN,

Laura must not learn the contents of this letter. Your hopes would forever be cut off! I wish her to cleave to you, not by some sense of misplaced duty or to save your wealth, but by affection alone.

If within a period of one year from the date of your marriage, Laura shall have presented you with a Son and Heir, I may assume that Love has found a way, and you will not be disappointed.

Meanwhile, Laura shall remain the executrix of my will and guardian of my fortune, as before stated.

I feel it only fair to warn you, my grandson, that your failure to become the father of a male heir to Duff-Drummond will cut you off from all my wealth, forever.

Affectionately,
GRANNY.

172

Duff-Drummond's face was livid when he looked up from the page. His lips moved but no sound came.

"I wish I could say, 'I'm sorry!'" murmured Sir Henry.

Duff-Drummond's flush changed to deathly pallor. He flung the letter-codicil on the desk, leaned across the silver inkwell, the handsome clock, the delft tobacco jar— all Sir Henry's precious knickknacks. "You egged her on to this! You and your mania. You should've been head-master of a London board school!"

"I repeat: I was glad to help your grandmother," retorted Sir Henry. "Her lips, not mine, dictated the terms of this will!"

"You put her up to it," raged Duff-Drummond, "or else Granny was insane! Is a man like a bull or a stallion that he can breed at will?—years of servitude to the bed of my gaoler and paymaster! I'll not endure it!"

"How easy to shorten the term," suggested the solicitor with a faint smile. "One lucky strike on your prison bars . . . you're a free man and a rich one! A million pounds are wrapped in the swaddling clothes of the babe who will be your son and heir!" But Sir Henry saw that his listener was too rebellious to be swayed by reason.

"It's the principle!" roared Duff-Drummond. "I won't be beholden to a woman!"

"No? Seems to me that in the past—what I'm trying to say is . . . your granny's fortune is all hers. The only bequest from Duff-Drummond side, your domain in Scot-land."

"A hulk of stone, rocky fields, three hundred pounds a year!" scoffed Duff-Drummond.

"Exactly!" said Sir Henry with irrefutable logic. "La Monette's wealth came from her first and second hus-bands. Your father was poor. You've done nothing to in-crease the wealth of your domain. In plain words, your luxuries, even your necessities, have come from a woman's hands."

"Call me a pimp and have done with it!" shouted Duff-Drummond.

"Easy . . . easy, Colin!" soothed Sir Henry. "I'm merely trying to point out that for a little while the substitution of a charming wife's soft hand for your granny's iron rod should not be too much to endure. And I assure you Miss Macneil is innocent of plotting. She knows less about your grandmother's will than you do."

Duff-Drummond paced the floor in anger. "Even if Laura is innocent, and I doubt it—women are so subtle, she was always granny's pet—I can't accept the yoke! I'll take this will and have it nullified."

"Impossible, Colin!"

"But— But—" Duff-Drummond's fist struck the desk with a force that set the knickknacks jingling. "A peasant gel—mistress of my fortune! It's intolerable!"

"Your grandmother thought otherwise. She told me she held Miss Macneil in highest esteem. She said she was a model of womanly virtue, common sense, kindness, love, Scots pride! La Monette was keen about Scots pride."

"Scots pride be damned!" blasted Duff-Drummond. "I tell you—" His tirade was interrupted by a knock. The clerk looked in.

"It is the young person again, Sir Henry. She is waiting in the outside office . . . says it is most urgent."

The clerk's face took on an expression, smug and confidential. "It's Miss Macneil, Sir Henry."

"Laura . . . here?" exclaimed Duff-Drummond. "What new trick is this?"

"No trick!" exclaimed Sir Henry. "A happy coincidence! Quick! In here!" He motioned Colin into an adjoining chamber, hardly larger than a closet, opened a square in the paneling to reveal a wooden grillwork. "I call this, the 'ear.' Perhaps you had better lend yours."

The Olympian Sir Henry Banks rose when Laurie entered. There was a subtle difference in his manner—differ-

174

ence compounded of a man's homage to a woman, the bowing to a patron—also the jollity of an elder offering sweets to a child.

"Ah, Miss Macneil! My heartfelt congratulations!"

"What for, Sir Henry?" Laurie's bluntness had the desired effect, jarring the man-of-law out of his so lofty calm.

"What for, my dear young woman! Is not your coming marriage to Lord Duff-Drummond a matter of congratulations?"

"My marriage?" Laurie sank into the chair the courtly Sir Henry held for her. "I haven't seen Lord Duff-Drummond or heard from him since the day you read the will."

"Oh! But I have, Miss Macneil. The poor fellow is heartbroken. He knows not how or where to begin pleading forgiveness for his rude behavior. Colin always kicks against the pricks. He resented his grandmother's . . . er . . . close wording of her testament."

Laurie's blood seemed turning to sparkling wine in her veins. Did this high-browed gentleman speak the truth? Could she believe the unbelievable? She'd sat too long in agony of waiting not to doubt.

"Sir Henry . . . I fear I'm skeptical! Did Lord Duff-Drummond give you leave to make these statements about his repentance, his broken heart?"

"I'm scarcely the man to invent such terms, Miss Macneil."

"But . . ." Laurie argued against her own wild hope, ". . . if I say no to Lady Inverkleith's proposal, that I . . . I . . ."

"That you marry Lord Duff-Drummond?" prompted the solicitor.

"Thank you, Sir Henry," said Laurie swallowing hard. "What I'm trying to say is . . . surely the will can be set aside . . . or whatever the legal term may be. You told me Lady Inverkleith had been kind enough to bequeath me a small sum of money. That would be more than I ever dreamed of. I'll waive all other bequests—the jewels—though I'd like to keep Prince. Oh, Sir Henry, I desire nothing that belongs to Lord Duff-Drummond! Most of all I do not want a husband who must force himself to . . ."

"Fulfill the marriage bond?" prompted Sir Henry with a grave face.

"Yes," said Laurie blushing. "I'd rather forfeit all—"

"Unfortunately, that is not possible, Miss Macneil," said the solicitor firmly. "No will written by Henry Banks can be broken."

"Not even if I refuse to take one penny? Not even if I go far, far away?"

"Even so!"

"But . . . surely my feelings must also be considered!"

"Not at all, Miss Macneil. It was Lady Inverkleith's intention to insure the continuance of an ancient and noble line. She chose you. At the same time she wanted her fortune to go to her grandson and his heirs, with certain conditions that to her seemed to be for his own good."

Laurie tried to conceal her inner turmoil as she said, "Sir Henry, you take it for granted Lord Duff-Drummond wants to marry me, that he is willing, that he will submit to his grandmother's decree. One thing more —how could Lady Inverkleith assume that I am a fit administrator . . . executrix . . . or stewardess of so vast a fortune?"

"Dear Miss Macneil!" said Sir Henry. "I like modesty in a young woman. Naturally, Lady Inverkleith did not assume that you would act without an adviser. She named your humble servant. You need only call on me."

"I . . . I could never feel sure I was doing the right thing!" stammered Laurie. "I'd always fear to vex Lord Duff-Drummond if I said no. And if I did not approve of his expenditures, I'd certainly say no!"

Sir Henry swallowed his surprise, that there lived a

woman so ingenuous, so honest, so candid as Laura Macneil. "Let us presume for the sake of presuming Colin is able to convince you of his honest intentions. The poor boy was sorely vexed that his grandmother should have . . . er . . . stolen his thunder as 'twere! He wanted to press his own suit with you. Would you believe me when I tell you that he was mortally afraid his grandmother would not agree to your marriage? The old lady was hard to please—"

"Lord Duff-Drummond afraid?" murmured Laurie. Her doubts battled on the last breach. "Surely, Lord Duff-Drummond has never known the meaning of the word 'afraid.' He would have found some way to approach me."

"You forget . . . you vanished!" said Sir Henry quickly. "Colin had planned to press his suit the moment he returned to London."

"Oh, why did he go!" cried Laurie wringing her hands.

The astute Sir Henry brought out deadly artillery. "My dear Miss Macneil, I'll betray a secret, but I feel it is time. You know Lady Inverkleith's yearly ballet? All those beggar children she bade to the feast?"

"Yes, I know."

"Poor Colin could not endure the sight of so much misery. When he was young, it made him physically ill! He has a tender heart, you know! Colin's theory . . . the little good his grandmother did was . . . too little. To open a vista of Paradise to the eyes of the poor and then close the window was downright cruelty! That is the real reason why he always absents himself from London over Christmas and Boxing Day, goes boar-hunting in Chartley Forest, a rugged sport in rain and snow. Colin once said to me, 'Anything is better than to see those poor little devils, without shoes . . . in rags.'"

"Lord Duff-Drummond said that?" cried Laurie.

"My word of honor, he did!" the solicitor answered.

Laurie sat for a moment in silence. O mystery of the

human heart! Could it be true that Colin possessed compassion for the needy that burning will to improve, and uplift? If this were so . . .

The solicitor knew the signs of a woman's weakening. "Surely you can't object to seeing Lord Duff-Drummond, discussing this matter in a sane, reasonable manner? Think what you could do, in the way Lady Inverkleith always hoped—improve the domain, give opportunity to the people, restore Scots pride as she phrased it. I'm certain Lord Duff-Drummond would approve. He is intelligent. He's had enough of wasteful living. Every man has two sides and Colin is no exception. I imagine that when he was a boy, he must have dreamed that he was Drake on the quarterdeck of his flagship—Cromwell, ridin' vengeance through the Shires. Knock the world to pieces— that's Colin! Tell me, Miss Macneil—how much of the globe is made of air, wind, mist—so with a man!" The girl was listening like the serpent to the charmer's reed. Sir Henry pressed his advantage.

"How Lady Inverkleith would weep! She hoped . . . she *knew* that you were the one to bring about a change in her grandson! 'Henry,' she said to me, 'that young woman has every attribute of wife, sweetheart and companion that Colin would wish, every virtue the mother of Duff-Drummond race should possess.' "

The eavesdropping Duff-Drummond had heard enough of Henry Banks' rhetoric. He wiped the perspiration from his brow, straightened his coat, and taking a deep breath, he emerged from the closet.

The man-of-law lingered long enough to admire a Marble Venus, suddenly come to life, a statue that shed real tears and heaved a royal bosom. A statue that cried, "Colin!"

Sir Henry slipped into the closet, eyes to the grille, and watched loverly doings.

"Laura, forgive me!" said Colin—the young blackguard.

178

"I . . . forgive you? Can you forgive me?" Venus sobbed.

"No, I'm at fault. I've been battling with my pride. It was my pride, Laurie! At last I can speak, tell you what's here." Duff-Drummond touched his breast. "I was unbearably rude, my feelin's overcame me that Granny should trust me so little—I who was on the verge of askin' her consent to take you for my bride. Laura! You do believe me?" Colin reached, but the young woman stood aside.

"I must think. Don't gadge me!" The Scots word meaning to "dictate impertinently" was not unknown to Sir Henry.

"Gabbock me!" laughed Colin. "Nae, Laurie! I dinna wish tae gadge ye. Ding-me-yavel, if I wudna douk willin' to a doll so fair! Let me call the bridesman, my bonnie! When shall it be? 'Nab that darlin' lass as quick as you can,' said Granny! How obedient am I! Gie me the kissie that says, 'I do!' "

Sir Henry did not grasp the half of their Scots gibberish but the pantomime was easy to understand, titivating to observe! Old blood stirred when the two began to kiss. Gad! This was no 'prentice job. Surely they'd done it before—damn Colin's slick lies! And the girl—passionate, glorious, a lioness in love! Sir Henry chuckled. This jungle queen of the tawny mane would present her Leo with a lion-kit nine months from mating time. What more delightful finis to La Monette's last Ballet, entitled *The Prince and the Pauper!*

"How soon, my darling?" said Colin at the end of a long embrace. Away they went—exit *au pas de galop.*

"Ah me!" sighed Sir Henry. Returning to his gray chambers, empty now except for a whiff of feminine perfume, he poured himself a thimbleful of brandy and drank it standing—"To Young Love."

"What day shall we set for the wedding?" said the

Laird to his blushing fiancée. "Will Wednesday be too soon? Wednesday evening at nine. Don't trouble your pretty head, I'll make all the arrangements."

As if by magic, the change began. This time the Laird was the magician.

A staff of new servants appeared. Cold rooms warmed. Candelabra glowed. Greenhouses gave up their fragrant treasure. Working night and day, a crew of decorators transformed Lady Inverkleith's bedroom and boudoir. "Milord's orders," said their foreman.

The new steward whom his lordship engaged turned out to be the eagle-eyed clerk Cibber from Sir Henry Banks' office.

"I took the liberty of engaging a maid for Miss Macneil —Pritchet, fresh from three years' service to Lady Alycia Montgomery—the Lady Montgomery of Wendover Castle, Buckshire."

Could all this be real, or was it a dream? Her darling had said, "Is Wednesday too soon?" Laurie pinched herself—yes, she was awake! But her doubts remained until Wednesday at noon a messenger came with a box from Mrs. Jack of Jermyn Street—a large box covered with white moiré silk. Carefully packed in layers of white paper, a bridal dress of ivory satin, bridal shoes, white silk stockings, a bridal wreath of white blossoms. A letter was at the bottom of the box.

> Your bridesman and maid will come at nine o'clock tonight. Be ready.
>
> THE LAIRD.

Take up the dress, shake out the folds, slip on the dress. Beautiful! Try on the wreath! Your cheeks are the color of chalk! Your belly is like a ball of lead! Take off the dress! Sit with hands clasped and knees a-tremble. What if it were only a dream, after all?

"Would Miss Macneil like supper?" said maid Pritchet.

"No thank you, Pritchet."

"Hot water, miss?"

"Yes, please. And bring the poodle's meal."

Laurie fed Prince, walked him and put him to bed. It was only seven. How slow the hours in passing!

"Your bath, miss. May I help, miss?"

"No thank you, Pritchet."

Bathe and preen like a dove. Comb your hair and dress it. Take it down and do it over again—there was still too much time!

> Blythe Bessie in the milking shiel
> Says: "I'll be wed, come o't what will . . ."

"Come, Blythe Bessie!" Laurie smiled to her mirror. "Quit mooning . . . put on the bride's gown!"

False white for an unchaste bride—but it was the Laird who had taken her maidenhood and made her the mother of his child. Sobered by this thought, Laurie paused. Must she confess to her husband? Confess and brand the child begotten out of wedlock, or hold her tongue?

Laurie heard a sound that made her blood quicken— the pipes, the pipes of Scotland skirling, "Fye, let's a' to the bridal!"

She ran to the window and saw the flare of torches. The music of the pipes was growing louder. She burst out of her room and ran down the long curved staircase, but even before she could reach the bottom, a footman had hastened to open the door. She saw Count Jean d'Antimes on the threshold.

Obeying some ancient law that she must have learned long before she was born, she folded her hands over her bosom and drifted light as a snowflake across the vast hall, her eager eyes searching for those emblems of her own dear land, the glint of a dirk, the waving of a plaid, the gleam of firearms.

"I am your bridesman!" said Count Jean d'Antimes with

181

a sweep of his Bond Street hat to the ground. "Pray link your arm in mine." Who had coached this Frenchman in the customs of the Scots bridals? He turned and handed the end of a long white scarf to a young girl in a white dress. "Your bridesmaid."

"Margit!" cried Laurie in delight. "Cousin Margit!"

"Yes!"

"Oh, Margit! I'm happy it's you!"

"Jinny brought me to London. Come. They're waiting!"

Laurie locked her arms in those of her bridesman. The pipes that had been grumbling like old men in church-meeting now spoke out loudly, "Fye, let's a' to the bridal!" and the wedding company set forth with the proper, right foot. In the rear flitted two young girls, holding a second white scarf between them, so that the bride and her bridesman and maid were "all hemmed in with purity."

The night was damp and cold, but Laurie felt no cold. For all she knew she might be walking in the May dew at Ben Fada! At every step she felt the scarf, symbol of a maid's chastity, holding her in check. Where would the bridesman take the bride? The gardens had a different look. They were a quarter-way to the rose arbor—now at the rambler arch! Then she saw the Laird waiting at the cross-path to the swan-lake. Two torch-bearers stood by to light him. How magnificently arrayed was he, to meet his bride. The Highland full-dress sat him with ease. Caught with the Twig of Juniper, the tartan Duff-Drummond swung airily from his left shoulder. A jewel flashed in the cock of his bonnet. Silver buckles gleamed on his shoes; at his throat, laces like the snowdrift. He wore gloves as pure white as the bride's gown and his left hand rested on the hilt of his dorlach—the huntsman's dagger that every Highlander carries—princely Highland bride-groom!

The pipes began to skirl the March of Clan Duff-Drummond, "Buadgh No Bas!" Laurie would long remember how Colin smiled as he walked beside her with measured step. She would remember other things too—the mountain fragrance of a silver spruce that brushed her shoulder as she went by; the cold that pierced the thin soles of her slippers; above all, her astonishment when the *clachan* came into view, candles softly gleaming on the white hair of a minister with open Book. Yesterday there was no church at this place! For all she knew, it might have been dropped from the skies!

The pipers droned softly outside while bridesman and maid delivered the bride to the altar. Laurie saw the dark cheek of the Laird pale and his eye deepen to midnight hue when he took her hand. Then she heard the dominie's deep voice . . . a Scots wedding was not mere giving and taking of vow but a state of blessedness. In that sweet, solemn moment the might of Spirit came to transform and inspire the sons and daughters of Earth, according to Heaven's design.

"O Lord of Lights, illumine the way of these two, that they may find contentment and increase and in the end, life everlasting under Thy perfect Rule . . ." The dominie touched their bent heads and announced, startlingly, "Now ye are no more two, but one flesh, and so be it, Amen and Amen!"

The full clamor of the pipes was hurled at the married pair when they stepped out to the threshold of the magic *clachan*. The park echoed with the Clansmen's shouts, "Buadgh no bas! Buadgh no bas!"

Laurie then saw that the two scarves had been whisked aside—symbol that the way was now open for the bridegroom.

"I claim bridesman's right!" cried Count Jean d'Antimes. He smacked a resounding kiss on her lips.

"Come, Lady Laura!" Her husband flung his tartan around her shoulders and swept her away. The next she knew, she was rocking down the drive in a carriage. Horsemen in flying tartans rode on the left and right. They had just passed the gates of Hathmore House when her husband parted the folds of the tartan, slipped his arm around his bride.

"Now we're tethered, cae ye not let those rosy lips fondle me agin!"

Laurie thrilled with gladness that he had not kissed her before the company as it was often done. Here in the racing darkness, she let love's water flood her downstream.

"Damn it! Here we are!"

"Where?" she murmured, waking from her dream.

"The house of Krik Fordyce of Clan Barra—your distant kinsman. Remember the saying, 'Sorry the bride who crosses her ane stane with the first foot'?"

Laurie knew of the custom. After a Highland wedding, the company was wont to adjourn to the nearest inn or to the house of a male relative of the bride; it was considered ill luck for her to cross first the "stanes" of her own doorstep.

"Your hand, Lady Laura," said Duff-Drummond. He led his wife up the marble steps. "Krik Fordyce!" he called, "I bring the fairest bride e'er mothered by Mother Scotland!"

Their host of the strange-sounding name was silhouetted against the light, behind him a crowd of guests. He handed a plate of oat-cakes across the threshold and Jean d'Antimes and bridesmaid Margit laughingly obeyed the ancient rite and broke a cake over Laurie's head to signify that the bride would never lack. A glass of uisgha made the round, passing sunways in obedience to the age-old Druid law of *deas'oil,* meaning to walk with the sun, from East to West. This law used to govern every detail of the Celt's life, so much so that one might think the law still reigned. Entire peoples migrated from East to West. The West was always the "last look"—the sunset like a symbol of man's yearning for heaven.

Their lips met with the ceremonial cup of uisgha, man and wife were invited in.

The host whom Lord Colin called "Krik" was wearing the blue-on-blue and scarlet of the Macneil and a sprig of the Macneil Wild Thyme over his heart. He was older than Colin. Tawny-haired and amber-eyed, muscular though not tall, he was a handsome man!

A stately gentleman with bushy brows and rugged features was named Duinne Uassel Hamilton. His son, a fine-looking young man with ruddy complexion and red-gold hair, kissed the bride's wrist. "Sir Ian Hamilton, son of the Duinne Uassel." Laurie heard the most fabled names of Scotland. Melford, Macray, Macfie, Macewan, the Earl of Dunbar, Lord Graham of Montrose, Grant of Strathspey. She picked out the colors of other clans. Brodie and Wallace! Buchanan and Lamond! Stewart and Gunn! She was not prepared to see so many ladies in ballroom array and glittering jewels. Lady Hamilton, Lady Wallace, Lady Stewart greeted her with friendly smiles. "Congratulations and heartfelt wishes for your future wedded life, Lady Duff-Drummond," said Lady Lamond, who was radiant in yellow satin.

Laurie stared at the approach of a tiny, vivacious creature in rose and diamonds. Jinny Baird—looking like a queen in miniature.

"Come, Laurie! Come to the boudoir and tell me how all this came about? Last night, Colin . . . I mean . . . well, I might as well call him Colin now! He's me new coz!"

Jinny sat at the mirror and chattered on. "We never thought we'd find you . . . Say, coz . . . why didn't you wear some of your jewels? I hear Lady Inverkleith left you a fortune in diamonds! See mine? Lolly gave 'em to me. I always told you I'd be a big success! Lolly . . . Lord Sitley . . . is a patron of the drama. I may have to nab *him* for a husband, now you've nabbed Duff-Drummond!"

Laurie was relieved to see her cousin Margit enter the

room. "Isn't it a dream!" cried Margit. "The three of us, in London . . ."

"And Margit with a love hanging to her skirts," said Jinny with a teasing smile in the direction of her sister. "Guess who he is, Laurie?"

"Jinny! I forbid you to say!" cried Margit with a blush.

"It's Count d'Antimes. That's who it is," said Jinny, unheeding. "The man is mad about her! Sighs! Sonnets! Flowers! 'Twas your hubby who brought the Count to my house . . . a duck of a place . . . Number 6, St. James Street. Of course if I marry Lolly Sitley, I'll have a palace like Hathmore House."

More bewildered than she liked to show, Laurie suggested that they join the company.

"Chafin' to see your Duff-Drummond, eh?" said Jinny. There was a gleam in her green eyes. "She's right, Margit. It's not wise to leave Duff-Drummond alone! Come! I to Lord Sitley. Sister Margit to Count d'Antimes. Laurie to her Duff!"

An odd feeling—not jealousy, something less, something more—was dissipated when Laurie entered the ballroom and found her husband waiting on the threshold.

"Half a reel," said Duff-Drummond in his wife's ear. "Then we'll slip away."

One reel became two, then three, and with every stop of the bagpipes Duff-Drummond drank a fresh draught of uisgha. He was walking on air when he handed his bride into the carriage and gave the order, "Home." A Scotsman is seldom sober at his wedding—even Laurie's head was spinning from a few mouthfuls of the stuff that she had been forced to swallow at her host's urging. She clapped her hands to her ears when her merry husband began to bawl at the top of his lungs:

"MASQUERADES, Grand parades!
Plenty of news, all to amuse!

186

Monkey Jacco, all the crack-o!
Monkey Jacco, all the crack-o!"

"Colin, dearest, you will wake the household!"

"Wake Granny's ghost?" Duff-Drummond cupped his
hands around his lips and hollered through the hall,
"Granny! O Granny! Are you satisfied?" He made believe
hark for the answer. "'Not yet!' says Granny!" He guffawed. "By Gad, she will be, ere dawn doth appear!"

But her husband's merry mood changed on the threshold
of the bridal chamber. "Like it?" he said, drawing his wife
into his arm.

"It's beautiful!" cried Laurie in amazement.

Lady Inverkleith's rose-and-gilt bedroom had been
transformed. The walls were hung with blue silk, here and
there a motif of silver. The hangings and bed curtains were
blue with heavy silver fringe. The downy carpet was
white. "The latest style," said Duff-Drummond with a
satisfied smile. "It becomes you, Laura."

"So many white roses!" cried Laurie, faint with delight
that her husband should have done all this for her sake.

"Roses no whiter than your skin," whispered Duff-
Drummond in her ear. Caught in old madness, Laurie
clung to the man she idolized. "Darling . . .

"Till a' the sands gang dry,
And the rocks melt wi' the sun;
I will luve thee still . . ."

"Ha'e ye nought but poetry for the Laird?" said Duff-
Drummond playfully. "Here! Help me off wi' my jock and
kiltie!"

As often as she had lain in these arms and drunk in
these kisses, Laurie knew her love for the man—her husband now—would never wane. As often as he'd carried her
to the mountaintop of rapture, each flight higher than the
one before, each culminating kiss sweeter, each embrace

187

more passionate, she knew there was yet another and greater delight to come. Her yearning heart and hungry hope discovered new heights. But surprised by her own delight and impatient of her lover-husband's silent frenzy, Laurie sought to make him share her transport— Oh! If he would only speak his tenderness, echo her thoughts— "Love, how could I leave thee? My treasure . . . master of my life!"

Duff-Drummond in the darkness, said not a word. Sober, his every faculty centered upon one goal, the Laird willed that to be which must be . . . a son! This blond garden, this teeming bed of roses and snow was but the golden transmitter of the life that shot from his loins. A son—by heaven, a son! Two women to content—one dead at near a hundred, the other, a living, loving, panting slave. Content the two with one lucky hit! An heir for Granny, a suckling babe to swing on these sweet tits—keep this busy-head busier. Let Highland Laurie have what she had begged and somehow missed 'til now—a child!

Thirteen

Three Nights

FEBRUARY STORMS RAGED. THE TREES OF HATHMORE PARK tossed wild arms to gray skies. In milord and milady's chamber summer reigned!

Roses, now red, now white—the fruits of summer! Melons! Grapes! Champagne wine of summer evenings!

"Dearest, is there anything you care for . . . strawberries, perhaps? Do you prefer red meat to game?" Duff-Drummond coaxed his bride with delicacies and pampered her with kisses.

They played with Prince. The Laird's mood changing, he sent the doggie away and called for his piper, "Blaw me a strathspey, Fergus!" The piper stood outside the door and piped.

"Come here, Laura! Into my arms!" It seemed to Laura that her present state of intense feeling was separate from all outside impressions. This was the Isle of Love—bounded by a sea of bliss. Her lover-husband seemed content to stay at her side, proving his contentment o'er and o'er. Lazing afternoons by the fireside, he drew her down beside him and let his kisses stray on her white bosom. At night, he was the eagle, she the lark, taken while singing! One twenty-four hour passed—she marveled that he showed no fatigue, no sign of restlessness. Another round of the clock—he was no less ardent. The third day he said, "Have Cibber fetch up your jewels, my darling."

189

They were in each other's arms when the steward knocked.

"Set 'em down outside!" called Duff-Drummond. He bounded out of bed, fetched and unlocked the boxes.

"This . . . here!" he laughed and hung a pearl choker around her middle. "Diamonds, pearls, rubies, all mixed. See! They cover you completely. I find not a single inch left to kiss." He set a diadem on her head and clasped bracelets around her slender ankles. He covered her fingers and toes with rings, her arms with bracelets and necklaces. Then he placed two branched candlesticks at either side of the bed and stood back to view his handiwork. "You look like a lady in enamel, set with jewels! Do the stones warm to your flesh? They seem to glitter with new fire!"

"The weight bears me down!" laughed Laurie. "Come free me!"

"Lovely shackles," said Duff-Drummond. His tone changed. "Darling . . . why sit upon these baubles . . . leave 'em in the vault? I could use the money this old-fashioned stomacher would bring."

Laurie sat up. The jewels slithered down her breast and arms. "This might be a good time to talk about money, my darling."

Her husband eyed her. "If you say so?"

"You haven't made your wishes clear, Colin. Remember, I'm so inexpert . . . a child, in the matter of money."

"Your frankness is gratifying," said Duff-Drummond. "Perhaps you are unaware that Granny kept me pretty tight. I made a few debts . . . justifiable debts of course. My stables cost like the devil."

"I think perhaps Lady Inverkleith would have wanted to put her jewels to some better use than . . . a racing stable," said Laurie.

Duff-Drummond was examining the diamond stomacher he'd declared "old fashioned." He looked up. "Really? What better use, my dear?"

190

"Good works on your lands and for your people."

"Yes, of course!" Duff-Drummond agreed. "There's money aplenty for good works. I merely suggested that this stomacher would not be missed. You'll never wear it. Pearls are more becoming. Pearls and these emeralds, which are a perfect compliment to red-gold hair. Never mind. Think no more of it."

Duff-Drummond placed the jewels in the cases but he kept out a five-strand necklace of pearls and a parure of emeralds and diamonds.

"Wear your jewels, my sweet. Keep 'em here, locked in your cupboard. Granny did. Don't forget, she left her treasure to you to do exactly as you wish."

Laurie was contrite. Had she been too severe? "Colin, if you need money, tell me, darling."

"Gad! I could use five thousand . . . no mistake!"

"What must I do so that you may have five thousand pounds?"

"Write a memo to Henry: 'Pay to my husband Lord Duff-Drummond the sum of five thousand pounds.' This letter paper will do. Is the quill sharp? Here . . . the ink!"

Another enchanted night. Colin was never more tender, never gayer or more loverly.

"I was born the day we met!" thought the enraptured Laurie. "With every kiss, I'm born again!"

The morning of the third day, Duff-Drummond rose and padded to the window on bare feet. Pushing the curtains aside, he looked out. "Laura! The storm is over!"

He came and gave her a good-morning kiss. "Forgive me if I leave you for a few hours. I've business to attend to. À *bientôt*, my chérie."

Charming hours were passed between her husband's farewell and his returning kiss. Laurie rose and made herself beautiful. This done, she let Prince into the boudoir and played with him for a half-hour. Wearying of play, she sent the doggie for a romp in the gardens with a young footman.

She'd been wondering if there were not in Lady Inverkleith's huge collection of books, one book that would inform her on the state of a pregnant woman and give her some indication of the progress of the babe.

Seldom used nowadays, the great library was chilly and uncomfortable. Where to begin?

Try the As for Anatomy? Adams, Ady, Alanus de Insulis —all poets. Laurie went to the shelf that held the letter Ms for Medicine. There, among Marcus Aurelius and Merrick, was a beautifully bound and crested work entitled *The Anatomy of Man,* by B. S. Albinus. Opening the book, she found an unsealed letter under the cover—the date was April 5, 1760.

> LADY INVERKLEITH,
> MADAM,
>
> The B. S. Albinus, Leyden Edit., 1747 was placed on order by the deceased Lord Hathmore, in 1750. We have only recently been able to acquire the Work in good condition, at the Price of £11.5.0. If you wish other bindings in substitution for those with the crest of Prince Hohenstein von Bitzleben, I will be happy to have the change made at slight extra cost.
>
> > Your humble servant,
> > F. T. BOGGS—Paternoster Row.

Laurie poured spellbound over the engraved plates that enriched the work. Never had she suspected that bone and muscle, artery and vein, the structure of the skin, the intricate shape and operation of a heart-valve and vital organ could be transformed into beauty. The engraver, Jan Vandelaar of Leyden, had used his genius to reveal the mystery of the sexes in exquisite and luminous detail. Every organic function of womanhood was here set forth from the change that comes when the mammae or milk-secreting organs of the female are made to serve their purpose, the growth of the embryo and the condition of the womb in each successive stage of pregnancy.

What a windfall! She was on her way upstairs when a footman admitted a visitor.

"Margit!" Laurie ran down to greet her cousin.

"Laurie," said Margit after they had embraced, "forgive me if I break in on your honeymoon, but I'm in great need of advice."

After breathless questions, breathless answers—"Darling Laura, are you happy?"

"Divinely happy!"

"I should not have asked. Your happiness is written on your face! I'm the most troubled girl in the world, Laurie! I've had a proposal."

"Count d'Antimes?"

"Yes."

"Troubled? Why? He is a fine young man."

"Oh, yes!" cried Margit. "He is a wonderful young man. But Jinny says I shouldn't marry him, that I should wait until a rich suitor comes along."

"Not Jinny—*you* are the one to decide," said Laurie. "Listen only to your heart, Coz!"

"I do! I do! And my heart tells me Jean is the one!" said Margit with an adorable blush.

How different Margit's tender love story from her sister's mad escapades!

"I think we fell in love the first moment we met . . . Jean didn't dare speak. I had to encourage him and I did, without shame. He feared he was too poor—you see he comes of an émigré family who lost all in the French Revolution. Then guess what!" Margit's dark eyes began to glow. "The day after Lady Inverkleith died, her solicitor sent Jean a packet containing five thousand pounds."

"Wonderful Monette!" murmured Laurie.

"Our benefactress!" cried Margit. "And do you know what Jean wants to do with the money? He wants to migrate to the United States of America, to a place called Virginia, and buy property . . ."

"And . . . he wants a wife to accompany him, a girl named Margit Colquohoun?"

"Yes! Oh, Laurie, is it wrong of me to love Jean?" Margit burst into tears.

"No . . . no!" soothed Laurie.

"Jinny says I'm a little fool. She says I can choose among London's rich men. I don't want a rich man, I want Jean!"

"How is Jinny?" asked Laurie. "She was boasting she'd marry Lord Sitley."

"She will too!" said Margit sorrowfully. "An old man with a paunch who sneezes snuff all over his waistcoat, but Lord Sitley is rich, rich!"

"Does Jinny remember she once had a husband named Wattie Baird?"

"Didn't she tell you?" exclaimed Margit. "Poor Wattie was crushed under a cannon wheel. Jinny is a widow, free to marry whom she pleases. And she has plenty of suitors —a stream of 'em from morn 'til night! But none so rich as Lord Sitley."

Laurie could hardly wait to tell her husband the sweet story of Margit's romance with his friend, Count Jean d'Antimes.

"I guessed as much," chuckled Duff-Drummond when he heard the news. "Jean's been as close as a clam of late. To America? Not a bad idea. With five thousand, Jean could establish himself. He never liked the London climate. He'd never go back to France. Come here, wife! Where's that kiss?"

A rattling at the door froze the lover's gesture. Gillie Fergus stood in the doorway with two heavy portmanteaux hanging from his big hands. "Laird . . . where do 'e wish me to drr-rap Mr. Fordyce's bags?"

"Idiot! Ask the steward!" roared Duff-Drummond. When

194

the gillie backed across the threshold and hooked the door shut with his foot, he burst into laughter. "What a lout, that Fergus! Forgive me, darling . . . Fordyce leased his house for the season. He's on his way to Newmarket. He'll stay at Gin Lodge. I invited him to be with us until he's ready to leave. We may have more than one dinner guest tonight—don't know how many. Cibber is making the arrangements."

More than one dinner guest? Laurie quaked when she saw the assembled company! The Prince of Wales—"Eh! Eh! Chawmin'! Chawmin', Lady Duff-Drummond! About that haggis . . . you never did pass on it. I fear my chef could not reach the mark . . . no . . . no . . . he couldn't reach the mark."

But Laurie's gaze sped over the Prince's shoulder to a group of ladies—four in number. Gorgeous flower-bed of color, grace and exotic detail, they centered their eyes upon her with an intensity that was more than mere curiosity. She could not help but feel a sense of fright, as when a child is confronted by a new and, to his understanding, ferocious animal!

"My dear Laura," said her husband. "I wish you to meet some of my friends of the fairer sex. Then we'll pass on to those lesser creations, the male of the species."

Laurie gave back the curtsies of Diana, Duchess d'Alboli; Lady Arabella Dorkington; a stunning woman named Mrs. Maude Lowes; a beauty, the Lady Jane de Cruselle.

"How kind of you to come, ladies," she murmured and straightway she realized she'd said the wrong thing. The ladies set up a titter, smiled behind their plumed fans, exchanged amused glances.

"How quaint!" murmured the Duchess.

"Quite!" laughed Lady Dorkington.

"A mere child!" declared Mrs. Maude Lowes.

"But charming. Very, very charming!" murmured Jane de Cruselle. Her tone somehow belied the flattery.

At a loss what to say next, Laurie looked to her husband but he'd turned away to speak to the Prince.

"Do you remember me?" said a tall young man with ruddy hair and piercing blue eyes.

"Sir Ian Hamilton," smiled Laurie. "You were at my wedding feast."

"A fine feast, Lady Duff-Drummond. We stayed 'til dawn and found Krik Fordyce's whiskey of the best!"

"Come, my dear," said Duff-Drummond. "Others wish to pay their respects." He named the gentlemen one by one—"Sir Julian Struthers, Colonel Gwillim Folke of the Welsh Fusiliers; Lord Harry Grafton, the Earl of Mawebury, Sir Will Barré, Captain Jamie Haspers." Even the inexperienced Laurie could tag these notables as the crème de la crème of the sporting world—how white their hands, and what handsome rings! Their coats fitted snug as paint upon the wall. Their boots sparkled highlights. Their locks were clipped, hair for hair in the new blowaway style. They were poured into their trousers, the elastickers more revealing than Adam's fig-leaf. Fascinating the expression on each face—a vacuous stare, fashionable indifference but they did stare!

Presiding opposite her husband in the chair that was once Lady Inverkleith's throne, Laurie could hardly keep her mind on what his highness was saying—again and again, her gaze sought out the four ladies who were distributed among the greater number of men. The Duchess d'Alboli was thirty-five or more—a sovereign woman with a sultry smile, a mass of dark hair that she wore dressed in a myriad of little curls wrapped like knobs and fixed to her head in helmet shape. Her gown as daring as it was elegant. She wore dazzling jewels in her ears and on her wrists—not a jewel on her bosom. Seated at her host's right, she never ceased to engage him in banter to which he responded with amused laughter. The lady on Duff-Drummond's left was Jane de Cruselle—beautiful in the way a hummingbird or a cloud is beautiful. She did not make conversation but from time to time her large sad eyes turned to her host with a message only he could interpret.

Mrs. Maude Lowes was in the driver's seat of table-talk —theme of her conversation, horses. She and the Prince kept up a running comment on the races, this or that stable, this or that horse which was sold to this or that buyer. A handsome, florid woman, Mrs. Lowes—tawny hair, high complexion, muscular arms and hands. Last but not least, the Lady Arabella. To Laurie's way of thinking she was the most appealing of the four. She was also the most exquisitely gowned—sea-green gauze and diamonds, an arrangement of little diamond wings in her hair.

Nobody talked to Laurie except her left-hand partner, Sir Ian Hamilton, and there was an occasional "Eh! Eh!" from the Prince.

But young Sir Ian kept her constantly engaged with conversation about their native Scotland. Glad to hide her lack of ease, Laurie talked her favorite theme—the need for schools in the Highlands, the need for Scots to learn the English language.

However she was not displeased when dinner ended— she hadn't foreseen a new ordeal! Contrary to habit when Lady Inverkleith was hostess, the gentlemen remained, the ladies adjourned to the drawing room.

"My dear, you must not forget to give me the address of your little seamstress!" said the Duchess Diana, eyeing Laurie's simple gown—one of those Lady Inverkleith had given her. "One has such trouble finding, nowadays. I have my gowns made over for my country cousins. Of course, the good faiseuses won't do remodeling!"

"Are those not Lady Inverkleith's emeralds, Lady Laura," said Lady Arabella, eyeing her hostess' necklace. "They must be! The settin' is at least a hundred years old! Delightful old-fashioned, ain't it?"

"D'you ride, child?" asked Mrs. Maude Lowes in her strident voice. "Better learn! The Duff likes a woman who can handle a horse."

"I detest horses," murmured Lady Jane de Cruselle. "The odor's so frightful unpleasant! Tell me, Lady Laura, when will you hold your first evenin'? Will it be a grand ball, a rout, a masque . . . or music?"

None of the ladies waited for an answer, their questions were launched like spitballs—they didn't stop to see if they'd hit their target. Yes, target was the word! These four women were trying in subtle feminine way to humiliate and offend their hostess—why?

Laurie was vastly relieved when the gentlemen joined the ladies. From then on, all was smooth sailing. The company adjourned to the cardroom—except Sir Ian Hamilton.

"I hate cards," he said with a smile. "Do you like music? I play after a fashion. . . . How long since Lady Inverkleith's claviers have been tuned?"

Laurie had seldom visited the music room where string, wind and brass instruments neighbored with spinet, harpsichord, clavichord—a collection of bagpipes. Here, the antique patina of fiddles, violas and cellos glowed softly behind handsome glass cases and the brasses were kept bright with meticulous care, but the spinet and clavichord jangled out of tune when Sir Ian touched the keys.

"I could play you a tune on the bagpipes, but I daresay you'd not thank me," he laughed.

"Contrarily! I love the pipes. How did you ever master the difficult art?"

"I learned from my father's piper, the great Neil Reid," said Hamilton. "I can play the piob more, almost every kind of pipe that was ever invented, but I prefer the uilleann, one can get sweeter music from it. Here's an instrument that belonged to La Monette's adored Laird Duff-Drummond. She often asked me to play it when I came to call. Long before my time, she used to play the musette. It

198

was the style. In her day ladies of the court of Louis XV vied with one another to excel on their pet instrument, the wealth of decoration on the silk-embroidered bags."

Sir Ian removed a set of pipes from its case. "Shakespeare called the uilleann 'woolen pipes.' Remember the place where Shylock says, and I quote loosely, '... there's no firm reason to be rendered, why one man can't abide a pig, another, a harmless necessary cat, another a woolen pipe.' Shakespeare should have spelled the word u-i-l-l-e-a-n-n. He's made many a commentator burn the midnight oil trying to find out what he meant by the word 'woolen.'"

The lordly young piobaire set the bellows under his arm, slipped the ribbons in place. Soon a sprightly air issued from the pipes. The player was a master of curls and tipping.

"I wish I could learn to play!" cried Laurie when Sir Ian's rendition of an Irish rinncefada ended.

"Oh! but you *can* learn!" said Sir Ian. He slipped off the ribbons and offered Laurie the piper's stool.

"Sit as upright as possible! This ribbon is fastened around your waist . . . so. This one is brought over the arm . . . thus." Suiting the action to the word, Sir Ian arranged the ribbons over Laurie's bare shoulder and around her still-slender waist. "Now, press the bellows with your arm, up and down, easy and regular until the bag is full of wind."

Laurie did as she was told and much to her astonishment the limp bag swelled. "Now," said Sir Ian, "slip the upper part of the chanter with that hand where the bag rests, by lacing the tips of your fingers on the holes . . . keep the bag well secured with one arm . . . blow constant and steady with the other. See! You're piping! Now, the lower chanter . . . now with the tips of the fingers as with the other hand . . . it must be done so. Allow me to put your fingers in place, Lady Laura. See, the little finger

199

on the lower hole and the middle part of the other three fingers on the next holes . . . keep the thumb behind, to support the chanter. No . . . no . . . the drones are not to be kept over the hand but under, so as to rest near the body . . . so!"

Sir Ian's warm hands over hers, his broad torso so close that she could almost hear his heartbeat, Laurie blew a few weakling notes.

"You'd make a fine lady piper, and a beautiful one," said Sir Ian in her ear.

"Thank you for the lesson, Sir Ian!" said Laurie, her color heightening. "I think I'll listen, instead of trying to master the art."

She tried to extricate herself from the ribbons; Sir Ian had to help untie the one around her waist. As he freed her, she turned and saw her husband on the threshold of the music room.

"Our guests were asking for you, Laura," said Duff-Drummond. "I thought you'd retired."

"I've been giving Lady Laura first lessons in the piper's art," said Sir Ian in his quiet way.

"Colin, dearest," said Laurie to her husband that night when they had retired. "Did you approve of me?"

"Approve?"

"My behavior. My manners. My looks."

"Behavior . . . perfect. Manners refined. Looks . . . unmatched," Duff-Drummond declared. "One thing only . . ."

"What is it, dearest?"

"Why'd you have to devote your entire evening to Hamilton?"

"Nobody else seemed to want my 'devotion,'" Laurie answered in her usual direct way.

"But you showed such marked favor to Hamilton."

"He was courteous and interesting."

"Indeed?"

"Oh, yes! He has modern ideas about agriculture—tree husbandry, schools."

"Really? Well, the next time, pay more attention to the Prince and less to Hamilton."

"Colin! Are you jealous?" Laurie laughed.

Her husband's answer was to tumble her on the bed. "Damned if I couldn't be! You've that about you . . . deep-good like an apple plucked from a frost-struck tree! One bite, a man craves another and another. Kiss me, Laura!"

"Wait!" cried Laurie. "Tell me, Colin. Why did you invite those four ladies? They didn't like me, and I was ill-at-ease with them."

"Diana? Maude? Arabella? Jane? They thought you were charming. Can you blame any woman for being jealous of you?"

Fourteen

Honeymoon in Newmarket

COME WITH COLIN AND ME, LAURA," SAID KRIK FORDYCE. "I start tomorrow at eight o'clock. We'll travel like kings in my new curricle."

Suddenly, she hardly knew how, Laurie was Newmarket-bound.

Straddling the border between Cambridgeshire and Suffolk County, some twelve miles distant from the ivied courts of Cambridge University, the little town of Newmarket is charmed, but not awed, by the sight of kingly visitors, their equerries, friends and favorites. Hither came sportsman-King James I, in ringleted wig and riding boots to canter from King's House on a fine spring morning out to a heath west of town and mount the stands to view, through an admiral's telescope, the progress of the gees around the race-course. Hither came gambler-King Charles II, with mistress Nell Gwynn and his pet spaniels, to wager on the nags.

The town was neither charmed nor awed to hear the clatter of Mr. Fordyce's trotters on the cobblestones of High Street. But Mr. Fordyce's new-style carriage brought several patrons out of the White Hart Inn. "I sye, gov'nor, there's a smart turn-out. 'Ow do ye nyme it? 'Tain't a proper rig!"

Mr. Fordyce graciously described the elegant two-wheeled vehicle.

"This is a curricle. Some call it a cabriolet." He pointed

to the underpinnings. "Observe the elliptical springs that take the place of the usual heavy wood-and-iron perch and cross beds?" He was talking to experts who squatted on their haunches to look underneath. "Note the ornamental bar across the horses' backs which is connected by a leather brace to a spring under the pole?"

The experts rose, eyes following Mr. Fordyce's gloved forefinger. "The bar gives the proper balance and makes Obadiah Elliot's patented invention safer than any other previous type of two-wheeler. Note the folding hood which protects the passengers from the weather? A touch here . . . the hood collapses." Suiting the action to the word, Fordyce let down the hood, causing Colin and Laurie to pop into the open like a jack-in-the-box.

"I sye, gov'nor! Do the 'an'some filly go wi' Mr. Obadiah Elliot's patent invention?"

Fordyce smiled at the quip and said, "Colin, drive Lady Laura the rest of the way. I'll step into the White Hart a moment."

Colin of Newmarket was the sporting gentleman complete! Greatcoat of rough woolens. Cavalier hat with pheasant feather stuck in the band, leather "bricks," highly polished boots, sturdy gauntlets. Sportsman Colin transferred to the driver's seat and flicked the horses with the fly. "I'll show you famed Newmarket Course, my dear." He drove to the outskirts of the town. "See! Here it is! They keep it springy by planting earthworms that bore up and down, to break air into the turf. . . . See that embankment over there? It runs from the Cambridge Fens to Wood Ditton. Some call it the Devil's Dyke, others the Ditch, and all riders salute it in passing."

"Why?" asked Laurie faintly. She'd begun to weary.

"Because the stonework under the sward is supposed to be the remains of an ancient wall or entrenchment which divided the Eastern and Western Anglican tribes. People thought it brought them luck to salute the Ditch. Someday if you attend the races, you will see the jockeys salute the Ditch as they pass." Colin glanced at his watch. "We may as well be trottin' on . . ." He left the earthworms to their silent travail and the shades of the East and West Anglican tribes to the quiet of their stoneworks.

Here, at last, was Gin Lodge. The house, a boxlike edifice of stone, squatted behind a hedge of juniper bush eight feet high. The walls were covered with climbing ivy, so little trimmed that the windows looked like sleepy eyes peering from under uncombed locks. No sooner did the curricle wheel through a stone gate than several men ran out. Among them, three boys—or so Laurie thought until she got a closer view. Then she saw that they were those old-young men, the jockeys.

"Hullo, Dawson! Hullo, Vyner! Tom Cannon!" called Duff-Drummond, this last to a stoutish man of middle age who wore boots as fine as those of the most fastidious gentleman. "My trainer, Mr. Cannon, Laura. Tom . . . the Lady Duff-Drummond."

Mr. Cannon took to himself the honor of handing milady down from the rig. Stable-boys seized her boxes and carried them into the house. Hands in pockets, caps pushed back, the visors upstanding like the over-part of a crane's bill, thin jaws working—sucking on gaunt cheeks as though to get some nourishment from their own saliva—the ever-hungry "jocks" danced a shuffling dance on soft-soled boots and crowded around their master. The questions they tossed at him were put in a language Laurie did not understand.

"How'd Canie do, sir? We heerd he wanted to send in his cap and jacket."

"Frais'll cut it so in the decider, Finch wouldn't push to a finish."

"How's Philemon?" said Duff-Drummond to his trainer.

"Fine! Fine, m'lud."

"Will he be ready for the Craven?"

"That he will, m'lud."

A rustic servant-girl showed milady the way up a flight of creaky stairs to a bedroom on the first floor. The ceiling was so low that a tall man would graze it with his head. A four-poster bed of cottage make occupied most of the floor space. Rag rugs, a pewter bowl and pitcher, two chairs and a large oaken clothes-chest, the odor of the room— odor of wood-smoke and horse manure—prodded Laurie with a sharp remembrance!

"Please bring fuel and light a good fire," she said to the gaping servant-girl, as she threw open the windows. From a gold-topped bottle, she doused the walls, the rugs, the feather-bedding with eau-de-toilette.

The servant-girl was still glued to the spot, her nostrils quivering, a look of ecstasy on her plain face. Laughing, Laurie shook a few drops of the magic mist upon her apron. She gave a smile that fairly cracked her jaw, and hurried away to fetch fuel.

"Lavender Mist," said the inscription on the fancy perfume bottle that Laurie had purchased at a Bond Street shop. The bottle must be of more worth than the contents. It was made of baked earth, but the shape, the lavender-tinted glaze, the violet-tinted stopper made it eye-catching. "A mélange of wild lavender and other secret herbs blended with Turkish attar of roses," said the perfumer, transporting Laurie to the meadows above Ben Fada blue with wild lavender in season.

Her husband's footsteps pounding the stairs made her heart beat faster. She had changed her travel dress for a robe of greeny-blue velvet—"marvelous fetchin'" Mrs. Jack called it.

"My robin's egg, and I'm the one to suck it dry!" Colin slipped the bolt. Here was her bra' bridegroom again! Forgotten the fatigue of travel. Kisses were like no other kind of repose! Nay—after one kiss, she could have danced all night!

But to love was better! Her husband's dear arms were the best resting-place, his broad shoulder the finest pillow.

"Laura . . ." said Duff-Drummond in the dark of night. "Do you wish as I do that heaven would crown our affections with an heir?"

Was this the moment to confess? Trembling, Laurie answered, "Of course, dearest!"

"A fine son . . . ?"

"A son . . . a daughter . . . I'd welcome both!"

"I want a son!" said her husband emphatically.

"I'll try to oblige, milord!" laughed Laurie.

"I'm serious! Give me a son and I'll . . . I'll . . ."

"What?" breathed Laurie.

"Anything you wish!"

"Would you gang hame wi' me to the Hielands?" said Laurie tenderly. "I'd like our son to see the light of day on Scots soil, on Duff-Drummond domain."

" 'Twould be better to see your term through in London where good doctors are at hand."

"There are good doctors in Scotland," Laurie demurred.

"Need we decide tonight?" argued Duff-Drummond irritably. "There's no immediate prospect for medical care is there?"

"If he only knew!" thought Laurie. "Wait! Wait!" No! No! This was not the time to confess!

The people of Newmarket talked horses, thought horses, dreamed horses. Horses were their torment and their hope. The condition of a mare in foal, the pedigree of a stallion seemed of greater moment than the health of a queen or the affairs of a king. To win a race was as important as to win a battle. A "favorite" was a horse; not the mistress of a prince.

The men of Gin Lodge were no different from their neighbors. Here on these one hundred sixty acres were to be found the rivalry, ambition and pride of racing men everywhere.

Laurie took all this into account while listening to her husband. Walking with jaunty step and hat well cocked, trainer Tom Cannon and Jockey Vyner trailing, Colin did stable honors.

"My mare, Lady Grey. Here is Blue Boy. Next stall is Highland Lad . . . Lucky Shilling . . . Jane O'Dare, the gelding Laddie Jack. . . . Here is Philemon, my favorite."

Even Laurie's inexperienced eye could pick out the bay stallion's good points. "He *is* beautiful, Colin!"

Her husband's warm rejoinder told her how pleased he was. "Thought you'd like him. This is the horse I intend to save, come what may!"

"Save?"

"I'm hard-pressed for funds, my dear. I may have to sell." Colin turned to Krik Fordyce who had come out to join them. "What news, Krik?"

"Bad news, I fear."

"Really?"

"Yes. I pleaded with Judd. He's quite set."

"I'll not come down on my price, fifteen hundred guineas."

"Certainly not! Gwillim will give seventeen hundred if you'll take it in several payments."

Laurie began to see through Messieurs' transparent ruse —so Krik Fordyce was her husband's accomplice in the game "Get the Money"!

Why didn't Colin come out with it—say frankly, "I need money!" She resolved to wait until he did.

This was honeymoon day—all spring sunshine and tender merriment—"My sweet" this, and "My darling" that. As if by chance, Colin arranged for an alfresco picnic at the little stand-house overlooking his half-mile private track where the horses were exercising.

"You love racing, don't you Colin?" said Laurie fondly.

"Of course! One must race to keep one's head above water."

"Race . . . and win?"

"Win, of course."

"But you lose!"

"Naturally. Fortune's a fickle jade. One can't win always. I've had a losing streak but I had neither Philemon nor Jockey Vyner. That lad is so enduring he can walk hundreds of miles with his mount, keep 'em under constant watch. D'you know what he did for Sunderland? He took Princess Alice after winning the Epsom stakes and traveled by road to Newcastle-on-Tyne to meet his next engagement. The journey took him almost a month in easy stages. From Middleham, he walked him o'er moss and fell to Scotland. Snail's pace. That requires stamina and patience."

Laurie knew what he meant. When would he ask for money? A whispered conference with Fordyce who had ridden to Newmarket town that afternoon precipitated events. Laurie knew by their long faces that some creditor's patience must have shortened.

Even then Colin did not hurry. He watched her like a hawk, waiting to pounce on a moment of her weakness. This moment came at dusk. More weary of "walking" the stables, the race-track, the barns, than she cared to admit, Laurie had retired and thrown herself on the bed half-dressed. Soon she must tell! Colin proposed to teach her how to ride, the sport might be perilous for the child. As always her pulses quickened at the sound of her husband's step on the stair. He burst in and saw her.

"Tired, my love?"

"A little!"

"Then I'll be tired too!"

With what lightning speed Milord could divest himself of boots and breeches!

"I like to make love in the afternoon," he said, nuzzling her breast with his shapely nose. "A good half-hour folded between day and night. Fine sport, eh? The gel can't say no—there she lies, limp victim. Sweet prey! Wreathe those arms around your cavalier. With me now! First a trot and then a canter! Now we gallop . . . gallop!"

Dusk had deepened when at last they lay quietly, hand clasping hand.

Colin sighed. "Love me, Laura?"

"You must know."

"If you love me you'll lift a burden off my mind."

"Yes, my darling?"

"I'm in need of several thousand to tide me over until Philemon is ready. You'll see my point when I tell you its the soundest investment one could make, and quite in keeping with Granny's wishes!"

"Indeed?"

"Oh, yes! Krik Fordyce and Tom Cannon will bear me out—invested now, that money will come back a hundred-fold during this year's racing calendar."

"How much money do you need, Colin?"

"Twelve thousand, my dear—a bagatelle."

"It seems to me," Laurie teased, "and I have heard others say, that a horse-racing venture is not a sound investment." She kept her voice steady but her eyes were dancing at sight of her husband's quick change of humor, from gay to grave. "You call Gin Lodge a 'rackity-rick' place without comforts, a camp for trainers and jockeys, but the upkeep must be considerable. You feed twenty-three horses which have brought you no earnings. The proof—you owe twelve thousand."

The sum of his pleasures must stack high—very high, for Colin did not erupt in anger. Affably he said, "Some owners maintain stables larger than mine. Gin Lodge is a modest outlay."

"How modest, Colin?"

"Oh . . . two . . . three thousand guineas a year foots the bill."

"But you owe twelve thousand!"

"One strikes a betting snag here and there."

Before leaving London, Laurie had gone to Sir Henry Banks for precise instructions in her role of executrix-administrator of Lady Inverkleith's fortune. "If you need money, you've but to sign your name on a slip addressed to me: 'Dear Henry . . . pay to my order or to the order of whom you wish the sum of——.' Simple, is it not?"

Laurie had brought a writing case from London. It was made of leather and shaped like a miniature desk top. The cover unlocked to disclose a silver inkwell with screw-top and quill pens. One lifted the little felt-covered board. Underneath was letter paper with the crest of Duff-Drummond.

The pen scratched! "Here, dearest!" Laurie handed her husband what she had written.

> DEAR SIR HENRY, please pay to the order of Lord Duff-Drummond the sum of twelve thousand pounds and oblige,
> LAURA LADY DUFF-DRUMMOND.

Surprise left Duff-Drummond speechless. He stared at the order with popping eyes, he swept her in his arms and kissed her. "My darling. I've a pressing errand." He began to dress in haste.

"Mr. Judd?" asked Laurie mischievously. Her husband turned.

"Where did you hear the name of Judd?"

"Seems to me, from Krik Fordyce."

"Observant Puss in Boots, aren't you?"

"I observe what concerns you!"

"Dear Laura! I'll send a boy with this little present for Mr. Judd."

A merrier dinner party was n'er put together for Duff-Drummond, Laura and Fordyce. It struck Laurie as she listened to the gentlemen laugh, jest, click glasses to Beauty and the horses, that she had not yet skimmed the top of her husband's nature. Reared in a parsimonious

Highland home and taught all too soon that her lot was to battle poverty, how could she understand a man for whom disaster spelled losing a racehorse? Colin had never known the fear of being "with nae hame, nae safety"; he'd never felt the bite of winter, never wearied in menial tasks, never pulled in his belt to stay the pangs of hunger. To understand Colin better, she must climb in imagination to that plane of fortune where the necessary of a favored few is the superfluous of the many unfavored. Not "Where'll I find three shiller to pay the landlord?" but "Where'll I get a thousand to pay a card debt?" How the Laird must chafe under the yoke of the lassie who had once caught his "rovin' e'e." All-considered, Granny Monette had played her grandson a bad trick! "Now be good, or you'll have no porridge!" She must try to be more understanding, more openhanded.

Lying that night in her husband's arms, "Colin dearest," murmured Laurie, "tell me when you need money. I dislike my role of Keeper of the Keys. I'd give it up if I could." Dead silence—then a whispered "Another five . . . six thousand . . . would see me out of all inconvenience." Colin answered almost as if he were testing his hearing.

"I'll write another note for Sir Henry."

Colin at dusk had been the sporting gentleman who walks in on a chance mistress. Colin at midnight was a goddess' lover.

"Laura! My Venus! Fulfill my pride and hope! Mother me a son!"

"When shall I speak?" Laurie asked of a sickle of moon that clipped through the juniper hedge.

"Not yet," the moon seemed to answer.

Driving a light carriole, Colin took his wife exploring the countryside. Maytime had brought the trees to flower. The hawthorne was whiter than the driven snow. Lazing on the banks of a babbling brook, he listened while she talked of her plan a-borning—a way to increase the rev-

211

enue of the domain—make Highland lavender water, using some of the alcohol that now went into the brewing of inferior whiskey and the flowers of lavender that bloomed in the hills.

Engaged in exploring the secrets of his wife's gown—thirty-six buttons to be exact, he counted 'em one by one as he popped 'em from their buttonholes—Duff-Drummond listened absent-mindedly. "What would our good Angusmen say if you rob 'em of their uisgha to make that sweet-stinkin' stuff?"

" 'Twould only take a part," said Laurie, buttoning buttons as quickly as her husband got them undone.

"Hey! Whose bosom is this? Mine, I'll have you know! Here! My seal upon it! This one, too! I play no favorites when it comes to my wife's fair possessions."

"Colin! Be sensible! Listen to me!" pleaded Laurie.

"It's not my ears that do the kissin'!"

Laurie forgot her plans in the delight of loverly caresses! How entrancing to gaze into the lacework canopy overhead and let the beloved do his sweet will!

"D'you know, Laura, I can almost forgive Granny!" Colin whispered as he trussed her habit.

"Almost? When will you forgive altogether?"

Colin punctuated his sentence with a more virile caress. "I . . . may let you know . . . someday!"

The waters of the brook seemed to pour from their banks and drown Laurie—new Ophelia finding sweet oblivion in her lover's arms.

But late that night, she harked back to her plan. "If only we could bring new manufactures to the braes. I've thought of something else, a small industry to use those mountains of deer horn heaped where the hunters left 'em. One could teach the men how to polish horn and make pretty and useful things during the winter months."

"Polish horns?" Colin was far behind, yet far ahead. "I say . . . it occurs to me, we have a clay pit somewhere North of Grailie. I remember visiting it when I was a boy

212

and taking a bucketful which I wet and molded into manikins. Granny's bailie said then that it was the stuff of which good earthenware is made. Why not develop your own kiln? Make your own bottles for your lavender water?"

"You'll help me, darling?" cried Laurie in joyous excitement. "Oh, Colin! How much we could do if we worked together."

"Aye," drawled her husband. "How much indeed! Come . . . enough of lavender water . . . bottles . . . deer's horn. We've a more important manufacture—right at hand!"

That night, it seemed to Laurie, her husband wrung her dry! She'd reached a peak beyond which rapture must decline. Her weary limbs groaned. Was this not the time for an ardent spouse to favor the expectant mother?

At dawn, she cautiously freed herself from her sleeping husband's embrace and rose from the rustic bed. The room was close. She felt the need of fresh air. She'd not gone halfway to the shuttered window when she reeled and sank into a chair.

Her husband leaped to her aid. "Darling! What is it? Are you ill?"

Smiling, "Not ill," Laurie answered, "I think I know what's the matter!"

"Is it—can it be?" Her husband's voice broke. "Are you by any chance . . . ?"

"Yes. I've known it for several days. I did not want to tell you until there was no room for doubt."

Laurie had been aware of her husband's longing for a child but she hadn't known how great that longing was! Seized with wild exuberance, he leaped and pranced around her and shouted. "No room for doubt! No room for doubt, she says! By the Great Horned Filibuck, I'm to have an heir!" He stopped his prancing and took her by the shoulders and shook her lightly. "Let it be a son! I want no female! A son, d'you hear? A son!"

Fifteen

A Million for an Heir

"FIAT!" SAID DUFF-DRUMMOND AS HE CAME SWAGGERING into Sir Henry Banks' chambers the morning after he'd brought his wife back to London. "It's done, Henry! It's done!"

"What's done, Colin?"

"Madame is pregnant!"

"O marvel!" said Sir Henry dryly, "I'd have given a thousand to one on Madame's pregnancy."

"One million pounds, Henry! You said one million pounds!" exclaimed Duff-Drummond rubbing his hands. "Gad! That's a heap of money. And what a pleasant time I had earning it!"

"Wait, it's not in your pocket. Lady Laura must present you with a boy."

"She will!" said Duff-Drummond confidently. "She does my bidding in everything."

"So I see," said the solicitor. "Her orders to pay keep pouring in . . . five thousand . . . twelve thousand . . . another five! Where d'you drop it, Colin?"

"Here . . . there."

"I see. Well, you're to be congratulated for having such a wife."

"I am indeed! Conceive, say I—the lady obliges! Ah, Henry! Duff-Drummond is quite a man!"

"Any carter could do as much."

"Don't minimize my talents, Henry!"

214

"What is it you want now, Colin?" said Henry Banks, annoyed by his client's flippancy.

"Nothing, except to announce the good news. Ah, yes! Lady Laura and I plan to undertake a program of rural improvement in the braes—tree planting, building, a school, manufactories."

"You . . . to the braes?" exclaimed Sir Henry who could not believe his ears.

"We start a week Wednesday. In time to see Lady Laura's cousin Margit married to Jean d'Antimes, then we coach it to Edinburgh then awa' to the Hielands! Duff-Drummond, Highland chieftain. Duff-Drummond buadgh no bas!"

"I don't believe it!" exclaimed Sir Henry.

Colin tossed a familiar sheet of crested stationery on the lawyer's desk. "Maybe this will convince you! Lady Laura's first contribution to the improvement of Highland life. Thirty thousand pounds! Pray send the cash to Hathmore House by tomorrow noon, my dear Henry." Duff-Drummond snapped the rim of his dapper beaver and swaggered out.

The wedding of Margit and Count d'Antimes was celebrated in St. James Church, Piccadilly. Duff-Drummond gave the bride away. Laurie was matron of honor. Actress Jinny Baird attracted all eyes as she paraded down the aisle on the arm of Lord Ludland Sitley—the gossips buzzed he was to be her Future.

After the wedding a fashionable mob crowded the drawing rooms of Hathmore House and drank many magnums of champagne to the health of the happy pair. Most honored guest—the Prince of Wales. Among hundreds of handsome wedding gifts showered on the popular d'Antimes and his lovely bride, his highness' royal offering shone—a monumental epergne of silver and crystal.

"Prinny must have dug it out of the closet labeled 'Unusables!'" grinned Duff-Drummond. "Margit can use it for a bird-bath."

"Your gift and Laura's was the best!" said Margit. "Beautiful furniture and linen for our home."

"I'm happy you liked it," said Laurie.

"Thrifty gel!" said Duff-Drummond in his wife's ear, "you scrambled the furniture out of Granny's attics!"

"Every piece was of value!" Laurie argued. "I called in an antiquarian. Margit's bed is authentic Louis XV. She'll be the envy of all the Virginia ladies."

Laurie had another surprise for the bride and groom. A wedding haggis! When Prince George heard this, he elbowed his way to the table where d'Antimes was about to officiate with the carving knife. "Eh! Eh! A haggis! Lady Laura, I claim the first slice!"

His highness nibbled, stuffed his mouth, asked for more. "Roarin' good. I say!" He turned to the company. "Here, sons of Albion! Try a haggis of Scotland!"

Her husband's eyes caught Laurie's. "What a haggis can do!" he murmured as he clinked his glass to hers.

Most memorable part of Margit's wedding was the departure of the couple for their home in the New World. Their ship, the *Glasgow Queen*, sailed on the evening tide. The day had been clear and warm. Some of the sun's gold caught in the sails of the brigantine as they spread to the light breeze. The towers of Whitehall, the bridges were etched in sharp relief upon the gilded water of the Thames. That indefinable odor of brine and tar that haunts a port was strong upon the air.

The bridal pair stood elbow to elbow at the rail waving to those below. With rattle of iron, hissing of hawser and creaking of yards, the brig inched from the wharf, shuddered when the ebbing tide took hold of the hull, moved queenlike down the stream. "Goodbye! Goodbye!" said Margit's streaming scarf. "Goodbye! Goodbye!" said Jean's waving hat. The quick spring dusk came down in violet folds. Soon, the *Glasgow Queen* was a silhouette against a twilight sky.

"Now," said Laurie tearfully, "we can start for Scotland!"

Lady Inverkleith's departures used to be a spectacle for gaping audiences. But Lord and Lady Duff-Drummond slipped out of London in a manner most casual—the Prince of Poodles, Laurie, Colin in a well-slung traveling coach of sober black. How unlike Lady Inverkleith's pell-mell start with eight doggies in her Ark on wheels!

Milord had sent steward Cibber on to Scotland, "to arrange a proper welcome." Maid Pritchet, a chef and butler traveled in the luggage wagon. Gillie Fergus rode horseback, his pipes slung over his shoulder.

"Are you comfortable, my dear?"

"Quite, darling."

"Not weary?"

"Not weary at all!"

The miles were left behind. Soon the border was crossed and London Colin became the Laird in Scots dress, with Scots manners.

Laurie would not have liked to return to the braes without her husband. With him, she feared nothing!

He'd planned like a general. "We'll make our choice of a physician and midwife in Edinburgh. We'll look for a good nanny for the babe."

"I want to suckle him myself," said Laurie.

"*Him?* Ah, Laura!" Duff-Drummond exclaimed, "Are you sure the child will be a boy?"

"I'm sure for your sake," said Laura sweetly.

Her husband covered her hand with kisses. "Laura! Laura! My Queen of Hearts. It shall be a boy!"

Laurie saw Edinburgh Castle loom in the spring haze with indescribable emotion.

"It is now I feel like a Scotswoman!" she murmured to her husband.

The coach crossed Nor'Loch Bridge and halted at Number 28 George Street where Cibber was waiting.

"The house still smells of dog!" said Duff-Drummond as he crossed the threshold.

"I aired, milord," said Cibber. "I burned pitch and incense."

"Twenty generations of poodles can't be aired awa'!" laughed Duff-Drummond. He picked up his wife and carried her to the room that once was Lady Inverkleith's bedchamber. What memories here! Mementoes of a lifetime.

"I say, let's sell this old house," said Duff-Drummond as he sipped a glass of brandy and nibbled a wafer.

"Why?" Laurie asked.

"It's like a museum of antiquities."

"I like it."

"Then keep it, my dear."

Laurie could hardly believe her eyes and ears! What more dutiful, loving, solicitous husband than Colin! He was a model! A paragon!

During the week's sojourn in Edinburgh he devoted himself to his wife's health and comfort.

"I've good news for you, Laurie," he said one morning when he returned from town. "I've found an excellent physician. Name's Dr. Jamie Ayre. He's not an old fogy . . . up to the the latest tricks in obstetrics. He'll provide his own midwife. And for a nanny . . . why not let Nanny Biel pick a likely young woman from our villages? It would create good will . . . Nanny Biel will know the right one."

Heaven forgive Lady Duff-Drummond for gloating a teeny bit the afternoon her carriage stopped at the door of the Royal Scot in Edinburgh.

Her Uncle Thomas Colquohoun came running out, wiping his hands on his apron before settling his neckcloth.

"Weel, weel! Laurie! I mean, your ladyship!"

"Laurie will do, Uncle."

"Thank ye, Laurie! Ye ne'er was a prr-oud soul! Step right in."

With Prince straining at the leash, "I came to call on Aunt Emma, thank you, Uncle Thomas," said Laurie. "How is she?"

Trotting beside his niece like a jibbing horse, the master of the Royal Scot tapped his temple with one finger. "Bad! Verra bad."

Emma Colquohoun had gone to a world where a teapot with a broken spout, a clock without hands were more real than the comforts of her surroundings. She dined, not upon the fare that came up from the Royal Scot kitchen, but upon a menu concocted by spirits whispering from within. Her Golconda treasure was kept in an iron-bound chest without lock or key. Her odd contentment was reflected in the childish joy upon her face when Laurie agreed to share her secret store of goodies, a stick of rock candy, a moldy scone, a rind of cheese.

"She's mad," said Kate with a steely gleam in her eyes. "She should go to Bedlam."

"If you ever dare, Kate Colquohoun!" said Laurie indignantly, "I will bring you and your father to justice and prove that your mother is harmless."

A look of fear crossed the girl's plain face. "I dinna say I'd put her in Bedlam. I only said she *ought* to go there. I treat her weel. She walks out wi' the skudgy to take the air every day. Father gies her money for tea. She brings back crusts o' scones and hides 'em 'til the room is o'errun wi' mice."

On the stairs Laurie passed the girl whom Kate named, in contempt, "skudgy"; there but for a rebel soul went Lady Laura Duff-Drummond! The girl was under twenty, a Highland lass with powerful arms and the empty stare of kine.

"What is thy name?" asked Laurie.

"Bonnie, milady."

"Where is thy hame?"

"I hae nae hame, milady. I was found."

Dame Memory sat at Laurie's side to Kirrimuir. She had left these scenes a broken thing, filled with hurt and dismay. She returned in the fullness of wifehood—a mother-to-be. Chieftainess of her people!

As the carriage rolled into the widening vale, she saw the Rock and its sister crag, the high meadows where she'd gone gathering the May dew, the nestling roofs of slate, the barns and sheds—how would the people of the Five Villages receive the Laird's wife, whom they had known as a dairymaid?

The answer to her question was not long in coming. Nearing Ben Fada, the horses pricked up their ears at the sound of bagpipes.

"Hark!" said Duff-Drummond. "They're playing 'Hail to the Chief.' I see Cibber has done his work well!" He bawled, "Stop the coach!" sprang out and mounted a black stallion that gillie Fergus had led all the way from Kirrimuir. "'Twould n'er do for the Duinne Uassel to show himself to the people from a coach window!" Duff-Drummond touched his cocked bonnet and rode ahead with his gillie.

It seemed to Laurie's moist eyes that thousands were gathered along the route. Women waved evergreen branches. Children tossed flowers through the carriage window. She smiled as she recognized familiar faces—spinster Janet who did not believe in signs and omens! Silver-haired Nan who believed too much! Young Davy, Nanny Biel and her son Malcolm waved from the gate of the grange. Laurie waved back and threw kisses from the depth of her full heart!

What a wonder to see the Laird caracoling on his lively steed! His smiles, his gestures, "Thank you! Thank you!" blessed the crowd. But the cavalcade did not stop! How the horses strained up the stony way to the castle. Here, scenes were strongly etched in memory. Laurie shuddered as she passed the site of her struggle with gillie Angus— the place where Clargy and Angus fell. But no! She must forget the past, look ahead to the rosy future! Bailiff Malcolm came to announce that a party of neighboring lairds, Hamilton, Melfont, Dalgethy and others had come to hold a feast of welcome. Preparations were complete and victuals and drink were ready.

Fatigued by the long journey and by the strain of her own emotions, Laurie begged to be excused and retired early.

Did the ghost of a frightened sinner still lurk in this scarlet-hung bed chamber?

"Dear Lord, forgive!" she prayed, "I'll spend my life atoning for my sin."

She was dozing when a familiar shawled figure stole into the room.

"Nanny Biel!"

"Welcome hame, milady!" said the old nurse.

Laurie wept as she embraced her friend and protectress.

How strange, the sound of "milady" on the lips of Nanny Biel who used to give orders to dairymaid Laurie. But there was no question about it; the wife of the Laird must put herself in the place where these simple folk of the braes wanted her to be. From now on she'd hear "your ladyship" and "milady" on every lip and this was right and proper so long as the concept of lord and peasant lasted.

It came to Laurie forcefully that she had not wanted title or rank, that they had been thrust upon her. Highest honor—to serve her darling husband and her children. Finest title—Benefactress of the Poor. But the time had not come to break down every barrier. Perhaps it might never come, for in truth the world was full of followers— and of Leaders, few! Laurie, though she'd been a dairymaid and skudgy, was now Lady Duff-Drummond and so she must remain until this earth changed to the Golden City.

"Sit by my bed, Nanny Biel," she said softly. "How is your health? How did you pass the winter?"

"I kna' not the name, bad health, lass, pardon . . . milady. Old Nanny is made o' granite. Let me hear milady's news."

"Nanny," said Laurie with a happy smile, "confess, you fixed it so I'd go to Lady Inverkleith."

The old woman gave her a sidelong glance, in her twinkling eyes, shrewdness and kindness. "Aye, wud ye let the ewe stray after she's bin covered by the prize ram? Wud ye lose the lamb, pride o' the flock?"

"I was not in a family way when I left Ben Fada, Nanny!" said Laurie with a painful flush.

"Aye . . . but later . . . those nichts i' the ram's bosom! My son Malcolm's eye was not closed. He knew milady's condition."

"Malcolm?"

"Aye. And he told Lady Inverkleith."

"How . . . how could he have known?"

"A purr-rson named Madame . . . Madame . . . a furrin name. She came to wash and cut the dogs' coats."

"Madame Deréchault?"

"Aye." Nanny Biel reached into her pocket and took out a silver brooch—the Twig of Juniper. "I went to the castle while a' the folk were drinkin' and dancin'. I found this . . . beside the couch o' fox skins. I found a weddin' haggis wi' two slices cut. I found a strr-range cage . . . niver saw the likes . . . and a key tha' fitted a wee lock." Nanny's expression was more eloquent than words. "When the ithers went oop to the Rock, they found a' in order . . . the bed fresh made. Naebody e'er knew or guessed. Later, my sharp son Malcolm found out wha' went on at Hathmore House."

222

Pinning the precious silver Juniper Twig to her gown, Laurie tried to conceal her blushes. What a fool she'd been, to think that her secret could go undiscovered. Malcolm had not been Lady Inverkleith's confidential courier and steward for nought—and Colin, believing his nightly visits were a deep mystery to everyone but themselves!

"Nanny," said Laurie, "will it be a boy?"

"Nu . . . I'm no prophet!" laughed Nanny Biel, "but there's someone waitin' behind yon door."

"Nan!" laughed Laurie.

"Your ladyship's pardon . . . the lass was tha' set! She cudna wait to kiss milady's hand."

"Nan . . . kiss my hand?"

"Let her!" said the wise old woman.

When Nan entered she was pale with excitement. "Lady Laurie! I bid you welcome!" She made as if to kiss milady's hand but Laurie kissed her cheek. "What new spells have you for a bairn, Nan? Be it a boy or a girl?"

"Spells for a bairn!" said the girl, looking at her with misty blue eyes. "I've a spell that does not fail. See these magic straws? I place them crosswise on the floor. If the Laird enters and the straws fly apart and dinna meet or touch, 'twill be a bairn. If they do meet or touch at any part . . . 'twill be a lass."

Laurie had forgotten all about the magic straws when her husband came to bed. He slammed the door with a good slam. "Jove! I bet Ian Hamilton a hundred he couldn't floor me in a wrestling match, but we were both too full o' uisgha to carry through! We'll have to decide it some other time."

Laurie suddenly remembered Nan's magic spell. "Take the candle, Colin. See if you can find two long straws on the floor."

"Straws? Why? What for?"

"You wish to know the sex of our child, don't you?"

223

"Yes."

"Then do as I say."

A comical sight—the Laird crawling on hands and knees and sneezing at the candle-flame.

"Here's one straw. I can't find any more."

"One is enough," said Laurie, smiling. "If you believe in Scots magic, our baby will be a boy."

Dr. Jamie Ayre and a midwife came pony-back to Ben Fada at the end of June. Laurie liked the doctor at first meeting. She had given orders to rebuild and refurbish an abandoned cottage at the crossroads between Ben Fada and Fairlie for his accommodation. The house had a genteel look but Laurie had another idea in mind—to add a large room with several beds for the sick. Dr. Jamie Ayre would not only be her ladyship's private physician but also physician to the villages.

"Would you like to stay on in Angushire, Dr. Ayre?" she asked the young practitioner.

"That's accorr-rdin' to the inducements, Lady Duff-Drummond.

"What would your earnings be, in Edinburgh?"

"Farthin's, your ladyship. I'd planned to migrate to the Carolinas. But I'd prefer to stay in my native Scotland. I was born in Montrose and I've family there still."

"You give me little to go on, Dr. Ayre," smiled Laurie. "What is a fair year's earnings for a physician?"

"If milady provides me with surgical instruments, a woman helper or two, drugs, and . . . say the keep o' twelve beds, the cost would be about a thousand pounds a year."

"*Your* salary, Doctor Ayre?" laughed Laurie. "You ask only for others."

"Salary? I want the worr-rk done! Too long, our Scots have suffered. Our children die young, for want of care. Our women die in childbirth!"

Here was a man after Laurie's heart! She spoke to her husband about him.

"Beds? Medical care for the peasantry? Fancy, ain't it? We'd set a dangerous precedent. Our neighbors would howl!"

"But . . . Colin! Isn't it good to set precedents? Let the neighbors howl!"

"Oh, very well. Do as you think best." Duff-Drummond brushed the matter aside. "By the by, dear . . . there's something I'd like to discuss . . . the thirty thousand. How much will you need? Say . . . two . . . three thousand?"

"But . . . the rest?" said Laurie, in surprise.

"You spoke of setting up manufactures . . . buying seedlings in England for plantin' here. You talked about bringing new and better stock to the braes . . . buildin' a school . . . God knows what all! You'd have to purchase supplies in the Lowlands. The bulk of the money could be used for such purposes. I may make a flying trip to London where I can readily buy what you need."

"You . . . you plan to go back to London?"

"Only for a flying trip. As I said, I've business to attend to. We let everything drop, raced up north at a moment's notice."

Laurie's heart sank. "How soon would you return, dearest?"

"Oh! In a month . . . six weeks . . . meanwhile you can amuse yourself with all your plans and novelties."

"But Colin! I'll need more than five thousand pounds."

Her husband's brow furrowed. "Six or seven thousand will be ample. Even if you carpet the meadows with velvet, you couldn't spend more." He clasped her in his arms. "Besides, my dear, your condition will not allow you to strain too much. Your first care must be for the child."

Laurie resisted the pressure of arms she adored, the kiss that made wirra-warra in her brain. "Darling, added to all the money you've received, another five thousand should be ample for a month's stay in London."

"But you are asking me to purchase all kinds of supplies, livestock, building materials."

"Send the bills to Sir Henry."

"Very well, but you . . . write him a love letter. 'Dear Henry, please pay . . . etcetera.'"

"Oh, very well!" laughed Laurie, "you may deliver the letter with your own hands."

Even so, Laurie was teased, coaxed, caressed into a compromise. Her husband left only four thousand pounds in Cibber's strongbox—took the rest to London.

Struggling with her tears, she watched him ride away one fine morning—cavalier figure of a Chieftain with his piobaire Fergus in tow. No. She must not weep. Lady Laura Duff-Drummond faced a new life. No dream too vast! And Colin would help make that dream come true. How she'd watch for his return! Not even the stone-cold Lady Mala Liath of legend yearned more for the rising of the sun than Lady Laura for her husband's homecoming.

Sixteen

Duff-Drummond Runs Wild

SIR HENRY BANKS OWNED A COZY COTTAGE ON THAMESIDE to which he fled for rest and quiet during the summer months. Tabled on the terrace overlooking the sun-dappled waters of the Thames, he'd finished breakfast. Now he turned to the swans, waiting for his crusts. The black swan was the enemy of the white. Handsome fellow with red beak and angry red eye! Sir Henry tossed a crust far out to stream. The black spread mighty wings and pounced upon it—choked it down and eyed his rival as if to say, "I got there first!"

"Will that be all, sir?" said Sir Henry's butler.

"Yes thank you. The newspapers if you please."

Sir Henry clipped and lighted his favorite cheroot and leisurely opened the *Morning Post*.

First he glanced at the court calendar—mighty dull readin' these days, with one George locked in a tower and another George hidin' his antics from the public press. Sir Henry glanced at the racing news, noted that Duff-Drummond's stables had had another win with a nag named Philemon. He turned to the gossip column.

"What's this . . . what's this?" Sir Henry muttered. "Lord Duff-Drummond entertaining at Hathmore House!" The last he'd heard, Colin had gone to Scotland with his wife!

Further on down the column there was another mention of Lord Duff-Drummond.

His Royal Highness the Duke of Gloucester will entertain Lady Jane de Cruselle, Mrs. Carrie Farnley, the Duchess d'Alboli, Lady Arabella Dorkington, Mrs. Maude Lowes, Lord Duff-Drummond at Maryon Cottage for the running of the Gold Cup.

Four of the ladies mentioned were favorites of Duff-Drummond—the dark, beautiful Duchess Diana d'Alboli, reknowned for her Borgian temper and her Medicean vanity, Lady Dorkington whom intimates nicknamed "Kinkajou" because of her quick gestures and ceaseless chatter. Maude Lowes rode her lovers like a Norse goddess her winged steed! And the swanlike Jane de Cruselle, lovely disciple of Nymphe.

So—Colin was not in Scotland! Sir Henry's displeasure increased when he opened his mail pouch and found it stuffed with bills—Duff-Drummond's bills for cattle, seed, machines, tools, lumber, and of all things, schoolbooks—to the astonishing total of twenty-one thousand pounds.

Sir Henry sent a messenger to Hathmore House with a note.

> DEAR COLIN,
> A matter of some urgency having arisen I'd be obliged if you can arrange to see me at your convenience.

Duff-Drummond arrived driving a pair of elegant bays in tandem harness. His "spider" groom sat on the box with folded arms and a set lip, as if the country air did not agree with his turned-up nose.

To a connoisseur of masculine fashion, Duff-Drummond presented a most pleasing appearance. He was wearing a dark green, long-waisted, single-breasted frock coat with large mother-of-pearl buttons; waistcoat of kerseymere, ornamented alternately with stripes of green and white;

228

smallclothes of white corduroy made moderately high and very long over the knee, buttoning in front over the shinbone; boots very short with long tops, only one outside strap to catch and one to the back, the latter being employed to keep the breeches in a longitudinal shape. Conical hat with wide brim; box coat of drab with fifteen capes and two tiers of pockets; a cravat of white muslin, spotted with black; and a bouquet of myrtle, pink and geranium in the buttonhole. His lordship's skin was tanned a healthy brown, his movements were brisk, but the pouches under his eyes were a sign of late hours, too much wine, too many women! Duff-Drummond tossed the reins to his groom and leaped to the ground.

"Take 'em around back. Rub 'em down. Water sparingly when they've cooled." He left his box coat on the seat and joined Sir Henry in the garden nook. "Aah!" he breathed as he tossed his hat on the greensward and threw himself in a wicker chair, "This is the life, Henry. Peace and quiet. Fresh air."

"I thought you were enjoying the fresh air of Angushire," said the solicitor.

"I was . . . but business brought me back to London."

"So I see!" Sir Henry tapped his portfolio. "This is why I asked for a meeting. These bills! May I inquire—does Lady Laura know what you're up to?"

"Of course. The bills are for my wife's orders."

"You took thirty thousand pounds to Scotland. I regret to appear . . . inquisitive, but I am still bound by your grannys' will. Where did the thirty thousand run to?"

"Oh," Duff-Drummond waved his hand. "Here . . . there . . . a mass of projects! Laura is building, you know. Big program! She begged me to come to London and make purchases, gave me free hand! The dear gel is beginning to see my point of view—what use is money in the bank? Circulation! That's our motto—circulation." Duff-Drummond seemed to have run out of arguments.

But Sir Henry was not satisfied. "I understood Lady Laura was to send me her signature for all money payments."

"Is that what's bothering you my dear Henry? Here!" Duff-Drummond handed over his usual—"Dear Henry, please . . ."

"But . . . Colin!"

"No sermons, Henry! My wife is the keeper of my fortune, is she not? She's executrix . . . stewardess . . . paymistress? If she sees fit to spend on threshing-mills, factories for Highland lavender water, Ayrshire cattle and syllabi for beginners, who are we to say no?"

"You'd find a way out of Tantalus' cave, wouldn't you, Colin!" exclaimed the ruffled Sir Henry. It was plain that Duff-Drummond had added some new tricks to his bag of old ones—purchasing agent indeed! Why didn't Lady Laura avail herself of a bona fide agent, the firm of Sir Henry Banks, whose honest and painstaking hand could reach into every avenue of trade or supply and buy at rock-bottom price? But a woman in love was blind! Blind in more ways than one!

"How is your wife's health?"

"Excellent. The incubation proceeds normally."

"Do you plan to join her soon?"

Duff-Drummond gave his old friend an under-the-lid look. "Come, come Henry, what else do you wish to know, the date of my son's christening?"

"Or your daughter!" said Sir Henry. It was a barbed shaft that made the Laird wince.

Colin left in a huff. Sir Henry knew he'd added a passenger to his friend's elegant turn-out—a passenger named Doubt. But it served Colin right.

Driving back to town in the cool of afternoon, Duff-Drummond's thoughts took a dark turn. Newmarket—Blue Boy with a bad ankle, Judd screaming for more substantial payments, what a waste to pay a money-lender, they

gripped you all the tighter! And money was everywhere—
even little Jinny Baird had hit a gold vein! She'd hooked
old Lolly Sitley, richest man in England except . . . Duff-
Drummond was too superstitious to say "myself." He
hadn't his million yet! Oft when the fun was at its height,
Diana, Arabella, Jane, Maude taking turns in his arms, he
was brought up by the same tormenting thought Henry
Banks had suggested, "or a daughter?" It would be world's
end if Laura failed to give him a son.

Only yesterday, he'd broken with common sense and
sneaked off like a lovelorn stable-boy to see a Gypsy.

MADAM SAYA—said a black sign. He'd expected to find
a hag with poll-parrot and black cat—Madam Saya was
young, with cherry lips, flashing black eyes and the supple
hands of a tambourine dancer.

"Come in, milord!" Her long, pleated skirt of orange silk
rustled across the neatly swept floor. There was no parrot,
no black cat. An aroma of spiced cooking filled the air.

"Pray sit down, milord." The Romany waved him to a
chair with the grace of a princess. "The tarots, milord!
Does milord come with a problem of the heart?"

"All I wish to know . . . the sex of my coming child!"

Brilliant eyes that had taken stock of his clothes now
fixed upon his signet ring. Duff-Drummond knew the
reputation of Romany fortune-tellers—traders in blackmail
as well as in black magic. He regretted not having turned
the signet around; there were those who could read a
coat-of-arms and so identify the wearer.

Madam Saya's nimble fingers had laid out the tarots.
"Milord wants a son?"

"I want to know which it will be?"

"Milord is a daring sportsman who has luck at his preferred sport." Well, that was an easy guess. He'd come in
riding boots, with a riding crop in hand—it was likely too
that the Romany could detect a lingering stable scent.

"That is not what I asked."

"Milord is beloved by many women," murmured Madam Saya. "I see a lady with dark hair, another with hair like gold, a third—"

"I am not here for heart prescriptions, Madam Saya. Can your cards tell me what I wish to know?"

The Romany's white teeth flashed in a smile. She pointed with her index. "See that card? It warns of disaster. Milord must take care!"

"Shall we come to the point?" he prompted.

The Romany had placed three more cards on the table. "Ah! Here he is! The Knave of Hearts . . . son you hope for. He will not be fair-haired like his mother—"

"How'd you know the mother was fair-haired?"

"Milord just told me!" the Romany answered. "Is there anything more milord wishes to know?"

He'd dropped a sovereign on the table, taken hat, stick and his leave. To believe a Romany fortune-teller was madness—but what if these descendants of ancient Egypt did have seers' powers? A son! If only one could be sure!

Duff-Drummond swung into the park, but this time he could take small pleasure from the admiring gaze of the strollers.

Of all the ills that hurt a man's peace, pressed his soul, wrung his mind, surely worry was the worst! One could take a pill for a sluggish liver—what cure for the worrier?

Here 'twas only the beginning of August. Presuming his wife had conceived after consummation of the nuptial vow on February 18th, or any time immediately thereafter, her delivery could not be before November. Would Judd wait? The rascal had due-bills mountain-high. Tailor and haberdasher, saddler and feed-merchant, jeweler, decorator, cabinet-maker, old Tat, screamin' for payment on recent purchases of horse flesh—and that necklace for Maude Lowes, greedy, handsome thing!

There was worse—Judd had collected m'lud's "small"

outstanding debts—consolidating he called it. Loans for
card debts and racing bets. Gad! Even debts of creditors
like Osborne the whip-maker! But Duff-Drummond had
forestalled the "consolidation" of Osborne by quick
thinking.

"How'd you like to go to Angushire and set up a manu-
factory of buck horn? Teach my men how to polish horn
and work wood and leather? Five hundred pounds outlay
. . . all the horn and hide and wood you want!"

It had taken old Osborne a week to let the idea sink
into his Perthshireman's brain. Now he was on his
way with his three whip-maker sons and a lame saddler, expert in setting the horn on the stick. There wasn't
another man in the Isles who could put the zing into a
whip like Osborne. One more plaything for Laura—Oh,
yes! He must remember to send for Boggs, the bookseller,
answer Laura's recent letter in which she inquired about
Third Readers for adults. She was hell-bent on going
through with her plan to make scholars of Angusmen and
women; the devil only knew what she'd cook up next.

Reverend Macbride and Dr. Jamie Ayre had become
fast friends who worked hand-in-glove to break down su-
perstition and encourage new endeavor. 'Twas Reverend
Macbride who advised sending to England for the first
schoolmaster ever to be seen in the Braes of Angus. "Our
people know the Gael, they must learn English!" The reverend had a preacher friend in Devon. The preacher had
a promising son who'd been trained for teaching.

More and more, Laurie was forced to leave the practical
program of planning and change in other hands. Her steward worked in harmony with Bailiff Malcolm and the Reverend Macbride. Any doubts she'd had that the Highland
folk would take to a London steward-of-the-household
were at rest when she saw how well Cibber got along
with the people of Duff-Drummond. Perhaps it was true

that a plain man knows an honest man on sight. Cibber was never overbearing, always kind, always ready to listen to a grievance. His businesslike manner won the confidence of everyone. A man without a grain of humor, he was molded by Nature to rule that strange below-stairs kingdom where life is carried on in patterns quite as exacting as those of a royal court. In less than a fortnight he had the staff complete, the Rock running like a well-oiled clock. And his knowledge was quite as astonishing as his tact in dealing with the dour men of Angus, especially when newcomers like a French perfume-maker named Pierre Vachon and his helper, one André Bérard, came trudging up the valley with mysterious packs on their backs.

Their speech, their looks put the inhabitants on guard "agin' foreigners."

"These men are sent by the Laird," Cibber explained in his gentle ways—he always set the Laird's authority and name foremost—"They are going to set up an industry for making Highland lavender water." Angusmen looked askance until André Bérard, who was a worker in clay and trained to know the properties of the soil, discovered a bed of limestone twelve feet thick on the Northeast side of Ben Fada.

"What can one do with limestone?" asked Laurie when her steward made the report. Even Cibber could not help smiling. "Enrich the land, your ladyship, to make the fields increase in yield and quality of crops. Lime can also be used for making mortar and to lime-cast a building. By steeping hides in a lime-pit, the hair is removed. Lime is a precious quality in water and makes sound teeth. May I also suggest that milady look at a sample of red earth Bérard brought from a place about a mile down the valley and not far from the stream bed. He says it is fine brick earth. I heard Mr. Forbes speak of bringing building materials to the braes. He mentioned that there was graystone

234

in the hills but that it would take years to cut enough for the schoolhouses, whereas a brick kiln would be a simple matter."

"Build out of brick!" cried Laurie in excitement. "We could build faster . . . stronger . . . not only the schoolhouse, the cottages too! A brick house with a slate roof—that would be a change! I like floors, windows with glass, a door that closes. I like a shed out back for washing and drying. Tell me, Cibber, would it not be feasible to build an outdoor comfort house of brick . . . with a hole in the ground? I once saw a picture . . ."

"It is quite feasible, milady," Cibber answered with a repressed smile.

"Then I'll write my husband to ask his builder to draw a plan of a pretty brick cottage—say, with kitchen and two rooms or three for sleeping."

"Milady would have her people 'in mansions dwell,'" quoted Cibber. He added, "Milady need not write the Laird. There are Angusmen who know how to use plumbline and rule. I suggest that milady let each head of family decide how large a house he needs, also that Bailiff Malcolm and I be permitted to plan the financial outlay. Milady must remember that someday her people will have to face the problem of paying higher rents. The cost must be measured against their ability to pay. If milady will pardon a man of figures and accounts, milady seems to take little heed of that side of the problem."

"You are right, Cibber," Laurie agreed, "all I know is that by default more than intention the Laird has long been in debt to his people and that he can now make good the obligation." Fearing to have gone too far, Laurie changed the subject abruptly. "How long will it take to build a kiln and start making bricks?"

"Not too long if milady calls upon all hands to help. The clay must be dug and brought to the kiln."

"Why not build the kiln near the clay?"

235

"It is more practical to do the opposite, milady, build the kiln near the source of labor. Then there is also the problem of fuel. We shall have to cut—"

"Cut nothing!" cried Laurie sharply. "You may bring fuel pony-back from Montrose."

"But the cost, milady!"

"The Laird cares nothing what it costs." As Laurie spoke she wondered if she were saying the truth. But it was too late to turn back.

Where had Cibber learned about tree-planting and other useful things pertaining to husbandry?

"Take no more seedlings than you can handle, men and women," said Cibber in his friendly way. "This is only a beginning. Don't overreach. The Laird wants the trees planted right. It is best to dig a hole four feet wide and four feet deep. Fill with moss and dung and throw in a piece of rusty iron if you can."

How true that Lady Inverkleith's gold was like manna to hungry wayfarers in the desert of Knowledge! There was no place where money could not do wonders.

Laurie's closest ally and most useful adviser was the Reverend Macbride. Never a pulpit-ranter, the spiritual leader of the Five Villages was a man of modern thought and foresight. "Gie our people hard toil and decent earning. Gie 'em what to build for. A view into the future. Betterment of their poor lot."

The reverend was of the opinion that a council of elders should be called. "One man from each village. Let your ladyship hear what they have to say. Test their doubts and listen to their suggestions."

At first, the elders were reluctant to believe that her ladyship's ideas for reforms and improvements were sincere. They marched into the parley room like pallbearers at a funeral, sat down and glowered. Laurie had seen them all before. The occasion was quite different. A trembling girl had stood before her secret seducer. Talk was of violent death and where the blame lay.

"I bade you elders come, because I want your counsel."

"Deeds, your ladyship, nae worr-rds are wh' a Scotsmon craves," broke in Abraham Warrack of Fairlie.

"Aye!" Donald Carmeichel of Ben Leva agreed.

"Aye!" said Neil Cotts of Cortach.

"Aye!" said John Endricht of Grailie.

"So say I," echoed Angus Pherson of Ben Fada.

These five were the chosen spokesmen of the villages— the Elders, so-called—though only Cotts and Endricht could be called old. Carmeichel of Ben Leva, Pherson of Ben Fada, Warrack of Fairlie were knotty men in their prime, solid as the rocks of Stonehenge.

Donald Carmeichel sucked in his weatherbeaten cheeks. Neil Cotts coughed loudly, Abraham Warrack seemed to be waiting to hear more.

"The Laird plans to make many important changes. As you know, the Laird's grandmother, Lady Inverkleith, died and left money to spend on improving the lands. She was a woman of vast enterprise."

"Aye! Tha' she must 'a bin!" said Donald Carmeichel with a foxy smile. A chuckle greeted his sally.

"You do not believe me, sirs! The Laird Chieftain wishes to build a school for the free use of his tenants. He will build a modern wool mill and other factories. Each crofter will receive fruit trees for planting and a number of chickens. New milch cows are on the way, also five thousand of the best Merino sheep money can buy."

Abraham Warrack raised his hand. "Beggin' your ladyship's leave, why dinna the Laird say a' this ere he hasted awa' to Lunnun!"

"Aye!" spoke up Pherson. "Do 'e intend to raise our rents to pay for a' this gash?"

"Not one penny," said Laurie firmly. "Quite the contrary, some rents will be cut."

237

There was a long silence; doubting eyes spoke more eloquently than words. Laurie decided to make an about-face. "Men of Duff-Drummond, I ask your help. Tell me your needs, what *you* think can be done to provide a better living and keep the young people from leaving the braes?"

"Our roofs leak!" Elder Warrack answered. "Our cots are fallin' to ruins!"

"Re-open the slate quarry!" suggested Elder Donald Carmeichel.

"Who will work the quarry?" objected old John Endricht. "We've not even wedgin' tools, let alone workers!"

"And who will pay the wage?" Neil Cotts grumbled.

"The Laird," Malcolm answered.

John Endricht slapped the air like a man set upon by hornets. "I dinna believe! I canna gie ear to miracles!"

But soon they came to believe even in miracles. On orders from her ladyship, Malcolm reviewed contracts with the crofters, setting back rents and cutting tithes in half. A cavalcade of ponies did more to convince the doubters than a thousand promises. On their sturdy backs were roped an assortment of objects the likes of which had never been seen in the braes—tools, machines, a forge, a new kind of slow-burning stove to heat a building at moderate cost, a threshing mill that young Warrack adopted for his own.

Laurie poured her love and her news into letters to her husband.

> Send more and more tree plantings Dear Heart. Half a century of continuous planting will rid the land of bog and swamp dampness and clear up the persistent malady of ague that afflicts our peasantry as well as softening the rough climate of an unprotected land.

Was it foolish to write daily about such simple things as the Ayreshire herds that came straggling up the glen to be met with welcome of bagpipes and rejoicing of population? On the same page, details of school building costs and at page end, her loneliness and longing.

> I love you so Colin, my heart has shrunk with emptiness. Sweetheart of my life . . . I kiss your dear lips.

Colin answered.

> I thank you for keeping me posted on progress. I sent a new kind of stove that burns with even, slow heat but it can be made to give out a high degree of heat also. I long to embrace you, my sweet wife. . . . How is your health? Remember your condition and do not overdo.

Laurie's eyes sped to the bottom of the page. When . . . when would her husband come?

> I cannot make a start at this time . . . but soon, I hope . . .
> p.s. I enclose an account of recent purchases.
> A prize Ayreshire bull and six
> heifers £1200.14s 5d
> Twenty-eight work horses £2150. 4s 3d
> Twenty sacks of winter wheat
> seed .... £ 11. 3s 2d
> Andrew Miekle's new patent
> threshing-mill .... £ 300.12s 3d
> To Boggs and Sons, Booksellers:
> Three dozen Primers ⎫
> Three dozen First Readers ⎬ £ 16. 8s 4d
> Three dozen Second Readers ⎪
> Three dozen Third Readers ⎭

Perhaps if Colin knew how soon the child was due he'd not delay. Laurie began to wonder if bright-eyed Dr. Jamie Ayre were not aware of her advanced condition?

She put the query casually. "How soon may I expect the baby?"

"Can your ladyship give me exact dates?" said Dr. Ayre, "I know 'twill be sometime early in September but a precise review would help."

So—Dr. Jamie did know! Laurie answered with a blush. "My last period was December tenth."

"Just as I thought," said the physician matter-of-factly. "Your ladyship may expect delivery the first fortnight in September."

Medical calculus was barren stuff compared to memories of burning nights—tiptoe expeditions through the chilly corridors of Hathmore House—secret meetings with her lover. Laurie seemed to hear the creak of a door-hinge—the beloved's whisper, "May I come in!"

Day by day, she looked forward to her husband's return. She would hide her ungainly figure beneath a shawl of finest Highland weave. The old Rock gay with fall foliage. Knowing the exact day—he'd write of course, a watcher would be set upon the cliff—she'd call together a band of children to welcome their Laird with streamers and flowers. Oh, what a glad, glad moment!

The twentieth of August a courier came from London. Laurie seized upon her husband's letter with hands gone clumsy.

> SWEET WIFE,
>
> I had the good fortune to purchase another herd of fine Ayreshire cattle that I've sent by ship, via Montrose. I trust your condition is good and your spirits high. It will be impossible for me to go North at this time . . . hoping to be with you soon, say sometime around October 1st.
>
> I remain, your fond,
>
> COLIN.

Laurie wept. October would be too late. She needed her husband's support and love. What to do? Write a half-lie—the baby will be premature? No! No! The brave way, the right way, tell no lies, stop pining for the absent one, live as Nature ruled, for the child and for the child alone.

Laurie was too shaken to sit at the prayerful laying of the corner-stone for the school building. She feared she'd break down from weakness and shed tears before the assembled clansmen and their wives.

The school would be rushed to completion before the winter snows.

Young schoolmaster Daniel Clovelly from Ilfracombe in Devon brought his first report to her ladyship. Forty-seven children were eager to enter classes. Twenty-five adults were clamoring for instruction at evening classes.

"We'll soon have pupils enough to fill a school in each of the Five Villages," said schoolmaster Clovelly. The report gave Laurie deep satisfaction. This was right. This was as it should be.

"I've three scholars outstanding," said Mr. Clovelly.

"Let me guess!" smiled Laurie. "One is Davy the poet."

"Yes, milady. The lad has extraordinary talent, I might even say genius. He's already mastered his letters with but a little help from me. But we need books . . . books and more books!"

Laurie remembered the vast, shadowy library in Hathmore House—thousands and thousands of tomes gathering dust.

"We'll have books before long. Lots of 'em. Who are the other two promising pupils?"

"A girl named Nan," said the schoolmaster. "Doctor Ayre sent her to me. She shows remarkable aptitude for sick-care. Ayre is quite smitten with her blond charms! And there's a youth of Fairlie named Abraham Warrack, son of Elder Warrack."

It never occurred to Laurie until Mr. Clovelly pointed it out that mechanical genius was also inborn.

"'Machines! Tha's wha' we need,' young Abe Warrack says," said the schoolmaster. "He talks of water conduits, dams, container walls for places where the casual eye sees only trickling brook, a pond, a rain-bitten shoulder of earth. One might well dub him our Highland Leonardo! Warrack should have tools, a forge, a blast furnace, a thousand-weight of pig iron to work with instead of scratching the earth for a meager crop. Here's an example of his native understanding. One day I sketched a rough outline of a steam boiler. Much to my amazement, he asked no questions. 'Aye,' he mumbled as he studied the drawing, 'fire under a kettle. The steam fills the emptiness, but it canna escape e'er it gies the push! Power cooms frae tha' push. Aye! A mon cude move a mountain wi' sich a machine.' What would Laddie Abe say if he could study the drawings of Jamie Watts' inventions, see his steam-driven carrier that supplants the horse-drawn vehicle?"

Mr. Clovelly's explanations were incomprehensible to Laurie but one thing she did grasp. Even though at present young Abraham Warrack could neither read nor write, with the help of an enthusiast like the schoolmaster, he would soon learn.

At last Laurie had all the time she needed for reading. She read the Bible more often than any other book. Evenings, she sat by the fire and dreamed. The child would be a boy, of course; his name, Donald Duff-Drummond of Gillian and Barra! She was not afraid. She'd learned from the Albinus folios what to expect and how the child would be brought into the world—or so she thought. The reality was quite different! A week before the birth, heavy rains fell and deprived her of her daily outings. Her spirits sank. She longed for her husband with bitter longing.

The babe's weight had increased unbearably. She found

herself wishing for the moment when she would be light and free again.

"You need not fear," said Doctor Jamie, "you are in splendid condition."

The last day she awoke at dawn and as she lay staring at the ceiling, she felt an ache between those two wing-shaped bones that the Albinus told her were the pelvis. Thinking that perhaps she had slept in an awkward position, she arose and began moving about as usual. But though the ache seemed to go, she felt a sensation as of a hand, gripping her lower spine from the inside.

"Call Doctor Ayre," she said to her maid as soon as she got her breath.

He came at once. "This may be your time," he said, with a reassuring smile. "Now lie back and let go! Banish all thought of fear. This is woman's greatest moment, her happiest, if she meets it in the right frame of mind."

The doctor had transformed the Laird's bedroom into a snug, clean "spital" room. Here in this bed, Laurie had lain with her love—here she'd bear his child.

Not even a queen could have better care and attendance. Doctor Ayre and Mother Spencer the midwife, Nanny Biel and the young nursemaid of her choice. This "Nanny" had recently lost her bairn. Nanny Biel pronounced her name "Mengies," though it was written "Menzies." The bereft woman's pride and happiness to serve "the little Laird" were touching.

The Rs rippled from Mother Spencer's tongue and she'd an iron hand that did not go with her round, pink face, china blue eyes, her crinkly white hair, her ready smile.

"Coom now, your ladyship, sit there patient!" she said, "I'll rr-ready the bed, i' the pr-r-roper way."

Laurie sat in an easy chair clasping her arms about her enormous belly while Mother Spencer and the doctor placed three wide, wooden boards on top of the mattress and a quilt on top of the boards—then Nanny Menzies and

Mother Spencer covered boards and mattress with three layers of spotless linen sheets.

"Coom now!" said Mother Spencer, "to bed wi' ye!" She covered her patient lightly.

"Try to melt on those boards, your ladyship," said Doctor Jamie.

"Melt? They're hard as . . . as boards!" Laurie laughed in spite of herself.

"Butter can melt on a board. So must you."

"Very well, I'll try."

"Mind you breathe easily . . . steadily. Breathe in and out like a climber going up a mountain."

"Like a climber?"

Laurie tried to melt. Then in imagination, she began to climb the Rock. Here she was at the turn of the path. She could see granite walls towering above her clear to the sky.

"Drink this, my bonnie," said Mother Spencer. It was sweetened barley water.

The pains came every now and then. Laurie found that she could draw several long, easy breaths in between and this brought back her strength for the next one. Neither Doctor Ayre nor Mother Spencer spoke as they busied themselves with their duties.

Laurie could hear the fire crackling on the hearth. An age of time passed—time that she could count by the ebb and flow of the labor. Why was the path to the Rock so steep! She began to fidget and pant.

Looking down at her, Mother Spencer nodded and said approvingly, "You're making fine headway!"

"How long, Doctor?" whispered Laurie after a long pain.

"Less than you think!"

"How long?"

"Four . . . five hours."

"So little?" she gasped in relief. She'd thought it would

be longer. The Albinus folio showed birth in three stages—the first stage, the opening or widening of the cervix; the second stage, from full opening to the pushing out of the babe; and the third stage, from the birth to the pushing out of the afterbirth.

"The doctor will be back soon," said Mother Spencer when Doctor Jamie left the room.

The path to the Rock was steeper—but steeper to the Laird himself! Would she ever reach him? Why had she chosen a hot day for the climb? Mother Spencer wiped the sweat from her brow with a cloth wrung out in vinegar and herb extract.

It seemed suddenly that all pain was gone.

"I . . . I feel nothing!" she gasped in amazement.

"Good! Now for the delivery!" Doctor Jamie washed and washed his hands in the basin. Why didn't he hurry?

The pain came back—a different kind of pain this time, not so great that she couldn't bear it. She wondered if she were more fortunate than others? Often she'd heard the women in the Royal Scot kitchens describing childbirth with gory detail and harrowing grimace.

"Push and bear down, my bonnie," said Mother Spencer, as she pressed her iron hands against the small of her patient's back, almost lifting her off the board bed. "Take hold of my shoulders and push and bear down!" Was the end near? Later, Laurie was to smile at her false hope.

Now she could climb the Rock only on hands and knees. Every stone bruised! But the tower was there. In the tower . . . Colin waited. She longed to touch the cold granite walls and feel the rough texture of the stone under her palm . . . then to grasp her husband's hand!

"Let loose and scream an' ye will, my bonnie!" said Mother Spencer. Laurie did not need to be told. There was relief in a good scream—relief from nature's rack and wheel on which she was riding. Her cries were not from pain—she felt little pain! All she wanted was to reach the topmost stone of the Rock, there to lay her babe in her husband's arms. And in the midst of this fantasy of climbing she remembered the Albinus—first the babe's head. She pushed with might and main!

"Out! Out, son!" she screamed. It never occurred to her that the child might be a daughter.

"Look," said Mother Spencer, lifting her head, "a wee bairn!"

The babe shone with pearly luster. Joined to herself by the cord, he moved one tiny foot. She saw the flash of deft scissors. Snowdrop soft and mild, the child was free—born, living, perfect! She closed her eyes and pushed once more as Doctor Jamie told her, feeling no more unease, only weariness and longing to be alone.

Nanny Biel brought the swaddled child. "'Twas the stroke o' the day when he coom," she said, "a good omen!"

Dark of hair, her son was the blessed "first-foot" of the morning. He had crossed the earthy threshold a quarter after the stroke of midnight. Laurie turned away. Where was her Laird? Was love a scorn that man could so lightly toss it aside! Then while she kept out her dark thoughts, loud and proud, a piper began to play. She saw the flame of clavie fire dancing on the walls of the room. The clansmen had come to honor their future Duinne Uassel. They filled the hall, the steps, the corridor outside the bedchamber!

"Who is the piper?" asked Laurie through her tears.

"I never saw him before, your ladyship," said Nanny Biel, "but Davy is carrying the clavie and his face is blacker than Beltane from the smoke of the tar. Does the racket annoy your ladyship? I'll send 'em awa'."

"Let them stay. Have Cibber break out a barrel of uisgha, that they may drink to little Sir Donald's health."

The day after the birth, Laurie dispatched the physi-

cian's certificate of her son's birth to London, in care of
Sir Henry Banks. She could not bring herself to add a
word—later, she'd write the absent one . . . the careless
one!

Seventeen

The Laird's Ship Comes In

CERTAINLY THE SPIRITS OF THE EAST AND WEST ANGLICAN tribes were abroad in Newmarket country this morning! Paddocks and stables lost in fog, fog hanging in the trees, billowing on the meadow-edge, creeping along the hedges, spears of rain slanting down, the chill struck to the very bone!

Duff-Drummond drew his chin into the warmth of his greatcoat collar, flexed and unflexed cold fingers in his pockets, stomped and muttered his discomfort. "Mind Philemon doesn't take a chill when he's through with his gallop!"

" 'Sfair damp, that it is," Trainer Tom Cannon agreed, "I'd kep' 'im in the paddock, but he wanted to run!" The big bay swung around the turn. Tom Cannon hailed Jockey Vyner. "Bring 'em in!"

In the chill of this rain-drenched morning Duff-Drummond eyed the horse with no interest. He stood motionless, his thoughts groping, troubled, drawing from some depth of spirit a sense of weariness, boredom.

Philemon had come to glory on the turf. Acclaimed the greatest horse since Eclipse, he left all competitors so far behind that—in the words of an old crone who had witnessed his victory at Epsom—"I seen a bay horse runnin' at a monstrous rate. Then I seen another horse a great way behind, tryin' to catch 'im"; but she was sure he would never catch the bay if he "run to world's end."

Winning was not the whole of it. Duff-Drummond had tossed his winnings back into his racing establishment, letting Tom Cannon take on more studs, more racing stock, more men and boys for paddock and stables. He now had twenty new brood mares, and forty to fifty yearlings, five new stallions, twenty-eight cart horses. The latter were constantly employed to do necessary work upon the training course and gallops, removing soil, rolling turf, making roads and carting tar. Tom Cannon fed his young stock which was "still in the gristle and not yet hardened into the bone of maturity" the finest Scottish oats, imported from the Carse o' Gowrie, and old hay mixed with carrots or vetches. The foals were given rich Alderney milk and tempting foods were set within their reach. All this cost a mint o' money!

The end of the racing season found the owner with empty pockets, bills piling high, Judd crying, "Foreclosure!" If only he could be sure the child would be a son!

Cursing himself for an idiot, Duff-Drummond had played it heads or tails, counting the number of stallion colts in his stables, counting the number of children playing along the wayside—whether boys or girls were the most in number! To see a man first thing in the morning was a good omen, the opposite—bad! He nursed his own foolish beliefs and superstitions with ill-temper for no confidence could be derived from them, any more than respite from his money worries could be found in the sorcery or promise of a Romany gypsy.

A calendar carried in his pocket was marked with crosses—a cross for each month except November which he marked day by day. Laura's delivery should not be later than November. He had calculated the time it would take for the news to reach London. Bad weather would slow the mails. Taking count of every accident, he should know the best or the worst by December first.

"Comin', milord?" said Tom Cannon. He had tossed a

thick blanket over the bay stallion and sent him back to his stall.

Duff-Drummond stomped through the fog. How long could a man endure the uncertainty? His nerves were ready to snap. What was today? Only September 24th? How much longer must one wait . . .

"A mon coom fra Lunnon', Laird," said gillie Fergus, catching his master's hat on the fly as he entered the cottage.

"London? Where is he?"

"I' the kitchen, Laird."

"Fetch him!"

The "mon" was a messenger from Sir Henry Banks. He carried a sealed letter from the Braes—

> Born this day of Our Lord, September 16, 1806
> to Laura Macneil
> and Colin, Lord Duff-Drummond of Gillian and
> Barra, a son, Donald.

"I've got a son!" Duff-Drummond muttered thickly. Wild clamoring in his brain—the years of waiting to lay hands on Granny's million! Nine months' guesswork! Nine months? But the babe was born September 16th! That either made him a seven-months-old child or Laura had been caught before their marriage! By the Great Horned Filibuck, she had! He knew when—'twas that night—aye! Now it was clear why she'd run away! She feared the shame! Poor gel! He'd have married her all the sooner! A million pounds for one lucky strike! From now on he'd spit on money-lenders! He'd thumb his nose at every female, young or old, who ever tried to shackle his hands, bend his will, force his affections! "Colin do this . . . Colin do that!" *By the gods, from now on nobody would tell him what to do!* He was a free man! A rich man! A man with a million pounds! The master turned to his gillie and said with a shaking voice, "Bring around my horse. We'll ride to Newmarket and catch the Night Mail to London."

Unshaven and uncombed, Duff-Drummond swaggered into his solicitor's chambers. Sir Henry had just sat down to peruse the morning mail; his client's disheveled appearance startled him. "Colin! Has something gone wrong?"

"Something's gone right at last! Henry! I've got a son!" Duff-Drummond flung himself into a chair like a man winded from a race.

Sir Henry shook his hand. "Congratulations, Colin! But it's no surprise to me . . . a wife like Lady Laura!" And to himself the solicitor was saying, "Like the devil, Colin gets what he wants! How does he do it? Always to get what he wants when he wants it and with no sacrifice to himself!" "Mother and child in good health?" he queried aloud.

"So I presume." Duff-Drummond handed the birth certificate across the desk. "Legalize this, Henry . . . do the right thing . . . the boy's name up for Eton and Oxford . . . you know."

"With pleasure, Colin!" Sir Henry awaited his client's next demand. It came without delay.

"About the release of Granny's money . . . ?"

"It shall be done at once. Your signature is all that is needed at Barclay's Bank."

Duff-Drummond looked as though he could not believe his ears. "All the money?"

"Well . . . as for deposits . . . there's over six hundred thousand to your account. The remainder is in real estate, and stock in the India Company. I'll render a complete statement. But remember, yours and Lady Laura's expenditures since your marriage have mounted to quite a penny, fifty-nine thousand and over."

Duff-Drummond rose. "Do me another favor, Henry. Write to inform Lady Laura of the change, that I am now keeper of the purse! Ask for a precise list of her spending. Naturally, I shall not continue to sprinkle the braes with my good money!"

Sir Henry Banks could not but marvel at Duff-Drummond's single-mindedness. "Do you not intend to go to Scotland for the christening?"

"I . . . ? No. I'll leave domestic ceremonial to my wife and the clan. Long live the Albanach!"

"What is the Albanach?"

"A man of Scotland." Duff-Drummond yawned cavernously. "I'm weary to the bone. This windfall comes in the nick of time. My favorite money-lender was on the verge of puttin' the seals on Gin Lodge and all my nags. He drools when he sees Philemon run! Fancies himself a turfman, Judd does. Now he'll have to close out some other victim."

Sir Henry had never seen Duff-Drummond's handsome face shine as it did now—not with the tender glow of fatherhood, but with the satanic light of greed!

Duff-Drummond hired a hackney to Portland Place— the d'Alboli palace. He felt the need of a mature woman's understanding—he was shaken to the core by the events of the past twenty-four hours.

"Di-di!"—his favorite name for his earliest mistress. "Congratulate me. I've just come into my million."

"*Mon coeur!*" Diana sometimes affected the French language, sometimes the Italian. "I congratulate you from the bottom of a heart that burns for you, as it has always burned. Come, *amor mio.* Come upstairs, shave . . . bathe . . . we'll lunch and talk."

Cleansed and restored to his normal temper, Duff-Drummond viewed his mistress through the ruby-tinted wineglass, remarking to himself how a shade more coloring spoiled her fetching pallor. Di-di's ivory—her rivals called it sallow—skin was her greatest pride. More delicate than parchment, softer than the petal of a tea-rose, her complexion had the texture of a portrait by Leonardo—indeed, Diana took from the *cinquecento* rather than from the world of moderns!

"Amor mio!" Di-di rose and wreathed soft arms around her lover's neck. "Come . . . rest awhile."

But Duff-Drummond was not in the mood for Di-di's "rest."

"Forgive me, love! I've a rendezvous with my banker."

"But, amor . . . why? The day is young and I've been lonely."

"I can't stay," said Duff-Drummond trying to extricate himself from the lock of his lady's tenacious fingers.

"Darling . . . a half-hour with thy Di-di? Please . . ."

Duff-Drummond surrendered, but without the usual rapture in Di-di's embrace. Somehow everything was changed—or was it he that had changed? Her kisses seemed insipid, unwanted.

And Di-di was famed for never having enough! "Kiss me! Again! Again! Angelo! Caro! Adorato!"

Och! So much blather! Duff-Drummond shook his limbs free of ivory-tinted limbs that snaked around him.

"I *must* go, Di-di."

"When shall I see you again?" said the naked lady, trailing him to the door. "Tomorrow? The day after? Promise me, love! The day after tomorrow, for dinner."

"Beautiful no longer!" thought Duff-Drummond as he looked down into the pleading woman's face. "She's like a much-traveled road—no surprises. No new vistas."

He escaped into the fresh air. Today, he was all a-jangle. There was one woman though, a woman whose conversation never cloyed.

Mrs. Maude Lowes was not an unusual figure in London society, a woman of undistinguished origin who had come up in the world by means of her brazen courage and court jester's wit. She'd married three husbands; the last died obscurely on an Indian battlefield. All three were poor men. But Maude had sources of revenue—her rich lovers. She'd sucked Duff-Drummond like an egg, and he'd sucked the money-lenders for her sake.

Before going to call on Maude, Duff-Drummond drove to Carewe the jeweler in Bond Street.

"I'd like earrings to match the necklace I bought . . . remember that ruby trinket, Mr. Carewe."

He selected the jewels then asked, "Show me what you have in christening cups."

One cup caught his eye—plain, handsome. "Engrave it with my arms . . . pack it for shipment to Scotland. It's for my newborn son."

Mrs. Lowes' butler said madame was at home.

"You're lucky!" thought Duff-Drummond as he walked into his hostess' sitting room.

"Why?" said Maude with a welcoming smile.

"This." Duff-Drummond tossed a jewel box into her lap. Yes, Maude knew how to flatter and pamper a man into tiptop humor. She never asked before—only afterward did she fire her guns.

"Darling . . ." murmured the lady in the gathering twilight, "I find myself somewhat embarrassed . . . a nasty streak of bad luck."

"How much?" said Duff-Drummond resignedly and he congratulated himself that Maude was the only woman in his deer park who had ever called him for funds.

"Two thousand . . . say three."

"Nasty streak indeed!"

"I'll pay you back," said Maude with the aplomb of a pickpocket.

"Of course. Of course, my love." Duff-Drummond was in a hurry to leave before some new caprice was born.

"Colin," said Maude, "have you given any more thought to our plan to be married as soon as your son is born?"

"No, my sweet."

Duff-Drummond went home in a sour frame of mind, changed and drove to his club where the first person he met was Krik Fordyce.

"The heir has arrived, Krik."

"A boy? Bless me! What good news! Lady Laura's health?"

"Excellent."

"Congratulations, Colin. When are you leaving?"

"Leaving?"

"For Scotland?"

"Look here, Krik," said Duff-Drummond irritably. "Why take it for granted that I'm to trace off to Scotland?"

"But . . . your wife . . . your son?"

Colin's chin set in a familiar thrust that Krik Fordyce knew all too well. "Present my compliments to Lady Laura when you write," he said and strolled away.

His appetite for cards failing, Duff-Drummond dined alone and went home to bed. Fatigue closed his eyelids immediately. He did not waken until sunrise—damn it, why couldn't he sleep until noon? He'd nothing to do— nothing at all, except to go to the bank and get money, pay a money-lender—vastly uninteresting! How much more stimulating to draw foils with Judd and fence it out—"Can I or can't I get an extension of my loan?"

Duff-Drummond turned over with a flop, and watched a ray of the sun point like a golden wand to his desk on which was piled a mountain of unopened letters. The sunray inched along the wall and across the satin coverlet, swinging slowly upward until it smote the would-be sleeper in the eye. It stole across the headboard and slanted downward to the rug—a fly buzzed into the heart of a woolen rose woven in far Turkestan, preened gossamer wings, scraped tiny feet, rubbed its pin-head and buzzed away.

The racing calendar ended—damn Philemon who ran

odds-even from victory to victory, making his owner monotonously the winner.

Duff-Drummond hung on the bell-pull and when gillie Fergus answered his ring, "My bath . . . the new coat with shot gray silk revers . . ." yawned the Master.

"Aye, Laird!" Fergus placed a letter on the desk. The letter bore the seal of the Duke of Hamilton.

> DEAR SIR COLIN,
>
> Will you do me the honor of dining at Marbone House this Thursday, at eight? I wish to discuss a plan that I am certain is near to your heart as it is to mine . . . Scots representation in Parliament. As you know, poor Lochlinoch's death has left your shire's seat open. I'll say no more on paper but you'll grasp my meaning.
>
> > Sincerely,
> >
> > HAMILTON.

So—the old Ringmaster of the Scottish Show was trying to bring him into his circus! Duff-Drummond to stand for Angusshire in Westminster Parliament? The Duke fools himself! Why should the Duff bear Covenanters' burden? He'd write a letter . . . "Aware of Your Grace's meaning, I beg to be relieved of the honor . . . other commitments . . . pressing duties, etcetera, etcetera."

Fergus poured water into the Laird's copper tub. "Shall I pipe a wee?" he asked.

"Pipe if you will," Duff-Drummond answered. "Make it the Macrummum!"

Fergus took his favorite place on the window-box and began to sound the dirgelike wail.

"Quit it!" shouted Duff-Drummond, "D'you want to give me the megrims?"

Laurie's only comfort in loneliness was her son. Day by day, the bairn waxed stronger. She nursed him from her full breast—did he draw the milk of hope that fed her own soul? Hope that soon her husband would come to take his first-born in his arms?

She had relented and penned a wifely letter to her spouse.

> Little Donald is a beautiful child. He has your black hair and my blue eyes. Do try, dear Heart, and be here in time for the christening. Duff-Drummondmen expect and await your coming. As for me . . . I adore you! Can one say more?

Tyrant Love came with evening's soft airs to whisper the dearly Beloved's name. Fearsome the dawn, when the wakening mind starts to grope, the ear to hear, the pulse to throb, the ethereal to feel the flesh and the flesh to submit to the chain.

"Milady . . . Tam wishes to know, will your ladyship walk out today?"

"No, Pritchet."

Early and late, the strains of "Baw lula Law," "The Callum Gillie" and "Cock o' the North" poured from the pipes of Tam o'Stroma who had come to Ben Fada because he had heard that the Laird's newborn son had no piper. He had a chest like the Black Bear of the Mountains, and more wind than blows o'er Ben Muich Dhui's icebound summit. And how Tam strutted wi' the silk streamers of Duff-Drummond a-flyin' from the piob more —the great highland pipe that he played so well.

"Mail for your ladyship," said Cibber. "A parcel too." He emptied the pouch on the table.

Laurie's eye caught her husband's handwriting. She dared not open the letter in the steward's presence. When he had withdrawn, she pounced upon it.

> DEAR WIFE,
> I am rejoiced that Heaven has crowned our efforts with a son. The Christening mug here-

with, will serve the babe and later remind him of his father. I have the honor to be,

> your obedient servant,
> COLIN.

The christening mug was a beautiful thing—a christening mug and a letter!

Pritchet found her mistress lying on her bed. Beside her on the counterpane, a beautiful silver cup.

"Milady looked like she was asleep!" said Pritchet when she reported below stairs.

But Nanny Biel knew better and ran to her ladyship's chamber. "Lady . . . my sweet lass," she whispered, "Tell Nanny what's amiss?"

Laurie broke down. "The Laird isn't coming for the christening! He doesn't care! Neither does he love me!"

"Noo . . . noo . . ." comforted Nanny Biel, "I wudna say he luves thee not. Noo a mon luves . . . noo he tur-rns cauld." She added, nodding sagely, "Aye, milady, the Scotsmon is a queerr-r lot! Prr-roud like the lion, changin' like the snake i' the springtime. Peace! You have your bairn."

"I want my husband," cried Laurie.

"Patience . . ." soothed Nanny Biel. "The ram will stray, but he'll iver coom hame to the fauld."

What comfort in a folk-saying? Laurie had a more down-to-earth understanding of love—she did not care in the morning, care not in the afternoon. A plan of rebellion began to shape in her mind. Let the christening be done, then she'd take the bairn to London. Surely if Colin saw his lamb, his heart would swell with pride. Until now, Laurie reasoned, bachelor Colin had had no practice in fatherhood. Bereft of both parents in young age, he'd never known the meaning of the name Father. But with a loving heart to guide and the smile of a child to beckon, would he not delight in learning the joys of parenthood?

There was more—Laurie's hunger for her husband!

> Lanely night comes in,
> A' the rest are sleepin',
> I think on my bonnie lad,
> And I bleer my een wi' greetin'.

Malcolm ordered the christening according to Scots rites. The procession from castle to kirk would take place with the proper show.

Laurie was not a little surprised to welcome Sir Ian, heir to Hamilton, the Lairds Dalgethy, Melfont and Montrose, who came to honor the babe with the traditional gifts of gold purse, salt, a staff, a dirk.

Tam o'Stroma marched ahead with the piob more blawin' "Buadgh No Bas." Malcolm steadied the arm of Nanny Menzies who carried the babe, Laurie walked on the arm of Sir Ian Hamilton who served in his father's stead. Children tossed autumn branches in her path and greeted the child with joyful clamor. Little Donald was wrapped i' the Duff-Drummond tartan, a sprig o' juniper pinned to his breast. He never once opened his sleepy blue eyes while the christening took place.

Afterwards the company returned to the castle for a banquet. Games followed at which the lairds assisted and gave prizes.

Handsome Sir Ian could not admire baby Donald enough!

"You seem very fond of children," said Laurie who was flattered by the young man's praise of her babe.

"So fond, that I wish I could find me a wife like you, Lady Laura!" said the bold young man.

The lairds had not only come to feast, they had something else on their minds.

"The good news, Lady Laura . . . you've wrought amazing changes in your villages," said Lord Dalgethy. "May we look around?"

"They did not miss a nail . . . not a brace!" said Bailiff Malcolm who acted as the chieftains' guide. "I wish milady could have seen Sir Ian Hamilton's eyes pop when he saw the mechanical threshing mill. Abraham Warrack was wrestling with it when they came along. Suddenly it began to revolve with a frightful clatter."

"Did they admire the school, Malcolm?"

"I could not tell from the lairds' faces, milady, but they traded some mighty sharp looks!"

A mere two days after the christening, Lady Laura and her suite rolled southward and to make the voyage easy, a lovely false summer gilded the oaks and bronzed the heather. Three times Laurie had made this journey—first with Bailiff Ronald Clargy, the second time in lonely fear and shame, the third in pride and joy with her beloved by her side. Why was there not a greater sense of pride and fulfillment in her heart today? She traveled with her darling boy—how Nanny Menzies fussed over the bairn! The faithful Cibber rode on one side of the carriage, stout-lunged Tam o'Stroma on the other. In the vehicle behind, maid Pritchet, the dog Prince, and those of the servant staff who would be needed in London.

The weather held to perfection until the cavalcade reached the last post inn outside London. Then the heavens opened and the rain poured down.

"Wouldn't your ladyship prefer to spend the night here?" said Cibber. "Travel on by daylight?"

"How many more miles?" asked Laurie.

"Twenty-five miles to Charing Cross."

"Then press on!" said Laurie. She could not endure any delay. On—on to her goal! But travel was hard. The sudden downpour turned the road to mud. And Baby, who had been a model until now, began to fret.

Laurie cared neither for the discomforts of travel nor for the bad weather. When at eleven o'clock at night, the coach wheels rumbled on London cobblestones, she could hardly contain her joy.

Familiar landmarks came to view through the rain-spattered coach windows—there the majestic bulk of St. Paul's, here, Hyde Park. At the corner of Berkeley Street the coach stopped.

Cibber tapped on the window—poor man, he was wet through. "There's a block of carriages all down Berkeley Street, milady. It may take an hour or more to push to the gates of Hathmore House."

"Can't we detour?" asked Laurie.

"Impossible, milady. They're lined up three abreast."

Cibber's horse shied as a daring coachman with cracking whip cut in too close.

Suddenly Laurie remembered the garden gate—there it was! One hop across the pavement—if the gates were open, she could enter by way of the garden.

"Cibber, try the gate!"

"I have keys . . . but milady will get wet!"

"Never mind." Laurie took the babe from the nurse and nestled him under her traveling cape. "Stay where you are, Nanny Menzies!"

"Milady!" cried the nurse. "The bairn!" But Laurie did not heed. Stepping out of the coach, she darted between the carriages and reached the gate. It raining harder than she thought!

"Let me go with you, milady," begged the steward.

"No. I know my way!" Laurie started up the path—how many times she'd strolled under these trees or sat on yonder bench while the poodles frisked and played! A sharp east wind drove the rain into her face and whipped her cape like pennants from the masthead. A sharper gust caught the brim of her bonnet and tossed it back, only the streamers and tie kept it from flying away. She splashed into a puddle and came out wet to the ankles. Never mind! The babe was warm and dry! She rounded the corner of the greenhouse and came to a full stop at the ballroom door. Hathmore House was a blaze of lights. Music wafted out of the windows. Never mind! It was too late to turn back!

Five hundred bejeweled women and their cavaliers were whirling in the contredanse when a buzz and titter almost drowned out the fiddles. The dancers paused to stare at the woman who entered the ballroom—wet, tossed and blown! Her blue cape clung clammily. Her bonnet was a soggy mass of buckram and wet ribbons that dangled halfway down her back. Her hair hung in dank strings around her face.

Krik Fordyce was chatting with a friend when he became aware that the music had stopped in the middle of a bar. He heard someone exclaim, "Look! Lady Duff-Drummond!" Elbowing his way through the fashionable mob he saw the bedraggled Lady Laura and hastened to her side. "I trust you had a pleasant . . ." Even as he spoke he knew how idiotic he must sound. Laura was fighting bravely for courage! "My arm, Lady Laura!" Oh! to get her out of sight—target of a thousand mocking eyes!

But the evening's host had also heard the buzz—he'd been hard at cards with the Prince for a partner and two unlucky adversaries. LADY DUFF-DRUMMOND? Could it be? Duff-Drummond excused himself to his highness and hurried to the ballroom. There stood his wife. He heard her speak through an unpleasant drumming in his ears. "Good evening, Colin. I brought you our son."

Eighteen

London Enjoys a Scandal

TAM O'STROMA'S GREAT HIGHLAND PIPE AND FERGUS' BAG-pipes quarreled in the stable-loft, Tam's lusty blast of "Cogadh na Sith"—War or Peace—drowned out Fergus' skirling of "Jackson's Morning Brush."

Milord's stable-boys took to fisticuffs with those of milady. Milord's chef, an irascible Southcountryman, traded tongue-lashings with milady's Frenchman. Subject of dispute—whether milady did right to "pop in" on her spouse without warning and so hold him up to the ridicule of society, the barbs of gazetteers, the penned shafts of newspaper caricaturists.

All over London the controversy raged. Society and the slums, the salons and the clubs took sides, some with *her*, some with *him*.

"She did right . . . the only thing she could do."

"She did wrong. She should have let her husband know she was coming."

Mrs. Crimms and Mrs. Mimms rattled teacups in Finsbury.

"She showed 'im no consideration at all!"

"Poor fing! . . . 'er wif a bybe! Wet to the skin, she was!"

Lady Blitherington and the Marchioness of Haute-Heels rattled coffee cups in their drawing rooms.

"What can one expect of a commoner, my deah? You knew, did you not? She comes of low stock!"

263

"Low or high-up, Lord Duff-Drummond should not have allowed the ball to stop, the company to leave."

"What could he have done?"

"Requested his wife to change into a ball-gown and join the entertainment."

"After that long run from the wilds of Scotland? And a babe-in-arms?" Lady Blitherington and the Marchioness put their bonnets together. "I have it from reliable source . . . Duff-Drummond only married her to ensure the succession! It seems his eccentric grandmother put it in her testament . . . that they must wed."

"She was Lady Inverkleith's kennel-woman."

"Yes, my dear. And one can well imagine what went on, one knows Duff-Drummond's reputation—the greatest heart-thief in England!"

The storm center was Hathmore House. Nipped in the bud were Laurie's hopes, killed all her joys.

"You made me a laughingstock!" raged her husband. "Fourteen long years since I came of age . . . I'd been waiting to bid London to my house . . . not Granny's house you understand . . . not a house mortgaged to my creditors . . . *my house*. And you walk in like a Nanny-nurse caught in a shower . . . 'I bring you our son!' Did you hear them laugh? I'll never live it down."

Surely, thought Laurie, there must be some meaning to this terrible anger—some meaning more pertinent than a man's wounded pride, a host's social setback! Her husband had stomped away in anger—did not return. His only remark when he looked at his son, "He seems a healthy lad!"

She began to glimpse the truth when a signature under a caricature brought back the past. James Gillray had come out in the *Gazeteer* with an etching entitled,

THE LATEST IN RIGS

The drawing showed a gentleman tandem-driver holding the reins on four bejeweled and befeathered centauresses.

Tethered behind the vehicle, a fifth nag-lady with a wobbly colt at her flank.

FOUR STEPPERS TO WHIP.
ONE TO DRAG.
WILL MILORD BANG-UP TO SALTHILL?

O James Gillray! Little did he know how deep his etcher's burin pierced a tender heart!

A cocky lady in a puce riding habit walked in on Lady Duff-Drummond and made things still clearer—Jinny, Lady Sitley.

"You knew Lolly and I got married, didn't you, Coz?" said Jinny.

"No," said Laurie.

"Well, no matter. We eloped, I've quit the stage, and so it's done! Sometimes I wonder if I did right? Poor Lolly was took with a fit right after the honeymoon. He can't move a hand . . . has to be dressed and fed. And I have to peg-it all day at Sitley Hall! Brr! I wanted to open a house in Mayfair and have all the world in my drawing room."

Listening to her cousin's complaints, Laurie remembered Robbie Burns.

> It's no in titles nor in rank;
> It's no in wealth like Lun'on Bank,
> To purchase peace and rest . . .

Jinny rose and paced restlessly around the room, touching the back of a chair, setting a crystal breloque tinkling on the mantlepiece, moving a statuette a little to the right, then to the left. "I *am* sweet to Lolly," she pouted. "I read to him after dinner. Then Roger and I put him to bed. Roger is the nurse I hired to take care of him. He is a wonderful young man . . . so big and strong, like a centaur of old."

"A centaur is a mythical horse with human body, arms
265

and head only," said Laurie without a smile. "You must have discovered a rare specimen!"

"Oh, you know what I mean!" cried Jinny impatiently. "Roger is handsome, dashing, powerful. He can take my ankles in the palm of one hand and the nape of my neck in the other and lift me high above his head. It gives me the most melligent feelin'! I haf-to make myself stiff as a poker while he carries me 'round the garden . . . me . . . floatin' an' swingin' through the air—then he lets me drop into his arms, and he kisses me . . . and we make love in the grotto where all the statues are. Roger takes off his clothing and I do too. We walk around and pose just like statues. One night a footman nearly caught us. We saw him just in the nick of time, walkin' on tiptoe across the lawn, lookin' in all directions. He came pretty close to the Grotto, but he didn't dare enter. It's like a haunted place at night!"

Jinny in her restless roving had paused at the desk on which lay the Albinus folio. As luck would have it, she opened to a certain page. Her fair skin flushed. "What filthy book is this?"

"Filthy?" echoed Laurie, "Why, it is a book on anatomy."

"You should be ashamed!" cried Jinny. "It's evil to leave a book of this kind in places where innocent persons can open it."

"Jinny, you can't mean what you say?"

"I most certainly do! Look at these nasty pictures! They are shockin'ly indecent!" Jinny fluttered through the precious engraved pages, closed the folio with a bang. "Filthy! That's what I call it. I'm surprised at you!"

Laurie could not believe her ears—Jinny of all people! "Haven't you ever seen a picture of the human body?"

"No! And I don't wish to!"

"But . . . ? You play statues—"

"Statues show the *outside* of a man, not the insides!"

Suddenly Jinney stopped raving, tossed her pert head knowingly. "Is that how you had a baby? By that book? I mean . . . learnin'?" She lowered her voice to a whisper. "Unless Lolly recovers from his fit—and he *must* if I'm to have his money—otherwise Percy Dinmont will get it, he's Lolly's heir."

Jinny's mention of a centaur had struck Laurie. She fetched out Gillray's barbed cartoon. "Jinny . . . have you seen this?"

"Of course!" Jinny giggled. "Everybody's seen it."

"Who are the women?"

"I'm no tattletale."

"Please, Jinny. It's important that I know."

Jinny shrugged, used her riding crop for a pointer. "The lead horse is the Duchess Diana d'Alboli, they say she's been Colin's off-and-on for years. The second is Maude Lowes, daughter of Lord Aldborough—no money! A born scrounger! The third is Arabella, Lady Dorkington. Her husband is locked up like King George, a case of madness. The one nearest Colin is Lady Jane de Cruselle, his latest. They're the four big gooseberries of wit, fashion, figure—say Coz, hae ye not seen 'Periwinkle's Postboard'? It's on the third page o' the *Post* every Friday. There's a rumor Periwinkle is a gent of fashion who took a false name, the better to tell all! Society fears him like Beelzebub, and there's not a lady who wouldn't give her best bangle to top his Scale of Bon Ton. But they say he can't be bought. Là! I'm late to my dressmaker." Jinny went switching away.

Let her be gone quickly ere the tears began to flow. But an odd change came over Laurie. After she had cleansed herself of the poison-scum of jealousy, she began to use her head. Did she or did she not love her husband? The answer was . . . yes! Did she or did she not want to go on loving him? Again the answer was yes.

What sacrifice would she make to win him from his

passions? There was no sacrifice too great! "Even pride?"
Even pride!

Laurie sent for a copy of last Friday's *Morning Post* and
turned to "Periwinkle's Postboard."

Scale of Bon Ton	Beauty	Figure	Elegance	Wit	Sense	Grace	Expression	Sensibility	Honesty
Duchess d'Alboli	20	17	13	5	3	12	2	4	3
Countess of Jersey	12	5	0	14	13	15	13	12	2
Countess of Bartenmore	4	2	5	2	3	7	4	9	15
Mrs. Maude Lowes	14	5	5	15	10	5	3	5	2
Arabella, Lady Dorkington	18	25	14	5	5	15	15	18	5
Lady Jane de Cruselle	20	20	20	5	6	20	15	17	5
Countess of Sefton	15	14	5	12	18	5	15	8	20
Mrs. Bouverie	5	8	7	9	10	5	5	8	20
Lady Harriet Foley	8	5	5	3	20	8	17	20	20

The page was a jumble of numbers at first glance, but
four names caught her eye: Duchess d'Alboli, Lady Jane
de Cruselle, Arabella, Lady Dorkington, Mrs. Maude
Lowes.

Locking her door, Laurie made a study of Periwinkle
and soon discovered a design, a chart as 'twere, of her
husband's preferences. The women he favored were firsts
in animal gifts—Beauty, Figure, Elegance. He held Wit,
Expression, Sensibility, Honesty in very low esteem.

Working with pencil and paper, she totted up the score.
Lady Jane de Cruselle topped 'em with 128 points. After
her, Lady Arabella with 120 points. Mrs. Maude Lowes
stood high in Beauty and Wit—her score was only 64. The
Duchess d'Alboli scored 79, mostly for Beauty, Figure and
Elegance.

In down-to-earth language, Duff-Drummond liked a beautiful face and a shapely body clad in glad trappings! But Laurie knew another Duff-Drummond—a gay and tender teaser, a lover passionate and warm of heart. Which was the true man, the tandem-driver of four mistresses or the man who had held Highland Laurie in his arms and whispered, "Beautiful!" Pray, what was beauty, except love's image stamped upon the retina of the beholder? He *must* have loved her! He must!

Laurie was not surprised to receive the visit of Sir Henry Banks, who loudly praised the new heir. When Nanny Menzies took the babe off to his own quarters, Sir Henry said, "Did you receive my letter, Lady Laura?"

"No, Sir Henry," Laura answered.

"Then I'll tell you its contents. I wrote to inform you that your stewardship of your husband's fortune ceased at the birth of your son. Colin now has full control."

"I'm glad!" cried Laura. "It was a thorn in Colin's side."

Sir Henry sniffed audibly. "I presume it might be a relief to you both. But I also have good news for you. Lady Inverkleith established a trust in chancery for you . . . a sum to convert to your child or children after your demise. Lady Inverkleith said expressly: 'The money is Laura's even though she should divorce my grandson, and remarry.' "

"Lady Inverkleith presumed too much!" murmured Laurie all taken aback.

"Lady Inverkleith knew her grandson," said Sir Henry. "However, let us hope for the best. You may be surprised to hear that Lady Inverkleith left you quite a fortune— two hundred thousand pounds invested at three per cent. Your income will be six thousand yearly. And of course you have the jewels, which are yours to dispose of as you please. All this makes you a rich woman in your own right." Sir Henry did not linger. "Be kind enough to call at my chambers for the signing of necessary papers. Then you may draw on your account immediately."

"Sir Henry! One moment, please!"

"Yes, Lady Laura?"

"The obligations I've undertaken on the domain? Whose are they? Mine or my husband's?"

"All obligations undertaken up and until the moment of the child's birth are your husband's. Anything thereafter is your responsibility and yours alone."

An immediate result of Laurie's distressed state of mind was to dry her milk. Result at long-last was listlessness and disinterest in life. A wet-nurse took over her duties to Master Donald. Who could take the place of her husband? Duff-Drummond stayed away—gave no sign. Where was he? She hadn't a notion until Krik Fordyce came to call.

"Colin goes boar-hunting every year in December. He and the Prince's party are in Chartley Forest now. Remember last year? He always used to skip out, so he'd not be forced to attend his grandmother's Boxing Day ballet. I don't know why it annoyed him so . . . I believe he thought her too old for such capers."

Fordyce looked over the rim of his glass of oporto. "I'd been hoping for an invitation to Lady Duff-Drummond's first London reception . . . ?"

Laurie smiled sadly. "I'm in no mood for receptions."

As her caller was taking leave, he let drop a casual remark. "I've always heard it said . . . the best way to fight fire is with fire!"

Fight fire with fire? Laurie prompty seized the meaning of the remark, and the effect was lightning! Krik was wise. Oh, so wise! Fight fire with fire!

Laurie called Cibber into consultation. Her first entertainment—a dinner party and "amusements" for a selected list of twenty-four guests.

"Would milady like to see the book?" said Cibber.

"What book?"

"The guest-book wherein milady's callers have written their names?"

The name that Laurie added to the list was Sir Ian Hamilton. "Send a card to Sir Ian," said Laurie. "Place him on my left. Invite the Scottish lairds and their ladies . . . whomever else you think may give luster to the evening."

"The Prince?" murmured Cibber.

"Send a card by all means," said Laurie. "He may come!"

Laurie then called for Mrs. Jack of Jermyn Street. The dressmaker informed milady in the tone of a conspirator, "I've a new designer, a young Frenchman just escaped 'cross Channel. A genius! A marvel! He'll be the *dernier cri* of Mayfair."

"May I engage this young designer's services, exclusively?" asked Laurie.

"Exclusively? . . . But, milady . . . Monsieur Albert is . . ."

"Never mind what he is. I want you to make me a wardrobe, outstanding, bold, different, a change of gowns three or four times a day. Furs galore . . . all the rest."

"I see, milady," said Mrs. Jack. "I think I can promise Monsieur Albert's exclusive services."

"Good! Now tell me, who is the leading jeweler?"

"Carewe of Bond Street, milady."

"The most dashing modiste?"

"Madame Genette of Firth Street, Soho."

"The best shoemaker?"

"Bootier Marcello of Bond Street."

"Hairdressers?"

"Dario from Rome." A smile loosened Mrs. Jack's tight lips. "Milady has the figger, the hair, the features . . . everything superior, natural, bewitching. All milady needs are the arts that I and my fellow *artistes* can supply."

Laurie penned a letter to Mr. James Gillray in care of the *Morning Post*.

Dear Mr. Gillray,

Do you remember the young thing of whom you made an amusing sketch in the Great Marlowe-to-London stagecoach? If you consent to portray her again, do me the favor of dining at Hathmore House this Wednesday week, eight o'clock,

> And gratify,
>> your unforgetting
>>> Laura, Lady Duff-Drummond.

By January 8th Lord Duff-Drummond came out of Chartley Forest with chapped hands, two tuskers' heads and a bad case of spleen to find his residence in an uproar, upholsterers and decorators in charge—where was his wife?

"Milady is in town, your lordship," said steward Cibber, "the dressmaker, I believe . . . or was milady going to driving school?"

"Driving school? My wife?"

"Yes, milord. Her ladyship has joined the Tandem Club."

The skeptical Duff-Drummond took only time to bathe and change—hied himself to Tattersall's. There, taking instructions from Lord Jim Sefton, most famous whip in the land, he saw his wife.

She'd adopted the favorite uniform of Tandem Club members—dark green, long-waisted, single-breasted frock coat with pearl buttons; waistcoat of kerseymere ornamented with stripes of green and white, knee-length habit skirt of white corduroy, boots with long tops buttoning over the shinbone, a conical hat that sat her fiery locks with supreme elegance. In the lady whip's buttonhole, a bouquet of myrtle, pink and geranium. Around her swanlike throat, a cravat of white muslin with green spots.

As the tandem swung 'round the turn, Duff-Drummond

saw a beau riding the step on whip-side. Yellow-gloved fists gripping the brasses, red hair showing under his conical hat, a big grin on his handsome face—Ian Hamilton!

"Ah! Colin!" hailed Mr. Osbaldston.

"Hullo, old chap!" greeted Captain Morgan. Aldborough, Fitz-Stanhope, Sir Wedderburn Webster—all able whips.

"See there, Colin! Lady Laura will outstrip us yet! With Jim Sefton and Ian Hamilton for coaches, we've little chance!" Morgan grinned and the gents applauded her ladyship.

It was at the turn of the ring that Laura saw her husband and pulled her pair of bays to a prancing stop. "Darling! Welcome home!"

"Thanks kindly."

"I trust you had a good hunt!"

"Excellent!"

Duff-Drummond was waiting for Ian Hamilton to swing down from his toehold.

"Hullo, Colin!" said that beau and stayed where he was.

Smiling, Laurie leaned across Hamilton's green sleeve and presented her ungloved hand for her husband to kiss.

"Would you mind removing . . . this!" said Duff-Drummond giving a smart tap on Hamilton's arm with his stick.

"Sorry, old chap!" grinned Hamilton. "I'm poised on my big toe as 'twere. You wouldn't want me to roll in the sawdust?"

And a laughing Laura patted her spouse's livid cheek. "Just a few more turns, Colin dear. I'll be with you!" Crack went the whip, Duff-Drummond stepped back just in time to avoid a spray of sawdust from the bay's hoofs.

How long had this been going on—Ian Hamilton posing as Laura's gallant? He recalled uncomfortably that Ian Hamilton had been at his son's Highland christening. Where else? In any case, 'twas Hamilton who handed the lady whip down from the box and escorted her to her waiting mate.

"Thank you, Ian . . . Tuesday again as we arranged! You and dear Jim Sefton! How could I have learned without you?"

Lady Laura waved farewell to the gentlemen and set to talking, her tongue running fast.

"You should have told me what great sport it is to drive a tandem! Wonderful excitin'! What d'you think of my bays? Sir Ian helped me pick 'em out. Do you like the design of my new cart? I think it's quite the kick! I combined the spring and harness of Fordyce's curricle—remember? Anyway it rides like a feather!"

Duff-Drummond was crimson-eared when he handed his spouse into his carriage.

"You must dote on making me the butt of London's jesters. You . . . driving a tandem!"

"Sir Ian and Lord Sefton think I've made good progress," said Laurie. "Of course now you've come home, you might give me some pointers!"

Duff-Drummond gave his wife a sharp look. What was she trying to do, tweak his nose?

"How is our son?"

"Donald is in the pink of health!"

"I thought you planned to breast-nurse him?"

"I did. But I changed my mind . . . decided to do like the rest of the fashionables, give him a wet-nurse. You see it took so much of my time having to nurse him every two hours or so."

Even as Laurie spoke, her heart cried the falsehood! She'd wept bitterly when the milky fountain ran dry. Her most precious moments were the babe's feeding time—what other time was there, save that which she dedicated to her son, that which she would have loved to dedicate to her husband? Och! the bairn's cooing was music to a mother's ear and the mark of the father was on him like the swirls on a seashell.

But she forced her eyes to keep their secret; she'd made

274

a plan and a Scotswoman does not stray from the path she's set if she believes she's gangin' the richt glae.

Duff-Drummond was also a Scot—and far too woman-wise to pop the question, "What's come over you, Laura?"

He said nothing until they reached Hathmore House.

"Look here, Laura . . . all these alterations going on downstairs. What are you planning?"

"I thought the mansion looked rather dreary," said Laurie, lightly. "I plan to entertain quite a bit this season. I'd *adore* hearing what you think of the new design. The Berreye Brothers say Empire is *the* thing. Empire, of course, adapted to English taste. You'll like the dining hall!"

"Who's to pay for all this?" snapped Duff-Drummond.

"Why . . . I will, darling!" cooed Laurie.

Again, Duff-Drummond was too able a wrestler to be caught off balance. "Very sumptuous on your part!" he said and stalked off to his own quarters. But the next day he solved the riddle of his wife's affluence in Henry Banks' chambers.

"Lady Inverkleith left two hundred thousand pounds to Lady Laura," said Sir Henry. "It is so invested that only the income, six thousand a year, may be touched during Lady Laura's life durant. Later the income will be divided between her children."

Duff-Drummond was so angry that he could not repress an oath. "Six thousand a year for a woman to squander!"

For once the solicitor's calm gave way to merriment. "On your lips, my dear fellow, the word 'squander' takes new meaning and authority. But I do believe your wife may go you one better. Have you seen her of late? Your pardon, Laird, but you may have stayed too long in Chartley Forest to bag that pair o' boar's tusks!"

Nineteen

A Feud of Fashion

STAYED TOO LONG IN CHARTLEY FOREST! HENRY BANKS'
thrust began to fester when Duff-Drummond renewed
old habits.

Duchess Diana d'Alboli to whose palace he scurried
seeking crumbs of information, greeted him with her finest
cinquecentesque rage!

"'Little Highland Lass!' you said. 'A simple creature,
knowing nothing about nothing.' D'you know what your
wife has done? She's cornered Monsieur Albert!"

"Cornered Monsieur Albert?" echoed the amazed Duff-
Drummond. "What d'you mean?"

"The great Albert! The genius par excellence! The magician of all magic!"

"Come, Di-di!" said Duff-Drummond. "Speak English if
you can."

"The dressmaker Albert, you fool!" shouted the Duchess.
*The greatest dressmaker to be seen in London since the
days of Madame Aurelie! And your wife has him!* He'll
make for no one else, understand? No one else!" The angry
Duchess came at him. "Faithless! Betrayer! Liar!" With
each epithet, she gave him a sharp push in the chest!
"You'd make me a laughing-stock, would you? Marry this
cowpen creature, would you? All to grab your Granny's
dirty million! And I . . . your Diana who gave you body
and soul! Not even the devil could make me sleep with

her after she's had a child, you promised. Pfah! I spit on your lies! I spit on you!" The Duchess spat *à l'Italienne.*

Duff-Drummond wiped his cheek with a slow gesture—a break with Di-di was long overdue! "Farewell, Diana," he said softly and turned on his heel.

But the duchess was not a woman to let loose without a struggle. "Colin, *amor!* How can you say farewell to your Di-di?"

"Very simple. Farewell, Diana!"

"No! No! You cannot! Look, *amor mio!*" Hooking her jeweled fingers into the corners of her décolleté, the Duchess ripped the gown and stood with bare bosom offered. "Strike me! But do not leave me!"

"O tempt me not!" said Duff-Drummond in a voice so gentle that Diana was deceived. "I'd send that she-demon's head rolling like a bowling ball!"

The Duchess did not flinch, but a spark of hope lighted her dark eyes as she spat out her favorite invectives, "Coward! Cad! Yellow-livered dog!"

"Swine?" suggested Duff-Drummond with a grin, "cow, *sale vache* if you prefer—sounds dreadful in French! Crapaud! That's a good 'n! Toad! Viper, liar! Rogue! Oh, yes —Judas! Help me! I'm runnin' out!"

Diana's chin quivered. "Ain't you goin' to beat me?"

Duff-Drummond shook his head.

"Don't you love me any more?"

He put away her clinging hands. "The answer is . . . again, no."

Would she fall in a faint? He was ill-prepared for her parting thrust. "I think you mean it!" said Diana hoarsely, "I think after all, you are in love with your dairymaid wife! And d'you know who she's mad about? That hulking Highlander, Ian Hamilton!"

Duff-Drummond's palm was still smarting from the slap that he pasted across the Duchess' cheek when he entered

Lady Arabella Dorkington's cardroom that evening. At the first opportunity, his hostess took the newcomer aside.

"Colin! Colin! How could you wrong me so?"

"What have I done to you?"

"Brazen! Do you not know? *She* has taken *my* box in Periwinkle's Scale of Bon Ton. A hundred and nineteen points and I've fallen to eighty-two. Of course, you know the reason. Thanks to the immense sums you've spent on her, she's received twenty added points for elegance."

"What gibberish is this?" asked Duff-Drummond angrily. "Periwinkle . . . points? Your box? Who took it and what box d'you mean?"

Lady Arabella thrust a clipping of the *Morning Post* under the amazed Duff-Drummond's eyes. "THIS!" she shrilled. "Your wife in fifth place! She's climbed from Number Nine to Number Five."

Duff-Drummond had never given more than a cursory glance at Periwinkle's so-called Scale of Bon Ton; now he scanned the feature closely. Arabella was not lying. Here was his wife's name in company with those of the most beautiful women of the realm—Duchess d'Alboli, Countess of Jersey, Countess of Bartenmore, Maude Lowes, Jane de Cruselle.

"You don't love me any more!" wailed the dethroned Arabella.

"Neither do you love me!" said Duff-Drummond sharply. "It's the talk of London that you've been chasing Humphrey Sibthorpe while I was boar-hunting."

"I . . . ? I detest Humphrey Sibthorpe!"

"I heard otherwise." When, after a blistering attack on the lady's claim to fidelity, Duff-Drummond walked out of Dorkington House, his spirits were lighter. Arabella always was a beautiful, sniveling bore! Fortunately, there were still two women who could amuse him—Maude Lowes and Jane de Cruselle. But tonight Duff-Drummond let Maudie and Jane wait, he went home.

Lady Laura's maid was coming out of her mistress' bedroom with an armful of clothing. She stepped aside to let his lordship pass.

"Colin! How nice to see you! Did you spend a pleasant evening?" called his wife from her bed.

Duff-Drummond eyed the studied elegance of his wife's night apparel, the studied carelessness of her coiffeur-dressed hair. "Did you?"

"Oh! Yes indeed! Fuseli was at the reception. He's Keeper of the Royal Academy. He did the most amusin' five-minute sketches. Look—that drawing on my desk."

Swiss-born Fuseli had presented the allegory with his usual brilliance and style—a godlike young man with dagger raised, ready to plunge into the heart of an older, sleeping man. Egging the slayer on, a beautiful woman with a lamp. Her face could easily be recognized as that of Laura. The young slayer was Ian Hamilton.

Duff-Drummond brought the sketch to his wife's bedside. "What's the meaning of this Punch and Judy show?"

"We were playing charades," said Laurie. "The sleeping man is Krik Fordyce. He took the part of King Candaules of Lydia, B.C. 710–668. I played his queen who instigated his murder. The slayer is of course, Ian Hamilton. Isn't the resemblance extraordinary? The company was enchanted. They took all of fifteen minutes and forty-eight guesses to solve the charade."

Duff-Drummond held his temper and his tongue. "I didn't know you'd turned patroness of the arts?"

"Oh, yes! I've always adored painting and sculpture!" said Laurie with all the gush of Jane de Cruselle and her artful sisters.

She was a damnably tempting dish tonight! Her skin glowed like a pearl. She'd pleasures of bosom that cried to be savored—and he'd been three weeks in Chartley Forest in all-male company. But the fancy headdress, the pose, irked Nimrod. He longed to take the lady down a peg.

"Is . . . *that* the latest rage of Periwinkle?" he poked the hairdresser's edifice with a probing finger.

"Yes," said Laura and smilingly dodged his hand.

"Beastly unbecomin'! I like you better this way!"

Duff-Drummond ran his ten fingers through the curly pile and strewed combs, pins and bandeau six ways to one.

"Colin!" laughed Laurie, "you're pulling my hair!"

"I'd like to wring your neck—that or . . ." One bound, he was up and balanced astride her. "What's got into that beautiful head, Laura? Hamilton's sirup o'flattery? Periwinkle's blather? Remember where I found you, toting the Bailie's milk pails! Remember our bout—between the Laird's bedposts!"

But Laura was not to be ridden like a donkey. "Let me go!" she laughed and kneed him from his silken saddle.

The fall made him rage. "Look here, my haughty!" He seized her in his arms and pressed kisses to her unyielding lips. "After all, I'm your husband!"

"Yes, sultan!" cried Laurie and pulling away she laughed merrily.

"Must I go back to my harem?"

"Suit yourself, sultan dear!"

"And let you and Hamilton dance it?"

"Lord Hamilton and I have many interests in common."

"Such as . . . adultery?"

"You're fibbing and you know it!" said Laura gaily. "Now will you go and let me get my beauty sleep?"

Duff-Drummond was not the man to be dismissed like a lackey. Foraging among ribbons and laces, he found what he sought, Laura's soft bosom, lost his head as completely as a schoolboy at his first encounter with Venus.

"Laura! Laura sweet!"

Suddenly his hands were empty. Laura had slipped out of bed on t'other side.

Nightdress pressed to her breast she said, "Please, Colin. I'm tired. Your new apartments are in the west wing. I trust you'll like the color scheme. The Berreye Brothers gave it long thought. Green, they said, was so soothing."

Too pent-up to sleep, Duff-Drummond called for his carriage and went seeking a corkscrew with which to un-bottle his temper. Cards, a wrestling match at Welsh Danny's, a dog-fight, a woman—one corkscrew was as good as another. But the bottle stayed full, Duff-Drummond's temper unchanged.

London rubbed its hands in glee while the feud be-tween Lord and Lady Duff-Drummond went merrily on. Did his lordship give a rout? Her ladyship gave one better. Did his lordship entertain at cards? Her ladyship's card evening was distinguished by fabulous wins, fabulous losses.

"To whose party are you going tonight, my dear?" said Lady Lace to Countess Velours.

"To Hers, of course. Her chef is quite *superior* and she provides the most priceless entertainments. Guess who will amuse us this time—Mr. James Gillray! He'll do us in cari-cature. You know Gillray. Dear fellow! One may truthfully say that his wit is helpin' to win the war against Nappy as much as dear, dear Wellesley's military leadership."

Duff-Drummond soon ceased striving to outdo his wife on the same date. The practice, while it intrigued the imagination, was fraught with quid pro quos. On a recent evening he'd invited the Prince. He was waiting at the head of the stairs to welcome his royal friend. Prinny came puffing upstairs. "He! He! Chawmin' evenin'! Eh, Colin? Hope you're invited to your wife's dinner party? He! He!" His Royal Highness walked straight on, into Lady Duff-Drummond's drawing room.

It was not alone in the drawing and ballroom that Lady Duff-Drummond excelled his lordship. Laurie had become a champion tandem-driver. Of course she'd had the good luck to lay hands on two magnificent horses. But luck notwithstanding, she'd taken the blue ribbon at the first spring trial—Lord Sefton grinning like a Manx cat and Sir Ian Hamilton standing by to receive Lady Laura's reins and hand her down from the box when the race was run.

The changeable spring brought changing weather. But Duff-Drummond did not blow a gale in his wife's ear. His anger was reserved for those moments when, alone or in company of one whom he trusted, he let rip with Boreas' blast.

"Damme, Henry, did you see Laura?" he said to his solicitor after the Countess Dorset's "at home," where they happened to meet.

"Yes," said Sir Henry Banks.

"She's running wild!"

"The company seemed to applaud."

"*That* company would applaud a monkey with a hat."

It seemed to Sir Henry that only a woman of regal bearing could have carried off the new, mad mode that Lady Laura had exhibited at the Countess Dorset's. And Laura was plentifully endowed by nature to display the new bodice in which *les fruits de Venus* were contained like love apples in a golden basket. The lady's tubelike skirt of buttercup satin brought her stately limbs into full outline. When she removed her cape, she revealed an admirable pair of arms clad in green leather gloves, a slender ankle crisscrossed with green laces. How important, the end-ribbons that taped a woman together like a Deed of Property! Lady Laura's hat too, a marvel of the modiste's cunning—it consisted of three tiers of variegated satins, green, coral, magenta, wound around with gold beads. What a fool was Colin to prefer any woman to this queen.

"Are you not exaggerating your wife's caprices?" said Sir Henry Banks mildly.

"I liked her better as she used to be, simple, unassuming, sincere."

"*You* liked your wife?" Sir Henry grinned. "It might appear that the lady would be justified in thinking you never liked her!"

"What do you know about how the lady thinks?" retorted Duff-Drummond.

"Oh! Nothing . . . nothing at all!" Sir Henry assured him.

"Some scullery gossip, I suppose? My wife . . . Ian Hamilton!"

"Dear boy, Lady Laura is by her very nature above suspicion!"

But Duff-Drummond knew differently. Not the female to stoop to base infidelity, Laura was ne'ertheless proud and pleased to have captured the homage of a man the likes of Hamilton. More by innuendo—a glance exchanged at the club, a nudge of elbows when he entered a drawing room—was the rumor implied that Lord Hamilton and Lady Duff-Drummond . . . Oh! nothing that one could put one's finger on, but there was seldom an evening when her ladyship was "at home" that the quick eye of Duff-Drummond could not pick out Ian Hamilton's carriage among the vehicles stationing outside Hathmore House.

In this mood Duff-Drummond was not able to endure the beak-snapping of the swanlike Jane de Cruselle.

"Where were you? You promised . . . I waited an hour."

He let her alone for a fortnight—dreary fortnight! Then one afternoon they came face to face at a rout. And Jane began a scene for the mob to hear and see.

"I kept your plate at my table Friday, Colin."

"I regret, Lady Jane. I sent my respects—"

"Respects! You're an ill-mannered oaf, sir!"

"Please, Jane! Don't bawl!"

"I'll bawl it to all London! You're an oaf! A Scottish oaf to boot!"

Jane cracked her negligent lover over the cheek with her fan, whereupon the lover snapped the fan in pieces and walked out in what a pipsqueak journalist called "a huff" in his news rag the next day.

In purple humor, Arabella, Diana, Jane written off the slate and only good old Maudie left—the trouble with Maudie, she was so devilish mercenary!—Duff-Drummond quit his club early one afternoon and went home with the vague idea of picking a fight with his wife. But her ladyship was "dining out."

Dame Melancholy climbed with milord to the nursery on the third floor of Hathmore House. He'd seen his son only three times—how much had the boy grown?

"Dearie me! The Laird!" fussed Nanny Menzies, rising from her chair by the fire.

"How's the boy?" asked the Laird, who was slightly winded.

"In fine health, Laird."

Duff-Drummond's sensitive nostrils breathed in a strangely pleasant fragrance—lavender, clean linen, milk— yet another indefinable scent that he'd found only in the stables of his pampered race-horses—scent of suckling foal, perfume of babyhood.

A night lamp shed a mild glow over a nest of blue and laces—the cradle.

"Wudna the Laird wish to see the bairn?" said Nanny Menzies. She beckoned and pushed the laces aside.

Looking down at his son, Duff-Drummond felt a tremor along his nerves—that small, rosy creature, a man-to-be?

" 'Tis time to feed him," said the nurse. "Will the Laird na like to take him up?"

With the assured touch that he would have used to heft a newborn colt, the father lifted his son out of the cradle. How light he was—yet how heavy! How frail and yet how strong! Wee fingers clung like leeches! A tiny arm swung like a flail.

"If the Laird wi' br-rring the babe to the fire?" said the nurse.

The infant opened round blue eyes, opened a rosebud mouth and said, "Da!" The name shook the father as in his mind's eye he glimpsed the morning light bathing the lochs, the high hills of his native land; in that instant he saw with shining clarity a vision of home and love, a sunnier life filled with soaring purpose, vision that faded soon.

"If the Laird wi' hand me the bairn . . ." said Nanny Menzies.

"Aye!" Duff-Drummond gave the child to the nurse's arms.

A determined woman, Maude Lowes had always assumed that her day would come when Duff-Drummond acceded to his grandmother's fortune. The Duff's passing fancies for this or that mistress, even his longtime adherence to the overripe Duchess d'Alboli gave Maude no concern. She had not demurred when he had announced his marriage to a wench of capricious Lady Inverkleith's choice. Now, for the first time in her life, Maude Lowes was afraid that her grip upon her lover was loosening.

What lover would storm into his mistress' boudoir at midnight, berate the female sex, the modes and women's fancies unless he were jealous of his wife? Maude Lowes knew the rumors—that The Hamilton's son was on the grid, the fire, Lady D-D's smile. She also knew that Lady Laura's name had stood at the top of "Periwinkle's Postboard" these four weeks. Who could have put it there except a small coterie of elegants—the arbiters of fashion? Lady Laura not only rated first Beauty, Grace, Elegance, Figure—also for Wit, Sense, Expression, Sensibility, Honesty! Who gave Periwinkle his pointers? 'Twas bruited that he was a composite of the Top Nineteen, as they called themselves—nineteen gentlemen who set the styles for women as well as in waistcoats, who decreed what rig should be driven, the angle of a part in the hair, the color à la mode!

Maude Lowes cared nought for "Periwinkle's Post-board," only for that peculiar rage of preference which blows upon the name of a woman and wafts her to an eminence far above that of her sisters in popularity. Would the same rage make Duff-Drummond turn his head—acknowledge his own wife as Leader of Bon Ton and Beauty?

Far too cunning to heckle a man in a temper, Maude ordered a light collation up from her kitchen and fed the Beast, then she patted her couch. "Come, Colin-o'-Mine," —her favorite nickname for the man she idolized. Having learned to handle high-bred horses in childhood, she used the same methods to manage men. No use spurring, whipping or prodding Colin—let the Duchess d'Alboli do that! No use boring him with tears like Arabella Dorkington or plying him with honey to spoil his stomach like Jane de Cruselle, a surfeit in the end. No, Maude held the rein lightly, left the whip at home, kept her sweets deep in her pocket; only if the stallion nuzzled did she give.

Knowing her man, she tried tactfully to discover the reason for his foul mood tonight. "I saw Lady Laura at Lady Elpinstone's reception. She's quite handsome these days . . . so individual! But Scots girls *are* that way, they've natural talents. Have you seen 'Periwinkle's Postboard' this week?"

"Hang Periwinkle!" growled Duff-Drummond.

"Perhaps this will amuse you, Gillray's latest." Maude handed her lover a clipping. This time the mordant pen of the caricaturist had drawn a tandem turnout with a lady at the ribbons, a Scots gentleman in Duff-Drummond tartan for her seat-cushion. Harnessed to the rig, four beautiful centauresses and the caption—verses guaranteed to sear the souls of the ladies for whom they were intended:

Talk not to me, Sir, of old-fashioned rule
Laughed at by children, joke of the school.
That rule was good for matrons of old,
Who knew no better than their servants to scold;
As for me, Zounds and Blood! Am I not fit to ride in,
And what's more, a quartette of jades to drive tandem?

"Interestin' experiment, eh, Colin?" purred Maude. "Parin' the rough edges off a Highland lassie . . . teachin' her how to behave in good company."

"I taught my wife nothing," said Duff-Drummond darkly.

"Oh! But you must have!" cooed Maude. "How could she have learned?"

"Damned if I know!" Duff-Drummond answered with a knife edge to his tone. "It may be that, as you say, she has natural talents."

Maude let a moment pass. "Of course Ian's rather good, too . . . about horses . . . elegance . . . the social graces. I daresay your wife has called on him for advice."

"Ummm," mumbled Duff-Drummond.

Maude knew she'd hit the rotten spot in the apple. "He's a nice boy, is Ian," she cooed. "And they say his father is overjoyed! The two of 'em are Covenanters . . . all for Scotland. Of course they'd be quick to see the advantage—"

"Advantage?" said Duff-Drummond, beginning to sense her meaning.

"An alliance with two hundred thousand guineas is not to be sneezed at, Colin!" said Maude. "The Hamiltons are not rich except in acres. The old Duke could use some ringing gold in his fight for Scots Rule. I hear your Highland lassie is all wrapped up in Caledonian capers . . . that she and the Hamiltons, Melfont, Dalgethy, Fraser . . . all the kilted clan are, so to speak, fellow conspirators."

Duff-Drummond's digestive juices had ceased to run. He felt a ball of lead where his pampered tummikins should be. "One hears ten rumors to the hour!" he growled. "My wife's interest in Scotland is natural. She's a Scot!"

"But of course!" cooed Maude. "And how clever of you to indulge her whims—let her buy threshing machines, build schools, Lord knows what-all! You're quite the smartest man I know, Colin-o'-Mine."

"Smart?"

"You never doubted your ability to win your freedom! Not *my* Colin! I confess, dear, I was worried when your granny forced you to marry the wench. But I see now . . . there's no woman who can force *your* hand! Tell me, dearest, how's Philemon? What are your chances for the coming season?" Even as she swung the conversation to the turf, Maude wondered what her lover was thinking behind that furrowed brow. She would have been amazed had she been able to read her lover's thoughts—Ian Hamilton and my wife . . . too much together . . . the fellow like a burr on Laura's sleeve. What if it's true that a divorce is in the offing . . . Maude trying to tease me into letting Laura fling it with Ian . . . slut that Maude is!

Suddenly awake to the meaning of his mistress' catlike purr—that the heir of Hamilton was not only plotting to annex his wife and her money but also his son, Duff-Drummond bounced to his feet. "No, by God! Not the boy!" he shouted.

"Colin!" cried Maude to her lover's back. "Where are you going?"

"Home!" said Duff-Drummond and banged the door behind him.

288

Twenty

The Best Laid Plans of Mice and Men

THREADING THROUGH MAYFAIR'S DARK STREETS AT MID-
night Sir Ian Hamilton's coachman drove his aristocratic passengers back to Hathmore House.

By the simple expedient of pressing the speaking tube
to his ear, the footman could hear all that was being said
inside the vehicle. "They ain't talkin'!" he reported to the
coachman.

"Mmm-mm listen again! Master looked to be in fine
fettle 'e did, tonight!"

"I sye they ain't talkin'!" insisted the footman, "Mum
as dummies, they are!"

Indeed Sir Ian Hamilton was not speaking for he had already spoken at the Ball, and had his answer. Laura cared
only for her husband!

Even though he was unfaithful, neglectful, a mountain of egotism, she loved him still, would love him always.

"Summer will soon be in. I long for the Braes of Angus,"
said she, the light of a street lantern illuminating her
adorable smile.

"Will Colin accompany you?"

"I trust so."

Hamilton choked back the words: *Let me squire you if
he does not*. "If Colin stays in London, will you stay too?"

"Yes."

The way she said it was the featherweight that tipped

the scales of Ian Hamilton's good sense—of what use to plead a lost cause? This woman was ever-faithful, a Penelope in love.

"Laura . . . tell me one thing and I'll hold my tongue forever. If you'd met me instead of Colin, could you have cared for me?"

Laura's eyes were tender. "Yes, Ian. I think so. I believe so. You are in every way admirable . . . a grand gentleman, a man."

The young Scot pressed his clenched fists between his knees until they hurt. "Thank you, Laura. I'll remember your words always." A bleak feeling of loss eternal and irreparable swept over him, that this bright beauty, this earnest heart could not belong to him. What deadly charm did a man like Colin exert that every woman should endure what he meted out in the name of love?

"May I come and fetch those plans for a school to be built on our domain?" he said when the carriage rolled up to the porte-cochère of Hathmore House.

"Yes, Ian," answered Laura. "There's one detail I wanted to discuss, the heating. You see, my husband's method is better. I'll show you the drawings."

Lord Duff-Drummond returned home a scant fifteen minutes after his wife and her escort had entered Hathmore House.

"Is Lady Duff-Drummond in?" asked his lordship of the footman who opened the door.

"Yes, milord. 'Er ladyship and Sir Ian is both in the small drawin' room!"

Duff-Drummond bit off a curse, handed his hat and cane to a second footman and ran up the grand staircase. Such was the rage that seethed in his soul, he'd have liked to smash the face of Neptune in plaster who stared at him with painted eyes. This was the last straw. Laura receiving Ian Hamilton at midnight!

"I cawn't grawsp a gent like milord," said one footman to the other.

" 'Oo can?"

" 'Er ladyship so 'andsome . . . beautiful one myte ryte-fully call 'er!"

"Yus."

"Masters won't be long, but we myte catch a few winks."

The two went back to their bench, leaned shoulder to shoulder for a cat-nap until called.

The long corridor that led to Lady Duff-Drummond's east wing was lighted with a few wicks that shed round spots of yellow on the crimson runner. In the silence Duff-Drummond could hear his own heart beating.

What to do . . . burst in upon the two . . . accuse 'em of . . . what? Knowing Laura he did not suspect her of mere vulgar infidelity. No! Laura's turning away would be of another kind, the break clean! Legal severance and farewell!

God, why did he fear to make a move? Was it because at long last he'd come to respect his wife; because at the bitter end the knowledge had been riven into his skull that Laura was not only a lovely, ardent mistress, a dutiful wife and mother, but also a great lady!

Scots leaders like The Hamilton, Lords Dalgethy and Melfont were not quick to bestow recognition upon one whom their blue-blood wives could call "a peasant maid." Neither was the serious-minded Ian Hamilton apt to settle his affections through caprice.

Although a leader in fashion, although a worthy claimant of Good Deeds' scroll of merit, Laura was more . . . much more—a first-rate adversary for Duff-Drummond— her weapon, the only one against which even a master of subtlety could not prevail, HONESTY. Who said: "Well-timed silence hath more eloquence than speech"? Tonight was not the time to burst into her ladyship's apartments breathing lordly wrath.

Tomorrow he'd talk to his wife . . . plead with her, declare his change of heart, tell her how much he needed her, loved her, adored her, wanted her. And if she demanded total surrender, he'd run up the white flag!

In this contrite mood, Duff-Drummond turned back to his west wing exile. But the sound of conversation halted him at the head of the grand staircase. Laura and Ian had come out of the intimate rose drawing room that milady preferred to more formal quarters. Dressed for the ball, Laura was magnificent in green taffeta and emeralds as she held out her hand for Hamilton's salute.

"I see no reason why our plans shouldn't work out very well, Ian."

"Yes, without a doubt the scheme is practical."

"I hope to see the outcome before fall."

"I'll do my best to hasten things."

"Goodnight, Ian."

"Goodnight, Laura."

The Duff's blood began to boil all over again as he watched Hamilton bearing down the corridor. Plans? . . . Outcome before fall? . . . So they wanted things hastened.

A long view opened into the past—hadn't he and Ian Hamilton always been striving one against the other? Wrestling, running, fencing, shooting, spear and stone-throwing—their friendly grudges dated back to the day when a boyish Ian challenged the older Colin to an uphill race . . . and won! In later years it was Welsh Danny's Wrestling Club . . . bets high on Duff-Drummond who was floored by Ian in seven minutes. In vain Duff-Drummond reasoned that his strength had been cut down by a drinking bout the night before; the result was the same. In sports, the heir of Hamilton always took the trophy. Should he also be allowed to capture the finest prize of all, the Duff's lady?

The two could not help but meet head-on.

"Ah there, Colin! Home at last?"

"Not soon enough!"

"What d'you mean?"

"Need I explain?" As if by accident, Duff-Drummond trod hard on Hamilton's foot encased in elegant evening shoe.

"I think an explanation would be in orr-rder!" burred Hamilton, the Scots accent always betraying him when he was angry. "And kindly remove your foot from off my foot!" With an easy roll of the shoulder he upset Duff-Drummond's balance and got his pinioned foot free.

Duff-Drummond seized Hamilton's lapels and crowded him against the wall. "I'm not joking, Ian! What plans are you and my wife making that must be put into such hasty operation?"

"Plans?" Hamilton eyed the fists that grasped his Bond Street lapels. "Do you mean those plans for a school—a stove that spreads heat over-all at low cost? Colin! Let go! You'll tear my coat!"

Grinding out an oath, Duff-Drummond held on all the tighter. "School? Stove? I know all about your scheming. Ian! I demand your word here and now you'll never see Lady Laura again."

"I make few promises, old fellow," said Hamilton in a mild voice—his color had turned pasty white, dangerous sign in a redhead!—"I'll be honored to wait on Lady Laura whenever she pleases!"

Duff-Drummond's temper boiled over. "Damn you, I'll fix it so she won't please!" He swung with his right, knocked Hamilton off balance. A sharp molding in the panel caught the young Scot between the shoulder blades and wrung a gasp of pain from his lips.

"Colin, old fellow," he said after he'd righted himself and smoothed his lapels into some semblance of their former elegant bulge, "I hate to bark my knuckles on your nose! Why can't we decide it Cumberland style?"

"Decide what?"

"Whether I shall see Lady Laura again."

Stripping to belts and in stocking feet, the wrestlers squared away in proper stance—was that a smile on Hamilton's lips?

"Remember, Colin my friend, three falls out of five . . . and as Welsh Danny would say, 'No kneeing or kidney blows. Fight fair, and may the best gent win!' "

Striving for a first "trip," thick welts sprang up along the ribs of the fair-skinned Hamilton and Duff-Drummond's shoulders purpled under the iron pressure of his adversary's biceps. Nimble footwork was soundless on the deep pile of the crimson runner—only an expert ear could have heard the creak of a backbone, a sob crushed from collapsed lungs.

Hamilton was trying for a back-heel maneuver to get a leg behind his opponent's heel on the outside. Failing this he tried the "hank," lifting the opponent off the ground after a sudden turn. But Duff-Drummond did not forget the counter-trick; deftly he kicked Hamilton behind where the knee bends and threw him backward, falling himself breast-down and holding.

"One fall!" counted Hamilton from where he lay. "The fall is fair!"

The opponents leaped to their feet and grappled for a second bout.

This time Duff-Drummond took the offensive with a cross-buttock throw. Hamilton landed on fingertips and knees and announced, "Match still stands one to one."

Seeing his enemy so strong and calm, Duff-Drummond grew angrier. Down went Ian on a lucky "chip," but he bounced like a ball, caught the donor unprepared and floored him.

"Two falls each!" counted Hamilton. "Remember, my friend, it's three out of five."

Duff-Drummond's most successful trick was always the swinging "hype"—he'd learned it from a Westmoreland man—lift the opponent, swing clear around, get the left knee under his right leg and carry it high for a throw! He made a try and failed.

"The Westmoreland, eh?" panted Hamilton in his ear. "I know that one too!"

Maddened by the scent of Ian's hair—a special aroma of the Red Scot that acts on the Black Scot like an irritant—Duff-Drummond tossed wrestlers' rules out the window and let knee and fist go to work for victory. Hamilton's surprise gave Duff-Drummond the immediate advantage, then he was thrown clear and out of reach of his opponent.

"So . . . it's free-for-all?"

"No hits barred!"

"I'm agreeable!"

Two gentlemen boxers put fists up. A slashing blow to Duff-Drummond's midriff banged the breath out of him. He danced away, recovered, came back and let Hamilton have a bruiser under the heart. In a clinch, they worked on each other's kidneys while chinning each other's clavicles.

"Off!" cried Hamilton and disengaged himself.

Duff-Drummond's right ripped again and Hamilton reeled, but with footing regained he raked Duff-Drummond's jaw in cat's-paw strike that snapped his head backward.

Thinking to end the encounter, Duff-Drummond bore in with bull-like charge, but Hamilton was ready. Arms locked upon heaving torsos, they punched and thugged it out along the crimson runner until their stockinged feet thumped the bare marble.

An Italian mosaic-master had created a design resembling waves that rippled down the grand staircase and joined in an oceanic fantasy across the wide hall. Hamilton slipped on the slick of a marble ripple, backed against the banister and losing foothold he toppled and would have fallen the twenty feet had not Duff-Drummond seized him by one knee and hauled him back. The effort unbalanced Duff-Drummond's own precarious equilibrium. Heel over emptiness, he grabbed to save himself, pulled his opponent in his down-the-stair tumble.

The two dozing footmen were roused by noises overhead.

"Robbers!"

"Robbers?"

Pulling their firearms, they dashed upstairs, but at the first landing they stopped in their tracks and flattened themselves against the wall just in time to avoid being hit by a tangled mass of muscle and silk that came hurtling by. Bang! went a bust of Apollo and crashed in fragments on the mosaic below. At the turn of the staircase the human mass picked itself apart.

" 'Is Lordship!"

"Sir Ian!"

Eyes bugging, the footmen watched the two gentlemen go at each other like Whitechapel rats—first his lordship's fist found its mark, then Sir Ian's left! A lightning jab, Duff-Drummond flailed the air with his arms, knocked a plaster Venus off her perch. The last of the plaster gods to fall was the King of the Sea. Yielding to the combined weight of the fighters, newel-post Neptune joined their headlong plunge into a marble ocean.

A little cloud of plaster dust rose out of the wreck.

"Two bob 'as it they've broke their bloody necks!" whispered one footman.

"I'm not tykin' no bets this time, 'Arry Raff!"

" 'Adn't we better look see?"

The trembling footmen crept down the stairs.

" 'Is lordship's 'ead . . . all bashed and gory!"

"Sir Ian's back oozin' blood!"

With a single breath, the two yelled, " 'Elp! Murder!" and made a dash for the service stairs.

Springtime's night breeze, the bright moonlight recalled another June when she had climbed to The Rock with a haggis.

Laurie closed the curtains and turned to her husband's bed. "Concussion of the cerebrum," the doctor gentlemen of Harley Street had decreed, nor would they venture to say when, even IF Lord Duff-Drummond would recover.

It seemed to Laurie that she was walking along a road to despair from which there was no returning. Colin an invalid, Colin gone, her life was finished! The future held no promise, the past, only memories, nor was it true that the bereaved could find consolation in memories of lost joys! Bobbie Burns had said it —

> Ay waukin, O
> Waukin still and weary,
> Sleep I can get nane
> For thinking on my dearie.

Nursing her grief, a multitude of questions crowded to Laurie's mind;—what if she had not fled to the Highlands like a coward? Did she deserve Lady Inverkleith's blessings? Had she acted like a fool, hoping to win back her husband's love by trying to rival his mistresses? Even Ian Hamilton had taught her remorse when he came with a broken arm, a wound in his back and said, "I was to blame! I pressed Colin too hard! He loves you, Laura. I know for I measured his love by the strength of his arm in battle!"

Choking back a sob, Laurie stumbled into her dressing-room, but grief overcame her. She bowed her head and wept out loud. Startled from sleep by the strange sound, the little dog Prince bounded out of his gilt bed, barking madly.

"Prince! Be quiet!" Laurie commanded but the poodle's bark filled the room with doggy clamor. He evaded his mistress's hand, scampered into the bedroom, hopped on his master's bed and demanded protection with loud yap-pings.

"Down Prince!" said a man's firm voice. Laurie stopped on the threshold. "Down Prince!" That voice again! "Down you beggar!" Colin's voice! But a moment before he had lain silent . . . a man of stone!

Laurie ran to her husband's bedside.

"Colin! Colin dearest! Are you . . . are you better?"

"Better? Better? I feel fine. Is that you, Laurie? What time is it?"

"Two o'clock, dearest." Laurie pleaded heaven not to withdraw this blessing!

Duff-Drummond's eyes shone clear in the candle light, color came to his cheeks, again his voice, "Get this hound off my neck, will you? Latch the door on him . . . and come back to bed!"

Yes! GREAT GLORY! Yes! The laird was come back to life! What had happened, a miracle? Or had Prince's shrill bark done what Colin always said it could do, "Raise the dead!" Laurie hugged the pet to her heart. "Thank you, Prince!" Calm at last, the poodle trotted back to his gilt bed.

"Laurie Lass!" called her husband, "Coom nu! The night is far gone and I need hottin'!"

"Yes, yes Laddie!" Laurie answered, "I'll coom! I'll coom!"